Charles James Lever

A Rent in a Cloud and St. Patrick's Eve

Charles James Lever

A Rent in a Cloud and St. Patrick's Eve

ISBN/EAN: 9783743330528

Manufactured in Europe, USA, Canada, Australia, Japa

Cover: Foto ©Andreas Hilbeck / pixelio.de

Manufactured and distributed by brebook publishing software
(www.brebook.com)

Charles James Lever

A Rent in a Cloud and St. Patrick's Eve

A RENT IN A CLOUD

AND

ST. PATRICK'S EVE.

BY

CHARLES LEVER,

AUTHOR OF
"FORTUNES OF GLENCORE,"
"HARRY LORREQUER,"
"SIR JASPER CAREW,"
"MAURICE TIERNAY,"
"A DAY'S RIDE,"
ETC.

NEW EDITION

LONDON:
CHAPMAN AND HALL, 193, PICCADILLY.

A RENT IN A CLOUD.

CHAPTER I.

THE WHITE HORSE AT COBLENTZ.

UT of a window of the Weissen Ross, at Coblentz, looking upon the rapid Rhine, over whose circling eddies a rich sunset shed a golden tint, two young Englishmen lounged and smoked their cigars; rarely speaking, and, to all seeming, wearing that air of boredom which, strangely enough, would appear peculiar to a very enjoyable time of life. They were acquaintances of only a few days. They had met on an Antwerp steamer—rejoined each other in a picture-gallery—chanced to be side by side at a table d'hôte at Brussels, and, at last, drifted into one of those intimacies which, to very young men, represents friendship. They agreed they would travel together, all the more readily that neither cared very much in what direction. "As for me," said Calvert, "it doesn't much signify where I pass the interval; but, in October, I must return to India and join my regiment."

"And I," said Loyd, "about the same time must be in England. I have just been called to the bar."

" Slow work that must be, I take it."

" Do you like soldiering ? " asked Loyd, in a low quiet voice.

" Hate it ! abhor it !   It's all very well when you join first.   You are so glad to be free of Woolwich or Sandhurst, or wherever it is.   You are eager to be treated like a man, and so full of Cox and Greenwood, and the army tailor, and your camp furniture, and then comes the dépôt and the mess.   One's first three months at mess seemed to be the cream of existence."

" Is it really so jolly ?   Are the fellows good talkers ? "

" About the worst in the universe; but to a young hand, they are enchantment.   All their discourse is of something to be enjoyed.   It is that foot-race, that game of billiards, that match at cricket, that stunning fine girl to ride out with, those excellent cigars Watkins is sending us ; and so on.   All is action, and very pleasant action too.   Then duty, though it's the habit to revile and curse it, duty is associated with a sense of manhood ; a sort of goosestep chivalry to be sure, but still chivalry.   One likes to see the sergeant with his orderly book, and to read, ' Ensign Calvert for the main guard.' "

" And how long does all this last ? "

" I gave it three months, some have been able to prolong it to six.   Much depends upon where the dépôt is, and what sort of corps you're in."

" Now for the reaction !   Tell me of that."

" I cannot ; it's too dreadful.   It's a general detestation of all things military, from the Horse Guards to the mess waiter. You hate drill—parade—inspection—the adjutant —the wine committee—the paymaster—the field-officer of the day—and the major's wife.   You are chafed about everything—you want leave, you want to exchange, you want to be with the dépôt, you want to go to Corfu, and you are sent to Canada. Your brother officers are the slowest fellows in the service; you are quizzed about them at the mess of the Nine Hundred and Ninth—"Yours" neither give balls nor private theatricals. You wish you were in the Cape Coast Fencibles—in fact, you feel that destiny has placed you in the exact position you are least fitted for."

"So far as I can see, however, all the faults are in yourself."

"Not altogether. If you have plenty of money, your soldier life is simply a barrier to the enjoyment of it. You are chained to one spot, to one set of associates, and to one mode of existence. If you're poor, it's fifty times worse, and all your time is spent in making five-and-sixpence a day equal to a guinea."

Loyd made no answer, but smoked on.

"I know," resumed the other, "that this is not what many will tell you, or what, perhaps, would suggest itself to your own mind from a chance intercourse with us. To the civilian the mess is not without a certain attraction, and there is, I own, something very taking in the aspect of that little democracy where the fair-cheeked boy is on an equality with the old bronzed soldier, and the freshness of Rugby or Eton is confronted with the stern experiences of the veteran campaigner; but this wears off very soon, and it is a day to be marked with white chalk when one can escape his mess dinner, with all its good cookery, good wine, and good attendance, and eat a mutton-chop at the Green Man with Simpkins, just because Simpkins wears a black coat, lives down in the country, and never was in a Gazette in his life. And now for *your* side of the medal—what is it like?"

"Nothing very gorgeous or brilliant, I assure you," said Loyd, gently; for he spoke with a low quiet tone, and had a student-like submissive manner, in strong contrast to the other's easy and assured air. "With great abilities, great industry, and great connexion, the career is a splendid one, and the rewards the highest. But between such golden fortunes and mine there is a whole realm of space. However, with time and hard work, and ordinary luck, I don't despair of securing a fair livelihood."

"After—say—thirty years, eh?"

"Perhaps so."

"By the time that I drop out of the army a retired lieutenant-colonel, with three hundred a year, you'll be in fair practice at Westminster, with, let us take it, fifteen hundred, or two thousand—perhaps five."

"I shall be quite satisfied if I confirm the prediction in the middle of it."

"Ah," continued the soldier. "There's only one road to success—to marry a charming girl with money. Ashley of ours, who has done the thing himself, says that you can get money—any man can, if he will; that, in fact, if you will only take a little trouble you may have all the attractions you seek for in a wife, plus fortune."

"Pleasant theory, but still not unlikely to involve a self-deception, since, even without knowing it, a man may be far more interested by the pecuniary circumstance."

"Don't begin with it; first fall in love—I mean to yourself, without betraying it—and then look after the settlement. If it be beneath your expectation, trip your anchor, and get out of the reach of fire."

"And you may pass your best years in that unprofitable fashion, not to say what you may find yourself become in the meanwhile."

The soldier looked at the other askance, and there was

in his sidelong glance a sort of irony that seemed to say, "Oh! you're an enthusiast, are you?"

"There you have me, Loyd," said he, hurriedly: "that is the weak point of my whole system; but remember, after all, do what one will, he can't be as fresh at five-and-thirty as five-and-twenty—he will have added ten years of distrusts, doubts, and dodges to his nature in spite of himself."

"If they must come in spite of himself, there is no help for it; but let him at least not deliberately lay a plan to acquire them."

"One thing is quite clear," said the other, boldly; "the change will come, whether we like it or not, and the wisest philosophy is to plan our lives so that we may conform to the alterations time will make in us. I don't want to be dissatisfied with my condition at five-and-forty, just for the sake of some caprice that I indulged in at five-and-twenty, and if I find a very charming creature with an angelic temper, deep blue eyes, the prettiest foot in Christendom, and a neat sum in Consols, I'll promise you there will soon be a step in the promotion of her Majesty's service, vice Lieutenant Harry Calvert, sold out."

The reply of the other was lost in the hoarse noise of the steam which now rushed from the escape-pipe of a vessel that had just arrived beneath the window. She was bound for Mayence, but stopped to permit some few passengers to land at that place. The scene exhibited all that bustle and confusion so perplexing to the actors, but so amusing to those who are mere spectators; for while some were eagerly pressing forward to gain the gangway with their luggage, the massive machinery of the bridge of boats was already in motion to open a space for the vessel to move up the stream. The young Englishmen were both interested in watching a very tall, thin old lady, whose efforts to gather together the members of her party, her luggage, and her followers, seemed to have overcome all the ordinary canons of politeness, for she pushed here and drove there, totally regardless of the inconvenience she was occasioning. She was followed by two young ladies, from whose courteous gestures it could be inferred how deeply their companion's insistance pained them, and how ashamed they felt at their position.

"I am afraid she is English," said Loyd.

"Can there be a doubt of it? Where did you ever see that reckless indifference to all others, that selfish disregard of decency, save in a certain class of our people? Look, she nearly pushed that fat man down the hatchway; and see, she will not show the steward her tickets, and she will have her change. Poor girls! what misery and exposure all this is for you!"

"But the steamer is beginning to move on. They will be carried off! See, they are hauling at the gangway already."

"She's on it; she doesn't care; she's over now. Well done, old lady! That back-hander was neatly given; and see, she has marshalled her forces cleverly: sent the light division in front, and brings up the rear herself with the luggage and the maids. Now, I call that as clever a landing on an enemy's shore as ever was done."

"I must say I pity the girls, and they look as if they felt all the mortification of their position. And yet, they'll come to the same sort of thing themselves one of these days, as naturally as one of us will to wearing very easy boots and loose-fitting waistcoats."

As he said this, the new arrivals had passed up from the landing-place, and entered the hotel.

"Let us at least be merciful in our criticisms on for-

eigners, while we exhibit to their eyes such national speci-
mens as these!" said Calvert. "For my own part, I
believe, that from no one source have we as a people
derived so much of sneer and shame, as from that which
includes within it what is called the unprotected female."

"What if we were to find out that they were Belgians,
or Dutch, or Americans? or better still, what if they
should chance to be remarkably good sort of English? I
conclude we shall meet them at supper."

"Yes, and there goes the bell for that gathering, which
on the present occasion will be a thin one. They're all
gone off to that fair at Lahnech." And so saying, Calvert
drew nigh a glass, and made one of those extempore
toilets which young men with smart moustaches are
accustomed to perform before presenting themselves to
strangers. Loyd merely took his hat and walked to
the door.

"There! that ought to be enough, surely, for all rea-
sonable captivation!" said he, laughingly.

"Perhaps you are right; besides, I suspect in the
present case it is a mere waste of ammunition;" and,
with a self-approving smile, he nodded to his image in the
glass, and followed his friend.

One line at this place will serve to record that Calvert
was very good looking; blue-eyed, blond-whiskered,
Saxon-looking withal; erect carriage and stately air,
which are always taken as favourable types of our
English blood. Perhaps a certain over-consciousness of
these personal advantages, perhaps a certain conviction
of the success that had attended these gifts, gave him
what, in slang phrase, is called a "tigerish" air : but it
was plain to see that he had acquired his ease of manner
in good company, and that his pretension was rather the
stamp of a class than of an individual.

Loyd was a pale, delicate-looking youth, with dark eyes set in the deepest of orbits, that imparted sadness to features in themselves sufficiently grave. He seemed what he was, an overworked student, a man who had sacrificed health to toil, and was only aware of the bad bargain when he felt unequal to continue the contest. His doctors had sent him abroad for rest, for that "distraction" which as often sustain its English as its French acceptance, and is only a source of worry and anxiety where rest and peace are required. His means were of the smallest—he was the only son of a country vicar, who was sorely pinched to afford him a very narrow support—and who had to raise by a loan the hundred pounds that were to give him this last chance of regaining strength and vigour. If travel therefore had its pleasures, it had also its pains for him. He felt, and very bitterly, the heavy load that his present enjoyment was laying upon those he loved best in the world, and this it was that, at his happiest moments, threw a gloom over an already moody and depressed temperament.

The sad thought of those at home, whose privations were the price of his pleasures, tracked him at every step; and pictures of that humble fireside where sat his father and his mother, rose before him as he gazed at the noble cathedral, or stood amazed before the greatest triumphs of art. This sensitive feeling, preying upon one naturally susceptible, certainly tended little to his recovery, and even at times so overbore every other sentiment, that he regretted he had ever come abroad. Scarcely a day passed that he did not hesitate whether he should not turn his steps homeward to England.

CHAPTER II.

THE PASSENGERS ON THE STEAMBOAT.

THE table d'hôte room was empty as the two Englishmen entered it at supper-time, and they took their places, moodily enough, at one end of a table laid for nigh thirty guests. "All gone to Lahneck, Franz?" asked Calvert of the waiter.

"Yes, Sir, but they'll be sorry for it, for there's thunder in the air, and we are sure to have a deluge before nightfall."

"And the new arrivals, are they gone too?"

"No, Sir. They are up stairs. The old lady would seem to have forgotten a box, or a desk, on board the steamer, and she has been in such a state about it that she couldn't think of supping; and the young ones appear to sympathise in her anxieties, for they, too, said, 'Oh, we can't think of eating just now.'"

"But of course, she needn't fuss herself. It will be detained at Mayence, and given up to her when she demands it."

A very expressive shrug of the shoulders was the only answer Franz made, and Calvert added, "You don't quite agree with me, perhaps?"

"It is an almost daily event, the loss of luggage on those Rhine steamers; so much so, that one is tempted to believe that stealing luggage is a regular livelihood here."

Just at this moment the Englishwoman in question entered the room, and in French of a very home manufacture asked the waiter how she could manage, by means of the telegraph, to reclaim her missing property.

A most involved and intricate game of cross purposes ensued ; for the waiter's knowledge of French was scarcely more extensive, and embarrassed, besides, by some specialities in accent, so that though *she* questioned and *he* replied, the discussion gave little hope of an intelligible solution.

"May I venture to offer my services, Madam ?" said Calvert, rising and bowing politely. "If I can be of the least use on this occasion——"

"None whatever, Sir. I am perfectly competent to express my own wishes, and have no need of an interpreter ;" and then turning to the waiter, added : "Montrez moi le telegraph, garçon."

The semi-tragic air in which she spoke, not to add the strange accent of her very peculiar French, was almost too much for Calvert's gravity, while Loyd, half pained by the ridicule thus attached to a countrywoman, held down his head and never uttered a word. Meanwhile the old lady had retired with a haughty toss of her towering bonnet, followed by Franz.

"The old party is fierce," said Calvert, as he began his supper, "and would not have me at any price."

"I suspect that this mistrust of each other is very common with us English : not so much from any doubt of our integrity, as from a fear lest we should not be equal in social rank."

"Well ; but really, don't you think that our externals might have satisfied that old lady she had nothing to apprehend on that score ?"

"I can't say how she may have regarded that point," was the cautious answer.

Calvert pushed his glass impatiently from him, and said, petulantly, "The woman is evidently a governess, or a companion, or a housekeeper. She writes her name in the book Miss Grainger, and the others are called Walter. Now, after all, a Miss Grainger might, without derogating too far, condescend to know a Fusilier, eh? Oh, here she comes again."

The lady thus criticised had now re-entered the room, and was busily engaged in studying the announcement of steamboat departures and arrivals, over the chimney.

"It is too absurd," said she, pettishly, in French, "to close the telegraph-office at eight, that the clerks may go to a ball."

"Not to a ball, Madam, to the fair at Lahnech," interposed Franz.

"I don't care, Sir, whether it be a dance or a junketing. It is the same inconvenience to the public; and the landlord, and the secretary, as you call him, of this hotel, are all gone, and nothing left here but you."

Whether it was the shameless effrontery of the contempt she evinced in these words, or the lamentable look of abasement of the waiter, that overcame Calvert, certain is it he made no effort to restrain himself, but, leaning back in his chair, laughed heartily and openly.

"Well, Sir," said she, turning fiercely on him, "you force me to say, that I never witnessed a more gross display of ill breeding and bad manners."

"Had you only added, Madam, 'after a very long experience of life,' the remark would have been perfect," said he, still laughing.

"Oh, Calvert!" broke in Loyd, in a tone of deprecation; but the old lady, white with passion, retired without waiting for that apology which, certainly, there was little prospect of her receiving.

"I am sorry you should have said that," said Loyd, "for though she was scarcely measured in her remark, your laughter was a gross provocation."

"How the cant of your profession sticks to you!" said the other. "There was the lawyer in every word of that speech. There was the 'case' and the 'set off.'"

Loyd could not help smiling, though scarcely pleased at this rejoinder.

"Take my word for it," said Calvert, as he helped himself to the dish before him, "there is nothing in life so aggressive as one of our elderly countrywomen when travelling in an independent condition. The theory is attack —attack—attack! They have a sort of vague impression that the passive are always imposed on, and certainly they rarely place themselves in that category. As I live, here she comes once more."

The old lady had now entered the room with a slip of paper in her hand, to which she called the waiter's atten tion, saying, "You will despatch this message to Mayence, when the office opens in the morning. See that there is no mistake about it."

"It must be in German, Madam," said Franz. "They'll not take it in in any foreign language."

"Tell her you'll translate it, Loyd. Go in, man, and get your knock-down as I did," whispered Calvert.

Loyd blushed slightly; but not heeding the sarcasm of his companion, he arose, and, approaching the stranger, said, "It will give me much pleasure to put your message into German, Madam, if it will at all conven ience you."

It was not till after a very searching look into his face, and an apparently satisfactory examination of his features, that she replied, "Well, Sir, I make no objection; there can be no great secrecy in what passes through a telegraph-office. You can do it, if you please."

Now, though the speech was not a very gracious acknowledgment of a proffered service, Loyd took the paper and proceeded to read it. It was not without an effort, however, that he could constrain himself so far as not to laugh aloud at the contents, which began by an explanation that the present inconvenience was entirely owing to the very shameful arrangements made by the steam packet company for the landing of passengers at intermediate stations, and through which the complainant, travelling with her nieces, Millicent and Florence Walter, and her maids, Susannah Tucker and Mary Briggs, and having for luggage the following articles——

"May I observe, Madam," said Loyd, in a mild tone of remonstrance, "that these explanations are too lengthy for the telegraph, not to say very costly, and as your object is simply to reclaim a missing article of your baggage——"

"I trust, Sir, that having fully satisfied your curiosity as to who we are, and of what grievance we complain, that you will spare me your comments as to the mode in which we prefer our demand for redress; but I ought to have known better, and I deserve it!" and, snatching the paper rudely from his hand, she dashed out of the room in passion.

"By Jove! you fared worse than myself," said Calvert, as he laughed loud and long. "You got a heavier castigation for your polite interference than I did for my impertinence."

"It is a lesson, at all events," said Loyd, still blushing for his late defeat. "I wonder is she all right up here," and he touched his forehead significantly.

"Of course she is.   Nay, more, I'll wager a Nap. that in her own set, amidst the peculiar horrors who form her daily intimates, she is a strong-minded sensible woman, 'that won't stand humbug,' and so on.   These are speci- alities; they wear thick shoes, woollen petticoats, and brown veils, quarrel with cabmen, and live at Clapham."

" But why do they come abroad ? "

" Ah ! that is the question that would puzzle nineteen out of every twenty of us.   With a panorama in Leicester- square, and a guide-book in a chimney-corner, we should know more of the Tyrol than we'll ever acquire junket- ing along in a hired coach, and only eager not to pay too much for one's 'Kalbsbraten' or 'Schweinfleisch,' and yet here we come in shoals,—to grumble and complain of all our self-imposed miseries, and incessantly lament the comforts of the land that we won't live in."

"Some of us come for health," said Loyd, sorrow- fully.

"And was there ever such a blunder?   Why the very vicissitudes of a continental climate are more trying than any severity in our own.   Imagine the room we are now sitting in, of a winter's evening, with a stove heated to ninety-five, and the door opening every five minutes to a draught of air eleven degrees below zero !   You pass out of this furnace to your bed-room, by a stair and corridor like the Arctic regions, to gain an uncarpeted room, with something like a knife-tray for a bed, and a poultice of feathers for a coverlet ! "

"And for all that we like it, we long for it; save, pinch, screw, and sacrifice Heaven knows what of home enjoy- ment just for six weeks or two months of it."

"Shall I tell you why?   Just because Simpkins has done it.   Simpkins has been up the Rhine and dined at the Cursaal at Ems, and made his little début at roulette

at Wiesbaden, and spoken his atrocious French at Frank-
fort, and we won't consent to be less men of the world
than Simpkins; and though Simpkins knows that it
doesn't 'pay,' and *I* know that it doesn't pay, we won't
'peach' either of us, just for the pleasure of seeing you,
and a score like you, fall into the same blunder, exper-
ience the same disasters, and incur the same disappoint-
ments as ourselves."

"No. I don't agree with you; or, rather, I won't
agree with you. I am determined to enjoy this holiday
of mine to the utmost my health will let me, and you
shall not poison the pleasure by that false philosophy
which, affecting to be deep, is only depreciatory."

"And the honourable gentleman resumed his seat, as
the newspapers say, amidst loud and vociferous cheers,
which lasted for several minutes." This Calvert said as
he drummed a noisy applause upon the table, and made
Loyd's face glow with a blush of deep shame and con-
fusion.

"I told you, the second day we travelled together, and
I tell you again now, Calvert," said he, falteringly,
"that we are nowise suited to each other, and never
could make good travelling companions. You know
far more of life than I either do or wish to know.
You see things with an acute and piercing clearness
which I cannot attain to. You have no mind for the
sort of humble things which give pleasure to a man
simple as myself; and, lastly, I don't like to say it,
but I must, your means are so much more ample than
mine, that to associate with you I must live in a style
totally above my pretensions. All these are confessions
more or less painful to make, but now that I have made
them, let me have the result, and say, good-bye—good-
bye."

There was an emotion in the last words that more than compensated for what preceded them. It was the genuine sorrow that loneliness ever impresses on certain natures; but Calvert read the sentiment as a tribute to himself, and hastily said, " No, no, you are all wrong. The very disparities you complain of are the bonds between us. The differences in our temperament are the resources by which the sphere of our observation will be widened— my scepticism will be the corrector of your hopefulness— and, as to means, take my word for it, nobody can be harder up than I am, and if you'll only keep the bag, and limit the outgoings, I'll submit to any shortcomings when you tell me they are savings."

" Are you serious—downright in earnest in all this ? " asked Loyd.

" So serious, that I propose our bargain should begin from this hour. We shall each of us place ten Napoleons in that bag of yours. You shall administer all outlay, and I bind myself to follow implicitly all your behests, as though I were a ward and you my guardian."

" I'm not very confident about the success of the scheme. I see many difficulties already, and there may be others that I cannot foresee ; still, I am willing to give it a trial."

" At last I realise one of my fondest anticipations which was to travel without the daily recurring miseries of money reckoning."

" Don't take those cigars, they are supplied by the waiter, and cost two groschen each, and they sell for three groschen a dozen in the Platz ; " and, so saying, Loyd removed the plate from before him in a quiet business-like way, that promised well for the spirit in which his trust would be exercised.

Calvert laughed as he laid down the cigar, but his obedience ratified the pact between them.

"When do we go from this?" asked he, in a quiet and half-submissive tone.

"Oh, come, this is too much!" said Loyd. "I undertook to be purser, but not pilot."

"Well, but I insist upon your assuming all the cares of legislation. It is not alone that I want not to think of the cash; but I want to have no anxieties about the road we go, where we halt, and when we move on. I want, for once in my life, to indulge the glorious enjoyment of perfect indolence—such another chance will scarcely offer itself."

"Be it so. Whenever you like to rebel, I shall be just as ready to abdicate. I'll go to my room now and study the map, and by the time you have finished your evening's stroll on the bridge, I shall have made the plan of our future wanderings."

"Agreed!" said Calvert. "I'm off to search for some of those cheap cigars you spoke of."

"Stay; you forget that you have not got any money. Here are six silver groschen; take two dozen, and see that they don't give you any of those vile Swiss ones in the number."

He took the coin with becoming gravity, and set out on his errand.

CHAPTER III.

FELLOW-TRAVELLERS' LIFE.

PARTLY to suit Calvert's passion for fishing, partly to meet his own love of a quiet, unbroken, easy existence, Loyd decided for a ramble through the lakes of Northern Italy ; and, in about ten days after the compact had been sealed, they found themselves at the little inn of the Trota, on the Lago d'Orta. The inn, which is little more than a cottage, is beautifully situated on a slender promontory that runs into the lake, and is itself almost hidden by the foliage of orange and oleander trees that cover it. It was very hard to believe it to be an inn with its trellised vine-walk, its little arched boat-house, and a small shrine beside the lake, where on certain saints' days, a priest said a mass, and blessed the fish and those that caught them. It was still harder, too, to credit the fact when one discovered his daily expenses to be all comprised within the limits of a few francs, and this with the services of the host, Signor Onofrio, for boatman.

To Loyd it was a perfect paradise. The glorious mountain range, all rugged and snow-capped—the deep-bosomed chestnut-woods—the mirror-like lake—the soft and balmy air, rich in orange odours—the earth teeming with violets—all united to gratify the senses, and wrap the mind in a dreamy ecstasy and enjoyment. It was equally a spot to relax in or to work, and although now more disposed for the former, he planned in himself to come back here, at some future day, and labour with all the zest that a strong resolve to succeed inspires.

What law would he not read? What mass of learned lore would he not store up! What strange and curious knowledge would he not acquire in this calm seclusion! He parcelled out his day in imagination; and, by rising early, and by habits of uninterrupted study, he contemplated that in one long vacation here he would have amassed an amount of information that no discursive labour could ever attain. And then, to distract him from weightier cares, he would write those light and sketchy things, some of which had already found favour with editors. He had already attained some small literary successes, and was like a very young man, delighted with the sort of recognition they had procured him; and last of all, there was something of romance in this life of mysterious seclusion. He was the hero of a little story to himself, and this thought diffused itself over every spot and every occupation, as is only known to those who like to make poems of their lives, and be to their own hearts their own epic.

Calvert, too, liked the place; but scarcely with the same enthusiasm. The fishing was excellent. He had taken a "four-pounder," and heard of some double the size. The cookery of the little inn was astonishingly good. Onofrio had once been a courier, and picked up some knowledge of the social chemistry on his travels. Beccafichi abounded, and the small wine of the Podere had a false smack of Rhenish, and then with cream, and fresh eggs, and fresh butter, and delicious figs in profusion, there were, as he phrased it, " far worse places in the hill country !"

Besides being the proprietor of the inn, Onofrio owned

a little villa, a small cottage-like thing on the opposite shore of the lake, to which he made visits once or twice a week, with a trout, or a capon, or a basket of artichokes, or some fine peaches—luxuries which apparently always found ready purchasers amongst his tenants. He called them English, but his young guests, with true British phlegm, asked him no questions about them, and he rarely, if ever, alluded to them. Indeed, his experience of English people had enabled him to see that they ever maintained a dignified reserve towards each other, even when offering to foreigners all the freedom of an old intimacy; and then he had an Italian's tact not to touch on a dangerous theme, and thus he contented himself with the despatch of his occasional hamper without attracting more attention to the matter than the laborious process of inscribing the words "Illustrissima Sign'. Grangiari," on the top.

It was about a month after they had taken up their abode at the Trota that Onofrio was seized with one of those fevers of the country which, though rarely dangerous to life, are still so painful and oppressive as to require some days of confinement and care. In this interval, Calvert was deprived of his chief companion, for mine host was an enthusiastic fisherman, and an unequalled guide to all parts of the lake. The young soldier, chafed and fretted out of all measure at this interruption to his sport, tried to read; tried to employ himself in the garden; endeavoured to write a long-promised letter home; and at last, in utter failure, and in complete discontent with himself and everything, he walked moodily about, discussing within himself whether he would not frankly declare to Loyd that the whole thing bored him, and that he wanted to be free.

"This sort of thing suits Loyd well enough," would he

say. "It is the life of Brazenose or Christchurch in a purer air and finer scenery. He can read five or six hours at a stretch, and then plunge in the lake for a swim, or pull an oar for half an hour, by way of refreshment. He is as much a man of reflection and thought as I am of action and energy. Yet, it is your slow, solemn fellow," he would say, "who is bored to death when thrown upon himself;" and now he had, in a measure, to recant this declaration, and own that the solitude was too much for *him*.

While he was yet discussing with himself how to approach the subject, the hostess came to tell him that Onofrio's illness would prevent him acting as his boatman, and begged the boat might be spared him on that day, to send over some fruit and fresh flowers he had promised to the family at St. Rosalia; "that is," added she, "if I'm lucky enough to find a boatman to take them, for at this season all are in full work in the fields."

"What would you say, Donna Marietta, if I were to take charge of the basket myself, and be your messenger to the villa?"

The hostess was far less astonished at his offer than he had imagined she would be. With her native ideas on these subjects, she only accepted the proposal as an act of civility, and not as a surprising piece of condescension, and simply said, "Onofrio shall thank you heartily for it when he is up and about again."

If this was not the exact sort of recognition he looked for, Calvert at all events saw that he was pledged to fulfil his offer; and so he stood by while she measured out peas, and counted over artichokes, and tied up bundles of mint and thyme, and stored up a pannier full of ruddy apples, surmounting all with a gorgeous bouquet of richly perfumed flowers, culled in all the careless profusion of that land of plenty. Nor was this all. She impressed upon him how he was to extol the excellence of this, and the beauty of that, to explain that the violets were true Parmesans, and the dates such as only Onofrio knew how to produce.

Loyd laughed his own little quiet laugh when he heard of his friend's mission, and his amusement was not lessened at seeing the half-awkward and more than half-unwilling preparations Calvert made to fulfil it.

"Confound the woman!" said he, losing all patience; "she wanted to charge me with all the bills and reckonings for the last three weeks, on the pretext that her husband is but ill-skilled in figures, and that it was a rare chance to find one like myself to undertake the office. I have half a mind to throw the whole cargo overboard when I reach the middle of the lake. I suppose a Nap. would clear all the cost."

"Oh, I'll not hear of such extravagance," said Loyd, demurely.

"I conclude I have a right to an act of personal folly, eh?" asked Calvert, pettishly.

"Nothing of the kind. I drew up our contract with great care, and especially on this very head, otherwise it would have been too offensive a bargain for him who should have observed all the rigid injunctions of its economy."

"It was a stupid arrangement from the first," said Calvert warmly. "Two men yet never lived, who could say that each could bound his wants by those of another. Not to say that an individual is not himself the same each day of the week. I require this on Tuesday, which I didn't want on Monday, and so on."

"You are talking of caprice as though it were necessity, Calvert."

"I don't want to discuss the matter like a special plea-der, and outside the margin of our conjoint expenses I mean to be as wasteful as I please."

"As the contract is only during pleasure, it can never be difficult to observe it."

"Yes, very true. You have arrived at my meaning by another road. When was it we last replenished the bag?"

"A little more than a week ago."

"So that there is about a fortnight yet to run?"

"About that."

Calvert stood in thought for a few seconds, and then, as if having changed the purpose he was meditating, turned suddenly away and hastened down to the boat quay.

Like many bashful and diffident men, Loyd had a false air of coldness and resolution, which impressed others greatly, but reacted grievously on his own heart in mo-ments of afterthought ; and now, no sooner had his com-panion gone, than he felt what a mockery it was for him to have assumed a rigid respect for a mere boyish agree-ment, which lost all its value the moment either felt it burdensome. "*I* was not of an age to play Mentor to *him*. It could never become me to assume the part of a guardian. I ought to have said the bargain ceases the instant you repudiate it. A forced companionship is mere slavery. Let us part the good friends we met; and so on." At last he determined to sit down and write a short note to Calvert, releasing him from his thraldom, and giving him his full and entire liberty.

"As for myself, I will remain here so long as I stay abroad, and if I come to the continent again, I will make for this spot as for a home : and now for the letter."

CHAPTER IV.

THE "LAGO D'ORTA."

LEAVING Loyd to compose his letter, we will follow Calvert, as, with vigorous stroke, he rushed his light boat through the calm water, leaving a long bright line of bubbles in his wake. Dressed in his blue flannel shirt and white trousers, a gay bunch of roses stuck jauntily in the side of his straw hat, there was an air of health, vigour, and dash about him, to which his full bright eye and upturned moustache well contributed. And, as from time to time he would rest on his oars, while his thin skiff cleaved her way alone, his bronzed and manly face and carelessly waving hair made up a picture of what we are proud to think is eminently British in its character. That is to say, there was about him much of what indicated abundance of courage, no small proportion of personal strength, and a certain sort of recklessness, which in a variety of situations in life is equivalent to power.

To any eye that watched him, as with scarce an effort he sent his boat forward, while the lazy curl of smoke that rose from his short pipe indicated ease, there would have seemed one who was indulging in the very fullest enjoyment of a scene second to none in Europe. You had but to look along the lake itself to see the most gorgeous picture of wooded islands and headlands glowing in every tint of colour from the pure white of the

oleander to the deep scarlet of the San Giuseppe, with, in
the distance, the snow-capped Alps of the St. Bernard,
while around and close to the very water's edge peeped
forth little villas, half smothered in orange-blossoms. Far
over the lake came their floating perfumes, as though to
lend enchantment to each sense, and steep the very soul
in a delicious luxury.

Now, as Calvert felt the refreshing breath of the gentle
air that stirred the water, he was conscious of a glorious
morning, and of something generally grand in the scene
about him ; but that was all. He had little romance—
less of the picturesque—in his nature. If his eyes fell on
the lake, it was to fancy the enjoyment of cleaving
through it as a swimmer ; if he turned towards the Alps,
it was to imagine how toilsome would prove the ascent ;
how deeply lay the snow on the wheels of the diligence ;
how many feet below the surface were buried the poles
that once marked out the road. But even these were but
fleeting fancies. His thoughts were seriously turned upon
his own future, which opened no bright or brilliant pro-
spect before him. To go back again to India, to return
to the old regimental drudgery, or the still more wearisome
existence of life in a remote detachment ; to waste what
he felt the best years of life in inglorious indolence, wait-
ing for that routine promotion that comes associated with
the sense of growing old ; and to trace at last the dim
vista of a return to England, when of an age that all
places and people and things have grown to be matters
of indifference. These were sad reflections. So sad,
that not even the bright scene around him could dispel.
And then there were others, which needed no speculation
to suggest, and which came with the full force of docu-
ments to sustain them. He was heavily in debt. He
owed money to the army agent, to the paymaster, to the

Agra Bank, to the regimental tailor, to the outfitter—to everyone, in short, who would suffer him to be a debtor. Bonds, and I O's, and promissory notes, renewed till they had nigh doubled, pressed on his memory, and confused his powers of calculation.

An old uncle, a brother of his mother's, who was his guardian, would once on a time have stood by him, but he had forfeited his good esteem by an act of deception with regard to money, which the old man could not forgive. "Be it so," said he; "I deemed my friendship for you worth more than three hundred pounds. You, it would seem, are differently minded; keep the money and let us part." And they did part, not to meet again. Calvert's affairs were managed by the regimental agent, and he thought little more of an old relative, who ceased to hold a place in his memory when unassociated with crisp inclosures "payable at sight."

"I wonder what would come of it if I were to write to him; if I were to put it to his humanity to rescue me from a climate where, after all, I might die—scores of fellows die out there. At all events, I detest it. I could say, 'My leave expires in October, if you would like to see me once more before I quit England for ever, for I am going to a pestilential spot—the home of the ague and jungle fever, and Heaven knows what else—your sister's son—poor Sophy's child.' That ought to touch him." And then he went on to think of all the tender and moving things he could write, and to picture to himself the agitation of him who read them; and thus speculating, and thus plotting, he swept his light boat along till she came close in to shore, and he saw the little villa peeping through the spray-like branches of a weeping ash that stood beside it. "Higher up," cried a voice, directing him. "Don't you know the landing-place yet?" And, startled by a voice not altogether strange to him, he looked round and saw the old lady of the Rhine steamer, the same who had snubbed him at Coblentz, the terrible Miss Grainger of the lost writing-case. It was some minutes before he remembered that he was performing the part of boatman, and not appearing in his own character. Resolved to take all the benefit of his incognito, he lifted his hat in what he fancied to be the true Italian style, and taking a basket in each hand, followed the old lady to the house.

"It is three days that we have been expecting you," said she, tartly, as she walked briskly on, turning at times to point a sarcasm with a fierce look. "You were punctual enough on Tuesday last, when you came for your rent. You were to the very minute then, because it suited yourself. But you are like all your countrymen—mean, selfish, and greedy. As to those pears you brought last, I have struck them off the account. You may bring others if you please, but I'll not pay for rotten fruit any more than I will for three journeys to Como for nothing — do you hear me, Sir? three journeys to look after my writing-desk, which I lost on the Rhine, but which I know was forwarded here, though I can't get it. Is it worth your while to answer? Oh, of course, your old excuse—you are forgetting your English—it is so long since you were a courier. You knew quite enough, when I came here, to make me pay more than double the proper rent for this miserable place, without a carpet, or——" Just as she reached thus far, she was joined by one of the young girls, whose looks had vastly changed for the better, and was now a strikingly fine and handsome girl.

"Milly," said the old lady, "take this man round by the kitchen garden, and get some one to take the fruit from him, and be sure you count the melons."

Not sorry for the change of companionship, Calvert followed Milly, who, not condescending to bestow a look on him, moved haughtily on in front.

"Leave your baskets yonder, my good man," said she, pointing to a bench under a spreading fig-tree; and Calvert, depositing his burden, drew himself up and removed his hat. "My aunt will pay you," said she, turning to go away.

"I'd far rather it had been the niece," said he, in English.

"What do you mean? Who are you?"

"A stranger, who, rather than suffer you to incur the privation of a breakfast without fruit, rowed across the lake this morning to bring it."

"Won't he go, Milly? What is he bargaining about?" cried Miss Grainger, coming up.

But the young girl ran hastily towards her, and for some minutes they spoke in a low tone together.

"I think it an impertinence—yes, an impertinence, Milly—and I mean to tell him so!" said the old lady, fuming with passion. "Such things are not done in the world. They are unpardonable liberties. What is your name, Sir?"

"Calvert, Madam."

"Calvert? Calvert? Not Calvert of Rocksley?" said she, with a sneer.

"No, Ma'am, only his nephew."

"Are you his nephew, really his nephew?" said she, with a half incredulity.

"Yes, Madam, I have that very unprofitable honour. If you are acquainted with the family, you will recognise

their crest ;" and he detached a seal from his watch-chain
and handed it to her.

"Quite true, the portcullis and the old motto, 'Ferme
en Tombant.' I know, or rather I knew your relatives
once, Mr. Calvert;" this was said with a total change of
manner, and a sort of simpering politeness that sat very
ill upon her.

Quick enough to mark this change of manner and
profit by it, he said, somewhat coldly, "Have I heard
your name, Madam? Will you permit me to know it?"

"Miss Grainger, Sir. Miss Adelaide Grainger"—
reddening as she spoke.

"Never heard that name before. Will you present me
to this young lady?" And thus with an air of pretension,
whose impertinence was partly covered by an appearance
of complete unconsciousness, he bowed and smiled, and
chatted away till the servant announced breakfast.

To the invitation to join them, he vouchsafed the
gentlest bend of the head, and a half smile of acceptance,
which the young lady resented by a stare that might have
made a less accomplished master of impertinence blush
to the very forehead. Calvert was, however, a proficient
in his art.

As they entered the breakfast-room, Miss Grainger
presented him to a young and very delicate-looking girl
who lay on a sofa propped up by cushions, and shrouded
with shawls, though the season was summer.

"Florence, Mr. Calvert. Miss Florence Walter. An
invalid come to benefit by the mild air of Italy, Sir, but
who feels even these breezes too severe and too bracing
for her."

"Egypt is your place," said Calvert; "one of those
nice villas on the sea slope of Alexandretta, with the palm-
trees and the cedars to keep off the sun;" and seating

himself by her side in an easy familiar way, devoid of all excess of freedom, talked to her about health and sickness in a fashion that is very pleasant to the ears of suffering. And he really talked pleasantly on the theme. It was one of which he had already some experience. The young wife of a brother officer of his own had gained, in such a sojourn as he pictured, health enough to go on to India, and was then alive and well, up in the Hill country above Simlah.

"Only fancy, aunt, what Mr. Calvert is promising me—to be rosy-cheeked," said the poor sick girl, whose pale face caught a slight pinkish tint as she spoke.

"I am not romancing in the least," said Calvert, taking his place next Milly at the table. "The dryness of the air, and the equitable temperature, work, positively, miracles;" and he went on telling of cures and recoveries. When at last he arose to take leave, it was amidst a shower of invitations to come back, and pledges on his part to bring with him some sketches of the scenery of Lower Egypt, and some notes he had made of his wanderings there.

"By-the-way," said he, as he gained the door, "have . your permission to present a friend who lives with me—a strange, bashful, shy creature, very good in his way, though that way isn't exactly my way; but really clever and well read, I believe. May I bring him? Of course I hope to be duly accredited to you myself, through my uncle."

"You need not, Mr. Calvert. I recognise you for one of the family in many ways," said Miss Grainger; "and when your friend accompanies you, he will be most welcome."

So, truly cordially they parted.

CHAPTER V.

OLD MEMORIES.

WHEN Calvert rejoined his friend, he was full of the adventure of the morning — such a glorious discovery as he had made. What a wonderful old woman, and what charming girls ! Milly, however, he owned, rather inclined to the contemptuous. " She was what you Cockneys call ' sarcy,' Loyd; but the sick girl was positively enchanting ; so pretty, so gentle, and so confiding withal. By-the-way, you must make me three or four sketches of Nile scenery—a dull flat, with a palm-tree, group of camels in the fore, and a pyramid in the background; and I'll get up the journal part, while you are doing the illustrations. I know nothing of Egypt beyond the overland route, though I have persuaded them I kept a house in Cairo, and advised them by all means to take Florence there for the winter."

" But how could you practise such a deception in such a case, Calvert ? " said Loyd, reproachfully.

" Just as naturally as you have ' got up ' that grand tone of moral remonstrance. What an arrant humbug you are, Loyd. Why not keep all this fine indignation for Westminster, where it will pay ? "

" Quiz away, if you like ; but you will not prevent me saying that the case of a poor sick girl is not one for a foolish jest, or a——"

He stopped and grew very red, but the other continued :—

"Out with it, man. You were going to say, a falsehood. I'm not going to be vexed with you because you happen to have a rather crape-coloured temperament, and like turning things round till you find the dark side of them." He paused for a few seconds and then went on : "If you had been in my place this morning, I know well enough what you'd have done. You'd have rung the changes over the uncertainty of life, and all its miseries and disappointments. You'd have frightened that poor delicate creature out of her wits, and driven her sister half distracted, to satisfy what you imagine to be your conscience, but which, I know far better, is nothing but a morbid love of excitement—an unhealthy passion for witnessing pain. Now, I left her actually looking better for my visit—she was cheered and gay, and asked when I'd come again, in a voice that betrayed a wish for my return."

Loyd never liked being drawn into a discussion with his friend, seeing how profitless such encounters are in general, and how likely to embitter intercourse; so he merely took his hat and moved towards the door.

"Where are you going? Not to that odious task of photography, I hope?" cried Calvert.

"Yes," said the other, smiling; "I am making a complete series of views of the lake, and some fine day or other I'll make water-colour drawings from them."

"How I hate all these fine intentions that only point to more work. Tell me of a plan for a holiday, some grand scheme for idleness, and I am with you; but to sit quietly down and say, 'I'll roll that stone up a hill next summer, or next autumn,' that drives me mad."

"Well, I'll not drive you mad. I'll say nothing about it," said Loyd, with a good-natured smile.

"But won't you make me these drawings, these jottings of my tour amongst the Pyramids?"

"Not for such an object as you want them to serve."

"I suppose, when you come to practise at the bar, you'll only defend innocence and protect virtue, eh? You'll, of course, never take the brief of a knave, or try to get a villain off. With your principles, to do so would be the basest of all crimes."

"I hope I'll never do that deliberately which my conscience tells me I ought not to do."

"All right. Conscience is always in one's own keeping—a guest in the house, who is far too well bred to be disagreeable to the family. Oh, you arch hypocrite! how much worse you are than a reprobate like myself."

"I'll not dispute that."

"More hypocrisy!"

"I mean that, without conceding the point, it's a thesis I'll not argue."

"You ought to have been a Jesuit, Loyd. You'd have been a grand fellow in a long black soutane, with little buttons down to the feet, and a skull-cap on your head. I think I see some poor devil coming to you about a 'cas de conscience,' and going away sorely puzzled with your reply to him."

"Don't come to me with one of yours, Calvert, that's all," said Loyd, laughing, as he hurried off.

Like many men who have a strong spirit of banter in them, Calvert was vexed and mortified when his sarcasm did not wound. "If the stag will not run, there can be no pursuit," and so was it that he now felt angry with Loyd, angry with himself. "I suppose these are the sort of fellows who get on in life. The world likes their quiet subserviency, and their sleek submissiveness. As for me, and the like of me, we are 'not placed.' Now for a line to my Cousin Sophy, to know who is the 'Grainger' who says she is so well acquainted with us all. Poor Sophy, it was a love affair once between us, and then it came to a quarrel, and out of that we fell into the deeper bitterness of what is called 'a friendship.' We never really hated each other till we came to that!"

"Dearest, best of friends," he began, "in my broken health, fortunes, and spirits, I came to this place a few weeks ago, and made, by chance, the acquaintance of an atrocious old woman called Grainger—Miss or Mrs., I forget which—who is she, and why does she know *us*, and call us the 'dear Calverts,' and your house 'sweet old Rocksley?' I fancy she must be a begging-letter impostor, and has a design—it will be a very abortive one—upon my spare five-pound notes. Tell me all you know of her, and if you can add a word about her nieces twain—one pretty, the other prettier—do so.

"Any use in approaching my uncle with a statement of my distresses — mind, body, and estate? I owe him so much gratitude that, if he doesn't want me to be insolvent, he must help me a little further.

"Is it true you are going to be married? The thought of it sends a pang through me, of such anguish as I dare not speak of. Oh dear! oh dear! what a flood of bygones are rushing upon me, after all my pledges, all my promises! One of these girls reminded me of your smile; how like, but how different, Sophy. Do say there's no truth in the story of the marriage, and believe me—what your heart will tell you I have never ceased to be—your devoted

"HARRY CALVERT."

"I think that ought to do," said he, as he read over the letter; "and there's no peril in it, since her marriage is fixed for the end of the month. It is, after all, a cheap luxury to bid for the lot that will certainly be knocked down to another. She's a nice girl, too, is Sophy, but, like all of us, with a temper of her own. I'd like to see her married to Loyd, they'd make each other perfectly miserable."

With this charitable reflection to turn over in various ways, tracing all the consequences he could imagine might spring from it, he sauntered out for a walk beside the lake.

"This box has just come by the mail from Chiasso," said his host, pointing to a small parcel, corded and sealed. "It is the box the signora yonder has been searching for these three weeks; it was broken when the diligence upset, and they tied it together as well as they could."

The writing-desk was indeed that which Miss Grainger had lost on her Rhine journey, and was now about to reach her in a lamentable condition—one hinge torn off, the lock strained, and the bottom split from one end to the other.

"I'll take charge of it. I shall go over to see her in a day or two, perhaps to-morrow;" and with this Calvert carried away the box to his own room.

As he was laying the desk on his table, the bottom gave way, and the contents fell about the room. They were a mass of papers and letters, and some parchments; and he proceeded to gather them up as best he might, cursing the misadventure, and very angry with himself for being involved in it. The letters were in little bundles, neatly tied, and docketed with the writers' names. These he replaced in the box, having inverted it, and placing all, as nearly as he could, in due order, till he came to a thick papered document tied with red tape at the corner, and entitled Draft of

3—2

Jacob Walter's Will, with Remarks of Counsel. "This we must look at," said Calvert. "What one can see at Doctors' Commons for a shilling is no breach of confidence, even if seen for nothing;" and with this he opened the paper.

It was very brief, and set forth how the testator had never made, nor would make, any other will, that he was sound of mind, and hoped to die so. As to his fortune, it was something under thirty thousand pounds in Bank Stock, and he desired it should be divided equally between his daughters, the survivor of them to have the whole, or, in the event of each life lapsing before marriage, that the money should be divided amongst a number of charities that he specified.

"I particularly desire and beg," wrote he, "that my girls be brought up by Adelaide Grainger, my late wife's half-sister, who long has known the hardships of poverty, and the cares of a narrow subsistence, that they may learn in early life the necessity of thrift, and not habituate themselves to luxuries, which a reverse of fortune might take away from them. I wish, besides, that it should be generally believed their fortune was one thousand pounds each, so that they should not become a prey to fortune-hunters, nor the victims of adventurers, insomuch that my last request to each of my dear girls would be not to marry the man who would make inquiry into the amount of their means till twelve calendar months after such inquiry, that time being full short enough to study the character of one thus palpably worldly-minded and selfish."

A few cautions as to the snares and pitfalls of the world followed, and the document finished with the testator's name, and that of three witnesses in pencil, the words "if they consent," being added in ink, after them.

" Twice fifteen make thirty—thirty thousand pounds—
a very neat sum for a great many things, and yielding,
even in its dormant state, about fifteen hundred a year.
What can one do for that?   Live, certainly — live
pleasantly, jovially, if a man were a bachelor.   At Paris,
for instance, with one's pleasant little entresol in the Rue
Neuve, or the Rue Faubourg St. Honoré, and his club,
and his saddle-horses, with even ordinary luck at billiards,
he could make the two ends meet very satisfactorily.
Then, Baden always pays its way, and the sea-side places
also do, for the world is an excellent world to the fellow
who travels with his courier, and only begs to be plucked
a little by the fingers that wear large diamonds.

" But all these enchantments vanish when it becomes a
question of a wife.   A wife means regular habits and
respectability.   The two most costly things I know of.
Your scampish single-handed valet, who is out all day
on his own affairs, and only turns up at all at some
noted time in your habits, is not one tenth as dear as
that old creature with the powdered head and the
poultice of cravat round his neck, who only bows when
the dinner is served, and grows apoplectic if he draws
a cork.

"It's the same in everything ! Your house must be
taken, not because it is convenient or that you like it, but
because your wife can put a pretentious address on her
card.   It must be something to which you can tag
Berkeley Square, or Belgravia.   In a word, a wife is a
mistake, and, what is worse, a mistake out of which there
is no issue."

Thus reasoning and reflecting—now, speculating on
what he should feel—now, imagining what "the world"
would say — he again sat down, and once more read
over Mr. Walter's last will and testament.

CHAPTER VI.

SOPHY'S LETTER.

IN something over a week the post brought two letters for the fellow-travellers. Loyd's was from his mother—a very homely affair, full of affection and love, and overflowing with those little details of domestic matters so dear to those who live in the small world of home and its attachments.

Calvert's was from his Cousin Sophy, much briefer, and very different in style. It ran thus:

"Dear Henry——"

"I used to be Harry," muttered he.

"Dear Henry,—It was not without surprise I saw your handwriting again. A letter from you is indeed an event at Rocksley.

"The Miss Grainger, if her name be Adelaide (for there were two sisters) was our nursery governess long ago. Cary liked, I hated her. She left us to take charge of some one's children—relatives of her own, I suspect—and though she made some move about coming to see us, and presenting 'her charge,' as she called it, there was no response to the suggestion, and it dropped. I never heard more of her.

"As to any hopes of assistance from papa, I can scarcely speak encouragingly. Indeed, he made no inquiry as to the contents of your letter, and only remarked afterwards to Cary that he trusted the correspondence was not to continue.

"Lastly, as to myself, I really am at a loss to see how my marriage can be a subject of joy or grief, of pleasure or pain, to you. We are as much separated from each other in all the relations of life, as we shall soon be by long miles of distance. Mr. Wentworth Graham is fully aware of the relations which once subsisted between us, —he has even read your letters—and it is at his instance I request that the tone of our former intimacy shall cease from this day, and that there may not again be any reference to the past between us. I am sure in this I am merely anticipating what your own sense of honourable propriety would dictate, and that I only express a sentiment your own judgment has already ratified.

"Believe me to be, very sincerely yours,

"SOPHIA CALVERT."

"Oh dear! When we were Sophy and Harry, the world went very differently from now, when it has come to Henry and Sophia. Not but she is right—right in everything but one. She ought not to have shown the letters. There was no need of it, and it was unfair! There is a roguery in it too, which, if I were Mr. Wentworth Graham, I'd not like. It is only your most accomplished sharper that ever plays 'cartes sur table.' I'd sorely suspect the woman who would conciliate the new love by a treachery to the old one. However, happily, this is his affair, not mine. Though I could make it mine, too, if I were so disposed, by simply reminding her that Mr. W. G. has only seen one half, and, by long odds, the least interesting half, of our correspondence, and that for the other he must address himself to me. Husbands have occasionally to learn that a small sealed packet of old letters would be a more acceptable present to the bride on her wedding morning than the prettiest trinket from the Rue de la Paix. Should like to throw this shell into the midst of the orange-flowers and the wedding favours, and I'd do it too, only that I could never accurately hear of the tumult and dismay it caused. I should be left to mere imagination for the mischief, and imagination no longer satisfies me."

While he thus mused, he saw Loyd preparing for one of his daily excursions with the photographic apparatus, and could not help a contemptuous pity for a fellow so easily amused and interested, and so easily diverted from the great business of life—which he deemed "getting on "—to a pastime which cost labour and returned no profit.

"Come and see 'I Grangeri' (the name by which the Italians designated the English family at the villa), it's far better fun than hunting out rocky bits, or ruined fragments of masonry. Come, and I'll promise you something prettier to look at than all your feathery ferns or drooping foxgloves."

Loyd tried to excuse himself. He was always shy and timid with strangers. His bashfulness repelled intimacy and so he frankly owned that he would only be a bar to his friend's happiness, and throw a cloud over this pleasant intercourse.

"How do you know but I'd like that?" said Calvert with a mocking laugh. "How do you know but I want the very force of a contrast to bring my own merits more conspicuously forward?"

"And make them declare when we went away, that it is inconceivable why Mr. Calvert should have made a companion of that tiresome Mr. Loyd—so low-spirited and so dreary, and so uninteresting in every way?"

"Just so l And that the whole thing has but one explanation—in Calvert's kindness and generosity ; who, seeing the helplessness of this poor depressed creature, has actually sacrificed himself to vivify and cheer him. As we hear of the healthy people suffering themselves to be bled that they might impart their vigorous heart's blood to a poor wretch in the cholera."

"But I'm not blue yet," said Loyd laughing. "I almost think I could get on with my own resources."

"Of course you might, in the fashion you do at present ; but *that* is not life—or at least it is only the life of a vegetable. Mere existence and growth are not enough for a man who has hopes to fulfil, and passions to exercise, and desires to expand into accomplishments, not to speak of the influence that everyone likes to wield over his fellows. But, come along, jump into the boat, and see these girls ! I want you ; for there is one of them I scarcely understand as yet, and as I am always taken up with her sick sister, I've had no time to learn more about her."

"Well," said Loyd, "not to offer opposition to the notion of the tie that binds us, I consent." And sending back to the cottage all the details of his pursuit, he accompanied Calvert to the lake.

"The invalid girl I shall leave to your attention, Loyd," said the other, as he pulled across the water. "I like her the best ; but I am in no fear of rivalry in that quarter, and I want to see what sort of stuff the other is made of. So, you understand, you are to devote yourself especially to Florence, taking care, when opportunity serves, to say all imaginable fine things about me — my talents, my energy, my good spirits, and so forth. I'm serious, old fellow, for I will own to you I mean to marry one of them, though which, I have not yet decided on."

Loyd laughed heartily—far more heartily than in his quiet habit was his wont—and said, "Since when has this bright idea occurred to you?"

"I'll tell you," said the other gravely. "I have for years had a sort of hankering kind of half attachment to a cousin of mine. We used to quarrel, and make up, and quarrel again; but somehow, just as careless spend-thrifts forget to destroy the old bill when they give a renewal, and at last find a swingeing sum hanging over them they had never dreamed of, Sophy and I never entirely cancelled our old scores, but kept them back to be demanded at some future time. And the end has been, a regular rupture between us, and she is going to be married at the end of this month, and, not to be out-done on the score of indifference, I should like to an-nounce my own happiness, since that's the word for it, first."

"But have you means to marry?"

"Not a shilling."

"Nor prospects?"

"None."

"Then I don't understand——"

"Of course you don't understand. Nor could I make you understand how fellows like myself play the game of life. But let me try by an illustration to enlighten you. When there's no wind on a boat, and her sails flap lazily against the mast, she can have no guidance, for there is no steerage-way on her. She may drift with a current, or rot in a calm, or wait to be crushed by some heavier craft surging against her. Any wind—a squall, a hurricane—would be better than that. Such is my case. Marriage without means is a hurricane; but I'd rather face a hurricane than be water-logged between two winds."

"But the girl you marry——"

"The girl I marry—or rather the girl who marries *me* —will soon learn that she's on board a privateer, and that on the wide ocean called life there's plenty of booty to be had, for a little dash and a little danger to grasp it."

"And is it to a condition like this you'd bring the girl you love, Calvert?"

"Not if I had five thousand a year. If I owned that, or even four, I'd be as decorous as yourself; and I'd send my sons to Rugby, and act as poor-law guardian, and give my twenty pounds to the county hospital, and be a model Englishman, to your heart's content. But I haven't five thousand a year, no, nor five hundred a year ; and as for the poor-house and the hospital, I'm far more likely to claim the benefit than aid the funds. Don't you see, my wise-headed friend, that the whole is a question of money? Morality is just now one of the very dearest things going, and even the rich cannot always afford it. As for me, a poor sub in an Indian regiment, I no more affect it than I presume to keep a yacht, or stand for a county."

"But what right have you to reduce another to such straits as these? Why bring a young girl into such a conflict?"

"If ever you read Louis Blanc, my good fellow, you'd have seen that the right of all rights is that of ' associated labour.' But come, let us not grow too deep in the theme, or we shall have very serious faces to meet our friends with, and yonder, where you see the drooping ash trees, is the villa. Brush yourself up, therefore, for the coming interview; think of your bits of Shelley and Tennyson, and who knows but you'll acquit yourself with honour to your introducer."

"Let my introducer not be too confident," said Loyd, smiling ; " but here come the ladies."

As he spoke, two girls drew nigh the landing-place, one leaning on the arm of the other, and in her attitude showing how dependent she was for support.

"My bashful friend, ladies !" said Calvert, presenting Loyd.   And with this they landed.

CHAPTER VII.

DISSENSION.

THE knowledge Calvert now possessed of the humble relations which had subsisted between Miss Grainger and his uncle's family, had rendered him more confident in his manner, and given him even a sort of air of protection towards them. Certain it is, each day made him less and less a favourite at the villa, while Loyd, on the other hand, grew in esteem and liking with everyone of them. A preference which, with whatever tact shrouded, showed itself in various shapes.

"I perceive," said Calvert one morning, as they sat at breakfast together, "my application for an extension of leave is rejected. I am ordered to hold myself in readiness to sail with drafts for some regiments in Upper India!" he paused for a few seconds, and then continued. "I'd like anyone to tell me what great difference there is in real condition between an Indian officer and a transported felon. In point of daily drudgery there is little, and as for climate the felon has the best of it."

"I think you take too dreary a view of your fortune. It is not the sort of career I would choose, nor would it suit me, but if my lot had fallen that way, I suspect I'd not have found it so unendurable."

"No. It would not suit you. There's no scope in a

soldier's life for those little sly practices, those small artifices of tact and ingenuity, by which subtlety does its work in this world. In such a career, all this adroitness would be clean thrown away."

"I hope," said Loyd, with a faint smile, "that you do not imagine that these are the gifts to achieve success in any calling."

"I don't know—I am not sure, but I rather suspect they find their place at the Bar."

"Take my word for it, then, you are totally mistaken. It is an error just as unworthy of your good sense as it is of your good feeling!" And he spoke with warmth and energy.

"Hurrah! hurrah!" cried Calvert. "For three months I have been exploring to find one spot in your whole nature that would respond fiercely to attack, and at last I have it."

"You put the matter somewhat offensively to me, or I'd not have replied in this fashion—but let us change the topic, it is an unpleasant one."

"I don't think so. When a man nurtures what his friend believes to be a delusion, and a dangerous delusion, what better theme can there be than its discussion?"

"I'll not discuss it," said Loyd, with determination.

"You'll not discuss it?"

"No!"

"What if I force you? What if I place the question on grounds so direct and so personal that you can't help it?"

"I don t understand you."

"You shall presently. For some time back I have been thinking of asking an explanation from you—an explanation of your conduct at the villa. Before you had established an intimacy there, I stood well with everyone. The old woman, with all her respect for my family and connexions, was profuse in her attentions. Of the girls, as I somewhat rashly confided to you, I had only to make my choice. I presented you to them, never anticipating that I was doing anything very dangerous to them or to myself, but I find I was wrong. I don't want to descend to details, nor inquire how and by what arts you gained your influence; my case is simply with the fact that, since *you* have been in favour, *I* have been out of it. My whole position with them is changed. I can only suggest now what I used to order, and I have the pleasure, besides, of seeing that even my suggestion must be submitted to you and await your approval."

"Have you finished?" said Loyd, calmly.

"No, far from it! I could make my charge extend over hours long. In fact, I have only to review our lives here for the last six or seven weeks, to establish all I have been saying, and show you that you owe me an explanation, and something more than an explanation."

"Have you done now?"

"If you mean, have I said all that I could say on this subject, no, far from it. You have not heard a fiftieth part of what I might say about it."

"Well, I have heard quite enough. My answer is this, you are totally mistaken; I never, directly or indirectly, prejudiced your position. I seldom spoke of you, never slightingly. I have thought, it is true, that you assumed towards these ladies a tone of superiority, which could not fail to be felt by them, and that the habit grew on you, to an extent you perhaps were not aware of; as, however, they neither complained of, nor resented it, and as, besides, you were far more a man of the world than myself, and consequently knew better what the usages of society permitted, I refrained from any remark, nor, but for your present charge, would I say one word now on the subject."

"So, then, you have been suffering in secret all this time over my domineering and insolent temper, pitying the damsels in distress, but not able to get up enough of Quixotism to avenge them?"

"Do you want to quarrel with me, Calvert?" said the other calmly.

"If I knew what issue it would take, perhaps I could answer you."

"I'll tell you, then, at least so far as I am concerned, I have never injured, never wronged you.   I have therefore nothing to recall, nothing to redress, upon any part of my conduct.   In what you conceive you are personally interested, I am ready to give a full explanation, and this done, all is done between us."

"I thought so, I suspected as much," said Calvert, contemptuously. "I was a fool to suppose you'd have taken the matter differently, and now nothing remains for me but to treat my aunt's nursery governess with greater deference, and be more respectful in the presence —the august presence—of a lawyer's clerk."

"Good-bye, Sir," said Loyd, as he left the room.

Calvert sat down and took up a book, but though he read three full pages, he knew nothing of what they contained.   He opened his desk, and began a letter to Loyd, a farewell letter, a justification of himself, but done more temperately than he had spoken; but he tore it up, and so with a second and a third.   As his passion mounted, he bethought him of his cousin and her approaching marriage.   "I can spoil some fun there," cried he, and wrote as follows:

"Lago d'Orta, August 12.

"Dear Sir,—In the prospect of the nearer relations which a few days more will establish between us, I venture to address you thus familiarly. My cousin, Miss Sophia Calvert, has informed me by a letter I have just received that she deemed it her duty to place before you a number of letters written by me to her, at a time when there subsisted between us a very close attachment. With my knowledge of my cousin's frankness, her candour, and her courage—for it would also require some courage—I am fully persuaded that she has informed you thoroughly on all that has passed. We were both very young, very thoughtless, and, worse than either, left totally to our own guidance, none to watch, none to look after us. There is no indiscretion in my saying that we were both very much in love, and with that sort of confidence in each other that renders distrust a crime to one's own conscience. Although, therefore, she may have told you much, her womanly dignity would not let her dwell on these circumstances, explanatory of much, and palliative of all that passed between us. To you, a man of the world, I owe this part declaration, less, however, for your sake or for mine, than for her, for whom either of us ought to make any sacrifice in our power.

"The letters she wrote me are still in my possession. I own they are very dear to me; they are all that remain of a past, to which nothing in my future life can recall the equal. I feel, however, that your right to them is greater than my own, but I do not know how to part with them. I pray you advise me in this. Say how you would act in a like circumstance, knowing all that has occurred, and be assured that your voice will be a command to your very devoted servant,

"H. C.

"P.S.—When I began this letter, I was minded to say my cousin should see it: on second thoughts, I incline to say not, decidedly not."

When this base writer had finished writing he flung down the pen, and said to himself, half aloud, "I'd give something to see him read this!"

With a restless impatience to do something—anything, he left the house, walking with hurried steps to the little jetty where the boats lay. "Where's my boat, Onofrio?" said he, asking for the skiff he generally selected.

"The other signor has taken her across the lake."

"This is too much," muttered he. "The fellow fancies that because he skulks a satisfaction, he is free to practise an impertinence. He knew I preferred this boat, and therefore he took her."

"Jump in, and row me across to La Rocca," said he to the boatman. As they skimmed across the lake, his mind dwelt only on vengeance, and fifty different ways of exacting it passed and repassed before him. All, however, concentrating on the one idea—that to pass some insult upon Loyd in presence of the ladies would be the most fatal injury he could inflict, but how to do this without a compromise of himself was the difficulty.

"Though no woman will ever forgive a coward," thought he, "I must take care that the provocation I offer be such as will not exclude myself from sympathy." And, with all his craft and all his cunning, he could not hit upon a way to this. He fancied, too, that Loyd had gone over to prejudice the ladies against him by his own version of what had occurred in the morning. He knew well how, of late, he himself had not occupied the highest place in their esteem—it was not alone the insolent and overbearing tone he assumed, but a levity in talking of things which others treated with deference, alike offensive to morals and manners—these had greatly lowered him in their esteem, especially of the girls, for old Miss Grainger, with a traditional respect for his name and family, held to him far more than the others.

"What a fool I was ever to have brought the fellow here! What downright folly it was in me to have let them ever know him. Is it too late, however, to remedy this? Can I not yet undo some of this mischief?" This was a new thought, and it filled his mind till he landed. As he drew quite close to the shore he saw that the little awning-covered boat, in which the ladies occasionally made excursions on the lake, was now anchored under a large drooping ash, and that Loyd and the girls were on board of her. Loyd was reading to them; at least so the continuous and equable tone of his voice indicated, as it rose in the thin and silent air. Miss Grainger was not there—and this was a fortunate thing—for now he should have his opportunity to talk with her alone, and probably ascertain to what extent Loyd's representations had damaged him.

He walked up to the villa, and entered the drawing-room, as he was wont, by one of the windows that opened on the green sward without. There was no one in the room, but a half-written letter, on which the ink was still fresh, showed that the writer had only left it at the instant. His eye caught the words, "Dear and Reverend Sir," and in the line beneath the name Loyd. The temptation was too strong, and he read on :

"Dear and Reverend Sir,—I hasten to express my entire satisfaction with the contents of your letter. Your son, Mr. Loyd, has most faithfully represented his position and his prospects, and, although my niece might possibly have placed her chances of happiness in the hands of a wealthier suitor, I am fully assured she never could have met with one whose tastes, pursuits, and general disposition——"

A sound of coming feet startled him, and he had but time to throw himself on a sofa, when Miss Grainger entered. Her manner was cordial—fully as cordial as usual—perhaps a little more so, since, in the absence of her nieces, she was free to express the instinctive regard she felt towards all that bore his name.

"How was it that you did not come with Loyd?" asked she.

"I was busy, writing letters I believe—congratulations on Sophy's approaching marriage; but what did Loyd say —was that the reason he gave?"

"He gave none. He said he took a whim into his head to row himself across the lake; and indeed I half suspect the exertion was too much for him. He has been coughing again, and the pain in his side hasreturned."

"He's a wretched creature—I mean as regards health and strength. Of course he always must have been so: but the lives these fellows lead in London would breach the constitution of a really strong man."

"Not Loyd, however; he never kept late hours, nor had habits of dissipation."

"I don't suppose he ever told you that he had," said he, laughing. "I conclude that he has never shown you his diary of town life."

"But do you tell me, seriously, that he is a man of dissipated habits?"

"Not more so than eight out of every ten, perhaps, in his class of life. The student is everywhere more given to the excitements of vice than the sportsman. It is

the compensation for the wearisome monotony of brain
labour, and they give themselves up to excesses from
which the healthier nature of a man with country tastes
would revolt at once. But what have I to do with his
habits? I am not his guardian nor his confessor."

"But they have a very serious interest for *me*."

"Then you must look for another counsellor. I am
not so immaculate that I can arraign others; and, if I
were, I fancy I might find some pleasanter occupation."

"But if I tell you a secret, a great secret——"

"I'd not listen to a secret. I detest secrets, just as I'd
hate to have the charge of another man's money. So, I warn
you, tell me nothing that you don't want to hear talked
of at dinner, and before the servants."

"Yes; but this is a case in which I really need your
advice."

"You can't have it at the price you propose. Not to
add, that I have a stronger sentiment to sway me in
this case, which you will understand at once, when I
you tell that he is a man of whom I would like to speak
with great reserve, for the simple reason that I don't like
him."

"Don't like him! You don't like him!"

"It does seem very incredible to you; but I must re-
peat it, I don't like him."

"But will you tell me why? What are the grounds of
your dislike?"

"Is it not this very moment I have explained to you
that my personal feeling towards him inspires a degree of
deference which forbids me to discuss his character?
He may be the best fellow in Europe, the bravest, the
boldest, the frankest, the fairest. All I have to say is,
that if I had a sister, and he proposed to marry her,
I'd rather see her a corpse than his wife; and now you

have led me into a confession that I told you I'd not
enter upon. Say another word about it, and I'll go and
ask Loyd to come up here and listen to the discussion,
for I detest secrets and secrecy, and I'll have nothing to
say to either."

" You'd not do anything so rash and inconsiderate ? "

" Don't provoke me, that's all. You are always telling
me you know the Calverts, their hot-headedness, their
passionate warmth, and so on. I leave it to yourself,
is it wise to push me further ? "

" May I show you a letter I received yesterday morn-
ing, in reply to one of mine ? "

" Not if it refers to Loyd."

" It does refer to him."

" Then I'll not read it. I tell you for the last
time, I'll not be cheated into this discussion. I don't
desire to have it said of me some fine morning, 'You
talked of the man that you lived with on terms of in-
timacy. You chummed with him, and yet you told stories
of him.'"

" If you but knew the difficulty of the position in which
you have placed me——"

" I know at least the difficulty in which you have placed
me, and I am resolved not to incur it. Have I given to
you Sophy's letter to read ? " said he with a changed
voice. " I must fetch it out to you and let you see
all that she says of her future happiness." And thus,
by a sudden turn, he artfully engaged her in recollections
of Rocksley, and all the persons and incidents of a re-
mote long ago !

When Loyd returned with the girls to the house, Cal-
vert soon saw that he had not spoken to them on the
altercation of the morning—a reserve which he ungene-
rously attributed to the part Loyd himself filled in the

controversy. The two met with a certain reserve; but which, however felt and understood by each, was not easily marked by a spectator. Florence, however, saw it, with the traditional clearness of an invalid. She read what healthier eyes never detect. She saw that the men had either quarrelled, or were on the brink of a quarrel, and she watched them closely and narrowly. This was the easier for her, as at meal times she never came to table, but lay on a sofa, and joined in the conversation at intervals.

Oppressed by the consciousness of what had occurred in the morning, and far less able to conceal his emotions or master them than his companion, Loyd was disconcerted and ill at ease : now answering at cross-purposes, now totally absorbed in his own reflections. As Calvert saw this, it encouraged him to greater efforts to be agreeable. He could, when he pleased, be a most pleasing guest. He had that sort of knowledge of people and life which seasons talk so well, and suits so many listeners. He was curious to find out to which of the sisters Loyd was engaged, but all his shrewdness could not fix the point decisively. He talked on incessantly, referring occasionally to Loyd to confirm what he knew well the other's experience could never have embraced, and asking frankly, as it were, for his opinion on people he was fully aware the other had never met with.

Emily (or Milly, as she was familiarly called) Walter showed impatience more than once at these sallies, which always made Loyd confused and uncomfortable, so that Calvert leaned to the impression that it was she herself was the chosen one. As for Florence, she rather enjoyed, he thought, the awkward figure Loyd presented, and she even laughed outright at his bashful embarrassment.

"Yes," said Calvert to himself, "Florence is with me. She is my ally.   I'm sure of her."

"What spirits he has," said Miss Grainger, as she brought the sick girl her coffee.   "I never saw him in a gayer mood.   He's bent on tormenting Loyd though, for he has just proposed a row on the lake, and that he should take one boat and Loyd the other, and have a race.   He well knows who'll win."

"That would be delightful, aunt.   Let us have it by all means.   Mr. Calvert, I engage *you*.   You are to take *me*.   Emily will go with Mr. Loyd."

"And I'll stand at the point and be the judge," said Miss Grainger.

Calvert never waited for more, but springing up, hastened down to the shore to prepare the boat.   He was soon followed by Miss Grainger, with Florence leaning on her arm, and looking brighter and fairer than he thought he had ever seen her.

"Let us be off at once," whispered Calvert, "for I'd like a few hundred yards' practice—a sort of trial gallop —before I begin;" and, placing the sick girl tenderly in the stern, he pulled vigorously out into the lake.   "What a glorious evening!" said he.   "Is there anything in the world can equal one of these sunsets on an Italian lake, with all the tints of the high Alps blending softly on the calm water?"

She made no answer; and he went on enthusiastically about the scene, the hour, the stillness, and the noble sublimity of the gigantic mountains which arose around them.

Scarcely, however, had Calvert placed her in the boat, and pulled out vigorously from the shore, than he saw a marked change come over the girl's face.   All the laughing gaiety of a moment back was gone, and an expression of anxiety had taken its place.

"You are not ill?" asked he, eagerly.

"No. Why do you ask me?"

"I was afraid—I fancied you looked paler. You seem changed."

"So I am," said she, seriously. "Answer me what I shall ask, but tell me frankly."

"That I will; what is it?"

"You and Loyd have quarrelled—what was it about?"

"What a notion! Do you imagine that the silly quizzing that passes between young men implies a quarrel?"

"No matter what I fancy; tell me as candidly as you said you would. What was the subject of your disagreement?"

"How peremptory you are," said he laughing. "Are you aware that to give your orders in this fashion implies one of two things—a strong interest in me, or in my adversary?"

"Well, I accept the charge; now for the confession."

"Am I right, then, dearest Florence?" said he, ceasing to row, and leaning down to look the nearer at her. "Am I right, then, that your claim to this knowledge is the best and most indisputable?"

"Tell me what it is!" said she, and her pale face suddenly glowed with a deep flush.

"You guessed aright, Florence, we did quarrel; that is, we exchanged very angry words, though it is not very easy to say how the difference began, nor how far it went. I was dissatisfied with him. I attributed to his influence, in some shape or other, that I stood less well here—in *your* esteem, I mean—than formerly; and he somewhat cavalierly told me if there were a change I owed it to myself, that I took airs upon me, that I was haughty, presuming, and fifty other things of the same sort ; and so, with an interchange of such courtesies, we grew at last to feel very warm, and finally reached that point where men—of the world, at least—understand discussion ceases, and something else succeeds."

" Well, go on," cried she, eagerly.

" All is told ; there is no more to say.   The lawyer did not see the thing, perhaps, in the same vulgar light that I did ; he took his hat, and came over here.   I followed him, and there's the whole of it."

" I think he was wrong to comment upon your manner, if not done from a sense of friendship, and led on to it by some admission on your part."

" Of course he was ; and I am charmed to hear you say so."

She was silent for some time, leaning her head on her hand, and appearing deep in thought.

" Now that I have made *my* confession, will you let me have one of *yours ?* " said he, in a low, soft voice.

" I'm not sure ; what's it to be about ? "

" It's about myself I want to question you."

" About yourself !   Surely you could not have hit upon a sorrier adviser, or a less experienced counsellor than I am."

" I don't want advice, Florence, I only want a fact ; and from all I have seen of you, I believe you will deal fairly with me."

She nodded assent, and he went on :

" In a few weeks more I shall be obliged to return to India ; to a land I dislike, and a service I detest : to live amongst companions distasteful to me, and amidst habits and associations that, however endurable when I knew no better, are now become positively odious in my eyes.   This is my road to rank, station, and honour. There is, however, another path ; and if I relinquish this career, and give up all thought of ambition, I might remain in Europe—here, perhaps, on this very lake side —and lead a life of humble but unbroken happiness— one of those peaceful existences which poets dream of, but never realise, because it is no use in disparaging the cup of life till one has tasted and known its bitterness; and these men have not reached such experience — *I* have."

He waited for her to speak—he looked eagerly at her for a word—but she was silent.

"The confession I want from you, Florence, is this: could you agree to share this life with me?"

She shook her head and muttered, but what he could not catch.

"It would be too dreary, too sad-coloured, you think?"

"No," said she, "not that."

"You fear, perhaps, that these schemes of isolation have never succeeded: that weariness will come when there are no longer new objects to suggest interest or employment?"

"Not that," said she, more faintly.

"Then the objection must be myself. Florence, is it that you would not, that you could not, trust me with your happiness?"

"You ask for frankness, and you shall have it. I cannot except your offer. My heart is no longer mine to give."

"And this—this engagement, has been for some time back?" asked he, almost sternly.

"Yes, for some time," said she, faintly.

"Am I acquainted with the object of it? Perhaps I have no right to ask this. But there is a question I have full and perfect right to ask. How, consistently with

such an engagement, have you encouraged the **attentions**
I have paid you?"

"Attentions! and to me! Why, your attentions **have**
been directed rather to my sister—at least, she always
thought so—and even these we deemed the mere passing
flirtations of one who made no secret of saying that he
regarded marriage as an intolerable slavery, or rather, the
heavy price that one paid for the pleasure of courtship."

"Are the mere levities with which I amused an hour
to be recorded against me as principles?"

"Only when such levities fitted into each other so
accurately as to show plan and contrivance."

"It was Loyd said that. That speech was his. I'd
lay my life on it."

"I think not. At least, if the thought were his, he'd
have expressed it far better."

"You admire him, then?" asked he, peering closely
at her.

"I wonder why they are not here," said she, turning
her head away. "This same race ought to come off by
this time."

"Why don't you answer my question?"

"There he goes! Rowing away all alone, too, and
my aunt is waving her handkerchief in farewell. See
how fast he sends the boat through the water. I wonder
why he gave up the race?"

"Shall I tell you? He dislikes whatever he is chal-
lenged to do. He is one of those fellows who will never
dare to measure himself against another."

"My aunt is beckoning to us to come back, Mr. Cal-
vert."

"And my taste is for going forward," muttered he,
while at the same time he sent the boat's head suddenly
round, and pulled vigorously t owards the shore.

"May I trust that what has passed between us is a secret, and not to be divulged to another—not even to your sister?"

"If you desire—if you exact."

"I do, most decidedly. It is shame enough to be rejected. I don't see why my disgrace is to be paraded either for pity or ridicule."

"Oh, Mr. Calvert——"

"Or triumphed over," said he sternly, as he sent the boat up to the side of the little jetty, where Miss Grainger and her niece awaited them.

"Poor Loyd has just got bad news from home," said Miss Grainger, "and he has hastened back to ask, by telegraph, if they wish him to return."

"Anyone ill, or dying?" asked Calvert carelessly.

"No, it's some question of law about his father's vicarage. There would seem to be a doubt as to his presentation—whether the appointment lay with the patron or the bishop."

Calvert turned to mark how the girls received these tidings, but they had walked on, and with heads bent down, and close together, were deep in conversation.

"I thought it was only in my profession," said Calvert sneeringly, "where corrupt patronage was practised. It is almost a comfort to think how much the good people resemble the wicked ones."

Miss Grainger, who usually smiled at his levities, looked grave at this one, and no more was said, as they moved on towards the cottage.

CHAPTER VIII.

GROWING DARKER.

T was late at night when Calvert left the villa, but, instead of rowing directly back to the little inn, he left his boat to drift slowly in the scarce perceptible current of the lake, and wrapping himself in his cloak, lay down to muse or to sleep.

It was just as day broke that he awoke, and saw that he had drifted within a few yards of his quarters, and in a moment after he was on shore.

As he gained his room, he found a letter for him in Loyd's hand. It ran thus:

"I waited up all night to see you before I started, for I have been suddenly summoned home by family circumstances. I was loth to part in an angry spirit, or even in coldness, with one in whose companionship I have passed so many happy hours, and for whom I feel, notwithstanding what has passed between us, a sincere interest. I wanted to speak to you of much which I cannot write—that is to say, I would have endeavoured to gain a hearing for what I dare not venture to set down in the deliberate calm of a letter. When I own that it was of yourself, your temper, your habits, your nature, in short, that I wished to have spoken, you will, perhaps, say that it was as well time was not given me for such temerity. But bear in mind, Calvert, that though I am free to admit all your superiority over myself, and never would presume to compare my faculties or my abilities with yours—though I know well there is not a single gift or grace in which you are not my master, there is one point in which I have an advantage over you—I had a mother! You, you have often told me, never remember to have seen yours. To that mother's trainings I owe anything of good, however humble it be, in my nature, and, though the soil in which the seed has fallen be poor and barren, so much of fruit has it borne that I at least respect the good which I do not practise, and I reverence that virtue to which I am a rebel. The lesson, above all others, that she instilled into me, was to avoid the tone of a scoffer, to rescue myself from the cheap distinction which is open to everyone who sets himself to see only ridicule in what others respect, and to mock the themes that others regard with reverence. I stop, for I am afraid to weary you—I dread that, in your impatience, you will throw this down and read no more—I will only say, and I say it in all the sincerity of truth, that if you would endeavour to be morally as great as what your faculties can make you intellectually, there is no eminence you might not attain, nor any you would not adorn.

" If our intimacy had not cooled down of late, from what causes I am unable to tell, to a point in which the first disagreement must be a breach between us, I would have told you that I had formed an attachment to Florence Walter, and obtained her aunt's consent to our marriage ; I mean, of course, at some future which I cannot define, for I have my way to make in the world, and, up to the present, have only been a burden on others. We are engaged, however, and we live on hope. Perhaps I presume too far on any interest you could feel for me when I make you this communication. It may be that you will say, 'What is all this to me?' At all events, I have told you what, had I kept back, would have seemed to myself an uncandid reservation. Deal with it how you may.

"There is, however, another reason why I should tell you this. If you were unaware of the relations which exist between our friends and myself, you might unconsciously speak of me in terms which this knowledge would, perhaps, modify—at least, you would speak without the consciousness that you were addressing unwilling hearers. You now know the ties that bind us, and your words will have that significance which you intend they should bear.

"Remember, and remember distinctly, I disclaim all pretension, as I do all wish, to conciliate your favour as regards this matter; first, because I believe I do not need it; and secondly, that if I asked for, I should be unworthy of it. I scarcely know how, after our last meeting, I stand in your estimation, but I am ready to own that if you would only suffer yourself to be half as good as your nature had intended you and your faculties might make you, you would be conferring a great honour on being the friend of yours truly,

"Joseph Loyd."

"What a cant these fellows acquire!" said Calvert as he read the letter and threw it from him. "What mock humility! what downright and palpable pretension to superiority through every line of it ! The sum of it all being, I can't deny that you are cleverer, stronger, more active, and more manly than me; but, somehow, I don't exactly see why or, how, but I'm your better! Well, I'll write an answer to this one of these days, and such an answer as I flatter myself he'll not read aloud to the company who sit round the fire at the vicarage. And so, Mademoiselle Florence, this was your anxiety, and this the reason for all that interest about our quarrel which I was silly enough to ascribe to a feeling for myself. How invariably it is so ! How certain it is that a woman, the weakest, the least experienced, the most commonplace, is more than a match in astuteness for a man, in a question where her affections are concerned. The feminine nature has strange contradictions. They can summon the courage of a tigress to defend their young, and the spirit of a Machiavelli to protect a lover. She must have had some misgiving, however, that, to prefer a fellow like this to me would be felt by me as an outrage. And then the cunning stroke of implying that her sister was not indisposed to listen to me. The perfidy of that !"

Several days after Loyd's departure, Calvert was lounging near the lake, when he jumped up, exclaiming, "Here comes the postman ! I see he makes a sign to me. What can this be about ? Surely, my attached friend has not written to me again. No, this is a hand that I do not recognise. Let us see what it contains." He opened and read as follows :

"Sir,—I have received your letter. None but a scoundrel could have written it ! As all prospect of connexion with your family is now over, you cannot have a pretext for not affording me such a satisfaction as, had you been a gentleman in feeling as you are in station, it would never have been necessary for me to demand from you. I leave this, to-morrow, for the continent, and will be at Basle by Monday next. I will remain there for a week at your orders, and hope that there may be no difficulty to their speedy fulfilment.

"I am, your obedient and faithful servant,

"WENTWORTH GORDON GRAHAM."

5

"The style is better than yours, Master Loyd, just because it means something. The man is in an honest passion and wants a fight. The other fellow was angry, and begged me not to notice it. And so, Sophy, I have spoiled the wedding favours, and scattered the bridesmaids! What a heavy lesson for an impertinent note. Poor thing! why did she trust herself with a pen? Why did she not know that the most fatal of all bottles is the ink bottle? Precious rage old Uncle Geoffrey must be in. I'd like to have one peep at the general discomfiture —the deserted dinner-table, and the empty drawing-room. They deserve it all! they banished *me*, and much good have they got of it. Well, Mr. Wentworth Gordon Graham must have his wicked way. The only difficulty will be to find what is so absurdly misnamed as a friend. I must have a friend; I'll run up to Milan and search the hotels: I'll surely find some one who will like the cheap heroism of seeing another man shot at. This is the season when all the fellows who have no money for Baden come across the Alps. I'm certain to chance upon one to suit me."

Having despatched a short note, very politely worded, to Mr. Graham, to the post office, Basle, he ordered a carriage, and set out for Milan.

The city was in full festivity when he arrived, over-joyed at its new-born independence, and proud of the presence of its king. The streets were crowded with a holiday population, and from all the balconies and windows hung costly tapestries, or gay coloured carpets. Military music resounded on all sides, and so dense was the throng of people and carriages, that Calvert could only proceed at a walking pace, none feeling any especial care to make way for a dusty traveller, seated in one of the commonest of country conveyances.

As he moved slowly and with difficulty forwards, he

suddenly heard his name called; he looked up, and saw a well known face, that of a brother officer, who had left India on a sick leave along with himself.

"I say, old fellow!" cried Barnard, "this is your ground; draw into that large gate to your right, and come up here."

In a few seconds, Calvert, escorted by a waiter, was shown to his friend's apartment.

"I never dreamed of meeting you here, Calvert."

"Nor I of finding you lodged so sumptuously," said Calvert, as his eyes ranged over the splendid room, whose massive hangings of silk, and richly gilt ceiling, gave that air of a palace one so often sees in Italian hotels.

"Luck, Sir, luck. I'm married, and got a pot of money with my wife." He dropped his voice to a whisper, while, with a gesture of his thumb towards an adjoining room, he motioned his friend to be cautious.

"Who was she?"

"Nobody; that is, not anyone you ever heard of. Stockport people, called Reppingham. The father, a great railway contractor, vulgar old dog—begun as a navvy—with one daughter, who is to inherit, they say, a quarter of a million; but, up to this, we've only an allowance—two thousand a year. The old fellow, however, lives with us—a horrible nuisance." This speech, given in short, abrupt whispers, was uttered with many signs to indicate that the respected father-in-law was in the vicinity. "Now, of yourself, what's your news? What have you done last, eh?"

"Nothing very remarkable. I have been vegetating on a lake in the north of Italy, trying to live for five shillings a day, and spending three more in brandy, to give me courage to do it."

5—2

"But your leave is up; or perhaps you have got **a** renewal."

"No, my leave goes to the fifteenth of October."

"Not a bit of it; we got our leave on the same day, passed the Board the same day, and for exactly the same time. My leave expired on the tenth of August. I'll show you the paper; I have it here."

"Do so. Let me see it."

Barnard opened his desk, and quickly found the paper he sought for. It was precisely as Barnard said. The Board of Calcutta had confirmed the regimental recommendation, and granted a two-years' leave, which ended on the tenth of August.

"Never mind, man," said Barnard; "get back to London as hard as you can, furbish up some sick certificate to say that you were unable to quit your bed——"

"That is not so easy as you imagine; I have a little affair in hand, which may end in more publicity than I have any fancy for." And he told him of his approaching meeting with Graham, and asked him to be his friend.

"What was the quarrel about?" asked Barnard.

"A jealousy; he was going to marry a little cousin I used to flirt with, and we got to words about it. In fact, it is what Sir Lucius would call a very pretty quarrel, and there's nothing to be done but finish it. You'll stand by me, won't you?"

"I don't see how I can. Old Rep, our governor, never leaves me. I'm obliged to report myself about four times a day."

"But you know that can never go on. You needn't be told by me that no man can continue such a system of slavery, nor is there anything could recompense it. You'll have to teach her better one of these days; begin

at once. My being here gives you a pretext to begin.
Start at once—to-day. Just say, 'I'll have to show
Calvert the lions ; he'll want to hunt up galleries,' and
such-like."

"Hush ! here comes my wife. Fanny, let me present
to you one of my oldest friends, Calvert. It's a name
you have often heard from me."

The young lady—she was not more than twenty—was
pleasing-looking and well mannered. Indeed, Calvert
was amazed to see her so unlike what he expected ; she
was neither pretentious nor shy ; and, had his friend not
gone into the question of pedigree, was there anything to
mark a class in life other than his own. While they
talked together they were joined by her father, who,
however, more than realised the sketch drawn by Bar-
nard.

He was a morose, down-looking old fellow, with a
furtive expression, and a manner of distrust about him
that showed itself in various ways. From the first, though
Calvert set vigorously to work to win his favour, he
looked with a sort of misgiving at him. He spoke very
little, but in that little there were no courtesies wasted ;
and when Barnard whispered, " You had better ask him
to dine with us, the invitation will come better from
you !" the reply was, " I won't; do you hear that ? I
won't."

" But he's an old brother-officer of mine, Sir ; we served
several years together."

" The worse company yours, then."

" I say, Calvert," cried Barnard, aloud, " I must give
you a peep at our gay doings here. I'll take you a
drive round the town, and out of the Porta Orien-
tale, and if we should not be back at dinner-time,
Fanny——"

"We'll dine without you, that's all!" said the old man ; while, taking his daughter's hand, he led her out of the room.

"I say, Bob, I'd not change with you, even for the difference," said Calvert.

"I never saw him so bad before," said the other, sheepishly.

"Because you never tried him! Hitherto you have been a spaniel, getting kicked and cuffed, and rather liking it; but, now that the sight of an old friend has rallied you to a faint semblance of your former self, you are shocked and horrified. You made a bad start, Bob ; that was the mistake. You ought to have begun by making him feel the immeasurable distance there lay between him and a gentleman ; not only in dress, language, and behaviour, but in every sentiment and feeling. Having done this, he would have tacitly submitted to ways that were not his own, by conceding that they might be those of a class he had never belonged to. You might, in short, have ruled him quietly and constitutionally. Now you have nothing for it but one thing."

"Which is——"

"A revolution! Yes, you must overthrow the whole government, and build up another out of the smash. Begin to-day. We'll dine together wherever you like. We'll go to the Scala if it's open. We'll sup——"

"But Fanny?"

"She'll stand by her husband. Though, probably, she'll have you 'up' for a little private discipline afterwards. Come, don't lose time. I want to do my cathedral, and my gallery, and my other curiosities in one day, for I have some matters to settle at Orto before I start for Basle. Have they a club, a casino, or anything of the sort here, where they play?"

"There is a place they call the Gettone, but I've never been there but once."

"Well, we'll finish there this evening; for I want to win a little money, to pay my journey."

"If I can help you——"

"No, no. Not to be thought of. I've got some fifty Naps by me—tame elephants—that are sure to entrap others. You must come with me to Basle, Bob. You can't desert me in such a crisis," said Calvert, as they left the inn together.

"We'll see. I'll think over it. The difficulty will be——"

"The impossibility is worse than a difficulty; and that is what I shall have to face if you abandon me. Why, only think of it for a moment. Here I am, jilted, out of the army—for I know I shall lose my commission—without a guinea; you'd not surely wish me to say, without a friend! If it were not that it would be so selfish, I'd say the step will be the making of you. You'll have that old bear so civilised on your return, you'll not know him."

"Do you really think so?"

"I know it. He'll see at once that you'll not stand this sort of bullying. That if you did, your friends would not stand it. We shan't be away above four days, and those four days will give him a fright he'll never forget."

"I'll think over it."

"No. You'll do it—that's better; and I'll promise you—if Mr. Graham does not enter a fatal objection—to come back with you and stand to you through your troubles."

Calvert had that about him in his strong will, his resolution, and his readiness at reply, which exercised no mean despotism over the fellows of his own age. And it

was only they who disliked and avoided him who ever
resisted him.   Barnard was an easy victim, and before the
day drew to its close, he had got to believe that it was
by a rare stroke of fortune Calvert had come to Milan—
come to rescue him from the "most degrading sort
of bondage a good fellow could possibly fall into."

They dined splendidly, and sent to engage a box at the
Opera; but the hours passed so pleasantly over their
dinner, that they forgot all about it, and only reached the
theatre a few minutes before it closed.

"Now for the—what do you call the place?" cried
Calvert.

"The Gettone."

"That's it.   I'm eager to measure my luck against
these Milanais.   They say, besides, no fellow has such a
vein as when his life is threatened; and I remember my-
self, when I had the yellow fever at Galle, I passed
twenty-one times at écarté, all because I was given
over!"

"What a fellow you are, Calvert!" said the other,
with a weak man's admiration for whatever was great,
even in infamy.

"You'll see how I'll clear them out.   But what have I
done with my purse?   Left it on my dressing table.   I
suppose they are honest in the hotel?"

"Of course they are.   It's all safe; and I've more
money about me than you want.   Old Rep handed me
three thousand francs this morning to pay the bill, and
when I saw you, I forgot all about it."

"Another element of luck," cried Calvert, joyously.
"The money that does not belong to a man always wins.
Why, there's five thousand francs here," said Calvert, as
he counted over the notes.

"Two of them are Fanny's.   She got her quarter's

allowance yesterday. Stingy, isn't it? Only three hundred a year."

"It's downright disgraceful. She ought to have eight at the very least; but wait till we come back from Basle. You'll not believe what a change I'll work in that old fellow, when I take him in hand."

By this time they had reached the Gettone, and, after a brief colloquy, were suffered to pass up stairs and enter the rooms.

"Oh, it's faro they play; my own game," whispered Calvert. "I was afraid the fellows might have indulged in some of their own confounded things, which no foreigner can compete in. At faro I fear none."

While Barnard joined a group of persons round a roulette-table, where fashionably-dressed women adventured their franc pieces along with men clad in the most humble mode, Calvert took his place among the faro players. The boldness of his play, and the reckless way he adventured his money, could not conceal from their practised acuteness that he was master of the game, and they watched him attentively.

"I think I have nearly cleaned them out, Bob," cried he to his friend, as he pointed to a heap of gold and silver, which lay promiscuously piled up before him.

"I suppose you must give them their revenge?" whispered the other, "if they wish for it."

"Nothing of the kind. At a public table, a winner rises when he pleases. If I continue to sit here now, it is because that old fellow yonder has got a rouleau in his pocket which he cannot persuade himself to break. See, he has taken it out: for the fourth time, this is. I wonder can he screw up his courage to risk it. Yes! he has! There go ten pieces on the queen. Go back to your flirtation with the blonde ringlets, and don't disturb my game.   I must have that fellow's rouleau before I leave.   Go back, and I'll not tell your wife."

It was in something less than an hour after this that Barnard felt a hand laid on his shoulder, and looking up, saw Calvert standing over him.   "Well, it took you some time to finish that old fellow, Calvert !"

"He finished *me*, which was worse.   Have you got a cigar?"

"Do you mean that you lost all your winnings ?"

"Yes, and your five thousand francs besides, not to speak of a borrowed thousand from someone I have given my card to.   A bore, isn't it?"

"It's more than a bore—it's a bad business.   I don't know how I'll settle it with the landlord."

"Give him a bill, he'll never be troublesome : and, as to your wife's money, tell her frankly you lost it at play. Isn't that the best way, Madame?" said he, addressing a young and pretty woman at his side.   "I am advising my friend to be honest with his wife, and confess that he spent his money in very pleasant company.   Come along out of this stuffy place.   Let us have a walk in the fresh cool air, and a cigar, if you have one.   I often wonder," said he, as they gained the street, "how the fellows who write books and want to get up sensation scenes, don't come and do something of this sort.   There's a marvellous degree of stimulant in being cleaned out, not only of one's own cash, but of one's credit ; and by credit I mean it in the French sense, which says, 'Le crédit est l'argent des autres.'"

"I wish you had not lost that money," muttered the other.

"So do I.   I have combativeness very strong, and I hate being beaten by anyone in anything."

"*I'm* thinking of the money !" said the other, doggedly.

" Naturally, for it was yours. ' 'Twas mine, 'tis his,' as Hamlet has it. Great fellow, Hamlet! I don't suppose that anyone ever drew a character wherein Gentleman was so distinctly painted as Hamlet. He combined all the grandest ideas of his class with a certain 'disinvoltura' —a sort of high bred levity—that relieved his sternness, and made him much better company than such fellows as Laertes and Horatio."

" When you saw luck turning, why didn't you leave off ? "

" Why not ask why the luck turned before I left off ? That would be the really philosophic inquiry. Isn't it chilly ? "

" I'm not cold, but I'm greatly provoked."

" So am I for *you ;* for I haven't got enough to repay you, but trust me to arrange the matter in the morning. The landlord will see the thing with the eyes of his calling : he'll soon perceive that the son-in-law of a man who travels with two carriages, and can't speak one word of French, is one to be trusted. I mean him to cash a bill for us before I leave. Old Rep's white hat and brown spencer are guarantees for fifty thousand francs in any city of Europe. There's a solvent vulgarity in the very creak of his shoes."

" Oh ! he's not a very distinguished-looking person, cer- tainly," said Barnard, who now resented the liberty he had himself led the way to.

" There I differ with you ; *I* call him eminently distin- guished, and I'd rather be able to 'come' that cravat tie, and have the pattern of the dark-green waistcoat with the red spots, than I'd have—what shall I say ?—all the crisp bank paper I lost awhile ago. You are not going in, surely ? " cried he, as the other rang violently at the hotel.

"Yes; I am very tired of this fooling. I wish **you** hadn't lost that money."

"Do you remember how it goes, Bob?"

> His weary song,
> The whole day long,
> Was still l'argent, l'argent, l'argent!

She is complaining that though the linnet is singing in the trees, and the trout leaping in the river, her tiresome husband could only liken them to the clink of the gold as it fell on the counter? Why, man, you'll wake the dead if you ring in that fashion!"

"I want to get in."

"Here comes the fellow at last; how disgusted he'll be to find there's not a five-franc piece between us."

Scarcely was the door opened than Barnard passed in, and left him without even a good-night.

CHAPTER IX.

ON THE ROAD.

CALVERT'S first care as he entered his room was to ascertain if his purse was there. It was all safe and untouched. He next lit a cigar, and opening his window, leaned out to smoke. It was a glorious autumn night, still, starry and cloudless. Had anyone from the street beneath seen him there, he might have said, "There is some wearied man of brain-labour, taking his hour of tranquil thought before he betakes himself to rest ; or he is one of those contemplative natures who loves to be free to commune with his own heart in the silence of a calm night." He looked like this, and perhaps—who knows if he were not nearer it than we wot of?

It was nigh daybreak before he lay down to sleep. Nor had he been fully an hour in slumber when he was awoke, and found Barnard, dressed in a morning gown and slippers, standing beside his bed.

"I say, Calvert, rub your eyes and listen to me. Are you awake?"

"Not very perfectly ; but quite enough for anything you can have to say. What is it?"

"I am so fretted about that money."

"Why you told me that last night," said Calvert, addressing himself, as it were, again to sleep.

"Oh, it's all very fine and very philosophic to be indifferent about another man's 'tin;' but I tell you I don't know what to do, what to say about it. I'm not six weeks married, and it's rather early to come to rows and altercations with a father-in-law."

"Address him to me. Say ' Go to Calvert—he'll talk to you.' Do that like a good fellow and go to bed. Good-night."

"I'll not stand this sort of thing, Calvert. I'm not going to lose my money and be laughed at too !"

"You'll not stand what ? " cried Calvert, sitting up in bed, and looking now thoroughly awake.

"I mean," said the other, doggedly, "you have got me into a confounded scrape, and you are bound to get me out of it."

"That is speaking like a man of sense. It is what I intend to do; but can't we sleep over it first ? I want what the old ladies call my 'natural rest.'"

"There's no time for that. The old governor is always pottering about by six o'clock, and it's just as likely, as the landlord talks English, he'll be down by way of gossiping with him, and ask if the bill is settled."

"What an old beast he must be. I wonder you could have married into such a vulgar set."

"If you have nothing to say but abuse of my con-nections, I am not going to waste any more time here."

"There, that's a dear fellow; go to bed now, and call me somewhere towards four in the afternoon."

"This is rather more than a joke."

"To be sure it is, man ; it is dead sleepiness. Good-night."

"I see you have found your purse—how much had you in it ? "

"Count it, if you're curious," said Calvert, drowsily.

"Fifty-four Napoleons and a half," said the other,

slowly. "Look ye, Calvert, I'm going to impound this. It's a sorry instalment, but, as far as it goes——"

"Take it, old fellow, and leave me quiet."

"One word more, Calvert," said Barnard, seriously. I cannot muster courage to meet old Rep this morning, and if you like to start at once and settle this affair you have in Switzerland, I'm ready, but it must be done instanter."

"All right; I shall be ready within an hour. Tell the porter to send my bath up at once, and order coffee by the time you'll be dressed."

There was very little trace of sleep about Calvert's face now, as, springing from his bed, he prepared for the road. With such despatch, indeed, did he proceed, that he was already in the coffee-room before his friend had descended.

"Shall we say anything to the landlord before we start, Calvert?" whispered he.

"Of course; send Signor Angelo, or Antonio, or whatever his name, here. The padrone, I mean," said he to the waiter.

"He is called Luigi Filippo, Sir," said the man indignantly.

"A capital name for a rogue. Let us have him here."

A very burly consequential sort of man, marvellously got up as to beard, moustaches, and watch-chain, entered and bowed.

"Signor Luigi Filippo," said Calvert, "my friend here —the son of that immensely wealthy mi Lordo up stairs —is in a bit of scrape; he had an altercation last night with a fellow we take to be an Austrian spy."

The host spat out, and frowned ferociously.

"Just so; a dog of a Croat, I suspect," went on Calvert; "at all events, he must put a bullet in him, and to do so, must get over the frontier beyond Como ; we want therefore a little money from you, and your secrecy, till this blows over."

The host bowed, and pursed up his lips like one who would like a little time for reflection, and at last said, " How much money, Signor ? "

" What do you say, Bob ? will a hundred Naps do, or eighty ? "

" Fifty ; fifty are quite enough," cried Barnard.

"On a circular note, of course, Signor ? " asked the host.

" No, a draft at six days on my friend's father ; mi Lordo means to pass a month here."

"I don't think I'll do that, Calvert," whispered Barnard ; but the other stopped him at once with " Be quiet ; leave this to me."

" Though payable at sight, Signor Luigi, we shall ask you to hold it over for five or six days, because we hope possibly to be back here before Saturday, and if so, we'll settle this ourselves."

" It shall be done, gentlemen," said the host. " I'll go and draw out the bills, and you shall have the money immediately."

" How I touched the fellow's patriotism, Bob. It was the Austrian dodge stood us in stead, there.   I know that I have jeopardised your esteem for me by the loss of that money last night ; but do confess that this was a clever hit of mine."

" It's a bad business from beginning to end!" was however all that he could obtain from Barnard.

" Narrow-minded dog ! he won't see any genius in a man that owes him five shillings."

" I wish it was only five shillings."

"What an ignoble confession ! It means this, **that**

your friendship depends on the rate of exchanges, and that when gold rises—— But here comes Luigi Filippo. Now, no squeamishness, but write your name firmly. 'Cut boldly,' said the auger, 'and he cut it through.' Don't you remember that classic anecdote in your Roman history?"

It is a strange fact that the spirit of raillery, which to a dull man is, at first, but a source of irritation and fretfulness, will, when persevered in, become at last one of the most complete despotisms. He dreads it as a weapon which he cannot defend himself against ; and he comes to regard it as an evidence of superiority and power. Barnard saw the dominion that the other exercised over him, but could not resist it.

"Where to now?" asked he, as they whirled rapidly along the road towards Monza.

"First of all, to Orta. There is an English family I want to see. Two prettier girls you can't imagine—not that the news has any interest for you, poor caged mouse that you are—but I am in love with one of them. I forget which, but I believe it's the one that won't have me."

"She's right," said Barnard, with a half smile.

"Well, I half suspect she is. I could be a charming lover, but I fear I'd make only a sorry husband. My qualities are too brilliant for every-day use. It is your dreary fellows, with a tiresome monotony of nature, do best in that melancholy mill they call marriage. You, for instance, ought to be a model 'mari.'"

"You are not disposed to give me the chance, I think," said Barnard, peevishly.

"On the contrary, I am preparing you most carefully for your career. Conjugal life is a reformatory. You must come to it as a penitent. Now I'll teach you the first part of your lesson; your wife shall supply the second."

"I'd relish this much better if——"

"I had not lost that money, you were going to say. Out with it, man. When a fellow chances upon a witty thing, he has a right to repeat it; besides, you have reason on your side. A loser is always wrong. But after all, Bob, whether the game be war, or marriage, or a horse-race, one's skill has very little to say to it. Make the wisest combinations that ever were fashioned, and you'll lose sometimes. Draw your card at hazard, and you'll win. If you only saw the fellow that beat me t'other day in a girl's affections—as dreary a dog as ever you met in your life, without manliness, without 'go' in him—and yet he wasn't a curate. I know you suspect he was a curate."

"If you come through this affair all right, what do you intend to turn to, Calvert?" said the other, who really felt a sort of interest in his fortunes.

"I have thought of several things: the Church—the Colonies—Patent Fuel—Marriage—Turkish Baths, and a Sympathy Society for Suffering Nationalities, with a limited liability to all who subscribe fifty pounds and upwards."

"But, seriously, have you any plans?"

"Ten thousand plans! I have plans enough to ruin all Threadneedle Street; but what use are plans? What's the good of an architect in a land were there are no bricks, no mortar, and no timber? When I've shot Graham, I've a plan how to make my escape out of Switzerland; but, beyond that, nothing; not one step, I promise you. See, yonder is Monte Rosa; how grand he looks in the still calm air of the morning. What a gentleman a mountain is! how independent of the changeful fortunes of the plains, where grass succeeds tillage, and what is barley to-day, may be a brick-field to-morrow;

but the mountain is ever the same—proud and cold if you will, but standing above all the accidents of condition, and asserting itself by qualities which are not money-getting. I'd like to live in a land of mountains, if it were not for the snobs that come to climb them."

" But why should they be snobs ? "

" I don't know ; perhaps the mountains like it. There, look yonder, our road leads along that ledge till we reach Chiasso, about twelve miles off ; do you think you can last that long without breakfast ? There, there, don't make that pitiful face ; you shall have your beefsteak, and your chocolate, and your eggs, and all the other claims of your Anglo-Saxon nature, whose birthright it is to growl for every twenty-four hours, and 'grub' every two."

They gained the little inn at Orta by the evening, and learned, as Calvert expected, that nothing had changed in his absence—indeed what was there to change—so long as the family at the villa remained in the cottage. All was to Calvert as he left it.

Apologising to his friend for a brief absence, he took boat and crossed the lake. It was just as they had sat down to tea that he entered the drawing-room.

If there was some constraint in the reception of him, there was that amount of surprise at his appearance that half masked it. "You have been away, Mr. Calvert?" asked Miss Grainger.

" Yes," said he, carelessly, " I got a rambling fit on me, and finding that Loyd had started for England, I grew fidgety at being alone, so I went up to Milan, saw churches and galleries, and the last act of a ballet ; but, like a country mouse, got home-sick for the hard peas and the hollow tree, and hurried back again."

After some careless talk of commonplaces he managed

at last to secure the chair beside Florence's sofa, and affected to take an interest in some work she was engaged at. "I have been anxious to see you and speak to you, Florry," said he, in a low tone, not audible by the others. "I had a letter from Loyd, written just before he left. He has told me everything."

She only bent down her head more deeply over her work, but did not speak.

"Yes; he was more candid than you," continued he. "He said you were engaged—that is—that you had owned to him that you liked him, and that when the consent he hoped for would be obtained, you would be married."

"How came he to write this to *you?*" said she, with a slight tremor in her voice.

"In this wise," said he, calmly. "He felt that he owed me an apology for something that had occurred between us on that morning; and, when making his excuses, he deemed he could give no better proof of frankness than by this avowal. It was, besides, an act of fairness towards one who, trusting to his own false light, might have been lured to delusive hopes."

"Perhaps so," said she, coldly.

"It was very right of him, very proper."

She nodded.

"It was more—it was generous."

"He *is* generous," said she, warmly.

"He had need be."

"How do you mean, that he had need be?" asked she, eagerly.

"I mean this—that he will require every gift he has, and every grace, to outbalance the affection which I bear you — which I shall never cease to bear you. You prefer him. Now, you may regard me how you will

—I will not consent to believe myself beaten. Yes, Florence, I know not only that I love you more than he does, but I love you with a love he is incapable of feeling. I do not wish to say one word in his dispraise, least of all to you, in whose favour I want to stand well; but I wish you—and it is no unfair request—to prove the affection of the two men who solicit your love."

" I am satisfied with his."

"You may be satisfied with the version your own imagination renders of it. You may be satisfied with the picture you have coloured for yourself; but I want you to be just to yourself, and just to me. Now if I can show you in his own handwriting—the ink only dried on the paper a day ago—a letter from him to me, in which he asks my pardon in terms so abject as never were wrung from any man, except under the pressure of a personal fear?"

" You say this to outrage me. Aunt Grainger," cried she, in a voice almost a scream, " listen to what this gentleman has had the temerity to tell me. Repeat it now, Sir, if you dare."

" What is this, Mr. Calvert? You have not surely presumed——"

"I have simply presumed, Madam, to place my pretensions in rivalry with Mr. Loyd's. I have been offering to your niece the half of a very humble fortune, with a name not altogether ignoble."

"Oh dear, Mr. Calvert!" cried the old lady, "I never suspected this. I'm sure my niece is aware of the great honour we all feel—at least I do most sensibly—that, if she was not already engaged——Are you ill, dearest? Oh, she has fainted. Leave us, Mr. Calvert. Send Maria here. Milly, some water immediately."

For more than an hour Calvert walked the little grass-plot before the door, and no tidings came to him from those within. To a momentary bustle and confusion, a calm succeeded—lights flitted here and there through the cottage. He fancied he heard something like sobbing, and then all was still and silent.

"Are you there, Mr. Calvert?" cried Milly, at last, as she moved out into the dark night air. "She is better now—much better. She seems inclined to sleep, and we have left her."

"You know how it came on?" asked he in a whisper. "You know what brought it about?"

"No; nothing of it."

"It was a letter that I showed her—a letter of Loyd's to myself—conceived in such terms as no man of, I will not say of spirit, but a common pretension to the sense of gentleman, could write. Wait a moment, don't be angry with me till you hear me out. We had quarrelled in the morning. It was a serious quarrel, on a very serious question. I thought, of course, that all young men, at least, regard these things in the same way. Well, he did not. I have no need to say more; *he* did not, and consequently nothing could come of it. At all events, I deemed that the man who could not face an adversary had no right to brave a rival, and so I intimated to him. For the second time he differed with me, and dared in my own presence to prosecute attentions which I had ordered him to abandon. This was bad enough, but there was worse to come, for, on my return home from this, I found a letter from him in the most abject terms; asking my pardon—for what?—for my having insulted him, and begging me, in words of shameful humility, to let him follow up his courtship, and, if he could, secure the hand of your sister. Now she might,

or might not, accept my offer. I am not coxcomb enough
to suppose I must succeed simply because I wish success ;
but, putting myself completely out of the question, could
I suffer a girl I deemed worthy of my love, and whom I
desired to make my wife, to fall to the lot of one so base
as this? I ask you, was there any other course open to
me than to show her the letter? Perhaps it was rash ;
perhaps I ought to have shown it first of all to Miss
Grainger. I can't decide this point. It is too subtle for
me. I only know that what I did I should do again, no
matter what the consequences might be."

"And this letter, has she got it still ?" asked Milly.

"No, neither she nor any other will ever read it now.
I have torn it to atoms. The wind has carried the last
fragment at this moment over the lake."

"Oh dear ; what misery all this is," cried the girl in an
accent of deep affliction. "If you knew how she is
attached——" Then suddenly checking the harsh in-
discretion of her words, she added, "I am sure you did
all for the best, Mr. Calvert. I must go back now. You'll
come and see us, or perhaps you'll let me write to you,
to-morrow."

"I have to say good-bye, now," said he, sadly. "I may
see you all again within a week. It may be this is a
good-bye for ever."

He kissed her hand as he spoke, and turned to the
lake, where his boat was lying.

"How amazed she'll be to hear that she saw a letter—
read it—held it in her hands," muttered he, "but I'll
stake my life she'll never doubt the fact when it is told to
her by those who believe it."

"You seem to be in rare spirits," said Barnard when
Calvert returned to the inn. "Have you proposed and
been accepted ? "

"Not exactly," said the other, smiling, "but I have had a charming evening; one of those fleeting moments of that 'vie de famille' Balzac tells us are worth all our wild and youthful excesses."

"Yes!" replied Barnard, scoffingly; "domesticity would seem to be your forte. Heaven help your wife, say I, if you ever have one."

"You don't seem to be aware how you disparage conjugal life, my good friend, when you speak of it as a thing in which men of *your* stamp are the ornaments. It would be a sorry institution if its best requirements were a dreary temperament and a disposition that mistakes moodiness for morality."

"Good-night; I have had enough," said the other, and left the room.

"What a pity to leave such a glorious spot on such a morning," said Calvert, as he stood waiting while the post-horses were being harnessed. "If we had but been good boys, as we might have been—that is, if *you* had not fallen into matrimony, and *I* into a quarrel—we should have such a day's fishing here! Yonder, where you see the lemon-trees hanging over the rock, in the pool underneath there are some twelve and fourteen 'pounders,' as strong as a good-size pike; and then we'd have grilled them under the chestnut-trees, and talked away, as we've done scores of times, of the great figure we were to make —I don't know when or how, but some time and in some wise—in the world; astonishing all our relations, and putting to utter shame and confusion that private tutor at Dorking who *would* persist in auguring the very worst of us."

"Is that the bill that you are tearing up? Let me see it. What does he charge for that Grignolino wine and those bad cigars?" broke in Barnard.

" What do I know or care?" said Calvert, with a saucy laugh. " If you possessed a schoolboy's money-box with a slit in it to hold your savings, there would be some sense in looking after the five-franc pieces you could rescue from a cheating landlord, and add to your store; but when you know in your heart that you are never the richer nor the better of the small economies that are only realised at the risk of an apoplexy and some very profane expressions, my notion is, never mind them —never fret about them."

"You talk like a millionaire," said the other contemptuously.

"It is all the resemblance that exists between us, Bob; not, however, that I believe Baron Rothschild himself could moralise over the insufficiency of wealth to happiness as I could. Here comes our team, and I must say a sorrier set of screws never tugged in a rope harness. Get in first. I like to show all respect to the man who pays. I say, my good fellow," cried he to the postilion, " drive your very best, for mi Lordo here is immensely rich, and would just as soon give you five gold Marengos as five francs."

" What was it you said to him?" asked Barnard, as they started at a gallop.

" I said he must not spare his cattle, for we were running away from our creditors."

" How could you——"

"How could I? What nonsense, man! besides, I wanted the fellow to take an interest in us, and, you see, so he has. Old Johnson was right; there are few pleasures more exhilarating than being whirled along a good road at the top speed of post-horses."

" I suppose you saw that girl you are in love with?" said Barnard after a pause.

"Yes; two of them. Each of the syrens has got a lien upon my heart, and I really can't say which of them holds 'the preference shares.'"

"Is there money?"

"Not what a great Crœsus like yourself would call money, but still enough for a grand 'operation' at Homburg, or a sheep-farming exploit in Queensland."

"You're more 'up' to the first than the last."

"All wrong! Games of chance are to fellows like you, who must accept Fortune as they find her. Men of *my* stamp mould destiny."

"Well, I don't know. So long as I have known you, you've never been out of one scrape without being half way into another."

"And yet there are fellows who pay dearer for their successes than ever I have done for my failures."

"How so? What do they do?"

"They marry! Ay, Bob, they marry rich wives, but without any power to touch the money, just as a child gets a sovereign at Christmas under the condition he is never to change it."

"I must say you are a pleasant fellow to travel with."

"So I am generally reputed, and you're a lucky dog to catch me 'in the vein,' for I don't know when I was in better spirits than this morning."

CHAPTER X.

A DAYBREAK BESIDE THE RHINE.

THE day was just breaking over that wide flat beside the Rhine at Basle, as two men, descending from a carriage on the high road, took one of the narrow paths which lead through the fields, walking slowly, and talking to each other in the careless tone of easy converse.

“We are early, Barnard, I should say; fully half an hour before our time,” said Calvert, as he walked on first, for the path did not admit of two abreast. What grand things these great plains are, traversed by a fine river, and spreading away to a far distant horizon. What a sense of freedom they inspire; how suggestive they are of liberty; don’t you feel that?”

“I think I see them coming,” said the other. “I saw a carriage descend the hill yonder. Is there nothing else you have to say—nothing that you think of, Harry?”

“Nothing. If it should be a question of a funeral, Bob, my funds will show how economically it must be done; but even if I had been richer, it is not an occasion I should like to make costly.”

“It was not of that I was thinking. It was of friends or relations.”

“My dear fellow, I have few relatives and no friends. No man’s executorship will ever entail less trouble than mine. I have nothing to leave, nor any to leave it to."

"But these letters — the cause of the present meeting — don't you intend that in case of — in the event of——"

"My being killed. Go on."

"That they should be given up to your cousin ? "

"Nothing of the kind ever occurred to me. In the first place, I don't mean to be shot ; and in the second, I have not the very remotest intention of releasing the dear Sophy from those regrets and sorrows which she ought to feel for my death. Nay, I mean her to mourn me with a degree of affliction to which anxiety will add the poignancy."

"This is not generous, Calvert."

"I'm sure it's not. Why, my dear friend, were I to detect any such weakness in my character, I'd begin to fancy I might end by becoming a poltroon."

"Is that your man—he in the cloak—or the tall one behind him ?" said Barnard, as he pointed to a group who came slowly along through a vineyard.

"I cannot say. I never saw Mr. Graham to my knowledge. Don't let them be long about the preliminaries, Bob ; the morning is fresh and the ground here somewhat damp. Agree to all they ask, distance and everything, only secure that the word be given by you. Remember that, in the way I've told you."

As Calvert strolled listlessly along towards the river, Barnard advanced to meet the others, who, to the number of five, came now forward. Colonel Rochefort, Mr. Graham's friend, and Barnard were slightly acquainted, and turned aside to talk to each other in confidence.

"It is scarcely the moment to hope for it, Mr.

Barnard," said the other, " but I cannot go on without asking, at least, if there is any peaceful settlement possible ? "

" I fear not. You told me last night that all retraction by your friend of his offensive letter was impossible."

" Utterly so."

" What, then, would you suggest ? "

" Could not Mr. Calvert be brought to see that it was he who gave the first offence? That, in writing, as he did, to a man in my friend's position——"

" Mere waste of time, colonel, to discuss this ; besides, I think we have each of us already said all that we could on this question, and Calvert is very far from being satisfied with me for having allowed myself to entertain it. There is really nothing for it but a shot."

" Yes, Sir ; but you seem to forget, if we proceed to this arbitrament, it is not a mere exchange of fire will satisfy my friend."

" We are, as regards that, completely at his service; and if your supply of ammunition be only in proportion to the number of your followers, you can scarcely be disappointed."

The colonel reddened deeply, and in a certain irritation replied : " One of these gentlemen is a travelling companion of my friend, whose health is too delicate to permit him to act for him ; the other is a French officer of rank, who dined with us yesterday; the third is a surgeon."

" 'To us it is a matter of perfect indifference if you come accompanied by fifty, or five hundred ; but let us lose no more time. I see how I am trying my friend's patience already. Ten paces, short paces, too," began Barnard as he took his friend's arm.

"And the word?"

"I am to give it."

"All right; and you remember how?"

"Yes! the word is, One—two; at the second you are to fire."

"Let me hear you say them."

"One—two."

"No, no; that's not it. One-two — sharp; don't dwell on the interval; make them like syllables of one word."

"One-two."

"Yes, that's it; and remember that you cough once before you begin. There, don't let them see us talking together. Give me a shake hands, and leave me."

"That man is nervous, or I am much mistaken," said Graham's invalid friend to the colonel; and they both looked towards Calvert, who with his hat drawn down over his brows, walked lazily to his ground.

"It is not the reputation he has," whispered the colonel. "Be calm, Graham; be as cool as the other fellow."

The principals were now placed, and the others fell back on either side, and almost instantaneously, so instantaneously, indeed, that Colonel Rochefort had not yet ceased to walk, two shots rung out, one distinctly before the other, and Graham fell.

All ran towards him but Calvert, who, throwing his pistol at his feet, stood calm and erect. For a few seconds they bent down over the wounded man, and then Barnard, hastening back to his friend, whispered, "Through the chest; it is all over."

"Dead?" said the other.

He nodded, and taking his arm, said, "Don't lose a

moment; the Frenchman says you have not an instant to spare."

For a moment Calvert moved as if going towards the others, then, as if with a changed purpose, he turned sharply round and walked towards the high road.

As Calvert was just about to gain the road, Barnard ran after him, and cried out, "Stop, Calvert, hear what these men say; they are crying out unfair against us. They declare——"

"Are you an ass, Bob?" said the other, angrily. "Who minds the stupid speech of fellows whose friend is knocked over?"

"Yes, but I'll hear this out," cried Barnard.

"You'll do so without *me*, then, and a cursed fool you are for your pains. Drive across to the Bavarian frontier, my man," said he, giving the postilion a Napoleon, "and you shall have a couple more if you get there within two hours."

With all the speed that whip and spur could summon, the beasts sped along the level road, and Calvert, though occasionally looking through the small pane in the back of the carriage to assure himself he was not pursued, smoked on unceasingly. He might have been a shade graver than his wont, and preoccupied too, for he took no notice of the objects on the road, nor replied to the speeches of the postilion, who, in his self-praise, seemed to call for some expression of approval.

"You are a precious fool, Master Barnard, and you have paid for your folly, or you had been here before this."

Such were his uttered thoughts, but it cost him little regret as he spoke them.

The steam-boat that left Constance for Lindau was just getting under weigh as he reached the lake, and he immediately embarked in her, and on the same evening, gained Austrian territory at Bregenz, to pass the night. For a day or two, the quietness of this lone and little-visited spot suited him, and it was near enough to the Swiss frontier, at the Rhine, to get news from Switzerland. On the third day, a paragraph in the Basle Zeitung told him everything. It was, as such things usually are, totally misrepresented, but there was enough revealed for him to guess what had occurred. It was headed "Terrible Event," and ran thus:

"At a meeting which took place with pistols, this morning, between two English lords at the White Meadows, one fell so fatally wounded that his death ensued in a few minutes. An instantaneous cry of foul play amongst his friends led to a fierce and angry altercation, which ended in a second encounter between the first principal and the second of the deceased. In this the former was shot through the throat, the bullet injuring several large vessels, and lodging, it is supposed, in the spine. He has been conveyed to the Hôtel Royal, but no hopes of his recovery are entertained."

"I suspected what would come of your discussion, Bob. Had you only been minded to slip away with me, you'd have been in the enjoyment of a whole skin by this time. I wonder which of them shot him. I'd take the odds it was the Frenchman; he handled the pistols like a fellow who envied us our pleasant chances. I suppose I ought to write to Barnard, or to his people; but it's not an agreeable task, and I'll think over it."

He thought over it, and wrote as follows:

"Dear Bob,—I suspect, from a very confused paragraph in a stupid newspaper, that you have fought somebody and got wounded. Write and say if this be so, what it was all about, who did it, and what more can be done for you,

"By yours truly,

"H. C.

"Address, Como."

To this he received no answer when he called at the post-office, and turned his steps next to Orta. He did not really know why, but it was, perhaps, with some of that strange instinct that makes the criminal haunt the homes of those he has once injured, and means to injure more. There was, however, one motive which he recognised himself; he wished to know something of those at the villa; when they had heard from Loyd, and what? whether, too, they had heard of his own doings, and in what way? A fatal duel, followed by another that was like to prove fatal, was an event sure to provoke newspaper notice. The names could not escape publicity, and he was eager to see in what terms they mentioned his own. He trusted much to the difficulty of getting at any true version of the affair, and he doubted greatly if anyone but Graham and himself could have told why they were to meet at all. Graham's second, Rochefort, evidently knew very little of the affair. At all events, Graham was no longer there to give his version, while for the incidents of the duel, who was to speak? All, save Barnard, who was dying, if not dead, must have taken flight. The Swiss authorities would soon have arrested them if within reach. He might therefore reassure himself that no statement that he could not at least impugn could get currency just yet. " I will row over to the old Grainger "—so he called her—"and see what she has heard of it all."

7

It was nightfall as he reached the shore, and walked slowly and anxiously to the house. He had learned at Orta that they were to leave that part of the world in another fortnight, but whither for none knew. As he drew nigh, he determined to have a peep at the interior before he presented himself. He accordingly opened the little wicket noiselessly, and passed round through the flower-garden till he reached the windows of the drawing-room.

98　　　　　　*A Rent in a Cloud.*

It was nightfall as he reached the shore, and walked slowly and anxiously to the house. He had learned at Orta that they were to leave that part of the world in another fortnight, but whither for none knew. As he drew nigh, he determined to have a peep at the interior before he presented himself.

CHAPTER XI.

THE LIFE AT THE VILLA.

HE curtains were undrawn, and the candles were lighted. All within looked just as he had so often seen it. The sick girl lay on her sofa, with her small spaniel at her feet. Miss Grainger was working at a table, and Emily sat near her sister, bending over the end of the sofa, and talking to her. "Let me see that letter again, Florry," she said, taking a letter from the passive fingers of the sick girl. "Yes, he is sure it must have been Calvert. He says, that though the Swiss papers give the name Colnart, he is sure it was Calvert, and you remember his last words here as he went away that evening?"

"Poor fellow!" said Florence, "I am sure I have no right to bear him good will, but I am sorry for him— really sorry. I suppose, by this time, it is all over?"

"The wound was through the throat, it is said," said Miss Grainger. "But how confused the whole story is. Who is Barnard, and why did Calvert fight to save Barnard's honour?"

"No, aunt. It was to rescue Mr. Graham's, the man who was about to marry Sophia Calvert."

"Not at all, Milly. It was Graham who shot Barnard; and then poor Calvert, horrified at his friend's fate——"

Calvert never waited for more. He saw that there

was that amount of mistake and misunderstanding, which required no aid on his part, and now nothing remained but to present himself suddenly before them as a fugitive from justice seeking shelter and protection. The rest he was content to leave to hazard.

A sharp ring at the door-bell was scarcely answered by the servant, when the man came to the drawing-room door, and made a sign to Miss Grainger.

"What is it, Giacomo? What do you mean?" she cried.

"Just one moment, signora; half a minute here," he said.

Well accustomed to the tone of secrecy assumed by Italians on occasions the least important, Miss Grainger followed him outside, and there, under the glare of the hall-lamp, stood Calvert, pale, his hair dishevelled, his cravat loosened, and his coat-sleeve torn. "Save me! hide me!" said he, in a low whisper. "Can you—will you save me?"

She was one not unfitted to meet a sudden change; and, although secretly shocked, she rallied quickly, and led him into a room beside the hall. "I know all," said she. "We all knew it was your name."

"Can you conceal me here for a day—two days at furthest?"

"A week, if you need it."

"And the servant—can he be trusted?"

"To the death. I'll answer for him."

"How can you keep the secret from the girls?"

"I need not; they must know everything."

"But Florence; can she—has she forgiven me?"

"Yes, thoroughly. She scarcely knows about what she quarrelled with you. She sometimes fears that she wronged you; and Milly defends you always."

"You have heard—you know what has happened to me?"

"In a fashion: that is, we only know there has been a duel. We feared you had been wounded; and, indeed, we heard severely wounded."

"The story is too long to tell you now; enough, if I say it was all about Sophy. You remember Sophy, and a fellow who was to have married her, and who jilted her, and not only this but boasted of the injury he had done her, and the insult he had thrown on us. A friend of mine, Barnard, a brother officer, heard him—but why go on with this detail?—there was a quarrel and a challenge, and it was by merest accident I heard of it, and reached Basle in time. Of course, I was not going to leave to Barnard what of right belonged to me. There were, as you can imagine, innumerable complications in the matter. Rochefort, the other man's friend, and a French fellow, insisted on having a finger in the pie. The end of it was, I shot Graham and somebody else—I believe Rochefort—put a bullet into Barnard. The Swiss laws in some cantons are severe, and we only learned too late that we had fought in the very worst of them; so I ran, I don't know how, or in what direction. I lost my head for a while, and wandered about the Vorarlberg and the Splugen for a week or two. How I find myself now here is quite a mystery to me."

There was a haggard wildness in his look that fully accorded with all he said, and the old lady felt the most honest pity for his sufferings.

"I don't know if I'm perfectly safe here," said he, looking fearfully around him. "Are you sure you can conceal me, if need be?"

"Quite sure; have no fear about that. I'll tell the girls that your safety requires the greatest cau-

tion and secrecy, and you'll see how careful they
will be."

"Girls *will* talk, though," said he, doubtingly.

"There is the double security here—they have no one
to talk to," she said, with a faint smile.

"Very true. I was forgetting how retired your life
was here. Now for the next point. What are you to
tell them—I mean, how much are they to know?"

The old lady looked puzzled; she felt she might easily
have replied, "If they only know no more than I can tell
them, your secret will certainly be safe;" but, as she
looked at his haggard cheek and feverish eye, she shrunk
from renewing a theme full of distress and suffering.
"Leave it to me to say something—anything which shall
show them that you are in a serious trouble, and require
all their secrecy and sympathy."

"Yes, that may do—at least for the present. It will
do at least with Emily, who bears me no ill will."

"You wrong Florence if you imagine that *she* does.
It was only the other day, when, in a letter from Loyd,
she read that you had left the army, she said how sorry
she was you had quitted the career so suited to your
abilities."

"Indeed! I scarce hoped for so much of interest
in me."

"Oh, she talks continually about you; and always as
of one, who only needs the guidance of some true friend
to be a man of mark and distinction yet."

"It is very good, very kind of her," he said; and, for
an instant, seemed lost in thought.

"I'll go back now," said Miss Grainger, "and prepare
them for your coming. They'll wonder what has detained
me all this while. Wait one moment for me here."

Calvert, apparently, was too much engaged with his

own thoughts to hear her, and suffered her to go without a word. She was quickly back again, and beckoning him to follow her, led the way to the drawing-room.

Scarcely had Calvert passed the doorway, when the two girls met him, and each taking a hand, conducted him without a word to a sofa. Indeed, his sickly look, and the air of downright misery in his countenance, called or all their sympathy and kindness.

"I have scarcely strength to thank you!" he said to them, in a faint voice. Though the words were addressed to both, the glance he gave towards Florence sent the blood to her pale cheeks, and made her turn away in some confusion.

"You'll have some tea and rest yourself, and when you feel once quiet and undisturbed here you'll soon regain your strength," said Emily, as she turned towards the tea-table. While Florence, after a few moments' hesitation, seated herself on the sofa beside him.

"Has she told you what has befallen me?" whispered he to her.

"In part—that is, something of it. As much as she could in a word or two; but do not speak of it now."

"If I do not now, Florence, I can never have the courage again."

"Then be it so," she said eagerly. "I am more anxious to see you strong and well again, than to hear how you became wretched and unhappy."

"But if you do not hear the story from myself, Florence, and if you should hear the tale that others may tell of me—if you never know how I have been tried and tempted——"

"There, there—don't agitate yourself, or I must leave you; and, see, Milly is remarking our whispering together."

"Does she grudge me this much of your kind-
ness?"

"No; but—there—here she comes with your tea."
She drew a little table in front of him, and tried to per-
suade him to eat.

"Your sister has just made me a very generous prom-
ise, Emily," said he. "She has pledged herself—even
without hearing my exculpation—to believe me innocent;
and although I have told her that the charges that others
will make against me may need some refutation on my
part, she says she'll not listen to them. Is not that very
noble—is it not truly generous?"

"It is what I should expect from Florence."

"And what of Florence's sister?" said he, with a half
furtive glance towards her.

"I hope, nothing less generous."

"Then I am content," said he, with a faint sigh.
"When a man is as thoroughly ruined as I am, it might
be thought he would be indifferent to opinion in every
shape—and so I am, beyond the four walls of this room;
but here," and he looked at each in turn, "are the arbiters
of my fate; if you will but be to me dear sisters—kind,
compassionate, forgiving sisters—you will do more for this
crushed and wounded heart, than all the sympathy of the
whole world beside."

"We only ask to be such to you," cried Florence,
eagerly: "and we feel how proud we could be of such a
brother; but, above all, do not distress yourself now, by
a theme so painful to touch on. Let the unhappy events
of the last few weeks lie, if not forgotten, at least un-
mentioned, till you are calm and quiet enough to talk
of them as old memories."

"Yes! but how can I bear the thought of what others
may say of me—meanwhile?"

" Who are these others—we see no one, we go into no society ? "

" Have you not scores of dear friends, writing by every post to ask if this atrocious duellist be 'your' Mr. Calvert, and giving such a narrative, besides, of his doings, that a galley-slave would shrink from contact with such a man ? Do I not know well how tenderly people deal with the vices that are not their own ? How severe the miser can be on the spendthrift, and how mercilessly the coward condemns the hot blood that resents an injury, and how gladly they would involve in shame the character that would not brook dishonour ? "

" Believe me, we have very few ' dear friends ' at all," said Florence, smiling, " and not one, no, not a single one of the stamp you speak of."

" If you were only to read our humdrum letters," chimed in Emily, " you'd see how they never treat of anything but little domestic details of people who live as obscurely as ourselves. How Uncle Tom's boy has got into the Charterhouse ; or Mary's baby taken the chicken-pox."

" But Loyd writes to you—and not in this strain ? "

" I suspect Joseph cares little to fill his pages with what is called news," said Emily, with a laughing glance at her sister, who had turned away her head in some confusion.

" Nor would he be one likely to judge you harshly," said Florence, recovering herself. " I believe you have few friends who rate you more highly than he does."

" It is very generous of him ! " said Calvert, haughtily ; and then, catching in the proud glance of Florry's eyes a daring challenge of his words, he added, in a quieter tone, " I mean, it is generous of him to overlook how unjust I have been to him. It is not easy for men so different to measure each other, and I certainly formed an unfair estimate of him."

"Oh! may I tell him that you said so?" cried she, taking his hand with warmth.

"I mean to do it for myself, dearest sister. It is a debt I cannot permit another to acquit for me."

"Don't you think you are forgetting our guest's late fatigues, and what need he has of rest and quietness, girls?" said Miss Grainger, coming over to where they sat.

"I was forgetting everything in my joy, aunt," cried Florence. "He is going to write to Joseph like a dear, dear brother as he is, and we shall all be so happy, and so united."

"A brother? Mr. Calvert a brother?" said the old lady, in consternation at such a liberty with one of that mighty house, in which she had once lived as an humble dependant.

"Yes," cried he. "It is a favour I have begged, and they have not denied me."

The old lady's face flushed, and pride and shame glowed together on her cheeks.

"So we must say good-night," said Calvert, rising; "but we shall have a long day's talk together, to-morrow. Who is it that defines an aunt as a creature that always sends one to bed?" whispered he to Florence.

"What made you laugh, dear?" said her sister, after Calvert had left the room.

"I forget—I didn't know I laughed—he is a strange incomprehensible fellow—sometimes I like him greatly, and sometimes I feel a sort of dread of him that amounts to terror."

"If I were Joseph, I should not be quite unconcerned about that jumbled estimation."

"He has no need to be. They are unlike in every way," said she, gravely; and then, taking up her book, went on, or affected to go on reading.

"I wish Aunt Grainger would not make so much of him. It is a sort of adulation that makes our position regarding him perfectly false," said Emily. "Don't you think so, dear?"

Florence, however, made no reply, and no more passed that evening between them.

Few of us have not had occasion to remark the wondrous change produced in some quiet household, where the work of domesticity goes on in routine fashion, by the presence of an agreeable and accomplished guest. It is not alone that he contributes by qualities of his own to the common stock of amusement, but that he excites those around him to efforts, which develop resources they had not, perhaps, felt conscious of possessing. The necessity, too, of wearing one's company face, which the presence of a stranger exacts, has more advantages than many wot of. The small details whose discussion forms the staple of daily talk—the little household cares and worries—have to be shelved. One can scarcely entertain their friends with stories of the cook's impertinence, or the coachman's neglect, and one has to see, as they do see, that the restraint of a guest does not in reality affect the discipline of a household, though it suppress the debates and arrest the discussion.

It has been often remarked that the custom of appearing in parliament—as it was once observed—in court-dress, imposed a degree of courtesy and deference in debate, of which men in wide-awake hats and paletots are not always observant; and, unquestionably, in the little ceremonial observances imposed by the stranger's presence, may be seen the social benefits of a good

breeding not marred by over-familiarity. It was thus
Calvert made his presence felt at the villa. It was true
he had many companionable qualities, and he had, or at
least affected to have, very wide sympathies. He was
ever ready to read aloud, to row, to walk, to work in the
flower-garden, to sketch, or to copy music, as though each
was an especial pleasure to him. If he was not as high
spirited and light hearted as they once had seen him, it
did not detract from, but rather added to the interest he
excited. He was in misfortune—a calamity not the less
to be compassionated that none could accurately define
it ; some dreadful event had occurred, some terrible con-
sequence impended, and each felt the necessity of lighten-
ing the load of his sorrow, and helping him to bear his
affliction. They were so glad when they could cheer
him up, and so happy when they saw him take even
a passing pleasure in the pursuits their own days were
spent in.

They had now been long enough in Italy not to feel
depressed by its dreamy and monotonous quietude, but
to feel the inexpressible charm of that soft existence,
begotten of air, and climate, and scenery. They had
arrived at that stage—and it *is* a stage—in which the
olive is not dusky, nor the mountain arid : when the dry
course of the torrent suggests no wish for water. Life—
mere life—has a sense of luxury about it, unfelt in
northern lands. With an eager joy, therefore, did they
perceive that Calvert seemed to have arrived at the same
sentiment, and the same appreciation as themselves. He
seemed to ask for nothing better than to stroll through
orange groves, or lie under some spreading fig-tree,
drowsily soothed by the song of the vine-dresser, or the
unwearied chirp of the cicala. How much of good there
must be surely in a nature pleased with such tranquil

simple pleasures! thought they. See how he likes to watch the children at their play, and with what courtesy he talked to that old priest. It is clear dissipation may have damaged, but has not destroyed that fine temperament—his heart has not lost its power to feel. It was thus that each thought of him, though there was less of confidence between the sisters than heretofore.

A very few words will suffice to explain this: When Florence recovered from the shock Calvert had occasioned her on the memorable night of his visit, she had nothing but the very vaguest recollection of what had occurred. That some terrible tidings had been told her—some disastrous news in which Loyd and Calvert were mixed up: that she had blamed Calvert for rashness or indiscretion; that he had either shown a letter he ought never to have shown, or not produced one which might have averted a misfortune; and, last of all, that she herself had done or said something which a calmer judgment could not justify—all these were in some vague and shadowy shape before her, and all rendered her anxious and uneasy. On the other hand, Emily, seeing with some satisfaction that her sister never recurred to the events of that unhappy night, gladly availed herself of this silence to let them sleep undisturbed. She was greatly shocked, it is true, by the picture Calvert's representation presented of Loyd. He had never been a great favourite of her own; she recognised many good and amiable traits in his nature, but she deemed him gloomy, depressed, and a dreamer—and a dreamer, above all, she regarded as unfit to be the husband of Florence, whose ill health had only tended to exaggerate a painful and imaginative disposition. She saw, or fancied she saw, that Loyd's temperament, calm and gentle though it was, seemed to depress her sister. His views of life were very sombre, and no effort ever enabled him to look forward in a sanguine or hopeful spirit. If, however, to these feelings an absolute fault of character were to be added —the want of personal courage—her feelings for him could no longer be even the qualified esteem she had hitherto experienced. She also knew that nothing could be such a shock to Florence, as to believe that the man she loved was a coward; nor could any station, or charm, or ability, however great, compensate for such a defect. As a matter, therefore, for grave after-thought, but not thoroughly "proven," she retained this charge in her mind, nor did she by any accident drop a hint or a word that could revive the memory of that evening.

As for Miss Grainger, only too happy to see that Florence seemed to retain no trace of that distressing scene, she never went back to it, and thus every event of the night was consigned to silence, if not oblivion. Still, there grew out of that reserve a degree of estrangement between the sisters, which each, unconscious of in herself, could detect in the other. "I think Milly has grown colder to me of late, aunt. She is not less kind or attentive, but there is a something of constraint about her I cannot fathom," would Florence say to her aunt. While the other whispered, "I wonder why Florry is so silent when we are alone together? She that used to tell me all her thoughts, and speak for hours of what she hoped and wished, now only alludes to some common-place topic—the book she has just read, or the walk we took yesterday."

The distance between them was not the less wide that each had secretly confided to Calvert her misgivings about the other. Indeed, it would have been, for girls so young and inexperienced in life, strange not to have ccorded him their confidence. He possessed a large share of that quality which very young people regard as sagacity. I am not sure that the gift has got a special name, but we have all of us heard of some one "with such a good head," "so safe an adviser," "such a rare counsellor in a difficulty," "knowing life and mankind so well," and "such an aptitude to take the right road in a moment of embarrassment." The phœnix is not usually a man of bright or showy qualities; he is, on the contrary, one that the world at large has failed to recognise. If, however, by any chance he should prove to be smart, ready-witted, and a successful talker, his sway is a perfect despotism. Such was Calvert; at least such was he to the eyes of these sisters. Now Emily had confided to him that she thought Loyd totally unworthy of Florence. His good qualities were undeniable, but he had few attractive or graceful ones; and then there was a despondent, depressed tone about him that must prove deeply injurious to one whose nature required bright and cheery companionship. Calvert agreed with every word of this.

Florence, on her side, was, meanwhile, imparting to him that Loyd was not fairly appreciated by her aunt or her sister. They deemed him very honourable, very truthful, and very moral, but they did not think highly of his abilities, nor reckon much on his success in life. In fact, though the words themselves were spared her, they told her in a hundred modes that "she was throwing herself away;" and, strange as it may read, she liked to be told so, and heard with a sort of triumphant pride that she was going to make a sacrifice of herself and all her prospects—all for "poor Joseph." To become the auditor of this reckoning required more adroitness than the other case; but Calvert was equal to it. He saw where to differ, where to agree with her. It was a contingency which admitted of a very dexterous flattery, rather insinuated, however, than openly declared ; and it was thus he conveyed to her that he took the same view as the others. He knew Loyd was an excellent fellow, far too good and too moral for a mere scamp like himself to estimate. He was certain he would turn out respectable, esteemed, and all that. He would be sure to be a churchwarden, and might be a poor-law guardian ; and his wife would be certain to shine in the same brightness attained by him. Then stopping, he would heave a low, faint sigh, and turn the conversation to something about her own attractions or graceful gifts. How enthusiastically the world of " society " would one day welcome them —and what a " success " awaited her whenever she was well enough to endure its fatigue. Now, though all these were only as so many fagots to the pile of her martyrdom, she delighted to listen to them, and never wearied of hearing Calvert exalt all the greatness of the sacrifice she was about to make, and how immeasurably she was above the lot to which she was going to consign herself.

It is the drip, drip, that eats away the rock, and iteration ever so faint, will cleave its way at last : so Florry, without in the slightest degree disparaging Loyd, grew at length to believe, as Calvert assured her, that " Master Joseph " was the luckiest dog that ever lived, and had carried off a prize immeasurably above his pretensions.

Miss Grainger, too, found a confessor in their guest : but it will spare the reader some time if I place before him a letter which Calvert wrote to one of his most intimate friends a short time after he had taken up his abode at the villa. The letter will also serve to connect some past events with the present now before us.

The epistle was addressed Algernon Drayton, Esq., Army and Navy Club, London, and ran thus:

"My dear Algy,—You are the prince of 'our own correspondents,' and I thank you, ' imo corde,' if that be Latin for it, for all you have done for me. I defy the whole Bar to make out, from your narrative, who killed who, in that affair at Basle. I know, after the third reading of it, I fancied that I had been shot through the heart, and then took post-horses for Zurich. It was and is a master-piece of the bewildering imbroglio style. Cultivate your great gifts, then, my friend. You will be a treasure to the court of Cresswell, and the most injured of men or the basest of seducers will not be able at the end of a suit to say which must kneel down and ask pardon of the other. I suppose I ought to say I'm sorry for Barnard, but I can't. No, Algy, I cannot. He was an arrant snob, and, if he had lived, he'd have gone about telling the most absurd stories and getting people to believe them, just on the faith of his stupidity. If there is a ridiculous charge in the world, it is that of 'firing before one's time,' which, to make the most of it, must be a matter of seconds, and involves, besides, a question as to the higher inflammability of one's powder. I don't care who made mine, but I know it did its work well. I'm glad, however, that you did not deign to notice that contemptible allegation, and merely limited yourself to what resulted. Your initials and the stars showered over the paragraph, are in the highest walk of legerdemain, and I can no more trace relatives to antecedents, than I can tell what has become of the egg I saw Houdin smash in my hat.

"I know, however, I mustn't come back just yet. There is that shake-of-the-headiness abroad that makes

one uncomfortable. Fortunately, this is no sacrifice to
me. My debts keep me out of London, just as effectually
as my morals. Besides this, my dear Algy, I'm living in
the very deepest of clover, domesticated with a maiden
aunt and two lovely nieces, in a villa on an Italian lake,
my life and comforts being the especial care of the triad.
Imagine an infant-school occupied in the care of a young
tiger of the spotted species, and you may, as the Yankees
say, realise the situation. But they seem to enjoy the
peril of what they are doing, or they don't see it, I can't
tell which.

"'Gazetted out,' you say; 'Meno male,' as they say
here. I might have been promoted, and so tempted to
go back to that land of Bores, Bearers, and Bungalores,
and I am grateful to the stumble that saves me from a
fall. But you ask, what do I mean to do? and I own I
do not see my way to anything. Time was when gentle-
man-riding, coach-driving, or billiards, were on a par with
the learned professions; but, my dear Drayton, we have
fallen upon a painfully enlightened age, and every fellow
can do a little of everything.

"You talk of my friends? You might as well talk of
my Three per Cents. If I had friends, it would be
natural enough they should help me to emigrate as a
means of seeing the last of me; but I rather suspect that
my relatives, who by a figure of speech represent the
friends aforesaid, have a lively faith that some day or
other the government will be at the expense of my
passage—that it would be quite superfluous in them to
provide for it.

"You hint that I might marry, meaning thereby marry
with money; and, to be sure, there's Barnard's widow
with plenty of tin, and exactly in that stage of affliction
that solicits consolation; for when the heart is open to

sorrow, Love occasionally steps in before the door closes. Then, a more practical case. One of these girls here—the fortune is only fifteen thousand—I think over the matter day and night, and I verily believe I see it in the light of whatever may be the weather at the time: very darkly on the rainy days; not so gloomy when the sky is blue and the air balmy.

"Do you remember that fellow that I stayed behind for at the Cape, and thereby lost my passage, just to quarrel with—Headsworth? Well, a feeling of the same sort is tempting me sorely at this time. There is one of these girls, a poor delicate thing, very pretty and coquettish in her way, has taken it into her wise head to prefer a stupid loutish sort of young sucking barrister to me, and treats me with an ingenious blending of small compassion and soft pity to console my defeat. If you could ensure my being an afflicted widower within a year, I'd marry her, just to show her the sort of edged tool she has been playing with. I'm often half driven to distraction by her impertinent commiseration. I tried to get into a row with the man, but he would not have it. Don't you hate the fellow that won't quarrel with you, worse even than the odious wretch who won't give you credit?

"I might marry the sister, I suppose, to-morrow; but that alone is a reason against it. Besides, she is terribly healthy; and though I have lost much faith in consumption, from cases I have watched in my own family, bad air and bad treatment will occasionally aid its march. Could you, from such meagre data as these, help me with a word of advice? for I do like the advice of an unscrupulous dog like yourself—so sure to be practical. Then there is no cant between men like us—we play 'cartes sur table.'

"The old maid who represents the head of this house
8—2

has been confidentially sounding me as to an eligible investment for some thousands which have fallen in from a redeemed mortgage. I could have said, 'Send them to me, and you shall name the interest yourself;' but I was modest, and did not. I bethought me, however, of a good friend, one Algy Drayton, a man of large landed property, but who always wants money for drainage. Eh, Algy! Are your lips watering at the prospect? If so, let your ingenuity say what is to be the security.

"Before I forget it, ask Pearson if he has any more of that light Amontillado. It is the only thing ever sets me right, and I have been poorly of late. I know I must be out of sorts, because all day yesterday I was wretched and miserable at my misspent life and squandered abilities. Now, in my healthier moments, such thoughts never cross me. I'd have been honest if Nature had dealt fairly with me; but the younger son of a younger brother starts too heavily weighted to win by anything but a 'foul.' You understand this well, for we are in the same book. We each of us pawned our morality very early in life, and never were rich enough to redeem it. Apropos of pledges, is your wife alive? I lost a bet about it some time ago, but I forget on which side. I backed my opinion.

"Now, to sum up. Let me hear from you about all I have been asking; and, though I don't opine it lies very much in your way, send me any tidings you can pick up —to his disadvantage, of course—of Joseph Loyd, Middle Temple. You know scores of attorneys who could trace him. Your hint about letter writing for the papers is not a bad one. I suppose I could learn the trick, and do it at least as well as some of the fellows whose lucubrations I read. A political surmise, a spicy bit of scandal, a sensation trial, wound up with a few moral reflections upon how much better we do the same sort of things at home. Isn't that the bone of it? Send me—don't forget it—send me some news of Rocksley. I want to hear how they take all that I have been doing of late for their happiness. I have half of a letter written to Soph—a sort of mild condolence, blended with what the serious people call profitable reflections and suggestive hints that her old affection will find its way back to me one of these days, and that when the event occurs, her best course will be to declare it. I have reminded her, too, that I laid up a little love in her heart when we parted, just as shrewd people leave a small balance at their bankers' as a title to reopen their account at a future day.

"Give Guy's people a hint that it's only wasting postage-stamps to torment me with bills. I never break the envelope of a dun's letter, and I know them as instinctively as a detective does a swell-mobsman. What an imaginative race these duns must be. I know of no fellow, for the high flights of fancy, to equal one's tailor or bootmaker. As to the search for the elixir vitæ, it's a dull realism after the attempts I have witnessed for years to get money out of myself.

"But I must close this; here is Milly, whose taper fingers have been making cigarettes for me all the morning, come to propose a sail on the lake!—fact Algy!—and the wolf is going out with the lambs, just as prettily and as decorously as though his mother had been a ewe and cast 'sheep's eyes' at his father. Address me, Orta, simply, for I don't wish it to be thought here that my stay is more than a day by day matter. I have all my letters directed to the post-office.

"Yours, very cordially,

"HARRY CALVERT."

The pleasant project thus passingly alluded to was not destined to fulfilment; for as Calvert with the two sisters were on their way to the lake, they were overtaken by Miss Grainger, who insisted on carrying away Calvert, to give her his advice upon a letter she had just received. Obeying with the best grace he could, and which really did not err on the score of extravagance, he accompanied the old lady back to the house, somewhat relieved, indeed, in mind, to learn that the letter she was about to show him in no way related to him nor his affairs.

"I have my scruples, Mr. Calvert, about asking your opinion in a case where I well know your sympathies are not in unison with our own; but your wise judgment and great knowledge of life are advantages I cannot bring myself to relinquish. I am well aware that whatever your feelings or your prejudices, they will not interfere with that good judgment."

"Madam, you do me honour; but, I hope, no more than justice."

"You know of Florry's engagement to Mr. Loyd?" she asked, abruptly, as though eager to begin her recital; and he bowed. "Well, he left this so hurriedly about his father's affairs, that he had no time to settle anything, or, indeed, explain anything. We knew nothing of his prospects or his means, and he just as little about my niece's fortune. He had written, it is true, to his father, and got a most kind and affectionate answer, sanctioning the match, and expressing fervent wishes for his happiness—— Why do you smile, Mr. Calvert?"

"I was only thinking of the beauty of that benevolence that costs nothing; few things are more graceful than a benediction—nothing so cheap."

"That may be so. I have nothing to say to it," she rejoined, in some irritation. "But old Mr. Loyd's letter was very beautiful, and very touching. He reminded Joseph that he himself had married on the very scantiest of means, and that though his life had never been above the condition of a very poor vicar, the narrowness of his fortune had not barred his happiness. I'd like to read you a passage——"

"Pray do not. You have given me the key-note, and I feel as if I could score down the whole symphony."

"You don't believe him, then?"

"Heaven forfend! All I would say is, that between a man of his temperament and one of mine discussion is impossible; and if this be the letter on which you want my opinion, I frankly tell you I have none to give."

"No, no! this is not the letter; here is the letter I wish you to read. It has only come by this morning's post, and I want to have your judgment on it before I speak of it to the girls."

Calvert drew the letter slowly from its envelope, and, with a sort of languid resignation, proceeded to read it. As he reached the end of the first page, he said, "Why, it would need a lawyer of the Ecclesiastical Court to understand this. What's all this entangled story about irregular induction, and the last incumbent, and the lay impropriator?"

"Oh, you needn't have read that! It's the poor old gentleman's account of his calamity; how he has lost his vicarage, and is going down to a curacy in Cornwall. Here," said she, pointing to another page, "here is where you are to begin; 'I might have borne——'"

"Ah, yes!" said he, reading aloud; "'I might have borne up better under this misfortune if it had not occurred at such a critical moment of my poor boy's fate, for I am still uncertain what effect these tidings will have produced on you. I shall no longer have a home to offer the young people, when from reasons of health, or economy, or relaxation, they would like to have left the town and come down to rusticate with us. Neither will it be in my power to contribute—even in the humble shape I had once hoped—to their means of living. I am, in short, reduced to the very narrowest fortune, nor have I the most distant prospect of any better: so much for myself. As for Joseph, he has been offered, through the friendly intervention of an old college companion, an appointment at the Calcutta Bar. It is not a lucrative nor an important post, but one which they say will certainly lead to advancement and future fortune. Had it not been for his hopes—hopes which had latterly constituted the very spring of his existence—such an opening as this would have been welcomed with all his heart; but now the offer comes clouded with all the doubts as to how you may be disposed to regard it. Will you consent to separate from the dear girl you have watched over with such loving solicitude for years? Will she herself consent to expatriation and the parting from her sister and yourself? These are the questions which torture his mind, and leave him no rest day or night! The poor fellow has tried to plead his cause in a letter—he has essayed a dozen times—but all in vain. "My own selfishness shocks me," he says, "when I read over what I have written, and see how completely I have forgotten everything but my own interests." If he remain at home, by industry and attention he may hope, in some six or seven years, to be in a position to marry; but six or seven years are a long period of life, and sure to have their share of vicissitudes and casualties. Whereas, by accepting this appointment, which will be nearly seven hundred a year, he could afford at once to support a wife, of course supposing her to submit willingly to the privations and wants of such straitened fortunes. I have offered to tell his story for him—that story he has no strength to tell himself—but I have not pledged to be his advocate; for, while I would lay down my life to secure his happiness, I cannot bring myself to urge, for his sake, what might be unfair or ungenerous to exact from another.

"'Though my son's account of your niece leaves us nothing more to ask or wish for in a daughter, I am writing in ignorance of many things I would like to know. Has she, for instance, the energy of character that would face a new life in a new and far away land? Has she courage—has she health for it? My wife is not pleased at my stating all these reasons for doubt; but I am determined you shall know the worst of our case from ourselves, and discover no blot we have not prepared you for.'" Calvert muttered something here, but too inaudibly to be heard, and went on reading: "'When I think that poor Joe's whole happiness will depend on what decision your next letter will bring, I have only to pray that it may be such as will conduce to the welfare of those we both love so dearly. I cannot ask you to make what are called 'sacrifices' for us: but I entreat you let the consideration of affection weigh with you, not less than that of worldly interests, and also to believe that when one has to take a decision which is to influence a lifetime, it is as safe to take counsel from the heart as from the head— from the nature that is to feel, as from the intellect that is to plan.'

"I think I have read enough of this," said Calvert, impatiently. "I know the old gent's brief perfectly. It's the old story: first gain a girl's affections, and let her friends squabble, if they dare, about the settlements. He's an artful old boy, that vicar! but I like him, on

the whole, better than his son, for though he does plead
in formâ pauperis, he has the fairness to say so."

"You are very severe, Mr. Calvert.   I hope you are
too severe," said the old lady, in some agitation.

"And what answer are you going to give him?"
asked he, curtly.

"That is exactly the point on which I want your
advice; for though I know well you are no friend to
young Loyd, I believe you to be our sincere well-wisher,
and that your judgment will be guided by the honest
feelings of regard for us."

Without deigning to notice this speech, he arose and
walked up and down the room apparently deep in
thought.   He stopped at last, and said, abruptly, "I
don't presume to dictate to you in this business; but
if I were the young lady's guardian, and got such a
letter as this, my reply would be a very brief one."

"You'd refuse your consent?"

"Of course I would!   Must your niece turn adven-
turess, and go off to Heaven knows where, with God
knows whom?   Must she link her fortunes to a man who
confessedly cannot face the world at home, but must go
to the end of the earth for a bare subsistence?   What is
there in this man himself, in his character, station, abilities,
and promise, that are to recompense such devotion as
this?   And what will your own conscience say to the first
letter from India, full of depression and sorrow, regrets
shadowed forth, if not avowed openly, for the happy days
when you were all together, and contrasts of that time, with
the dreary dulness of an uncheered existence?   *I* know
something of India, and I can tell you it is a country
where life is only endurable by splendour.   Poverty in
such a land is not merely privation, it is to live in derision
and contempt.   Everyone knows how many rupees you

have per month, and you are measured by your means in everything. That seven hundred a year, which sounds plausibly enough, is something like two hundred at home, if so much. Of course you can override all these considerations, and, as the vicar says, 'Let the heart take precedence of the head.' *My* cold and worldly counsels will not stand comparison with *his* fine and generous sentiments, no more than I could make as good a figure in the pulpit as he could. But, perhaps, as a mere man of the world, I am his equal; though there are little significant hints in that very letter that show the old parson is very wide awake."

"I never detected them," said she, curtly.

"Perhaps not, but rely upon one thing. It was not such a letter as he would have addressed to a man. If *I*, for instance, had been the guardian instead of you, the whole tone of the epistle would have been very different."

"Do you think so?"

"Think so! I know it. I had not read ten lines till I said to myself, "This was meant for very different eyes from mine.'"

"If I thought that——"

"Go on," said he; "finish, and let me hear what you would say or do, when arrived at the conclusion I have come to."

So far, however, from having come to any decision, she really did not see in the remotest distance anything to guide her to one.

"What would you advise me to do, Mr. Calvert?" said she, at last, and after a pause of some time.

"Refer him to me; say the point is too difficult for you; that while your feelings for your niece might overbear all other considerations, those very feelings might be the sources of error to you. You might, for instance, concede too much to the claim of affection; or, on the other hand, be too regardful of the mere worldly consideration. Not that, on second thoughts, I'd enter upon this to him. I'd simply say a friend in whom I repose the fullest confidence, has consented to represent me in this difficult matter.   Not swayed as I am by the claims of affection, he will be able to give a calmer and more dispassionate judgment than I could.   Write to Mr. Calvert, therefore, who is now here, and say what the mere business aspect of the matter suggests to you to urge.   Write to him frankly, as to one who already is known to your son, and has lived on terms of intimacy with him.   His reply will be mine."

"Is not that a very cold and repelling answer to the good vicar's letter?"

"I think not, and I suspect it will have one good effect.   The parson's style will become natural at once, and you'll see what a very different fashion he'll write when the letter is addressed to me."

'"What will Florence say?"

"Nothing, if she knows nothing.   And, of course, if you intend to take her into your counsels, you must please to omit *me*.   I'm not going to legislate for a young lady's future with herself to vote in the division!"

"But what's to become of me, if you go away in the middle of the negotiation, and leave me to finish it?"

"I'll not do so.   I'll pledge my word to see you through it.   It will be far shorter than you suspect.   The vicar will not play out his hand when he sees his adversary.   You have nothing to do but write as I have told you; leave the rest to me."

"Florence is sure to ask me what the vicar has written; she knows that I have had his letter."

"Tell her it is a purely business letter; that his son

having been offered a colonial appointment, he wishes to ascertain what your fortune his, and how circumstanced, before pledging himself further. Shock her a little about their worldliness, and leave the remainder to time."

" But Joseph will write to her in the meanwhile and disabuse her of this."

" Not completely. She'll be annoyed that the news of the colonial place did not come first from himself; she'll be piqued into something not very far from distrust; she'll show some vexation when she writes; but don't play the game before the cards are dealt. Wait, as I say —wait and see. Meanwhile, give me the vicar's note, for I dread your showing it to Florry, and if she asks for it, say you sent it to Henderson—isn't that your lawyer's name?—in London, and told him to supply you with the means of replying to it."

Like a fly in a cobweb, Miss Grainger saw herself entangled wherever she turned, and though perhaps in her secret heart she regretted having ever called Calvert to her counsels, the thing was now done and could not be undone.

CHAPTER XII.

DARKER AND DARKER.

THERE was an unusual depression at the villa—each had his or her own load of anxiety, and each felt that an atmosphere of gloom was thickening around, and, without being able to say why or wherefore, that dark days were coming.

"Among your letters this morning was there none from the vicar, Mr. Calvert?" asked Miss Grainger, as he sat smoking his morning cigar under the porch of the cottage.

"No," said he, carelessly. "The post brought me nothing of any interest. A few reproaches from my friends about not writing, and relieving their anxieties about this unhappy business. They had it that I was killed—beyond that, nothing."

"But we ought to have heard from old Mr. Loyd before this. Strange, too, Joseph has not written."

"Stranger if he had! The very mention of my name as a referee in his affairs will make him very cautious with his pen."

"She is so fretted," sighed the old lady.

"I see she is, and I see she suspects, also, that you have taken me in your counsels. We are not as good friends as we were some time back."

"She really likes you, though—I assure you she does, Mr. Calvert. It was but t'other day she said, 'What would have become of us all this time back if Mad Harry

—you know your nickname—if Mad Harry had not been here?'"

"That's not liking! That is merely the expression of a weak gratitude towards the person who helps to tide over a dreary interval. You might feel it for the old priest who played piquet with you, or the Spitz terrier that accompanied you in your walks.

"Oh, it's far more than that. She is constantly talking of your great abilities—how you might be this, that and t'other. That, with scarcely an effort, you can master any subject, and without any effort at all always make yourself more agreeable than anyone else."

"Joseph excepted?"

"No, she didn't even except him; on the contrary, she said, 'It was unfortunate for him to be exposed to such a dazzling rivalry—that your animal spirits alone would always beat him out of the field.'"

"Stuff and nonsense! If I wasn't as much his superior in talent as in temperament, I'd fling myself over that rock yonder, and make an end of it!" After a few seconds' pause he went on: "She may think what she likes of *me*, but one thing is plain enough—she does not love *him*. It is the sort of compassionating, commiserating estimate imaginative girls occasionally get up for dreary depressed fellows, constituting themselves discoverers of intellect that no one ever suspected—revealers of wealth that none had ever dreamed of. Don't I know scores of such who have poetised the most commonplace of men into heroes, and never found out their mistake till they married them!"

"You always terrify me when you take to predicting, Mr. Calvert."

"Heaven knows, it's not my ordinary mood. One who looks so little into the future for himself has few temptations to do so for his friends."

"Why do you feel so depressed?"

"I'm not sure that I do feel depressed. I'm irritable, out of sorts, annoyed if you will; but not low or melancholy. Is it not enough to make one angry to see such a girl as Florry bestow her affections on that——Well, I'll not abuse him, but you *know* he is a 'cad'—that's exactly the word that fits him."

"It was no choice of mine," she sighed.

"That may be; but you ought to have been more than passive in the matter. Your fears would have prevented you letting your niece stop for a night in an unhealthy locality. You'd not have suffered her to halt in the Pontine Marshes; but you can see no danger in linking her whole future life to influences five thousand times more depressing. I tell you, and I tell you deliberately, that she'd have a far better chance of happiness with a scamp like myself."

"Ah, I need not tell you my own sentiments on that point," said she, with a deep sigh.

Calvert apparently set little store by such sympathy, for he rose, and throwing away the end of his cigar, stood looking out over the lake. "Here comes Onofrio, flourishing some letters in his hand. The idiot fancies the post never brings any but pleasant tidings."

"Let us go down and meet him," said Miss Grainger; and he walked along at her side in silence.

"Three for the Signor Capitano," said the boatman, "and one for the signorina," handing the letters as he landed.

"Drayton," muttered Calvert; "the others are strange to me."

"This is from Joseph. How glad poor Florry will be to get it."

"Don't defer her happiness, then," said he, half

sternly; "I'll sit down on the rocks here and con over my less pleasant correspondence." One was from his lawyer, to state that outlawry could no longer be resisted, and that if his friends would not come forward at once with some satisfactory promise of arrangement, the law must take its course. "My friends," said he, with a bitter laugh, "which be they?" The next he opened was from the army agents, dryly setting forth that as he had left the service it was necessary he should take some immediate steps to liquidate some regimental claims against him, of which they begged to enclose the particulars. He laughed bitterly and scornfully as he tore the letter to fragments and threw the pieces into the water. "How well they know the man they threaten!" cried he defiantly. "I'd like to know how much a drowning man cares for his duns?" He laughed again. "Now for Drayton. I hope this will be pleasanter than its predecessors." It was not very long, and it was as follows:

"'The Rag, Tuesday.

"Dear Harry,—Your grateful compliments on the dexterity of my correspondence in the Meteor arrived at an unlucky moment, for some fellow had just written to the editor a real statement of the whole affair, and the next day came a protest, part French, part English, signed by Edward Rochefort, Lieutenant-Colonel; Gustavus Brooke, D.L.; George Law, M.D.; Alberic de Raymond, Vicomte, and Jules de Lassagnac. They sent for me to the office to see the document, and I threw all imaginable discredit on its authenticity, but without success. The upshot is, *I* have lost my place as 'own correspondent,' and you are in a very bad way. The whole will appear in print to-morrow, and be read from Hudson's Bay to the Him-

9

alaya. I have done my best to get the other papers to disparage the statement, and have written all the usual bosh about condemning a man in his absence, and entreating the public to withhold its judgment, &c. &c.; but they all seem to feel that the tide of popular sentiment is too strong to resist, and you must be pilloried; prepare yourself, then, for a pitiless pelting, which, as parliament is not sitting, will probably have a run of three or four weeks.

"In any other sort of scrape, the fellows at the club here would have stood by you, but they shrink from the danger of this business, which I now see was worse than you told me. Many, too, are more angry with you for deserting B. than for shooting the other fellow; and though B. was an arrant snob, now that he is no more you wouldn't believe what shoals of good qualities they have discovered he possessed, and he is 'poor Bob' in the mouth of twenty fellows who would not have been seen in his company a month ago. There is, however, worse than all this : a certain Reppingham, or Reppengham, the father of B.'s wife, has either already instituted, or is about to institute, proceedings against you criminally. He uses ugly words, calls it a murder, and has demanded a warrant for your extradition and arrest at once. There is a story of some note you are said to have written to B., but which arrived when he was insensible, and was read by the people about him, who were shocked by its heartless levity. What is the truth as to this? At all events, Rep has got a vendetta fit on him, and raves like a Corsican for vengeance. Your present place of concealment, safe enough for duns, will offer no security against detectives. The bland blackguards with black whiskers know the geography of Europe as well as they know the blind alleys about Houndsditch. You must decamp, therefore; get across the Adriatic into Dalmatia, or into Greece. Don't delay, whatever you do, for I see plainly, that in the present state of public opinion, the fellow who captures you will come back here with a fame like that of Gérard the lion-killer. Be sure of one thing, if you were just as clean handed in this business as I know you are not, there is no time now for a vindication. You *must* get out of the way, and wait. The clubs, the press, the swells at the Horse Guards, and the snobs at the War-office, are all against you, and there's no squaring your book against such long odds. I am well aware that no one gets either into or out of a scrape more easily than yourself; but don't treat this as a light one: don't fancy, above all, that I am giving you the darkest side of it, for, with all our frankness and free speech together, I couldn't tell you the language people hold here about it. There's not a man you ever bullied at mess, or beat at billiards, that is not paying off his scores to you now! And though you may take all this easily, don't undervalue its importance.

"I haven't got—and I don't suppose you care much now to get—any information about Loyd, beyond his being appointed something, Attorney-General's ' devil,' I believe, at Calcutta. I'd not have heard even so much, but he was trying to get a loan, to make out his outfit, from Joel, and old Isaac told me who he was, and what he wanted. Joel thinks, from the state of the fellow's health, that no one will like to advance the cash, and if so, he'll be obliged to relinquish the place. You have not told me whether you wish this, or the opposite.

"I wish I could book up to you at such a moment as this, but I haven't got it. I send you all that I can scrape together, seventy odd; it is a post bill, and easily cashed anywhere. In case I hear of anything that may

9—2

be imminently needed for your guidance, I'll telegraph to you the morrow after your receipt of this, addressing the message to the name Grainger, to prevent accidents. You must try and keep your friends from seeing the London papers so long as you stay with them. I suppose, when you leave, you'll not fret about the reputation that follows you. For the last time, let me warn you to get away to some place of safety, for if they can push matters to an arrest, things may take an ugly turn.

"They are getting really frightened here about India at last. Harris has brought some awful news home with him, and they'd give their right hands to have those regiments they sent off to China to despatch now to Calcutta. I know this will be all 'nuts' to you, and it is the only bit of pleasant tidings I have for you. Your old prediction about England being a third-rate power, like Holland, may not be so far from fulfilment as I used to think it. I wonder shall we ever have a fireside gossip over all these things again? At present, all looks too dark to get a peep into the future. Write to me at once, say what you mean to do, and believe me as ever, yours,

"A. DRAYTON.

"I have just heard that the lawyers are in doubt as to the legality of extradition, and Braddon declares dead against it. In the case they relied on, the man had come to England after being tried in France, thinking himself safe, as 'autrefois acquit;' but they found him guilty at the Old Bailey, and——him. There's delicacy for you, after your own heart."

Calvert smiled grimly at his friend's pleasantry. "Here is enough trouble for any man to deal with. Duns, outlawry, and a criminal prosecution!" said he, as he replaced his letter in its envelope, and lighted his cigar. He had not been many minutes in the enjoyment of his weed, when he saw Miss Grainger coming hastily towards him. "I wish that old woman would let me alone, just now!" muttered he. "I have need of all my brains for my own misfortunes."

"It has turned out just as I predicted, Mr. Calvert," said she, pettishly. "Young Loyd is furious at having his pretensions referred to you, and will not hear of it. His letter to Florence is all but reproachful, and she has gone home with her eyes full of tears. This note for you came as an enclosure."

Calvert took the note from her hands, and laying it beside him on the rock, smoked on without speaking.

"I knew everything that would happen!" said Miss Grainger. "The old man gave the letter you wrote to his son, who immediately sat down and wrote to Florry. I have not seen the letter myself, but Milly declares that it goes so far as to say, that if Florry admits of any advice or interference on your part, it is tantamount to a desire to break off the engagement. He declares, however, that he neither can nor will believe such a thing to be possible. That he knows she is ignorant of the whole intrigue. Milly assures me that was the word, intrigue; and she read it twice over to be certain. He also says something, which I do not quite understand, about my being led beyond the bounds of judgment by what he calls a traditional reverence for the name you bear—but one thing is plain enough, he utterly rejects the reference to you, or, indeed, to anyone now but Florence herself, and says, 'This is certainly a case for your own decision, and I will accept of none other than yours.'"

"Is there anything more about me than you have said?" asked Calvert, calmly.

"No, I believe not. He begs, in the postscript, that the enclosed note may be given to you, that's all."

Calvert took a long breath ; he felt as if a weight had been removed from his heart, and he smoked on in silence.

"Won't you read it ? " cried she, eagerly. "I am burn: ing to hear what he says."

"I can tell you just as well without breaking the seal," said he, with a half scornful smile. "I know the very tone and style of it, and I recognise the pluck with which such a man, when a thousand miles off, dares to address one like myself."

"Read it, though ; let me hear his own words !" cried she.

"I'm not impatient for it," said he ; "I have had a sufficient dose of bitters this morning, and I'd just as soon spare myself the acrid petulance of this poor creature."

"You are very provoking, I must say," said she, angrily, and turned away towards the house. Calvert watched her till she disappeared behind a copse, and then hastily broke open the letter.

"Middle Temple, Saturday.

"Sir—My father has forwarded to me a letter which, with very questionable good taste, you addressed to him. The very relations which subsisted between us when we parted, might have suggested a more delicate course on your part. Whatever objections I might then, however, have made to your interference in matters personal to myself, have now become something more than mere objections, and I flatly declare that I will not listen to one word from a man whose name is now a shame and a disgrace throughout Europe. That you may quit the roof which has sheltered you hitherto without the misery of exposure, I have forborne in my letter to narrate the story which is on every tongue here; but, as the price of this forbearance, I desire and I exact that you leave the villa on the day you receive this, and cease from that day forth to hold any intercourse with the family who reside in it. If I do not, therefore, receive a despatch by telegraph, informing me that you accede to these conditions, I will forward by the next post the full details which the press of England is now giving of your infamous conduct and of the legal steps which are to be instituted against you.

"Remember distinctly, Sir, that I am only in this pledging myself for that short interval of time which will suffer you to leave the house of those who offered you a refuge against calamity—not crime—and whose shame would be overwhelming if they but knew the character of him they sheltered. You are to leave before night-fall of the day this reaches, and never to return. You are to abstain from all correspondence. I make no conditions as to future acquaintanceship, because I know that were I even so minded, no efforts of mine could save you from that notoriety which a few days more will attach to you, never to leave you.

"I am, your obedient servant,

"JOSEPH LOYD."

Calvert tried to laugh as he finished the reading of this note, but the attempt was a failure, and a sickly pallor spread over his face, and his lips trembled. "Let me only meet you, I don't care in what presence, or in what place," muttered he, "and you shall pay dearly for this. But now to think of myself. This is just the sort of fellow to put his threat into execution, the more since he will naturally be anxious to get me away from this. What is to be done? With one week more I could almost answer for my success. Ay, Mademoiselle Florry, you were deeper in the toils than you suspected. The dread of me that once inspired a painful feeling had grown into a sort of self-pride that elevated her in her own esteem. She was so proud of her familiarity with a wild animal, and so vain of her influence over him! So pleasant to say, 'See, savage as he is, he'll not turn upon *me!*' And now to rise from the table, when the game is all but won! Confound the fellow, how he has wrecked my fortunes! As if I had not enough, too, on my hands without this!" And he walked impatiently to and fro, like a caged animal in fretfulness. "I wanted to think over Drayton's letter calmly and deliberately, and here comes this order, this command, to be up and away—away from the only spot in which I can say I enjoyed an hour's peace for years and years, and from the two or three left to me, of all the world, who think it no shame to bestow on me a word or a look of kindness. The fellow is peremptory—he declares I must leave to-day." For some time he continued to walk, muttering to himself, or moodily silent. At last he cried out, "Yes; I have it! I'll go up to Milan, and cash this bill of Drayton's. When there I'll telegraph to Loyd, which will show I have left the villa. That done, I'll return here, if it be but for a day; and who knows what a day will bring forth?"

"Who has commands for Milan?" said he, gaily entering the drawing-room, where Miss Grainger sat, holding a half-whispering conversation with Emily.

"Milan! are you going to Milan?"

"Yes; only for a day. A friend has charged me with a commission that does not admit of delay, and I mean to run up this afternoon and be down by dinner-time to-morrow."

"I'll go and see if Florry wants anything from the city," said Miss Grainger, as she arose and left the room.

"Poor Florry! she is so distressed by that letter she received this morning. Joseph has taken it in such ill part that you should have been consulted by Aunt Grainger, and reproaches her for having permitted what she really never heard of. Not that, as she herself says, she admits of any right on his part to limit her source of advice. She thinks that it is somewhat despotic in him to say, 'You shall not take counsel except with leave from *me*.' She knows that this is the old vicar's doing, and that Joseph never would have assumed that tone without being put up to it."

"That is clear enough; but I am surprised that your sister saw it."

"Oh, she is not so deplorably in love as to be blinded."

CHAPTER XIII.

AGAIN TO MILAN.

"POOR Bob! You were standing on that balcony with a very jaunty air, smoking your cuba the last time I passed here," said Calvert, as he looked up at the windows of the Hôtel Royale at Milan, while he drove on to another and less distinguished hotel. He would have liked greatly to put up at the Royale, and had a chat with its gorgeous landlord over the Reppinghams, how long they stayed and whither they went, and how the young widow bore up under the blow, and what shape old Rep's grief assumed.

No squeamishness as to the terms that might have been used towards himself would have prevented his gratifying this wish. The obstacle was purely financial. He had told the host, on leaving, to pay a thousand francs for him that he had lost at play, and it was by no means convenient now to reimburse him. The bank had just closed as he arrived, so there was nothing for it but to await its opening the next morning. His steps were then turned to the Telegraph-office. The message to Loyd was in these words : "Your letter received. I am here, and leave to-morrow."

"Of course the fellow will understand that I have obeyed his high behest, and I shall be back at Orta in time to catch the post on its arrival, and see whether he has kept faith with me or not. If there be no newspapers there for the villa I may conclude it is all right." This brief matter of business over, he felt like one who had no further occasion for care. When he laid down his burden he could straighten his back, no sense of the late pressure remaining to remind him of the load that had pressed so heavily. He knew this quality in himself, and prized it highly. It formed part of what he used boastfully to call his " Philosophy," and he contrasted it proudly with the condition of those fellows, who instead of rebounding under pressure, collapsed, and sunk never to rise more. The vanity with which he regarded himself supplied him with a vindictive dislike to the world, who could suffer a fellow endowed and gifted as he was to be always in straits and difficulties. He mistook—a very common mistake by-the-way—a capacity to enjoy, for a nature deservant of enjoyment, and he thought it the greatest injustice to see scores of well-off people who possessed neither his own good constitution nor his capacity to endure dissipation uninjured. " Wretches not fit to live," as he said, and assuredly most unfit to live the life which he alone prized or cared for. He dined somewhat sumptuously at one of the great restaurants. " He owed it to himself," he said, after all that dreary cookery of the villa, to refresh his memory of the pleasures of the table, and he ordered a flask of Marco-brunner that cost a Napoleon.

He was the caressed of the waiters, and escorted to the door by the host. There is no supremacy so soon recognised as that of wealth, and Calvert, for a few hours, gave himself up to the illusion that he was rich. As the opera was closed, he went to one of the smaller theatres, and sat out for a while one of those dreariest of all dreary things, a comedy by the "immortal Goldoni!"

Immortal indeed, so long as sleep remains an endowment of humanity! He tried to interest himself in a plot wherein the indecency was only veiled by the dulness, and where the language of the drawing-room never rose above the tone of the servants'-hall, and left the place in disgust, to seek anywhere, or anyhow, something more amusing than this.

Without well knowing how, he found himself at the door of the Gettone, the hell he had visited when he was last at Milan.

"They shall sup me, at all events," said he, as he deposited his hat and cane in the ante-chamber. The rooms were crowded and it was some time before Calvert could approach the play-table, and gain a view of the company. He recognised many of the former visitors. There sat the pretty woman with the blonde ringlets, her diamond-studded fingers carelessly playing with the gold pieces before her; there was the pale student-like boy — he seemed a mere boy—with his dress-cravat disordered, and his hair dishevelled, just as he had seen him last; and there was the old man, whose rouleau had cost Calvert all his winnings. He looked fatigued and exhausted, and seemed as if dropping asleep over his game, and yet the noise was deafening—the clamour of the players, the cries of the croupier, the clink of glasses, and the clink of gold !

"Now to test the adage that says when a man is pelted by all other ill luck, that he'll win at play," said Calvert, as he threw, without counting them, several Napoleons on the table. His venture was successful, and so was another and another after it.

"This is yours, Sir," said she of the blonde ringlets, handing him a hundred franc-piece that had rolled amongst her own.

"Was it not to suggest a partnership that it went there?" said he, smiling courteously.

"Who knows?" said she, half carelessly, half invitingly.

"Let us see what our united fortunes will do. This old man is dozing and does not care for the game. Would you favour me with your place, Sir, and take your rest with so much more comfort, on one of those luxurious sofas yonder?"

"No!" said the old man, sternly. "I have as much right to be here as you."

"The legal right I am not going to dispute. It is simply a matter of expediency."

"Do you mean to stake all that gold, Sir?" interrupted the croupier, addressing Calvert, who, during this brief discussion, had suffered his money to remain till it had been doubled twice over.

"Ay, let it stay there," said he, carelessly.

"What have you done that makes you so lucky?" whispered the blonde ringlets. "See, you have broken the bank!"

"What have I done, do you mean in the way of wickedness?" said he, laughing as the croupiers gathered in a knot to count over the sum to be paid to him. "Nearly everything. I give you leave to question me— so far as your knowledge of the Decalogue goes—what have I not done?" And so they sauntered down the room side by side and sat down on a sofa, chatting and laughing pleasantly together, till the croupier came loaded with gold and notes to pay all Calvert's winnings.

"What was it the old fellow muttered as he passed?" said Calvert; "he spoke in German, and I didn't understand him."

"It was something about a line in your forehead that will bring you bad luck yet."

"I have heard that before," cried he, springing hastily up. "I wish I could get him to tell me more;" and he hastened down the stairs after the old man, but when he gained the street he missed him; he hurried in vain on this side and that; no trace of him remained. "If I were given to the credulous, I'd say that was the fiend in person," muttered Calvert, as he slowly turned towards his inn.

He tried in many ways to forget the speech that troubled him; he counted over his winnings; they were nigh fourteen thousand francs; he speculated on all he might do with them; he plotted and planned a dozen roads to take, but do what he might, the old man's sinister look and dark words were before him, and he could only lie awake thinking over them till day broke.

Determined to return to Orta in time to meet the post, he drove to the bank, just as it was open for business, and presented his bill for payment.

"You have to sign your name here," said a voice he thought he remembered, and, looking up, saw the old man of the play-table.

"Did we not meet last night?" whispered Calvert, in a low voice.

The other shook his head in dissent.

"Yes, I cannot be mistaken; you muttered a prediction in German as you passed me, and I know what it meant."

Another shake of the head was all his reply.

"Come, come, be frank with me; your secret, if it be one to visit that place, is safe with me. What leads you to believe I am destined to evil fortune?"

"I know nothing of you! I want to know nothing," said the old man, rudely, and turned to his books.

"Well, if your skill in prophecy be not greater than in

politeness, I need not fret about you," said Calvert laughing ; and he went his way.

With that superstitious terror that tyrannises over the minds of incredulous men weighing heavily on his heart, he drove back to Orta. All his winnings of the night before could not erase from his memory the dark words of the old man's prediction. He tried to forget, and then he tried to ridicule it. "So easy," thought he, "for that old withered mummy to cast a shadow on the path of a fellow full of life, vigour, and energy, like myself. He has but to stand one second in my sunshine ! It is, besides, the compensation that age and decrepitude exact for being no longer available for the triumphs and pleasures of life." Such were the sort of reasonings by which he sought to console himself, and then he set to plan out a future—all the things that he could, or might, or could not do.

Just as he drove into Orta the post arrived at the office, and he got out and entered, as was his wont, to obtain his letters before the public distribution had commenced.

CHAPTER XIV.

THE LAST WALK IN THE GARDEN.

THE only letter Calvert found at the post-office for the villa was one in the vicar's hand, addressed to Miss Grainger. Nothing from Loyd himself, nor any newspaper. So far, then, Loyd had kept his pledge. He awaited to see if Calvert would obey his injunctions before he proceeded to unmask him to his friends.

Calvert did not regard this reserve as anything generous—he set it down simply to fear. He said to himself, "The fellow dreads me; he knows that it is never safe to push men of my stamp to the wall; and he is wise enough to apply the old adage, about leaving a bridge to the retreating enemy. I shall have more difficulty in silencing the women, however. It will be a hard task to muzzle their curiosity; but I must try some plan to effect it. Is that telegram for me?" cried he, as a messenger hastened hither and thither in search for some one.

"Il Signor Grainger?"

"Yes, all right," said he, taking it. It was in these few words.

"They find it can be done—make tracks.

"DRAYTON."

"They find it can be done," muttered he. "Which means it is legal to apprehend me. Well, I supposed as much. I never reckoned on immunity; and as to getting away, I'm readier for it, and better provided too, than you think for, Master Algernon. Indeed, I can't well say what infatuation binds me to this spot, apart from the peril that attends it. I don't know that I am very much what is called in love with Florence, though I'd certainly marry her if she'd have me; but for that there are, what the lady novelists call, 'mixed motives,' and I rather suspect it is not with any especial or exclusive regard for her happiness that I'd enter into the holy bonds. I should like to consult some competent authority on the physiology of hatred—why it is that, though scores of fellows have injured me deeply in life, I never bore any, no, nor the whole of them collectively, the ill will that I feel for that man. He has taken towards me a tone that none have ever dared to take. He menaces me! Fifty have wronged, none have ever threatened me. He who threatens, assumes to be your master, to dictate the terms of his forbearance, and to declare under what conditions he will spare you. Now, Master Loyd, I can't say if this be a part to suit *your* powers, but I know well, the other is one which in no way is adapted to *mine*. Nature has endowed me with a variety of excellent qualities, but, somehow, in the hurry of her benevolence, she forgot patience! I suppose one can't have everything!"

While he thus mused and speculated, the boat swept smoothly over the lake, and Onofrio, not remarking the little attention Calvert vouchsafed to him, went on talking of "I Grangeri" as the most interesting subject he could think of. At last Calvert's notice was drawn to his words by hearing how the old lady had agreed to take the villa for a year, with the power of continuing to reside there longer if she were so minded.

The compact had been made only the day before, after Calvert had started for Milan, evidently—to his thinking—showing that it had been done with reference to something in Loyd's last letter. "Strange that she did not consult me upon it," thought he; "I who have been ᴛer chief counsellor on everything. Perhaps the lease of my confidence has expired. But how does it matter? A few hours more, and all these people shall be no more to me than the lazy cloud that is hanging about the mountain-top. They may live or die, or marry or mourn, and all be as nothing to me—as if I had never met them. And what shall *I* be to *them*, I wonder?" cried he, with a bitter laugh; "a very dreadful dream, I suppose; something like the memory of a shipwreck, or a fire from which they escaped without any consciousness of the means that rescued them! A horrid nightmare whose terrors always come back in days of depression and illness. At all events, I shall not be 'poor Calvert,' 'that much to be pitied creature, who really had some good in him.' No, I shall certainly be spared all commiseration of that kind, and they'll no more recur willingly to my memory than they'll celebrate the anniversary of some day that brought them shame and misfortune.

"Now then, for my positively last appearance in my present line of character! And yonder I see the old dame on the look-out for me; she certainly has some object in meeting me before her nieces shall know it.— Land me in that nook there, Onofrio, and wait for me."

"I have been very impatient for your coming," said she, as he stepped on shore; "I have so much to say to you; but, first of all, read this. It is from the vicar."

The letter was not more than a few lines, and to this

purport: he was about to quit the home he had lived in for more than thirty years, and was so overwhelmed with sorrow and distress, that he really could not address his thoughts to any case but the sad one before him. "'All these calamities have fallen upon us together; for although,' he wrote, 'Joe's departure is the first step on the road to future fortune, it is still separation, and at our age who is to say if we shall ever see him again?'"

"Skip the pathetic bit, and come to this. What have we here about the P. and O. steamers?" cried Calvert.

"'Through the great kindness of the Secretary of State, Joe has obtained a free passage out —a favour as I hear very rarely granted—and he means to pay you a flying visit; leaving this on Tuesday, to be with you on Saturday, and, by repairing to Leghorn on the following Wednesday, to catch the packet at Malta. This will give him three entire days with you, which, though they be stolen from us, neither his mother nor myself have the heart to refuse him. Poor fellow, he tries to believe—perhaps he does believe—that we are all to meet again in happiness and comfort, and I do my best not to discourage him; but I am now verging on seventy——'"

"How tiresome he is about his old age; is there any more about his son?" asked Calvert impatiently.

"Yes, he says here: 'Joe is, as you may imagine, full of business, and what between his interviews with official people, and his personal cares for his long journey, has not a moment to spare. He will, however, write to-morrow, detailing all that he has done and means to do. Of that late suggestion that came from you about referring us to a third party, neither Joseph nor myself desire to go back; indeed, it is not at a moment like the present we would open a question that could imperil the affections that unite us. It is enough to know that we trust each other, and need neither guarantees nor guidance.' "

"The old knave!" cried Calvert. "A priest is always a Jesuit, no matter what church he belongs to."

"Oh, Mr. Calvert."

"But he's quite right after all. I am far too worldly-minded in my notions to negotiate with men of such exalted ideas as he and his son possess. Besides, I am suddenly called away. I shall have to leave this immediately. They are making a fuss about that unfortunate affair at Basle, and want to catch me as a witness; and as my evidence would damage a fellow I really pity, though I condemn, I must keep out of the way."

"Well, you are certain to find us here whenever you feel disposed to have your own room again. I have taken the villa for another year."

Not paying the slightest attention to this speech he went on: "There is one point on which I shall be absolute. No one speaks of me when I leave this. Not alone that you abstain yourself from any allusion to my having been here, and what you know of me, but that you will not suffer any other to make me his topic. It is enough to say that a question of my life is involved in this request. Barnard's fate has involved me in a web of calumny and libel, which I am resolved to bear too, to cover the poor fellow's memory. If, however, by any indiscretion of my friends—and remember, it can only be of my friends under this roof—I am driven to defend myself, there is no saying how much more blood will have to flow in this quarrel. Do you understand me?"

"Partly," said she, trembling all over.

"This much you cannot mistake," said he, sternly; "that my name is not to be uttered, nor written, mind that. If, in his short visit, Loyd should speak of me, stop him at once. Say, 'Mr. Loyd, there are reasons why I will not discuss that person; and I desire that my wish be understood as a command.' You will impress your nieces with the same reserve. I suppose, if they hear that it is a matter which involves the life of more than one, that they will not need to be twice cautioned. Bear in mind this is no caprice of mine; it is no caprice of that Calvert eccentricity, to which, fairly enough sometimes, you ascribe many of my actions. I am in a position of no common peril; I have incurred it to save the fair fame of a fellow I have known and liked for years. I mean, too, to go through with it; that is, I mean up to a certain point to sacrifice myself. Up to a certain point, I say, for if I am pushed beyond that, then I shall declare to the world: Upon you and your slanderous tongues be the blame, not mine the fault for what is to happen now."

He uttered these words with a rapidity and vehemence that made her tremble from head to foot. This was not, besides, the first time she had witnessed one of those passionate outbursts for which his race was celebrated, and it needed no oath to confirm the menace his speech shadowed forth.

"This is a pledge, then," said he, grasping her hand. "And now to talk of something pleasanter. That old uncle of mine has behaved very handsomely; has sent me some kind messages, and, what is as much to the purpose, some money;" and, as he spoke, he carelessly drew from his pocket a roll of the bank-notes he had so lately won at play. "'Before making any attempt to re-enter the service,' he says, 'you must keep out of the way for a while.' And he is right there; the advice is excellent, and I mean to follow it. In his postscript he adds: 'Thank Grainger'—he means Miss Grainger, but you know how blunderingly he writes—'for all her kindness to you, and say how glad we should all be to see her at Rocksley, whenever she comes next to England.'"

The old lady's face grew crimson; shame at first, and pride afterwards, overwhelming her. To be called Grainger was to bring her back at once to the old days of servitude—that dreary life of nursery governess—which had left its dark shadow on all her later years; while to be the guest at Rocksley was a triumph she had never imagined in her vainest moments.

"Oh, will you tell him how proud I am of his kind remembrance of me, and what an honour I should feel it to pay my respects to him?"

"They'll make much of you, I promise you," said Calvert, "when they catch you at Rocksley, and you'll not get away in a hurry. Now let us go our separate ways, lest the girls suspect we have been plotting. I'll take the boat and row down to the steps. Don't forget all I have been saying," were his last words as the boat moved away.

"I hope I have bound that old fool in heavy recognisances to keep her tongue quiet; and now for the more difficult task of the young ones," said he, as he stretched himself full length in the boat, like one wearied by some effort that taxed his strength. "I begin to believe it will be a relief to me to get away from this place!" he muttered to himself, "though I'd give my right hand to pass the next week here, and spoil the happiness of those fond lovers. Could I not do it?" Here was a problem that occupied him till he reached the landing at the villa, but as he stepped on shore, he cried, "No, this must be the last time I shall ever mount these steps!"

Calvert passed the day in his room; he had much to think over, and several letters to write. Though the next step he was to take in life in all probability involved his whole future career, his mind was diverted from it by the thought that this was to be his last night at the villa—the last time he should ever see Florence. "Ay," thought he, "Loyd will be the occupant of this room in a day or two more. I can fancy the playful tap at this door, as Milly goes down to breakfast—I can picture the lazy fool leaning out of that window, gazing at those small snow-peaks, while Florence is waiting for him in the garden—I know well all the little graceful attentions that will be prepared for him, vulgar dog as he is, who will not even recognise the special courtesies that have been designed for him; well, if I be not sorely mistaken, I have dropped some poison in his cup. I have taught Florence to feel that courage is the first of manly attributes, and what is more to the purpose, to have a sort of half dread that it is not amongst her lover's gifts. I have left her as my last legacy that rankling doubt, and I defy her to tear it out of her heart! What a sovereign antidote to all romance it is, to have the conviction, or, if not the conviction the impression, the mere suspicion, that he who spouts the fine sentiments of the poet with such heartfelt ardour, is a poltroon, ready to run from danger and hide himself at the approach of peril. I have made Milly believe this; she has no doubt of it; so that if sisterly confidences broach the theme, Florence will find all her worst fears confirmed. The thought of this fellow as my rival maddens me!" cried he, as he started up and paced the room impatiently. "Is not that Florence I see in the garden? Alone, too! What a chance!" In a moment he hastened noiselessly down the stairs, opened the drawing-room window and was beside her.

"I hope the bad news they tell me is not true," she said, as they walked along side by side.

"What is the bad news?"

"That you are going to leave us."

"And are you such a hypocrite, Florry, as to call this bad news, when you and I both know how little I shall be needed here in a day or two? We are not to have many more moments together; these are probably the very last of them; let us be frank and honest. I'm not surely asking too much in that! For many a day you have sealed up my lips by the threat of not speaking to me on the morrow. Your menace has been, if you repeat this language, I will not walk with you again. Now, Florry, this threat has lost its terror, for to-morrow I shall be gone, gone for ever, and so to-day, here now, I say once more I love you! How useless to tell me that it is all in vain; that you do not, cannot return my affection. I tell you that I can no more despair that I can cease to love you! In the force of that love I bear you is my confidence. I have the same trust in it that I would have in my courage."

"If you but knew the pain you gave me by such words as these——"

"If you knew the pain they cost me to utter them!" cried he. "It is bringing a proud heart very low to sue as humbly as I do. And for what? Simply for time— only time. All I ask is, do not utterly reject one who only needs your love to be worthy of it. When I think of what I was when I met you first—you!—and feel the change you have wrought in my whole nature; how you have planted truthfulness where there was once but doubt; how you have made hope succeed a dark and listless in-difference—when I know and feel that in my struggle to be better it is you, and you alone, are the prize before me, and that if that be withdrawn life has no longer a bribe to my ambition—when I think of these, Florry, can you wonder if I want to carry away with me some small spark that may keep the embers alive in my heart?"

"It is not generous to urge me thus," said she in a faint voice.

"The grasp of the drowning man has little time for generosity. You may not care to rescue me, but you may have pity for my fate."

"Oh, if you but knew how sorry I am——"

"Go on, dearest. Sorry for what?"

"I don't know what I was going to say; you have agitated and confused me so, that I feel bewildered. I shrink from saying what would pain you, and yet I want to be honest and straightforward."

"If you mean that to be like the warning of the surgeon —I must cut deep to cure you—I can't say I have courage for it."

For some minutes they walked on side by side without a word. At length he said in a grave and serious tone, "I have asked your aunt, and she has promised me that, except strictly amongst yourselves, my name is not to be mentioned when I leave this. She will, if you care for them, give you my reasons; and I only advert to it now amongst other last requests. This is a promise, is it not?"

She pressed his hand and nodded.

"Will you now grant me one favour? Wear this ring for my sake; a token of mere memory, no more! Nay, I mean to ask Milly to wear another. Don't refuse me." He drew her hand towards him as he spoke, and slipped a rich turquoise ring upon her finger. Although her hand trembled, and she averted her head, she had not courage to say him no.

"You have not told us where you are going to, nor when we are to hear from you!" said she, after a moment.

"I don't think I know either!" said he in his usual reckless way. "I have half a mind to join Schamyl—I know him—or take a turn with the Arabs against the French. I suppose," added he, with a bitter smile, "it is my fate always to be on the beaten side, and I'd not know how to comport myself as a winner."

"There's Milly making a signal to us. Is it dinner-time already?" said she.

"Ay, my last dinner here!" he muttered. She turned her head away and did not speak.

On that last evening at the villa nothing very eventful occurred. All that need be recorded will be found in the following letter, which Calvert wrote to his friend Drayton, after he had wished his hosts a good-night, and gained his room, retiring, as he did, early, to be up betimes in the morning and catch the first train for Milan.

"Dear Drayton,—I got your telegram, and though I suspect you are astray in your 'law,' and don't believe these fellows can touch me, I don't intend to open the question, or reserve the point for the twelve judges, but mean to evacuate Flanders at once; indeed, my chief difficulty was to decide which way to turn, for having the whole world before me where to choose, left me in that indecision which the poet pronounces national when he says,

> I am an Englishman, and naked I stand here,
> Musing in my mind what raiment I shall wear!

Chance, however, has done for me what my judgment could not. I have been up to Milan and had a look through the newspapers, and I see what I have often predicted has happened. The Rajahs of Bengal have got sick of their benefactors, and are bent on getting rid of what we love to call the blessings of the English rule in India. Next to a society for the suppression of creditors, I know of no movement which could more thoroughly secure my sympathy. The brown skin is right. What has he to do with those covenanted and uncovenanted Scotchmen who want to enrich themselves by bullying him? What need has he of governors-general, political residents, collectors and commanders-in-chief? Could he not raise his indigo, water his rice-fields, and burn his widow, without any help of ours? particularly as our help takes the shape of taxation and vexatious interference.

"I suppose all these are very unpatriotic sentiments; but in the same proportion that Britons never will be slaves, they certainly have no objection to make others such, and I shudder in the very marrow of my morality to think that but for the accident of an accident I might at this very moment have been employed to assist in repressing the noble aspirations of niggerhood, and helping to stifle the cry of freedom that now resounds from the Sutlej to the Ganges. Is not that a twang from your own lyre, Master D.? Could our Own Correspondent have come it stronger?

"Happily, her Majesty has no further occasion for my services, and I can take a brief on the other side. Expect to hear, therefore, in some mysterious paragraph, 'That the mode in which the cavalry were led, or the guns pointed, plainly indicated that a European soldier held command on this occasion; and, indeed, some assert that an English officer was seen directing the movements on our flank.' To which let me add the hope that the —— Fusiliers may be there to see; and if I do not give the major a lesson in battalion drill, call me a Dutchman! There is every reason why the revolt should succeed. I put aside all the bosh about an en-slaved race and a just cause, and come to the fact of the numerical odds opposed. The climate intolerable to one, and easily borne by the other; the distance from which reinforcements must come; and, last of all, the certainty that if the struggle only last long enough to figure in two budgets, John Bull will vote it a bore, and refuse to pay for it. But here am I getting political when I only meant to be personal; and now to come back, I own that my resolve to go out to India has been aided by hearing that Loyd, of whom I spoke in my last, is to leave by the next mail, and will take passage on board the P. and O. steamer Leander, due at Malta on the 22nd. My in-tention is to be his fellow-traveller, and with this resolve I shall take the Austrian steamer to Corfu, and come up with my friend at Alexandria. You will perhaps be puzzled to know why the claims of friendship are so strong upon me at such a moment, and I satisfy your most natural curiosity by stating that this is a mission of torture. I travel with this man to insult and to outrage him; to expose him in public places, and to confront him at all times. I mean that this overland journey should be to him for his life long the reminiscence of a pilgrimage of such martyrdom as few have passed through, and I have the vanity to believe that not many men have higher or more varied gifts for such a mission than myself. My first task on reaching Calcutta shall be to report progress to you.

"I don't mind exposing a weakness to an old friend, and so I own to you I fell in love here. The girl had the obduracy and wrong headedness not to yield to my suit, and so I had no choice left to me but to persist in it. I know, however, that if I could only remain here a fortnight longer I should secure the inestimable triumph of rendering both of us miserable for life ! Yes, Drayton, that pale girl and her paltry fifteen thousand pounds might have spoiled one of the grandest careers that ever adorned history ! and lost the world the marvellous origin, rise, progress, and completion of the dynasty of the great English Begum Calvert in Bengal. Count upon me for high office whenever penny-a-lining fails you, and, if my realm be taxable, you shall be my Chancellor of the Exchequer !

"You are right about that business at Basle ; to keep up a controversy would be to invest it with more interest for public gossip. Drop it, therefore, and the world will drop it ; and take my word for it, I'll give them something more to say of me, one of these days, than that my hair trigger was too sensitive ! I'm writing this in the most romantic of spots. The moonlight is sleeping— isn't that the conventional ?—over the olive plain, and the small silvery leaves are glittering in its pale light. Up the great Alps, amongst the deep crevasses, a fitful flashing of lightning promises heat for the morrow ; a nightingale sings close to my window ; and through the muslin curtain of another casement I can see a figure pass and repass, and even distinguish that her long hair has fallen down, and floats loosely over neck and shoulders. How pleasantly I might linger on here, 'My duns forgetting, by my duns forgot.' How smoothly I might float down the stream of life, without even having to pull an oar ! How delightfully domestic and innocent and inglorious the whole thing ! Isn't it tempting, you dog? Does it not touch even *your* temperament through its thick hide of worldliness? And I believe in my heart it is all feasible, all to be done.

"I have just tossed up for it. Head for India, and head it is ! So that Loyd is booked for a pleasant journey, and I start to-morrow, to ensure him all the happiness in my power to confer. For the present, it would be as well to tell all anxious and inquiring friends, into which category come tailors, bootmakers, jewellers, &c., that it will be a postal economy not to address Mr. Harry Calvert in any European capital, and to let the 'bills lie on the table,' and be read this day six years, but add that if properly treated by fortune, I mean to acquit my debts to them one of these days.

"'That I 'wish they may get it' is, therefore, no scornful or derisive hope of your friend,

"H. CALVERT.

"If—not a likely matter—anything occurs worth mention, you shall have a line from me from Venice."

When he had concluded his letter, he extinguished his candles, and sat down at the open window. The moon had gone down, and, though star-lit, the night was dark. The window in the other wing of the villa, at which he had seen the figure through the curtain, was now thrown open, and he could see that Florence, with a shawl wrapped round her, was leaning out, and talking to some one in the garden underneath.

"It is the first time," said a voice he knew to be Emily's, "that I ever made a bouquet in the dark."

"Come up, Milly dearest; the dew is falling heavily. I feel it even here."

"I'll just fasten this rose I have here in his hat; he saw it in my hair to-night, and he'll remember it."

She left the garden, the window was closed. The light was put out, and all was silent.

CHAPTER XV.

SISTERS' CONFIDENCES.

THE day of Calvert's departure was a very sad one at the villa; so was the next and the next! It is impossible to repeat the routine of a quiet life when we have lost one whose pleasant companionship imparted to the hours a something of his own identity, without feeling the dreary blank his absence leaves, and, together with this, comes the not very flattering conviction of how little of our enjoyment we owed to our own efforts, and how much to his.

"I never thought we should have missed him so much," said Emily, as she sat with her sister beside the lake, where the oars lay along the boats unused, and the fishing-net hung to dry from the branches of the mulberry-tree.

"Of course we miss him," said Florence, peevishly. "You don't live in daily, hourly intercourse with a person without feeling his absence; but I almost think it is a relief," said she, slightly flushing.

"A relief, Florry! And in what way?"

"I don't know; that is, I'm not disposed to go into a nice analysis of Mr. Calvert's mind, and the effect produced upon my own, by the mere iteration of things I never agreed with. Besides, I don't want in the least to limit your regrets for him. He was one of your favourites."

"I always thought him more a favourite of yours than mine, Florry."

"Then I suspect you made a great mistake; but, really, I think we might talk of something else. Wha. about those hyacinths; didn't you tell me they ought to be moved?"

"Yes, Harry said they had too much sun there, and were losing colour in consequence."

"I can't imagine him a great authority in gardening."

"Well, but he really knew a great deal about it, and had an exquisite taste in the landscape part of it; witness that little plat under your window."

"The fuchsias are pretty," said she, with a saucy air. "Isn't the post late to-day?"

"It came two hours ago. Don't you remember my saying there were no letters, except two for Harry?"

"And where are you to forward them to him? Has he been confidential enough to tell you?"

"No; he said, if anything comes for me, keep it till you hear of me."

"He affected mystery. I think he imagined it gave something of romance to him, though a more prosaic, worldly character, never existed."

"I don't agree with you, Florry. I think it was the worldliness was the affectation."

Florence coloured deeply, but made no reply.

"And I'll tell you why I am convinced of it. In the mention of anything heroic or daring, or in allusion to any trait of deep devotion or pathetic tenderness, his lip would tremble and his voice falter, and then catching himself, and evidently ashamed of his weakness, he would come out with some silly, or even heartless remark, as though to mask his confusion and give him time to recover himself."

"I never noticed this," said Florence, coldly. "Indeed, I must confess to a much less critical study of his character than you have bestowed on him."

"You are unjust yourself. It was you first pointed out this trait in him to me."

"I forget it, then, that's all," said she, captiously.

"Oh, I knew he was ashamed of being thought romantic."

"I thought I had asked you to talk of something or somebody else, Milly. Let us, at least, select a topic we can think and speak on with some approach to agreement."

Accustomed to bear with Florence's impatience and her capricious humours as those of an invalid, Emily made no answer, but drew out her work from a basket and prepared to begin.

"You needn't hope to make much progress with your embroidery, Milly. You'll have no one to read out the Faust or the Winter Night's Tale to-day."

"Ah, that's true, and Joseph won't be here till Saturday," said she sighing, "not to say that I don't suspect he'll have much time to bestow on reading aloud."

"I thought you were going to say that he reads badly," said Florry, with a forced laugh.

"Oh no, Florry, I like his reading very much indeed; particularly of Tennyson and Browning."

"It is not so melodramatic as your friend Mr. Calvert's; but, in my poor estimation, it is in much truer taste."

"What a strange girl you are! Do you forget the evening you said, 'I'll not let Joseph read aloud any more; I detest to see him in any rivalry of which he has the worst?'"

"I must have said it in mockery, then, Milly, for I

know of nothing in which Mr. Calvert could claim superiority over him. I am aware this is not your opinion, Milly; indeed, poor Joseph has not many allies in this house, for even Aunt Grainger was one of the fascinated by our captivating guest."

"Well, but you know, dearest Florry, what a magic there is in the name Calvert to my aunt."

"Yes, I know and deplore it. I believe, too, from chance expressions she has let drop, that her relations with those very people suggest anything rather than proud or pleasant memories; but she is determined to think of them as friends, and is quite vain at having the permission to do so."

"Even Harry used to smile at her reverence for 'dear old Rocksley.'"

"The worse taste in him," said Florence haughtily.

"How bitter you are to the poor fellow," said the other, plaintively.

"I am not bitter to him. I think him a very accomplished, clever, amusing person, good-looking, manly, and so forth; and probably, if he hadn't persecuted me with attentions that I did not like or encourage, I might have felt very cordially towards him."

"Could he help being in love with you, Florry?"

"In love!" repeated she, in a voice of mockery and scorn.

"Ay, Florry, I never saw a man more thoroughly, devotedly in love. I could tell, as I entered the breakfast room, whether you had spoken to him in coldness or the reverse. His voice, as he read aloud, would betray whether you were listening with pleasure or indifference. You had not a mood of gay or grave that was not reflected in his face; and one day I remember, when I remarked on the capricious changes of his spirits, he said, 'Don't blame me; I am what she makes me: the happiest or the most miserable fellow breathing.' 'Well,' replied I, 'I fancied from your good spirits it was some pleasant tidings the post had brought you.' 'No,' said he, 'it was this;' and he drew a violet from his pocket, and showed it to me. I suppose you had given it to him."

"I dropped it, and he wouldn't give it back. I remember the day." And, as she spoke, she turned her head aside, but her sister saw that her cheek was crimson. Then suddenly she said, "How was it that you had such confidences together? I'm sure that, knowing my engagement, you must have seen how improper it was to listen to such nonsense on his part."

"I couldn't help it, Florry; the poor fellow would come to me with his heart almost breaking. I declare, there were times when his despair actually terrified me; and having heard from Aunt Grainger what dreadful passions these Calverts give way to—how reckless of consequences——"

"There, there, dear, spare me that physiology of the race of Calverts, of which I have gone through, I hope, every imaginable feature. To poor Aunt Grainger's eyes the dragon of the Drachenfels is a mild domestic creature in comparison with one of them." There was a jarring vibration in her sister's tone, that told it were safer not to prolong the discussion, and little more was said as they walked towards the house. At last Florence stopped short, and, pointing to the window of the room lately occupied by Calvert, said, "Joseph will dislike all those climbing creepers there, Milly; he hates that sort of thing. Let them be cut away."

"If you wish it, dearest; but is it not a pity? Only

think of all the time and pains it cost to train that jessamine——"

"Oh, if they have such tender memories for you, let them remain by all means; but I think it will be quite as well not to tell Joseph the reasons for which they were spared."

Though the speech was uttered in irritation, Emily affected to hear it without emotion, and said, "It was Harry's own desire that we should not speak of him to Joseph, and I mean to obey it."

CHAPTER XVI.

A LOVERS' QUARREL.

IN course of time Loyd arrived at the villa. He came tired and worn out by a fatiguing journey. There had been floods, broken bridges, and bad roads in Savoy, and the St. Gothard was almost impassable from a heavy snow-storm. The difficulties of the road had lost him a day, one of the very few he was to have with them, and he came, wearied and somewhat irritated, to his journey's end.

Lovers ought, perhaps, to be more thoughtful about "effect" than they are in real life. They might take a lesson in this respect with good profit from the drama, where they enter with all the aids that situation and costume can give them. At all events, Calvert would scarcely have presented himself in the jaded and disordered condition in which Loyd now appeared.

"How ill he looks, poor fellow," said Emily, as the two sisters left him to dress for dinner.

"I should think he may look ill. Fancy his travelling on, night and day, through rain and sleet and snow, and always feeling that his few hours here were to be shortened by all these disasters. And, besides all this, he is sorry now for the step he has taken; he begins to suspect he ought not to have left England; that this separation— it must be for at least two years—bodes ill to us. That it need not have been longer had he stayed at the home bar, and had, besides, the opportunity of coming out to see us in Vacation. That it was his friends who over-persuaded him ; and now that he has had a little time for calm reflection, away from them, he really sees no obstacles to his success at Westminster that he will not have to encounter at Calcutta."

"And will he persist, in face of this conviction ?"

"Of course he will ! He cannot exhibit himself to the world as a creature who does not know his own mind for two days together."

"Is that of more consequence than what would really serve his interests, Florry ?"

"I am no casuist, Milly, but I think that the impression a man makes by his character for resolution is always of consequence."

Emily very soon saw that her sister spoke with an unusual degree of irritation. The arrival of her lover had not overjoyed her; it had scarcely cheered her. He came, too, not full of high hopes and animated by the prospect of a bright future, speculating on the happy days that were before them, and even fixing the time they were to meet again, but depressed and dispirited, darkly hinting at all the dangers of absence, and gloomily telling over the long miles of ocean that were so soon to roll between them.

Now Florence was scarcely prepared for all this. She had expected to be comforted, and supported, and encouraged ; and yet from herself, now, all the encouragement and all the support was to be derived ! *She* was to infuse hope, to supply courage, and inspire determination. He was only there to be sustained and supported. It is true she knew nothing of the trials and difficulties which were before him, and she could neither discuss nor lighten them ; but she could talk of India as a mere neighbouring country, the "overland" a rather pleasant tour, and two years—what signified two years, when it was to be their first and last separation? For, if he could not obtain the leave he was all but promised, it was arranged that she should go out to Calcutta, and their marriage take place there.

He rallied at last under all these cheering suggestions, and gradually dropped into that talk so fascinating to Promessi Sposi in which affection and worldliness are blended together, and where the feelings of the heart and the furniture of the drawing-room divide the interest between them. There was a dash of romance, too, in the notion of life in the far East—some far-away home in the Neilgherries, some lone bungalow on the Sutlej— that helped them to paint their distant landscape with more effect, and they sat, in imagination, under a spreading plantain on the Himalaya, and watched the blood-red sunsets over the plains of Hindostan.

Time passed very rapidly in this fashion. Love is the very sublime of egotism, and people never weary of themselves. The last evening — sad things these last evenings—came, and they strolled out to take a last look on the lake and the snow-white Alps beyond it. The painful feeling of having so short a time to say so much was over each of them, and made them more silent than usual. As they thus loitered along, they reached a spot where a large evergreen oak stood alone, spreading its gigantic arms over the water, and from which the view of the lake extended for miles in each direction.

"This is the spot to have a summer-house, Florry," said Loyd; "and when I come back I'll build one here."

"You see there is a rustic bench here already. Harry made it."

Scarcely were the words uttered than she felt her cheek burning, and the tingling rush of her blood to her temples.

"Harry means Mr. Calvert, I conclude?" said he, coldly.

"Yes," said she, faintly.

"It was a name I have never uttered since I passed this threshold, Florry, and I vowed to myself that I would not be the first to allude to it. My pledge, however, went no further, and I am now released from its obligation. Let us talk of him freely."

"No, Joseph, I had rather not. When he was leaving this, it was his last wish that his name was not to be uttered here. We gave him our solemn promise, and I feel sure you will not ask me to forget it."

"I have no means of knowing by what right he could pretend to exact such a promise, which, to say the least, is a very unusual one."

"There was no question of a right in the matter. Mr. Calvert was here as our friend, associating with us in close intimacy, enjoying our friendship and our confidence, and if he had reasons of his own for the request, they were enough for us."

"That does not satisfy me, Florence," said he, gravely.

"I am sorry for it. I have no other explanation to give you."

"Well; I mean to be more explicit. Has he told you of a correspondence that passed between us?"

"Once for all, Joseph, I will not be drawn into this discussion. Rightfully, or the reverse, I have given my word, and I will keep it."

"Do you mean to say that to any mention of this man's name, or to any incident in which it will occur, you will turn a deaf ear, and not reply?"

"I will not speak of him."

"Be it so. But you will listen to me when *I* speak of him, and you will give my words the same credence you accord to them on other things. This is surely not asking too much ?"

"It is more, however, than I am willing to grant."

" This becomes serious, Florence, and cannot be dismissed lightly. Our relations towards each other are all but the closest that can bind two destinies. They are such as reject all secrecy—all mystery at all events. Now, if Mr. Calvert's request were the merest caprice, the veriest whim, it matters not. The moment it becomes a matter of peace of mind to me it is no longer a trifle."

" You are making a very serious matter of very little," said she, partly offended.

" The unlimited confidence I have placed, and desire still to place, in you, is not a little matter. I insist upon having a full explanation."

" You insist ?"

" Yes, I insist. Remember, Florence, that what I claim is not more my due for my sake than for your own. No name in the world should stand between yours and mine, least of all that of one whom neither of us can look on with respect or esteem."

" If this be the remains of some old jealousy——"

" Jealousy ! Jealousy ! Why, what do you mean ?"

" Simply that there was a time when *he* thought *you* his rival, and it was just possible you might have reciprocated the sentiment."

" This is intolerable," cried he. Then hastily checking his angry outburst, he added : " Why should we grow warm, Florence dearest, over a matter which can have but one aspect for us both ? It is of you, not of myself,

I have been thinking all this time.   I simply begged you to let me know what sort of relations existed between you and Mr. Calvert that should prevent you speaking of him to me."

"You said something about insisting.   Now, insisting is an ugly word.   There is an air of menace about it."

"I am not disposed to recal it," said he, sternly.

"So much the better; at least it will save us a world of very unpleasant recrimination, for I refuse to comply."

"You refuse!   Now let me understand you, for this is too vital a point for me at least to make any mistake about—what is it that you refuse?"

"Don't you think the tone of our present discussion is the best possible reason for not prolonging it?"

"No!   If we have each of us lost temper, I think the wisest course would be to recover ourselves, **and** see if we cannot talk the matter over in a better spirit."

"Begin then by unsaying that odious word."

"What is the word?"

"Insist!   You must not insist upon anything."

"I'll take back the word if you so earnestly desire it, Florence," said he gravely; "but I hope request will be read in its place."

"Now, then, what is it you request? for I frankly declare that all this time I don't rightly understand what you ask of me."

"This is worse than I suspected," said he angrily, "for now I see that it is in the mere spirit of defiance that you rejected my demand."

"Upon my word, Sir, I believe it will turn **out that** neither of us knew very much of the other."

"You think so?"

Yes; don't **you?**"

He grew very pale, and made no answer, though he twice seemed as if about to speak.

"I declare," cried she, and her heightened colour and flashing eye showed the temper that stirred her—"I declare I think we shall have employed all our lately displayed candour to very little advantage if it does not carry us a little further."

"I scarcely catch your meaning," said he, in a low voice.

"What I meant was, that by a little further effort of our frankness we might come to convey to each other that scenes like these are not pleasant, nor need they ever occur again."

"I believe at last I apprehend you," said he, in a broken accent. "You desire that our engagement should be broken off."

She made no answer, but averted her head.

"I will do my best to be calm, Florence," continued he, "and I will ask as much of you. Let neither of us sacrifice the prospect of a whole life's happiness for the sake of a petty victory in a very petty dispute. If, however, you are of opinion——" he stopped, he was about to say more than he had intended, more than he knew how to say, and he stopped, confused and embarrassed.

"Why don't you continue?" said she, with a cold smile.

"Because I don't know what I was about to say."

"Then shall I say it for you?"

"Yes, do so."

"It was this, then, or at least to this purport: If you, Miss Florence Walter, are of opinion that two people who have not succeeded in inspiring each other with that degree of confidence that rejects all distrust, are scarcely wise in entering into a contract of which truthfulness is the very soul and essence, and that, though not very gallant on *my* part, as the man to suggest it, yet in all candour, which here must take the place of courtesy, the sooner the persons so placed escape from such a false position the better."

"And part?" said he, in a hollow feeble voice.

She shrugged her shoulders slightly, as though to say that, or any similar word, will convey my meaning.

"Oh, Florence, is it come to this? Is this to be a last evening in its saddest, bitterest sense?"

"When gentlemen declare that they 'insist,' I take it they mean to have their way," said she, with a careless toss of her head.

"Good Heavens!" cried he in a passion, "have you never cared for me at all? or is your love so little rooted that you can tear it from your heart without a pang?"

"All this going back on the past is very unprofitable," said she coldly.

He was stung by the contemptuous tone even more than by the words she used. It seemed as though she held his love so lightly she would not condescend to the slightest trouble to retain it, and this too at a moment of parting.

"Florence!" said he, in a tone of deep melancholy, "if I am to call you by that name for the last time—tell me, frankly, is this a sudden caprice of yours, or has it lain rankling in your mind, as a thing you would conquer if you could, or submit to, if you must?"

"I suspect it is neither one nor the other," said she with a levity that almost seemed gaiety. "I don't think I am capricious, and I know I never harbour a long-standing grievance. I really believe that it is to your own heart you must look for the reasons of what has occurred between us. I have often heard that men are so ashamed of being jealous, that they'll never forgive anyone who sees them in the fit."

"Enough, more than enough," said he, trembling from head to foot. "Let us part."

"Remember, the proposal comes from you."

"Yes, yes, it comes from me. It matters little whence it comes."

"Oh, I beg your pardon, it matters a great deal, at least to me. I am not to bear the reproaches of my aunt and my sister for a supposed cruelty towards a man who has himself repudiated our engagement. It would be rather hard that I was to be deserted and condemned too."

"Deserted, Florry!" cried he, as the tears stood in his eyes.

"Well, I don't mean deserted. There is no desertion on either side. It is a perfectly amicable arrangement of two people who are not disposed to travel the same road. I don't want to imply that any more blame attaches to *you* than to *me*."

"How can any attach to me at all?" cried he.

"Oh, then, if you wish it, I take the whole of it."

"Shall I speak to your aunt, Miss Walter, or will you?"

"It does not signify much which of us is the first to acquaint her. Perhaps, however, it would come with more propriety from you. I think I see her yonder near the cypress-trees, and I'm sure you'll be glad to have it over. Wait one moment, this ring——" as she endeavoured to draw a small ruby ring from her finger, Loyd saw the turquoise which she wore on the other hand—— "this ring," said she, in some confusion, "is yours."

"Not this one," said he, sternly, as he pointed to the other.

"No, the ruby," said she, with an easy smile. "It was getting to hurt my finger."

"I hope you may wear the other more easily," said he with a bitter laugh.

"Thank you," said she, with a curtesy, and then turned away, and walked towards the house.

After Loyd had proceeded a few steps to overtake Miss Grainger, he stopped and hastened back to the villa. Such an explanation as he must make could, he felt, be only done by a letter. He could not, besides, face the questioning and cross-questioning the old lady would submit him to, nor endure the misery of recalling, at her bidding, each stage of their sad quarrel. A letter, therefore, he would write, and then leave the villa for ever, and without a farewell to any. He knew this was not a gracious way to treat those who had been uniformly affectionate and kind—who had been to him like dear sisters—but he dreaded a possible meeting. He could not answer for himself, either, as to what charges he might be led to make against Florence, or what weakness of character he might exhibit in the midst of his affliction. "I will simply narrate so much as will show that we have agreed to separate, and are never to meet more," muttered he. "Florence may tell as much more as she likes, and give what version of me she pleases. It matters little now how or what they think of one whose heart is already in the grave." And thus saying, he gained his room, and, locking the door, began to write. Deeply occupied in his task, which he found so difficult that several half-scrawled sheets already littered the table before him, he never felt the time as it passed. It was already midnight before he was aware of it, and still his letter was not finished. It was so hard to say enough and not too much; so hard to justify himself in any degree and yet spare *her*, against whom he would not use one word of reproach; so hard to confess the misery that he felt, and yet not seem abject in the very avowal.

Not one of his attempts had satisfied him. Some were too lengthy, some too curt and brief, some read cold, stern, and forbidding; others seemed like half entreaties for a more merciful judgment; in fact he was but writing down each passing emotion of his mind, and recording the varying passions that swayed him.

As he sat thus, puzzled and embarrassed, he sprung up from his chair with terror at a cry that seemed to fill the room, and make the very air vibrate around him. It was a shriek as of one in the maddest agony, and lasted for some seconds. He thought it came from the lake, and he flung open his window and listened, but all was calm and still, the very faintest night air was astir, and not even the leaves moved. He then opened his door, and crept stealthily out upon the corridor : but all was quiet within the house. Noiselessly he walked to the head of the stairs, and listened; but not a sound nor a stir was to be heard. He went back to his room, agitated and excited. He had read of those conditions of cerebral excitement when the nerves of sense present impressions which have no existence in fact, and the sufferers fancy that they have seen sights, or heard sounds, which had no reality.

He thought he could measure the agitation that distressed him by this disturbance of the brain, and he bathed his temples with cold water, and sat down at the open window to try to regain calm and self-possession. For a while the speculation on this strange problem occupied him, and he wandered on in thought to ask himself which of the events of life should be assumed as real, and which mere self delusions. "If, for instance," thought he, "I could believe that this dreadful scene with Florence never occurred, that it was a mere vision conjured up by my own gloomy forebodings, and my sorrow at our approaching separation—what ecstasy would be mine. What is there," asked he of himself aloud, "to show or prove that we have parted? What evidence have I of one word that may or may not have passed between us, that would not apply to that wild scream that so lately chilled my very blood, and which I now know was a mere trick of imagination?" As he spoke, he turned to the table, and there lay the proof that he challenged before him. There, beside his half-written letter, stood the ring he had given her, and which she had just given back to him. The revulsion was very painful, and the tears, which had not come before, now rolled heavily down his cheeks. He took up the ring and raised it to his lips, but laid it down without kissing it. These sent-back gifts are very sad things; they do not bury the memory of the loved one who wore them. Like the flower that fell from her hair, they bear other memories. They tell of blighted hopes, of broken vows, of a whole life's plan torn, scattered, and given to the winds. Their odour is not of love; they smell of the rank grave, whither our hearts are hastening. He sat gazing moodily at this ring—it was the story of his life. He remembered the hour and the place he gave it to her; the words he spoke, her blush, her trembling hand as he drew it on her finger, the pledge he uttered, and which he made her repeat to him again. He started. What was that noise? Was that his name he heard uttered? Yes, someone was calling him. He hastened to the door, and opened it, and there stood

Emily. She was leaning against the architrave, like one unable for further effort; her face bloodless, and her hair in disorder. She staggered forward, and fell upon his shoulder. "What is it, Milly, my own dear sister?" cried he; "what is the matter?"

"Oh, Joseph," cried she, in a voice of anguish, "what have you done? I could never have believed this of *you!*"

"What do you mean—what is it you charge me with?"

"*You*, who knew how she loved you—how her whole heart was your own!"

"But what do you impute to me, Milly dearest?"

"How cruel! How cruel!" cried she, wringing her hands.

"I swear to you I do not know of what you accuse me."

"You have broken her heart," cried she vehemently. "She will not survive this cruel desertion."

"But who accuses me of this?" asked he, indignantly.

"She, herself, does—she did, at least, so long as reason remained to her; but now, poor darling, her mind is wandering, and she is not conscious of what she says, and yet her cry is, 'Oh, Joseph, do not leave me. Go to him, Milly; on your knees beseech him not to desert me. That I am in fault I know, but I will never again offend him.' I cannot, I will not, tell you all the dreadful —all the humiliating things she says; but through all we can read the terrible trials she must have sustained at your hands, and how severely you have used her. Come to her, at least," cried she, taking his arm. "I do not ask or want to know what has led to this sad scene between you; but come to her before it be too late."

12

"Let me first of all tell you, Milly——" He stopped. He meant to have revealed the truth; but it seemed so ungenerous to be the accuser, that he stopped, and was silent.

"I don't care to hear anything. You may be as blameless as you like. What I want is to save her. Come at once."

Without a word he followed her down the stairs, and across the hall, and up another small stair. "Wait a moment," said she, opening the door, and then as quickly she turned and beckoned him to enter.

Still dressed, but with her hair falling loose about her, and her dress disordered, Florence lay on her bed as in a trance—so light her breathing you could see no motion of the chest. Her eyes were partly opened, and lips parted: but even these gave to her face a greater look of death.

"She is sleeping at last," whispered Miss Grainger. "She has not spoken since you were here."

Loyd knelt down beside the bed, and pressed his cheek against her cold hand; and the day dawn, as it streamed in between the shutters, saw him still there.

CHAPTER XVII.

PARTING SORROWS.

HOUR after hour Loyd knelt beside the bed where Florence lay, motionless and unconscious. Her aunt and sister glided noiselessly about, passed in and out of the room, rarely speaking, and then but in a whisper. At last a servant whispered in Loyd's ear a message. He started and said, "Yes, let him wait;" and then, in a moment after, added, "No, say no. I'll not want the boat—the luggage may be taken back to my room."

It was a few minutes after this that Emily came behind him, and, bending down so as to speak in his ear, said, "How I thank you, my dear brother, for this! I know the price of your devotion—none of us will ever forget it."

He made no answer, but pressed the cold damp hand he held to his lips.

"Does he know that it is nigh seven o'clock, Milly, and that he must be at Como a quarter before eight, or he'll lose the train?" said Miss Grainger to her niece.

"He knows it all, aunt; he has sent away the boat; he will not desert us."

"Remember, child, what it is he is sacrificing. It may chance to be his whole future fortune."

"He'll stay, let it cost what it may," said Emily.

"I declare I think I will speak to him. It is my duty

to speak to him," said the old lady, in her own fussy, officious tone. "I will not expose myself to the reproaches of his family—very just reproaches, too, if they imagined we had detained him. He will lose, not only his passage out to India, but, not impossibly, his appointment too. Joseph, Joseph, I have a word to say to you."

"Dearest aunt, I implore you not to say it," cried Emily.

"Nonsense, child. Is it for a mere tiff and a fit of hysterics a man is to lose his livelihood? Joseph Loyd, come into the next room for a moment."

"I cannot leave this," said he, in a low, faint voice: "say what you have to say to me here."

"It is on the stroke of seven."

He nodded.

"The train leaves a quarter before eight, and if you don't start by this one you can't reach Leghorn by Tuesday."

"I know it; I'm not going."

"Do you mean to give up your appointment?" asked she, in a voice of almost scornful reproach.

"I mean, that I'll not go."

"What will your friends say to this?" said she, angrily.

"I have not thought, nor can I think, of that now: my place is here."

"Then I must protest; and I beg you to remember that I have protested against this resolve on your part. Your family are not to say, hereafter, that it was through any interference or influence of ours that you took this unhappy determination. I'll write, this very day, to your father and say so. There, it is striking seven now!"

He made no reply; indeed, it seemed as if he had not heard her.

'You might still be in time, if you were to exert your-self," whispered she, with more earnestness.

"I tell you again," said he, raising his voice to a louder pitch, "that my place is here, and I will not leave her."

A low, faint sigh was breathed by the sick girl, and gently moving her hand, she laid it on his head.

" You know me then, dearest ? " whispered he. " You know who it is kneels beside you ? "

She made no answer, but her feeble fingers tried to play with his hair, and strayed, unguided, over his head.

What shape of reproach, remonstrance, or protest, Miss Grainger's mutterings took, is not recorded ; but she bustled out of the room, evidently displeased with all in it.

"She knows you, Joseph.   She is trying to thank you," said Emily.

" Her lips are moving : can you hear what she says, Milly ? "

The girl bent over the bed, till her ear almost touched her sister's mouth.   " Yes, darling, from his heart he does.   He never loved you with such devotion as now. She asks if you can forgive her, Joseph.   She remembers everything."

"And not leave me," sighed Florence, in a voice barely audible.

" No, my own dearest, I will not leave you," was all that he could utter in the conflict of joy and sorrow he felt.   A weak attempt to thank him she made by an effort to press his hand, but it sent a thrill of delight through his heart, more than a recompense for all he had suffered.

If Emily, with a generous delicacy, retired towards the window and took up her work, not very profitably perhaps, seeing how little light came through the nearly closed shutters, let us not show ourselves less discreet, and leave the lovers to themselves. Be assured, dear reader, that in our reserve on this point we are not less mindful of your benefit than of theirs. The charming things, so delightful to say and so ecstatic to hear, are wonderfully tame to tell. Perhaps their very charm is in the fact, that their spell was only powerful to those who uttered them. At all events, we are determined on discretion, and shall only own that, though Aunt Grainger made period-ical visits to the sick-room, with frequent references to the hour of the day, and the departures and arrival of various rail trains, they never heard her, or, indeed, knew that she was present.

And though she was mistress of those "asides" and that grand innuendo style which is so deadly round a corner, they never paid the slightest heed to her fire. All the adroit references to the weather, and the "glorious day for travelling," went for naught. As well as the more subtle compliments she made Florence on the appetite she displayed for her chocolate, and which were intended to convey that a young lady who enjoyed her breakfast so heartily need never have lost a man a passage to Calcutta for the pleasure of seeing her eat it. Truth was, Aunt Grainger was not in love, and consequently, no more fit to legislate for those who were than a peasant in rude health is to sympathise with the nervous irritability of a fine lady ! Neither was Milly in love, you will per-haps say, and *she* felt for them. True, but Milly might be—Milly was constitutionally exposed to the malady, and the very vicinity of the disease was what the faculty call a predisposing cause. It made her very happy to see Joseph so fond, and Florence so contented.

Far too happy to think of the price he paid for his happiness, Loyd passed the day beside her. Never before was he so much in love ! Indeed, it was not till the thought of losing her for ever presented itself, that he knew or felt what a blank life would hereafter become to him. Some quaint German writer has it that these little quarrels which lovers occasionally get up as a sort of trial of their own powers of independence, are like the attempts people make to remain a long time under water, and which only end in a profound conviction that their organisation was unequal to the test. But there is another form these passing differences occasionally take. Each of the erring parties is sure to nourish in his or her heart the feeling of being most intensely beloved by the other ! It is a strange form for selfishness to take, but selfishness is the most Protæan of all failings, and there never was seen the mask it could not fit to its face.

"And so you imagined you could cast me off, Florence !" " And you, Master Joseph, had the presumption to think you could leave me," formed the sum and substance of that long day's whispering. My dear, kind reader, do not despise the sermon from the seeming simplicity of the text. There is a deal to be said on it, and very pleasantly said, too. It is, besides, a sort of litigation in which charge and cross charge recur incessantly, and, as in all amicable suits, each party pays his own costs.

It was fortunate, most fortunate, that their reconciliation took this form. It enabled each to do that which was most imminent to be done—to ignore Calvert altogether, and never recur to any mention of his name. Loyd saw that the turquoise ring was no longer worn by her, and she, with a woman's quickness, noted his observation of the fact. I am not sure that in her eyes a recognition of his joy did not glisten, but she certainly never uttered a word that could bring up his name.

"So I am your guest, Madam, for ten days more!" said Loyd to Miss Grainger, as they sat at tea that night.

"Oh, we are only too happy. It is a very great pleasure to us, if—if we could feel that your delay may not prove injurious to you."

"It will be very enjoyable, at all events," said he, with an easy smile, and as though to evade the discussion of the other "count."

"I was thinking of what your friends would say about it."

"It is a very limited public, I assure you," said he, laughing, "and one which so implicitly trusts me, that I have only to say I have done what I believed to be right to be confirmed in their good esteem."

The old lady was not to be put off by generalities, and she questioned him closely as to whether an overland passage did not cost a hundred pounds and upwards, and all but asked whether it was quite convenient to him to disburse that amount. She hinted something about an adage of people who "paid for their whistle," but suggested some grave doubts if they ever felt themselves recompensed in after time by recollecting the music that had cost so dearly; in a word, she made herself supremely disagreeable while he drank his tea, and only too glad to make his escape to go and sit beside Florry, and talk over again all they had said in the morning.

"Only think, Milly," said she, poutingly, as her sister entered, "how Aunt Grainger is worrying poor Joseph, and won't let him enjoy in peace the few days we are to have together."

But he did enjoy them, and to the utmost. Florence very soon threw off all trace of her late indisposi-

tion, and sought, in many ways, to make her lover forget
all the pain she had cost him. The first week was one
of almost unalloyed happiness; the second opened with
the thought that the days were numbered. After Monday
came Tuesday, then Wednesday, which preceded Thurs·
day, when he was to leave.

How was it, they asked themselves, that a whole week
had gone over? It was surely impossible! Impossible
it must be, for now they remembered the mass of things
they had to talk over together, not one of which had been
touched on.

"Why, Joseph dearest, you have told me nothing about
yourself. Whether you are to be in Calcutta, or up the
country? Where, and how I am to write? When I
am to hear from you? What of papa—I was going to
say, our papa—would he like to hear from me, and
may I write to him? Dare I speak to him as a daugh-
ter? Will he think me forward or indelicate for it?
May I tell him of all our plans? Surely you ought to
have told me some of these things! What could we
have been saying to each other all this while?"

Joseph looked at her, and she turned away her head
pettishly, and murmured something about his being too
absurd. Perhaps he was; I certainly hold no brief to
defend him in the case: convict or acquit him, dear
reader, as you please.

And yet, notwithstanding this appeal, the next three
days passed over just as forgetfully as their predecessors,
and then came the sad Wednesday evening, and the
sadder Thursday morning, when, wearied out and ex-
hausted, for they had sat up all night—his last night—to
say good-bye.

"I declare he will be late again; this is the third time
he has come back from the boat," exclaimed Miss

Grainger, as Florence sank, half fainting, into Emily's arms.

"Yes, yes, dear Joseph," muttered Emily, "go now, go at once, before she recovers again."

"If I do not, I never can," cried he, as the tears coursed down his face, while he hurried away.

The monotonous beat of the oars suddenly startled the half-conscious girl; she looked up, and lifted her hand to wave an adieu, and then sank back into her sister's arms, and fainted.

Three days after, a few hurried lines from Loyd told Florence that he had sailed for Malta—this time irrevocably off. They were as sad lines to read as to have written. He had begun by an attempt at jocularity; a sketch of his fellow-travellers coming on board; their national traits, and the strange babble of tongues about them; but, as the bell rang, he dropped this, and scrawled out, as best he could, his last and blotted good-byes. They were shaky, ill-written words, and might, who knows, have been blurred with a tear or two. One thing is certain, she who read, shed many over them, and kissed them, with her last waking breath, as she fell asleep.

About the same day that this letter reached Florence, came another, and very different epistle, to the hands of Algernon Drayton, from his friend Calvert. It was not above a dozen lines, and dated from Alexandria:

"The Leander has just steamed in, crowded with snobs, civil and military, but no Loyd. The fellow must have given up his appointment or gone 'long sea.' In any case, he has escaped me. I am frantic. A whole month's plottings of vengeance scattered to the winds and lost! I'd return to England, if I were only certain to meet with him: but a Faquir, whom I have just consulted, says, 'Go east, and the worst will come of it!' and so I start in two hours for Suez. There are two here who know me, but I mean to caution them how they show it; they are old enough to take a hint.

"Yours, H. C.

"I hear my old regiment has mutinied, and sabred eight of the officers. I wish they'd have waited a little longer, and neither S. nor W. would have got off so easily. From all I can learn, and from the infernal fright the fellows who are going back exhibit, I suspect that the work goes bravely on."

CHAPTER XVIII.

TIDINGS FROM BENGAL.

AM not about to chronicle how time now rolled over the characters of our story. As for the life of those at the villa, nothing could be less eventful. All existences that have any claim to be called happy are of this type, and if there be nothing brilliant or triumphant in their joys, neither is there much poignancy in their sorrows.

Loyd wrote almost by every mail, and with a tameness that shadowed forth the uniform tenor of his own life. It was pretty nigh the same story, garnished by the same reflections. He had been named a district judge "up country," and passed his days deciding the disputed claims of indigo planters against the ryots, and the ryots against the planters. Craft, subtlety, and a dash of perjury, ran through all these suits, and rendered them rather puzzles for a quick intelligence to resolve, than questions of right or legality. He told, too, how dreary and uncompanionable his life was; how unsolaced by friendship, or even companionship; that the climate was enervating, the scenery monotonous, and the thermometer at a hundred and twenty or a hundred and thirty degrees.

Yet Loyd could speak with some encouragement about his prospects. He was receiving eight hundred rupees a month, and hoped to be promoted to some place, ending in Ghar or Bad, with an advance of two hundred more. He darkly hinted that the mutinous spirit of certain regiments was said to be extending, but he wrote this with all the reserve of an official, and the fear that Aunt Grainger might misquote him. Of course there were other features in these letters—those hopes and fears, and prayers and wishes, which lovers like to write, almost as well as read, poetising to themselves their own existence, and throwing a rose-tint of romance over lives as lead-coloured as may be. Of these I am not going to say anything. It is a theme both too delicate and too dull to touch on. I respect and I dread it.

I have less reserve with the correspondence of another character of our tale, though certainly, when written, it was not meant for publicity. The letter of which I am about to make an extract, and it can be but an extract, was written about ten months after the departure of Calvert for India, and, like his former ones, addressed to his friend Drayton :

"At the hazard of repeating myself, if by chance my former letters have reached you, I state that I am in the service of the Meer Morad, of Ghurtpore, of whose doings the *Times* correspondent will have told you something. I have eight squadrons of cavalry and a half battery of field-pieces—brass ten pounders—with an English crown on their breech. We are well armed, admirably mounted, and perfect devils to fight. You saw what we did with the detachment of the —th, and their sick convoy, coming out of Allehbad. The only fellow that escaped was the doctor, and I saved his life to attach him to my own staff. He is an Irish fellow, named Tobin, and comes from Tralee—if there be such a place—and begs his friends there not to say masses for him, for he is alive, and drunk every evening.   Do this, if not a bore.

"By good luck the Meer, my chief, quarrelled with the king's party in Delhi, and we came away in time to save being caught by Wilson, who would have recognised me at once.   By-the-way, Baxter of the 30th was stupid enough to say, 'Eh, Calvert, what the devil are you doing amongst these niggers?'   He was a prisoner, at the time, and, of course, I had to order him to be shot for his imprudence.   How he knew me I cannot guess; my beard is down to my breast, and I am turbaned and shawled in the most approved fashion.   We are now simply marauding, cutting off supplies, falling on weak detachments, and doing a small retail business in murder wherever we chance upon a station of civil servants.   I narrowly escaped being caught by a troop of the 9th Lancers, every man of whom knows me.   I went over with six trusty fellows, to Astraghan, where I learned that a certain Loyd was stationed as Government receiver. We got there by night, burned his bungalow, shot him, and then discovered he was not our man, but another Loyd.   Bradshaw came up with his troop.   He gave us an eight mile chase across country, and, knowing how the Ninth ride, I took them over some sharp nullahs, and the croppers they got you'll scarcely see mentioned in the government despatches.   I fired three barrels of my Yankee six-shooter at Brad, and I heard the old beggar offer a thousand rupees for my head.   When he found he could not overtake us, and sounded a halt, I screamed out, 'Threes about, Bradshaw.   I'd give fifty pounds to hear him tell the story at mess : 'Yes, Sir, begad, Sir, in as good English, Sir, as yours or mine, Sir : a fellow who had served the Queen, I'll swear.'

" For the moment, it is a mere mutiny, but it will soon be a rebellion, and I don't conceal from myself the danger of what I am doing, as you, in all likelihood, will suspect. Not dangers from the Queen's fellows—for they shall never take me alive—but the dangers I run from my present associates, and who, of course, only half trust me. . . . . . Do you remember old Commissary-General Yates—J.C.V.R. Yates, the old ass used to write himself? Well, amongst the other events of the time, was the sack and 'loot' of his house at Cawnpore, and the capture of his pretty wife, whom they brought in here a prisoner. I expected to find the poor young creature terrified almost out of her reason. Not a bit of it ! She was very angry with the fellows who robbed her, and rated them roundly in choice Hindostanee, telling one of the chiefs that his grandfather was a scorched pig. Like a woman, and a clever woman, too, though she recognised me—I can almost swear that she did— she never showed it, and we talked away all the evening, and smoked our hookahs together in Oriental guise. I gave her a pass next morning to Calcutta, and saw her safe to the great trunk road, giving her bearers as far as Behdarah. She expressed herself as very grateful for my attentions, and hoped at some future time—this with a malicious twinkle of her gray eyes—to show the 'Bahadoor' that she had not forgotten them. So you see there are lights as well as shadows in the life of a rebel.

I omit a portion here, and come to the conclusion, which was evidently added in haste.

" ' Up and away !' is the order. We are off to Bithoor. The Nana there—a staunch friend, as it was thought, of British rule—has declared for independence, and as there is plenty of go in him, look out for something ' sensational.'   You wouldn't believe how, amidst all these stirring scenes, I long for news—from what people call home—of Rocksley and Uncle G., and the dear Soph ; but more from that villa beside the Italian lake.   I'd give a canvas bag that I carry at my girdle with a goodly stock of pearls, sapphires, and rubies, for one evening's diary of that cottage !

"If all go on as well and prosperously as I hope for, I have not the least objection, but rather a wish that you would tell the world where I am, and what I am doing. Linked with failure, I'd rather keep dark ; but as a sharer in a great success, I burn to make it known through the length and breadth of the land that I am alive and well, and ready to acquit a number of personal obligations, if not to the very fellows who injured me, to their friends, relatives, and cousins, to the third generation.   Tell them, Algy, 'A chiel's amang ye, cutting throats,' and add, if you like, that he writes himself your attached friend,

"Harry Calvert."

This letter, delivered in some mysterious manner to the bankers at Calcutta, was duly forwarded, and in time reached the hands of Alfred Drayton, who confided its contents to a few "friends" of Calvert's—men who felt neither astonished nor shocked at the intelligence—shifty fellows, with costly tastes, who would live on society somehow, reputably, if they could—dishonourably if they must ; and who all agreed that "Old Calvert," as they called him — he was younger than most of them — had struck out a very clever line, and a far more re-munerative one than "rooking young Griffins at billiards" —such being, in their estimation, the one other alternative which fate had to offer him.   This was all the publicity, however, Drayton gave to his friend's achievements. Somehow or other, paragraphs did appear, not naming Calvert, but intimating that an officer, who had formerly served her Majesty, had been seen in the ranks of the insurgents of Upper Bengal. Yet Calvert was not suspected, and he dropped out of people's minds as thoroughly as if he had dropped out of life.

To this oblivion, for a while, we must leave him ; for even if we had in our hands, which we have not, any records of his campaigning life, we might scruple to occupy our readers with details which have no direct bearing upon our story. That Loyd never heard of him is clear enough. The name of Calvert never occurred in any letter from his hand. It was one no more to be spoken of by Florence or himself. One letter from him, however, mentioned an incident which, to a suspicious mind, might have opened a strange vein of speculation, though it is right to add that neither the writer nor the reader ever hit upon a clue to the mystery indicated. It was during his second year of absence that he was sent to Mulnath, from which he writes :

"The mutiny has not touched this spot ; but we hear every day the low rumbling of the distant storm, and we are told that our servants, and the native battalion that are our garrison, are only waiting for the signal to rise. I doubt this greatly. I have nothing to excite my distrust of the people, but much to recommend them to my favour. It is only two days back that I received secret intelligence of an intended attack upon my bungalow by a party of Bithoor cavalry, whose doings have struck terror far and near. Two companies of the —th, that I sent for, arrived this morning, and I now feel very easy about the reception the enemy will meet. The strangest part of all is, however, to come. Captain Rolt, who commands the detachment, said in a laughing jocular way, 'I declare, judge, if I were you, I would change my name, at least till this row was over.' I asked him 'Why?' in some surprise; and he replied, 'There's rather a run against judges of your name lately. They shot one at Astraghan last November. Six weeks back, they came down near Agra, where Craven Loyd had just arrived, district judge and assessor; they burnt his bungalow, and massacred himself and his household; and now, it seems, they are after *you.* I take it that some one of your name has been rather sharp on these fellows, and that this is the pursuit of a long meditated vengeance. At all events I'd call myself Smith or Brown till this prejudice blows over.'"

The letter soon turned to a pleasanter theme—his application for a leave had been favourably entertained. By October—it was then July—he might hope to take his passage for England. Not that he was, he said, at all sick of India. He had now adapted himself to its ways and habits, his health was good, and the solitude—the one sole cause of complaint—he trusted would ere long give way to the happiest and most blissful of all companionship. "Indeed, I must try to make you all emigrate with me. Aunt Grainger can have her flowers and her vegetables here in all seasons, one of my retainers is an excellent gardener, and Milly's passion for riding can be indulged upon the prettiest Arab horses I ever saw."

Though the dangers which this letter spoke of as impending were enough to make Florence anxious and eager for the next mail from India, his letter never again alluded to them. He wrote full of the delight of having got his leave, and overjoyed at all the happiness that he pictured as before him.

So in the same strain and spirit was the next, and then came September, and he wrote: "This day month, dearest—this day month, I am to sail. Already when these lines are before you, the interval, which to me now seems an age, will have gone over, and you can think of me as hastening towards you."

"Oh, aunt dearest, listen to this. Is not this happy news?" cried Florence, as she pressed the loved letter to her lips. "Joseph says that on the 18th—to-day is— what day is to-day? But you are not minding me, aunt. What can there be in that letter of yours so interesting as this?"

This remonstrance was not very unreasonable, seeing that Miss Grainger was standing with her eyes fixed steadfastly at a letter, whose few lines could not have taken a moment to read, and which must have had some other claim thus to arrest her attention.

"This is wonderful!" cried she, at last. •

"What is wonderful, aunt? Do pray gratify our curiosity!"

But the old lady hurried away without a word, and the door of her room, as it sharply banged, showed that she desired to be alone.

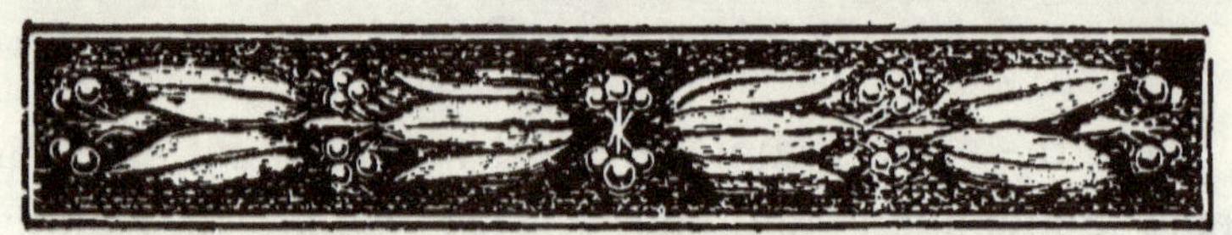

CHAPTER XIX.

A SHOCK.

O sooner did Mrs. Grainger find herself safely locked in her room, than she re-opened the letter the post had just brought her. It was exceedingly brief, and seemed hastily written:

"Strictly and imperatively private.

"Trieste, Tuesday morning.

"My dear Miss Grainger,—I have just arrived here from India, with important despatches for the government. The fatigues of a long journey have re-opened an old wound, and laid me up for a day; but as my papers are of such a nature as will require my presence to explain, there is no use in my forwarding them by another; I wait, therefore, and write this hurried note, to say that I will make you a flying visit on Saturday next. I say *you*, because I wish to see yourself and alone. Manage this in the best way you can. I hope to arrive by the morning train, and be at the villa by eleven or twelve at latest. Whether you receive me or not, say nothing of this note to your nieces; but I trust and pray you will not refuse half an hour to your attached and faithful friend,

"HARRY CALVERT."

It was a name to bring up many memories, and Miss

Grainger sat gazing at the lines before her in a state of wonderment blended with terror. Once only, had she read of him since his departure; it was, when agitated and distressed to know what had become of him, she ventured on a step of, for her, daring boldness, and to whose temerity she would not make her nieces the witnesses. She wrote a letter to Miss Sophia Calvert, begging to have some tidings of her cousin, and some clue to his whereabouts. The answer came by return of post; it ran thus:

"Miss Calvert has to acknowledge the receipt of Miss Grainger's note of the 8th inst.

"Miss Calvert is not aware of any claim Miss Grainger can prefer to address her by letter, still less, of any right to bring under her notice the name of the person she has dared to inquire after. Any further correspondence from Miss Grainger will be sent back unopened."

The reading of this epistle made the old lady keep her bed for three days, her sufferings being all the more aggravated, since they imposed secrecy. From that day forth she had never heard Calvert's name; and though for hours long she would think and ponder over him, the mention of him was so strictly interdicted, that the very faintest allusion to him was even avoided.

And now, like one risen from the grave, he was come back again! Come back to renew, Heaven could tell what sorrows of the past, and refresh the memory of days that had always been dashed with troubles.

It was already Friday. Where and how could a message reach him? She dreaded him, it is true: but why she dreaded him she knew not. It was a sort of vague terror, such as some persons feel at the sound of

the sea, or the deep-voiced moaning of the wind through
trees.   It conveyed a sense of peril through a sense of
sadness—no more.   She had grown to dislike him from
the impertinent rebuke Miss Calvert had administered to
her on his account. The mention of Calvert was coupled
with a darkened room, leeches, and ice on the head, and
worse than all, a torturing dread that her mind might
wander, and the whole secret history of the correspondence
leak out in her ramblings.

Were not these reasons enough to make her tremble
at the return of the man who had occasioned so much
misery?   Yet, if she could even find a pretext, could she
be sure that she could summon courage to say, " I'll not
see you ? "   There are men to whom a cruelly cold reply
is a repulse ; but Calvert was not one of these, and this
she knew well.   Besides, were she to decline to receive
him, might it not drive him to come and ask to see the
girls, who now, by acceding to his request, need never
hear or know of his visit?

After long and mature deliberation, she determined on
her line of action.   She would pretend to the girls that
her letter was from her lawyer, who, accidentally finding
himself in her neighbourhood, begged an interview as he
passed through Orta on his way to Milan, and for this
purpose she could go over in the boat alone, and meet
Calvert on his arrival.   In this way she could see him
without the risk of her nieces' knowledge, and avoid the
unpleasantness of not asking him to remain when he had
once passed her threshold.

" I can at least show him," she thought, " that our old
relations are not to be revived, though I do not altogether
break off all acquaintanceship.   No man has a finer sense
of tact, and he will understand the distinction I intend,
and respect it."   She also bethought her it smacked

somewhat of a vengeance—though she knew not precisely how or why—that she'd take Sophia Calvert's note along with her, and show him how her inquiry for him was treated by his family. She had a copy of her own, a most polite and respectful epistle it was, and in no way calculated to evoke the rebuke it met with. "He'll be perhaps able to explain the mystery," thought she, "and whatever Miss Calvert's misconception, he can eradicate it when he sees her."

"How fussy and important aunt is this morning!" said Florence, as the old lady stepped into the boat. "If the interview were to be with the Lord Chancellor instead of a London solicitor, she could not look more profoundly impressed with its solemnity."

"She'll be dreadful when she comes back," said Emily, laughing; "so full of all the law jargon that she couldn't understand, but will feel a right to repeat, because she has paid for it."

It was thus they criticised her. Just as many aunts and uncles, and some papas and mammas, too, are occasionally criticised by those younger members of the family who are prone to be very caustic as to the mode certain burdens are borne, the weight of which has never distressed their own shoulders. And this, not from any deficiency of affection, but simply through a habit which, in the levity of our day, has become popular, and taught us to think little of the ties of parentage, and call a father a Governor.

CHAPTER XX.

AGAIN AT ORTA.

"THERE is a stranger arrived, Signora, who has been asking for you," said the landlord of the little inn at Orta, as Miss Grainger reached the door. "He has ordered a boat, but feeling poorly, has lain down on a bed till it is ready. This is his servant," and he pointed as he spoke to a dark-visaged and very handsome man, who wore a turban of white and gold, and who made a deep gesture of obeisance as she turned towards him. Ere she had time to question him as to his knowledge of English, a bell rung sharply, and the man hurried away to return very speedily, and, at the same instant, a door opened and Calvert came towards her, and, with an air of deep emotion, took her hand and pressed it to his lips.

"This is too kind, far too kind and considerate of you," said he, as he led her forward to a room.

"When I got your note," she began, in a voice a good deal shaken, for there was much in the aspect of the man before her to move her, "I really did not know what to do. If you desired to see me alone, it would be impossible to do this at the villa, and so I bethought me that the best way was to come over here at once."

"Do you find me much changed?" he asked, in a low, sad voice.

"Yes, I think you are a good deal changed. You are browner, and you look larger, even taller, than you did, and perhaps the beard makes you seem older."

This was all true, but not the whole truth, which, had she spoken it, would have said, that he was far handsomer than before. The features had gained an expression of dignity and elevation from habits of command, and there was a lofty pride in his look which became him well, the more as it was now tempered with a gentle courtesy of manner which showed itself in every word and every gesture towards her. A slight, scarcely perceptible baldness, at the very top of the forehead, served to give height to his head, and add to the thoughtful character of his look. His dress, too, was peculiar, and probably set off to advantage his striking features and handsome figure. He wore a richly embroidered pelisse, fastened by a shawl at the waist, and on his head, rather jauntily set, a scarlet fez stitched in gold, and ornamented with a star of diamonds and emeralds.

"You are right," said he, with a winning but very melancholy smile. "These last two years have aged me greatly. I have gone through a great deal in them. Come," added he, as he seated himself at her side, and took her hand in his, "come, tell me what have you heard of me? Be frank; tell me everything."

"Nothing—absolutely nothing," said she.

"Do you mean that no one mentioned me?"

"We saw no one. Our life has been one of complete unbroken solitude."

"Well, but your letters; people surely wrote about me?"

"No," said she in some awkwardness, for she felt as though there was something offensive in this oblivion, and was eager to lay it to the charge of their isolation.

"Remember what I have told you about our mode of life."

"You read the newspapers, though ! You might have come upon my name in them !"

"We read none. We ceased to take them. We gave ourselves up to the little cares and occupations of our home, and we really grew to forget that there was a world outside us."

Had she been a shrewd reader of expression, she could not fail to have noticed the intense relief her words gave him. He looked like one who hears the blessed words Not Guilty ! after hours of dread anxiety for his fate. "And am I to believe," asked he, in a voice tremulous with joy, "that from the hour I said farewell, to this day, that I have been to you as one dead and buried and forgotten ?"

"I don't think we forgot you ; but we rigidly observed our pledge to you, and never spoke of you."

"What is there on earth so precious as the trustfulness of true friendship ?" burst he in, with a marked enthusiasm. "I have had what the world calls great successes, and I swear to you I'd give them all, and all their rewards twice told, for this proof of affection ; and the dear girls, and Florence—how is she ?"

"Far better than when you saw her. Indeed, I should say perfectly restored to health. She walks long walks, and takes rides on a mountain pony, and looks like one who had never known illness."

"Not married yet ?" said he with a faint smile.

"No ; he is coming back next month, and they will probably be married before Christmas."

"And as much in love as ever—he, I mean ?"

"Fully ; and she too."

"Pshaw ! She never cared for him ; she never could

care for him. She tried it—did her very utmost. I saw the struggle, and I saw its failure, and I told her so!"

"You told her so!"

"Why not? It was well for the poor girl that one human being in all the world should understand and feel for her. And she is determined to marry him?"

"Yes; he is coming back solely with that object."

"How was it that none of his letters spoke of me? Are you quite sure they did not?"

"I am perfectly sure, for she always gave them to me to read."

"Well!" cried he, boldly, as he stood up, and threw his head haughtily back, "the fellow who led Calvert's Horse—that was the name my irregulars were known by —might have won distinction enough to be quoted by a petty Bengal civil servant. The Queen will possibly make amends for this gentleman's forgetfulness."

"You were in all this dreadful campaign, then?" asked she eagerly.

"Through the whole of it. Held an independent command; got four times wounded: this was the last." And he laid bare a fearful cicatrice that almost surrounded his right arm above the wrist. "Refused the Bath."

"Refused it?"

"Why not? What object is it to me to be Sir Harry? Besides, a man who holds opinions such as mine, should accept no court favours. Colonel Calvert is a sufficient title."

"And you are a colonel already?"

"I was a major-general a month ago—local rank, of course. But why am I led to talk of these things? May I see the girls? Will they like to see me?"

"For that I can answer. But are your minutes not counted? These despatches?"

"I have thought of all that. This sword-cut has left a terrible 'tic' behind it, and travelling disposes to it, so that I have telegraphed for leave to send my despatches forward by Hassan, my Persian fellow, and rest myself here for a day or two. I know you'll not let me die unwatched, uncared for. I have not forgotten all the tender care you once bestowed upon me."

She knew not what to reply. Was she to tell him that the old green chamber, with its little stair into the garden, was still at his service? Was she to say, "Your old welcome awaits you there," or did she dread his presence amongst them, and even fear what reception the girls would extend to him?

"Not," added he, hastily, "that I am to inflict you with a sick man's company again. I only beg for leave to come out of a morning when I feel well enough. This inn here is very comfortable, and though I am glad to see Onofrio does not recognise me, he will soon learn my ways enough to suit me. Meanwhile, may I go back with you, or do you think you ought to prepare them for the visit of so formidable a personage?"

"Oh, I think you may come at once," said she, laughingly, but very far from feeling assured at the same time.

"All the better. I have some baubles here that I want to deposit in more suitable hands than mine. You know that we irregulars had more looting than our comrades, and I believe that I was more fortunate in this way than many others." As he spoke, he hastily opened and shut again several jewel-cases, but giving her time to glance— no more than glance—at the glittering objects they contained. "By-the-way," said he, taking from one of them a costly brooch of pearls, "this is the sort of thing they fasten a shawl with," and he gallantly placed it in her shawl as he spoke.

"Oh, my dear Colonel Calvert!"

"Pray do not call me colonel. I am Harry Calvert for you, just as I used to be. Besides, I wish for nothing that may remind me of my late life and all its terrible excitements. I am a soldier tired, very tired of war's alarms, and very eager for peace in its best of all significations. Shall we go?"

"By all means. I was only thinking that you must reconcile yourself not to return to-night, and rough it how best you can at the villa."

"Let me once see my portmanteau in the corner of my old green room, and my pipe where it used to hang beside my watch over the chimney, and I'll not believe that I have passed the last two terrible years but in a dream. You could not fancy how I attach myself to that spot, but I'll give you a proof. I have given orders to my agent to buy the villa. Yes; you'll wake some fine morning and find me to be your landlord."

It was thus they talked away, rambling from one theme to the other, till they had gone a considerable way across the lake, when once more Calvert recurred to the strange circumstance that his name should never have come before them in any shape since his departure.

"I ought to tell you," said she, in some confusion, "that I once did make an effort to obtain tidings of you. I wrote to your cousin Miss Sophia."

"You wrote to her!" burst he in, sternly; "and what answer did you get?"

"There it is," said she, drawing forth the letter, and giving it to him.

"'No claim! no right!' murmured he, as he re-read

the lines; "'the name of the person she had dared to inquire after;' and you never suspected the secret of all this indignant anger?"

"How could I? What was it?"

"One of the oldest and vulgarest of all passions—jealousy! Sophy had heard that I was attached to your niece. Some good-natured gossip went so far as to say we were privately married. My old uncle, who only about once in a quarter of a century cares what his family are doing, wrote me a very insulting letter, reminding me of the year-long benefits he had bestowed upon me, and, at the close, categorically demanded 'Are you married to her?' I wrote back four words, 'I wish I was,' and there ended all our intercourse. Since I have won certain distinctions, however, I have heard that he wants to make submission, and has even hinted to my lawyer a hope that the name of Calvert is not to be severed from the old estate of Rocksley Manor; but there will be time enough to tell you about all these things. What did your nieces say to that note of Sophy's?"

"Nothing. They never saw it. Never knew I wrote to her."

"Most discreetly done on your part. I cannot say how much I value the judgment you exercised on this occasion."

The old lady set much store by such praise, and grew rather prolix about all the considerations which led her to adopt the wise course she had taken.

He was glad to have launched her upon a sea where she could beat, and tack, and wear at will, and leave him to go back to his own thoughts.

"And so," said he, at last, "they are to be married before Christmas?"

"Yes; that is the plan."

"And then she will return with him to India, I take it."

She nodded.

"Poor girl! And has she not one friend in all the world to tell her what a life is before her as the wife of a third—no, but tenth-rate official—in that dreary land of splendour and misery, where nothing but immense wealth can serve to gloss over the dull uniformity of existence, and where the income of a year is often devoted to dispel the ennui of a single day? India, with poverty, is the direst of all penal settlements. In the bush, in the wilds of New Zealand, in the far-away islands of the Pacific, you have the free air and healthful breezes of heaven. You can bathe without having an alligator for your companion, and lie down on the grass without a cobra on your carotid; but, in India, life stands always face to face with death, and death in some hideous form."

"How you terrify me!" cried she, in a voice of intense emotion.

"I don't want to terrify, I want to warn. If it were ever my fate to have a marriageable daughter, and some petty magistrate—some small district judge of Bengal—asked her for a wife, I'd say to my girl, 'Go and be a farm servant in New Caledonia. Milk cows, rear lambs, wash, scrub, toil for your daily bread in some land where poverty is not deemed the 'plague;' but don't encounter life in a society where to be poor is to be despicable—where narrow means are a stigma of disgrace.'"

"Joseph says nothing of all this. He writes like one well contented with his lot, and very hopeful for the future."

"Hasn't your niece some ten or twelve thousand pounds?"

" Fifteen."

" Well, he presses the investment on which he asks a loan, just as any other roguish speculator would, that's all."

" Oh, don't say that, Mr. Calvert. Joseph is not a rogue."

" Men are rogues according to their capacity. The clever fellows do not need roguery, and achieve success just because they are stronger and better than their neighbours ; but I don't want to talk of Loyd ; every consideration of the present case can be entertained without him."

" How can that be, if he is to be her husband ? "

" Ah ! If—if. My dear old friend, when an if comes into any question, the wisest way is not to debate it, for the simple reason that applying our logic to what is merely imaginary is very like putting a superstructure of masonry over a house of cards. Besides, if we must talk with a hypothesis, I'll put mine, ' Must she of necessity marry this man, if he insists on it ? ' "

" Of course ; and the more, that she loves him."

" Loves him ! Have I not told you that you are mistaken there ? He entrapped her at first into a half admission of caring for him, and, partly from a sense of honour, and partly from obstinacy, she adheres to it. But she does so just the way people cling to a religion, because nobody has ever taken the trouble to convert them to another faith."

" I wish you would not say these things to me," cried she with much emotion. " You have a way of throwing doubts upon everything and everybody, that always makes me miserable, and I ask myself afterwards, Is there nothing to be believed ? Is no one to be trusted ? "

"Not a great many, I am sorry to say," sighed he. "It's no bright testimony to the goodness of the world, that the longer a man lives the worse he thinks of it. I surely saw the flutter of white muslin through the trees yonder. Oh dear, how much softer my heart is than I knew of! I feel a sort of choking in the throat as I draw near this dear old place. Yes, there she is— Florence herself. I remember her way of waving a handkerchief. I'll answer it as I used to do." And he stood up in the boat and waved his handkerchief over his head with a wide and circling motion. "Look! She sees it, and she's away to the house at speed. How she runs! She could not have mustered such speed as that when I last saw her."

"She has gone to tell Milly, I'm certain."

He made no reply, but covered his face with his hands, and sat silent and motionless. Meanwhile the boat glided up to the landing-place, and they disembarked.

"I thought the girls would have been here to meet us," said Miss Grainger, with a pique she could not repress; but Calvert walked along at her side, and made no answer.

"I think you know your way here," said she with a smile, as she motioned him towards the drawing-room.

CHAPTER XXI.

THE RETURN.

HEN Calvert found himself alone in the drawing-room, he felt as if he had never been away. Everything was so exactly as he left it. There was the sofa drawn close to the window of the flower-garden where Florence used to recline; there the little work-table with the tall glass that held her hyacinths, the flowers she was so fond of; there the rug for her terrier to lie on. Yonder, under the fig-tree, hung the cage with her favourite canary; and here were the very books she used to read long ago—Petrarch and Tennyson and Uhland. There was a flower to mark a place in the volume of Uhland, and it was at a little poem they had once read together. How full of memories are these old rooms, where we have dreamed away some weeks of life, if not in love, in something akin to it, and thus more alive to the influences of externals than if further gone in the passion! There was not a spot, not a chair, nor a window-seat that did not remind Calvert of some incident of the past. He missed his favourite song, "A place in thy memory, dearest," from the piano, and he sought for it and put it back where it used to be; and he then went over to her table to arrange the books as they were wont to be long ago, and came suddenly upon a small morocco case. He opened it. It was a miniature of Loyd, the man he hated the most on earth. It was an ill done portrait, and gave an affected thoughtfulness and elevation to his calm features which imparted insufferable pretension to them; Calvert held out the picture at arm's length, and laughed scornfully as he looked at it. He had but time to lay it down on the table when Emily entered the room. She approached him hurriedly, and with an agitated manner. "Oh, Colonel Calvert——" she began.

"Why not Harry, brother Harry, as I used to be, Milly dearest," said he, as he caught her hand in both his own. "What has happened to forfeit for me my old place in your esteem?"

"Nothing, nothing, but all is so changed; you have grown to be such a great man, and we have become lost to all that goes on in the world."

"And where is your sister, will she not come to see me?"

"You startled her, you gave her such a shock, when you stood up in the boat and returned her salute, that she was quite overcome, and has gone to her room. Aunt Grainger is with her, and told me to say—that is, she hoped, if you would not take it ill, or deem it unkind ——"

"Go on, dearest; nothing that comes from your lips can possibly seem unkind; go on."

"But I cannot go on," she cried, and burst into tears and covered her face with her hands.

"I never thought—so little forethought has selfishness —that I was to bring sorrow and trouble under this roof. Go back, and tell your aunt that I hope she will favour me with five minutes of her company; that I see what I greatly blame myself for not seeing before, how full of sad memories my presence here must prove. Go, darling, say this, and bid me good-bye before you go."

"Oh, Harry, do not say this. I see you are angry with us. I see you think us all unkind; but it was the suddenness of your coming; and Florence has grown so nervous of late, so disposed to give way to all manner of fancies."

"She imagines, in fact," said he, haughtily, "that I have come back to persecute her with attentions which she has already rejected. Isn't that so?"

"No. I don't think—I mean Florence could never think that when you knew of her engagement—knew that within a few months at furthest——"

"Pardon me, if I stop you. Tell your sister from me that she has nothing to apprehend from any pretensions of mine. I can see that you think me changed, Milly; grown very old and very worn. Well, go back, and tell her that the inward change is far greater than the outward one. Mad Harry has become as tame and quiet and commonplace as that gentleman in the morocco case yonder; and if she will condescend to see me, she may satisfy herself that neither of us in future need be deemed dangerous to the other."

There was an insolent pride in the manner of his delivery of these words that made Emily's cheek burn as she listened, and all that her aunt had often told her of "Calvert insolence" now came fully to her mind.

"I will go and speak to my aunt," she said at last.

"Do so," said he, carelessly, as he threw himself into a chair, and took up the book that lay nearest to him. He had not turned over many pages—he had read none—when Miss Grainger entered. She was flushed and flurried in manner; but tried to conceal it.

"We are giving you a very strange welcome, Colonel —Mr. Calvert; but you know us all of old, and you know that dear Florry is so easily agitated and overcome.

She is better now, and if you will come up stairs to the little drawing-room, she'll see you."

"I am all gratitude," said he, with a low bow : "but I think it is, perhaps, better not to inconvenience her. A visit of constraint would be, to me at least, very painful. I'd rather leave the old memories of my happiness here undashed by such a shadow. Go back, therefore, and say that I think I understand the reason of her reserve; that I am sincerely grateful for the thoughtful kindness she has been minded to observe towards me. You need not add," said he with a faint smile, "that the consideration in the present case was unnecessary. I am not so impressionable as I used to be ; but assure her that I am very sorry for it, and that Colonel Calvert, with all his successes, is not half so happy a fellow as mad Harry used to be without a guinea."

"But you'll not leave us ? You'll stay here to-night ?"

"Pray excuse me. One of my objects—my chief one —in coming over here, was to ask your nieces' acceptance of some trinkets I had brought for them. Perhaps this would not be a happy moment to ask a favour at their hands, so pray keep them over and make birthday presents of them in my name. This is for Florence—this, I hope Emily will not refuse."

"But do not go. I entreat you not to go. I feel so certain that if you stay we shall all be so happy together. There is so much, besides, to talk over ; and as to those beautiful things, for I know they must be beautiful——"

"They are curious in their way," said he, carelessly opening the clasp of one of the cases, and displaying before her amazed eyes a necklace of pearls and brilliants that a queen might wear.

"Oh, Colonel Calvert, it would be impossible for my

niece to accept such a costly gift as this.   I never beheld anything so splendid in my life."

" These ear-drops," he continued, " are considered fine. They were said to belong to one of the wives of the King of Delhi, and were reputed the largest pearls in India."

" The girls must see them ; though I protest and declare beforehand nothing on earth should induce us to accept them."

" Let them look well at them, then," said he, " for when you place them in my hands again, none shall ever behold them after."

" What do you mean ? "

" I mean that I'll throw them into the lake yonder. A rejected gift is too odious a memory to be clogged with."

" You couldn't be guilty of such rash folly ? "

" Don't you know well that I could ?   Is it to-day or yesterday that the Calvert nature is known to you ?   If you wish me to swear it, I will do so ; and, what is more, I will make you stand by and see the water close over them."

" Oh, you are not changed—not in the least changed," she cried, in a voice of real emotion.

" Only in some things, perhaps," said he, carelessly. " By-the-way, this is a miniature of me—was taken in India.   It is a locket on this side.   Ask Emily to wear it occasionally for my sake."

" How like ! and what a splendid costume ! "

" That was my dress in full state ! but I prefer my service uniform, and think it became me better."

" Nothing could become you better than this," said she, admiringly ; and truly there was good warrant for the admiration ; " but even this is covered with diamonds ! "

"Only a circlet and my initials. It is of small value. Thése are the baubles. Do what you will with them; and now good-bye. Tanti salutì, as we used to say long ago to the ladies—Tanti salutì de la parte mia. Tell Milly she is very naughty not to have given me her hand to kiss before we parted; but if she will condescend to wear this locket, now and then, I'll forgive her. Good-bye."

And, before Miss Grainger could reply, he had opened the window and was gone.

When Calvert reached the jetty the boatman was not there; but the boat, with her oars, lay close to the steps; the chain that attached her to an iron ring was, however, padlocked, and Calvert turned impatiently back to seek the man. After he had gone, however, a few paces, he seemed to change his mind, and turned once more towards the lake. Taking up a heavy stone, he proceeded to smash the lock on the chain. It was stronger than he looked for, and occupied some minutes; but he succeeded at last. Just as he threw into the boat the loose end of the broken chain, he heard steps behind him; he turned; it was Emily running towards him at full speed. "Oh Harry, dear Harry!" she cried, "don't go; don't leave us; Florence is quite well again, and as far as strength will let her, trying to come and meet you. See, yonder she is, leaning on aunt's arm." True enough, at some hundred yards off, the young girl was seen slowly dragging her limbs forward in the direction where they stood.

"I have come some thousand leagues to see *her*," said he, sternly, "through greater fatigues, and, perhaps, as many perils as she is encountering."

"Go to her; go towards her," cried Emily, reproachfully.

"Not one step; not the breadth of a hair, Milly," said he. "There is a limit to the indignity a woman may put upon a man, and your sister has passed it. If she likes to come and say farewell to me here, be it so; if not, I must go without it."

"Then I can tell you one thing, Colonel Calvert, if my sister Florence only knew of the words you have just spoken, she'd not move one other step towards you if, if——"

"If it were to save my life, you would say. *That* is not so unreasonable," said he, with a saucy laugh.

"Here is Florence come, weak and tottering as she is, to ask you to stay with us. You'll not have the heart to say No to her," said Miss Grainger.

"I don't think we—any of us—know much about Mr. Calvert's heart, or what it would prompt him to do," said Emily, half indignantly, as she turned away. And fortunate it was she did turn away, since, had she met the fierce look of Calvert's eyes at the moment, it would have chilled her very blood with fear.

"But you'll not refuse me," said Florence, laying her hand on his arm. "You know well how seldom I ask favours, and how unused I am to be denied when I do ask."

"I was always your slave—I ask nothing better than to be so still," he whispered in her ear.

"And you will stay?"

"Yes, till you bid me go," he whispered again; "but remember, too, that when I ask a favour I can just as little brook refusal."

"We'll talk of that another time. Give me your arm now, and help me back to the house, for I feel very weak and faint. Is Milly angry with you?" she asked, as they walked along, side by side.

"I don't know; perhaps so," said he, carelessly.

"You used to be such good friends. I hope you have not fallen out?"

"I hope not," said he, in his former easy tone; "or that if we have, we may make it up again. Bear in mind, Florence," added he with more gravity of manner, "that I am a good deal changed from what you knew me. I have less pride, cherish fewer resentments, scarcely any hopes, and no affections—I mean, strong affections. The heart you refused is now cold; the only sentiment left me, is a sense of gratitude. I can be very grateful; I am already so." She made no answer to this speech, and they re-entered the house in silence.

CHAPTER XXII.

A LETTER OF CONFESSIONS.

THE following letter from Calvert to Drayton was written about three weeks after the event of our last chapter:

"The Villa.

"My dear Algernon,—I knew my black fellow would run you to earth, though he had not a word of English in his vocabulary, nor any clue to you except your name and a map of England. It must have, however, been his near kinsman—the other 'black gentleman'—suggested Scarborough to him ; and, to this hour, I cannot conceive how he found you. I am overjoyed to hear that you could muster enough Hindostance to talk with him, and hear some of those adventures which my natural modesty might have scrupled to tell you. It would seem from your note, that he has been candour itself, and confessed much that a man of a paler and thinner skin might prefer to have shrouded or evaded. All true, D. ; we have done our brigandage on a grand scale, and divided our prize money without the aid of a prize-court. Keep those trinkets with an easy conscience, and if they leave your own hands for any less worthy still, re-member the adage, ' Ill got, ill gone,' and be comforted. I suppose you are right — you are generally right on a question of worldly craft and prudence—it is better not to attempt the sale of the larger gems in England. St. Petersburg and Vienna are as good markets, and safer.

"El. J. has already told you of our escape into Cashmere: make him narrate the capture of Mansergh, and how he found the Keyserbagh necklace under his saddle. A Queen's officer looting! Only think of the enormity! Did it not justify those proceedings in which Instinct anticipated the finding of a court-martial? The East, and its adventures—a very bulky roll, I assure you—must wait till we meet; and in my next I shall say where, and how, and when: for there is much that I . shall tell that I could not write even to you, Algernon. Respect my delicacy, and be patient.

"I know you are impatient to hear why I am not nearer England—even at Paris—and I am just as impatient to tell you. The address of this will show you where I am. All the writing in the world could not tell you why. No, Drayton; I lie awake at night, questioning, questioning, and in vain. I have gone to the nicest anatomy of my motives, dissecting fibre by fibre, and may I be—a Queen's officer—if I can hit upon an explanation of the mystery. The nearest I can come is, that I feel the place dangerous to me, and, therefore, I cling to it. I know well the feeling that would draw a man back to the spot where he had committed a great crime. Blood is a very glutinous fluid, and has most cohesive properties; but here, in this place, I have done no enormities, and why I hug this coast, except that it be a lee-shore, where shipwreck is very possible, I really cannot make out. Not a bit in love? No, Algy. It is not easy for a man like me to fall in love. Love demands a variety of qualities, which have long left me, if I ever had them. I have little trustfulness, no credulity; I very seldom look back, never look forward; I neither believe in another, nor ask belief in myself. I have seen too much of life to be a dreamer—reality with me denies all place to mere romance. Last of all I cannot argue from the existence of certain qualities in a woman to the certainty of her possessing fifty others that I wish her to have. I only believe what I see, and my moral eyes are affected with cataract; and yet, with all this, there's a girl here—the same, ay, the same, I told you of long ago—that I'd rather marry than I'd be King of Agra, with a British governor-general for my water-carrier! The most maddening of all jealousy is for a woman that one is not in love with! I am not mad, most noble Drayton, though I am occasionally as near it as is safe for the surrounders. With the same determination that this girl says she'll not have me, have I sworn to myself she shall be mine. It is a fair open game, and I leave *you*, who love a wager, to name the winner. I have seen many prettier women—scores of cleverer ones. I am not quite sure that in the matter of those social captivations into which manner enters, she has any especial gifts. She is not a horsewoman, in the real sense of the word, which, once on a time, was a sine quâ non of mine; nor, in fact, has she a peculiar excellence in anything, and yet she gives you the impression of being able to be anything she likes. She has great quickness and great adaptiveness, but she possesses one trait of attraction above all; she utterly rejects *me*, and sets all my arts at defiance. I saw, very soon after I came back here, that she was prepared for a regular siege, and expected a fierce love-suit on my part. I accordingly spiked my heavy artillery, and assumed an attitude of peace-like indolence. I lounged about, chiefly alone; neither avoided nor sought her, and, if I did nothing more, I sorely puzzled her as to what I could mean by my conduct. This was so far a success that it excited her interest, and I saw that she watched and was studying me. She even made faint attempts at little confidences: 'Saw I was unhappy—had something on my mind:' and, for the matter of that, I had plenty—plenty on my conscience, too, if nature had been cruel enough 'o have inflicted me with one. I, of course, said 'No' to all these insinuations. I was not happy nor unhappy. If I sat at the table of life, and did not eat, it was because I had no great appetite. The entertainment did not amuse me much, but I had nowhere particularly to go to. She went one day so far as to hint whether I was not crossed in love? But I assured her not, and I saw her grow very pale as I said it. I even suggested, that though one might have two attacks of the malady, like the measles, the second one was always mild, and never hurt the constitution. Having thus piqued her a little about myself, I gradually unsettled her opinion on other things, frightened her by how the geologists contradict Genesis, and gave her to choose between Monsieur Cuvier and Moses. As for India, I made her believe that we were all heartily ashamed of what we were doing there, spoke of the Hindoo as the model native, and said that if the story of our atrocities were written, Europe would rise up and exterminate us. Hence I had not taken the C.B., nor the V.C., nor any other alphabetical glories. In a word, Drayton, I got her into that frame of restlessness and fever in which all belief smacks of foolish credulity, and the commonest exercise of trust seems like the indulgence of a superstition.

"All this time no mention of Loyd, not a hint of his existence. Yesterday, however, came a fellow here, a certain Mr. Stockwell, with a note of introduction from

Loyd, calling him 'my intimate friend S., whom you have doubtless heard of as a most successful photographer. He is going to India with a commission from the Queen,' &c. We had him to dinner, and made him talk, as all such fellows are ready to talk, about themselves and the fine people who employ them. In the evening we had his portfolio and the peerage, and so delighted was the vulgar dog to have got into the land of coronets and strawberry-leaves, that he would have ignored Loyd if I had not artfuliy brought him to his recollection ; but he came to the memory of 'poor Joe,' as he called him, with such a compassionating pity, that I actually grew to like him. He had been at the vicarage, too, and saw its little homely ways and small economies ; and I laughed so heartily at his stupid descriptions and vapid jokes, that I made the ass think he was witty, and actually repeat them. All this time imagine Florry, pale as a corpse, or scarlet, either half fainting or in a fever, dying to burst in with an angry indignation, and yet restrained by maiden bashfulness. She could bear no more by eleven o'clock, and went off to bed under pretence of a racking headache.

" It is a great blow at any man's favour in a woman's esteem when you show up his particular friend, his near intimate ; and certes, I did not spare Stockwell. You have seen me in this part, and you can give me credit for some powers in playing it.

" ' Could that creature ever have been the dear friend of Joseph ?' said Milly, as he said good-night.

" ' Why not ?' I asked. 'They seem made for each other.'

" Florry was to have come out for a sail this morning with me, but she is not well—I suspect sulky—and has not appeared. I therefore give you the morning that I meant for her. Her excuses have amazed me; because, after my last night's success, and the sorry figure I had succeeded in presenting L. to her, I half hoped my own chances might be looking up. In fact, though I have . been playing a waiting game so patiently, to all appearance, I am driven half mad by self restraint. Come what may, I must end this; besides, to day is the fourth: on the tenth the steamer from Alexandria will touch at Malta; L. will therefore be at Leghorn by the fourteenth, and here two days after—that is to say, in twelve days more my siege must be raised. If I were heavily ironed in a felon's cell with the day of my execution fixed, I could not look to the time with one-half the heart-sinking I now feel.

" I'd give—what would I not give?—to have you near me, though in my soul I know all that you'd say; how you'd preach never minding, letting be, and the rest of it, just as if I could cut out some other work for myself to-morrow, and think no more of her. But I cannot. No Drayton, I cannot. Is it not too hard for the fellow who cut his way through Lahore with sixteen followers, and made a lane through her Majesty's light cavalry, to be worsted, defeated, and disgraced by a young girl, who has neither rank, riches, nor any remarkable beauty to her share, but is simply sustained by the resolve that she'll not have me? Mind, D., I have given her no opportunity of saying this since I came last here: on the contrary, she would, if questioned, be ready—I'd swear to it she would—to say, ' Calvert paid me no attentions, nor made any court to me.' She is very truthful in every-thing, but who is to say what her woman's instinct may not have revealed to her of my love? Has not the woman a man loves always a private key to his heart, and doesn't she go and tumble its contents about, just out of curiosity, ten times a day? Not that she'd ever find a great deal either in or on mine. Neither the indictments for murder or manslaughter, nor that other heavier charge for H. T., have left their traces within my pericardium, and I could stand to back myself not to rave in a compromising fashion if I had a fever to-morrow. But how hollow all this boasting, when that girl within the closed window-shutter yonder defies me—ay, defies me! Is she to go off to her wedding with the inner consciousness of this victory? There's the thought that is driving me mad, and will, I am certain, end by producing some dire mischief—what the doctors call a lesion—in this unhappy brain of mine. And now, as I sit here in listless idleness, that other fellow is hastening across Egypt, or ploughing his way through the Red Sea, to come and marry her! I ask you, D., what amount of philosophy is required to bear up under this?

"I conclude I shall leave this some time next week—not to come near England, though—for I foresee that it will soon be out where, how, and with whom I have been spending my holidays. Fifty fellows must suspect, and some half-dozen must know all about it. America, I take it, must be my ground—as well there as anywhere else —but I can't endure a plan, so enough of this. Don't write to me till you hear again, for I shall leave this certainly, though where for, not so certain.

"What a deal of trouble and uncertainty that girl might spare me if she'd only consent to say 'Yes.' If I see her alone this evening, I half think I shall ask her.

"Farewell for a while, and believe me,
"Yours ever,
"HARRY C.

"P.S. Nine o'clock, evening. Came down to dinner

looking exceedingly pretty, and dressed to perfection.
All spite and malice, I'm certain. Asked me to take
her out to sail to-morrow. We are to go off on an ex-
ploring expedition to an island—'que sais je?'

"The old Grainger looks on me with aunt-like eyes.
She has seen a bracelet of carbuncles in dull gold,
the like of which Loyd could not give her were he to
sell justice for twenty years to come. I have hinted
that I mean them for my mother-in-law whenever I
marry, and she understands that the parentage admits
of a representative. All this is very ignoble on my
part; but if I knew of anything meaner that would
ensure me success, I'd do it also.

" What a stunning vendetta on this girl, if she were
at last to consent, to find out whom she had married,
and *what.* Think of the winter nights' tales, of the
charges that hang over me, and their penalties. Im-
agine the Hue and Cry as light reading for the honey-
moon ! "

He added one line on the envelope, to say he would
write again on the morrow; but his promise he did
not keep.

CHAPTER XXIII.

A STORM.

THE boat excursion mentioned in Calvert's letter was not the only pleasure-project of that day. It was settled that Mr. Stockwell should come out and give Milly a lesson in photography, in which, under Loyd's former guidance, she had already made some progress. He was also to give Miss Grainger some flower-seeds of a very rare kind, of which he was carrying a store to the Pasha of Egypt, and which required some peculiar skill in the sowing. They were to dine, too, at a little rustic house beside the lake; and, in fact, the day was to be one of festivity and enjoyment.

The morning broke splendidly; and though a few clouds lingered about the Alpine valleys, the sky over the lake was cloudless, and the water was streaked and marbled with those parti-coloured lines which Italian lakes wear in the hot days of midsummer. It was one of those autumnal mornings in which the mellow colouring of the mature season blends with the soft air and gentle breath of spring, and all the features of landscape are displayed in their fullest beauty. Calvert and Florence were to visit the Isola de San Giulio, and bring back great clusters of the flowers of the "San Guiseppe" trees, to deck the dinner-table. They were also to go on as far as Pella for ice or snow to cool their wine, the voyage being, as Calvert said, a blending of the picturesque with the profitable.

Before breakfast was over the sky grew slightly overcast, and a large mass of dark cloud stood motionless over the summit of Monterone.

"What will the weather do, Carlo?" asked Calvert of the old boatman of the villa, as he came to say that all was in readiness.

"Who knows, 'cellenza?" said he, with a native shrug of the shoulders. "Monterone is a big traitor of a mountain, and there's no believing him. If that cloud scatters, the day will be fine; if the wind brings down fresh clouds from the Alps it will come on a 'burrasca.'"

"Always a burrasca; how I am sick of your burrasca," said he, contemptuously. "If you were only once in your life to see a real storm, how you'd despise those petty jobbles, in which rain and sleet play the loudest part."

"What does he say of the weather?" asked Florence, who saw that Calvert had walked on to a little point with the old man, to take a freer view of the lake.

"He says, that if it neither blows hard nor rains, it will probably be fine. Just what he has told us every day since I came here."

"What about this fine trout that you spoke of, Carlo?"

"It is at Gozzano, 'cellenza; we can take it as we go by."

"But we are going exactly in the opposite direction, my worthy friend; we are going to the island, and to Pella."

"That is different," said the old man, with another shrug of the shoulders.

"Didn't you hear thunder? I'm sure I did," cried Miss Grainger.

"Up yonder it's always growling," said Calvert, point-

15—2

ing towards the Simplon. "It is the first welcome travellers get when they pass the summit."

"Have you spoken to him, Milly, about Mr. Stockwell? Will he take him up at Orta, and land him here?" asked Miss Grainger, in a whisper.

"No, aunt; he hates Stockwell, he says. Carlo can take the blue boat and fetch him. They don't want Carlo, it seems."

"And are you going without a boatman, Florry?" asked her aunt.

"Of course we are. Two are quite cargo enough in that small skiff, and I trust I am as skilful a pilot as any Ortese fisherman," broke in Calvert.

"Oh, I never disputed your skill, Mr. Calvert."

"What, then, do you scruple to confide your niece to me?" said he, with a low whisper, in which the tone was more menace than mere inquiry. "Is this the first time we have ever gone out in a boat together?"

She muttered some assurance of her trustfulness, but so confusedly, and with such embarrassment, as to be scarcely intelligible. "There! that was certainly thunder!" she cried.

"There are not three days in three months in this place without thunder. It is the Italian privilege, I take it, to make always more noise than mischief."

"But will you go if it threatens so much?" said Miss Grainger.

"Ask Florry. For *my* part, I think the day will be a glorious one."

"I'm certain it will," said Florence, gaily; "and I quite agree with what Harry said last night. Disputing about the weather has the same effect as firing great guns: it always brings down the rain."

Calvert smiled graciously at hearing himself quoted.

It was the one sort of flattery he liked the best, and it rallied him out of his dark humour. "Are you ready?" —he had almost added "dearest," and only caught himself in time—perhaps, indeed, not completely in time— for she blushed, as she said, "Eccomi."

The sisters affectionately embraced each other. Emily even ran after Florence to kiss her once again, after parting, and then Florry took Calvert's arm, and hastened away to the jetty. "I declare," said she, as she stepped into the boat, "this leave-taking habit, when one is going out to ride, or to row, or to walk for an hour, is about the stupidest thing I know of."

"I always said so. It's like making one's will every day before going down to dinner. It is quite true you may chance to die before the dessert, but the mere possibility should not interfere with your asking for soup. No, no, Florry, you are to steer; the tiller is yours for to-day; my post is here;" and he stretched himself at the bottom of the boat, and took out his cigar. The light breeze was just enough to move the little lateen sail, and gradually it filled out, and the skiff stole quietly away from shore, without even a ripple on the water.

"What's the line, Florry? 'Hope at the helm, pleasure at the prow,' or is it love at the helm?"

"A bad steersman, I should say; far too capricious," cried she, laughing.

"I don't know. I think he has one wonderful attribute; he has got wings to fly away with whenever the boat is in danger, and I believe it is pretty much what love does always."

"Can't say," said she, carelessly. "Isn't that a net yonder? Oughtn't we to steer clear of it?"

"Yes. Let her fall off—so—that's enough. What a nice light hand you have."

" On a horse they tell me my hand is very light."

" How I'd like to see you on my Arab ' Said.' Such a creature ! so large-eyed, and with such a full nostril, the face so concave in front, the true Arab type, and the jaw a complete semicircle. How proud he'd look under you, with that haughty snort he gives, as he bends his knee. He was the present of a great Rajah to me—one of those native fellows we are graciously pleased to call rebels, because they don't fancy to be slaves. Two years ago he owned a territory about the size of half Spain, and he is now something like a brigand chief, with a few hundred followers."

" Dear Harry, do not talk of India—at least not of the mutiny."

" Mutiny ! Why call it mutiny, Florry ? Well, love, I have done," he muttered, for the word escaped him, and he feared how she might resent it.

" Come back to my lightness of hand."

" Or of heart, for I sorely suspect, Florence, the quality is not merely a manual one."

" Am I steering well ?"

" Perfectly. Would that I could sail on and on for ever thus :

> Over an ocean just like this,
> A life of such untroubled bliss."

Calvert threw in a sentimental glance with this quotation.

" In other words, an existence of nothing to do," said she, laughing, " with an excellent cigar to beguile it."

" Well, but ' ladye faire,' remember that I have earned some repose. I have not been altogether a carpet knight. I have had my share of lance and spear, and amongst fellows who handle their weapons neatly."

"You are dying to get back to Ghoorkas and Sikhs; but I won't have it. I'd rather hear Metastasio or Petrarch, just now."

"What if I were to quote something apposite, though it were only prose — something out of the Promessi Sposi ?"

She made no answer, and turned away her head.

"Put up your helm a little : let the sails draw freely. This is very enjoyable ; it is a right royal luxury. I'm not sure Antony ever had his galley steered by Cleopatra; had he ?"

"I don't know ; but I do know that I am not Cleopatra nor you Antony."

"How readily you take one up for a foolish speech, as if these rambling indiscretions were not the soul of such converse as ours. They are like the squalls, that only serve to increase our speed and never risk our safety, and, somehow, I feel to-day as if my temper was all of that fitful and capricious kind. I suppose it is the over-happiness. Are you happy, Florry ?" asked he, after a pause.

"If you mean, do I enjoy this glorious day and our sail, yes, intensely. Now, what am I to do? The sail is flapping in spite of me."

"Because the wind has chopped round, and is coming from the eastward. Down your helm, and let her find her own way. We have the noble privilege of not caring whither. How she spins through it now."

"It is immensely exciting," said she, and her colour heightened as she spoke.

"Have you superstitions about dates?" he asked, after another pause.

"No; I don't think so.   My life has been so uneventful.   Few days record anything memorable.   But why did you ask?"

"I am—I am a devout believer in lucky and unlucky days, and had I only bethought me this was a Friday, I'd have put off our sail till to-morrow."

"It is strange to see a man like you attach importance to these things."

"And yet it is exactly men like me who do so. Superstitions belong to hardy, stern, rugged races, like the northmen, even more than the natives of southern climes.   Too haughty and too self-dependent to ask counsel from others like themselves, they seek advice in the occult signs and faint whispers of the natural world. Would you believe it, that I cast a horoscope last night to know if I should succeed in the next project I undertook?"

"And what was the answer?"

"An enigma to this purpose : that if what I undertook corresponded with the entrance of Orion into the seventh house——Why are you laughing?"

"Is it not too absurd to hear such nonsense from you?"

"Was it not the grotesque homage of the witch made Macbeth a murderer?   What are you doing, child? Luff—luff up ; the wind is freshening."

"I begin to think there should be a more skilful hand on the tiller.   It blows freshly now."

"In three days more, Florence," said he gravely, "it will be exactly two years since we sailed here all alone. Those two years have been to me like a long, long life, so much of danger and trouble and suffering have been compassed in them.   Were I to tell you all, you'd own that few men could have borne my burden without being crushed by it. It was not death in any common shape that I confronted; but I must not speak of this. What I would say is, that through all the perils I passed, one image floated before me—one voice was in my ear. It was yours."

"Dear Harry, let me implore you not to go back to these things."

"I must, Florence—I must," said he, still more sadly. "If I pain you, it is only your fair share of suffering."

"My fair share! And why?"

"For this reason. When I knew you first, I was a worn-out, weary, heart-sick man of the world. Young as I was, I was weary of it all; I thought I had tasted of whatever it had of sweet or bitter. I had no wish to renew my experiences. I felt there was a road to go, and I began my life-journey without interest, or anxiety or hope. You taught me otherwise, Florence; you re-vived the heart that was all but cold, and brought it back to life and energy; you inspired me with high ambitions and noble desires; you gave confidence where there had been distrust, and hope where there had been indifference."

"There, there!" cried she, eagerly; "there comes another squall. You must take the helm; I am getting frightened."

"You are calmer than I am, Florence dearest. Hear me out. Why, I ask you—why call me back to an ex-istence which you intended to make valueless to me? Why ask me to go a road where you refuse to journey?"

"Do come here! I know not what I am doing. And see, it grows darker and darker over yonder!"

"You steered me into stormier waters, and had few compunctions for it. Hear me out, Florence. For you I came back to a life that I ceased to care for; for you I took on me cares, and dangers, and crosses, and conquered them all; for you I won honours, high rewards, and riches, and now I come to lay them at your feet, and say, 'Weigh all these against the proofs of that other man's affection. Put into one scale these successes, won alone for *you;* these trials, these wounds—and into the other some humdrum letters of that good-enough creature, who is no more worthy of *you* than he has the courage to declare it.'"

As he spoke a clap of thunder, sharp as a cannon-shot, broke above their heads, and a squall struck the boat aloft, bending her over till she half filled with water, throwing at the same time the young girl from her place to the lee-side of the boat.

Lifting her up, Calvert placed her on the seat, while he supported her with one arm, and with the other hand grasped the tiller.

"Is there danger?" whispered she faintly.

"No, dearest, none. I'll bale out the water when the wind lulls a little. Sit close up here, and all will be well."

The boat, however, deeply laden, no longer rose over the waves, but dipped her bow and took in more water at every plunge.

"Tell me this hand is mine, my own dearest Florence —mine for ever, and see how it will nerve my arm. I am powerless if I am hopeless. Tell me that I have something to live for, and I live."

"Oh, Harry, is it when my heart is dying with fear that you ask me this? Is it generous—is it fair? There! the sail is gone! the ropes are torn across."

"It is only the jib, darling, and we shall be better without it. Speak, Florence! say it is my own wife I am saving—not the bride of that man, who, if he were here, would be at your feet in craven terror this instant."

"There goes the mast!"

At the word the spar snapped close to the thwart and fell over the side, carrying the sail with it. The boat now lay with one gunwale completely under water, helpless and water-logged. A wild shriek burst from the girl, who thought all was lost.

"Courage, dearest—courage! she'll float still. Hold close to me and fear nothing. It is not Loyd's arm that you have to trust to, but that of one who never knew terror!"

The waves surged up now with every heaving of the boat, so as to reach their breasts, and, sometimes striking on the weather-side, broke in great sheets of water over them.

"Oh, can you save us, Harry—can you save us?" cried she.

"Yes, if there's aught worth saving," said he, sternly. "It is not safety that I am thinking of; it is what is to come after. Have I your promise? Are you mine?"

"Oh! do not ask me this; have pity on me."

"Where is your pity for me? Be quick, or it will be too late. Answer me—mine or his?"

"His to the last!" cried she, with a wild shriek; and clasping both her hands above her head, she would have fallen had he not held her.

"One chance more. Refuse me, and I leave you to your fate!" cried he, sternly.

She could not speak, but in the agony of her terror she threw her arms around and clasped him wildly. The dark dense cloud that rested on the lake was rent asunder by a flash of lightning at the instant, and a sound like a thousand great guns shook the air. The wind skimming the sea, carried sheets of water along and almost submerged the boat as they passed.

"Yes or no!" shouted Calvert, madly, as he struggled to disengage himself from her grasp.

"No!" she cried, with a wild yell that rung above all the din of the storm, and as she said it he threw her arms wide and flung her from him. Then, tearing off his coat, plunged into the lake.

The thick clouds as they rolled down from the Alps to meet the wind, settled over the lake, making a blackness almost like night, and only broken by the white flashes of the lightning. The thunder rolled out as it alone does in these mountain regions, where the echoes keep on repeating till they fill the very air with their deafening clamour. Scarcely was Calvert a few yards from the boat than he turned to swim back to her, but already was she hid from his view. The waves ran high, and the drift foam blinded him at every instant. He shouted out at the top of his voice; he screamed "Florence! Florence!" but the din around drowned his weak efforts, and he could not even hear his own words. With his brain mad by excitement, he fancied every instant that he heard his name called, and turned, now hither, now thither, in wild confusion. Meanwhile, the storm deepened, and the wind smote the sea with frequent claps, sharp and sudden as the rush of steam from some great steam-pipe. Whether his head reeled with the terrible uproar around, or that his mind gave way between agony and doubt, who can tell? He swam madly on and on, breasting the waves with his strong chest, and lost to almost all consciousness, save of the muscular effort he was making—none saw him more!

The evening was approaching, the storm had subsided, and the tall Alps shone out in all the varied colours of rock, or herbage, or snow-peak ; and the blue lake at the foot, in its waveless surface, repeated all their grand outlines and all their glorious tints. The water was covered with row-boats in every direction, sent out to seek for Florence and her companion. They were soon perceived to cluster round one spot, where a dismasted boat lay half-filled with water, and a figure, as of a girl sleeping, lay in the stern, her head resting on the gunwale. It was Florence, still breathing, still living, but terror-stricken, lost to all consciousness, her limbs stiffened with cold. She was lifted into a boat and carried on shore.

Happier for her the long death-like sleep—that lasted for days —than the first vague dawn of consciousness, when her senses returning, brought up the terrible memory of the storm, and the last scene with Calvert. With a heart-rending cry for mercy she would start up in bed, and, before her cry had well subsided, would come the consciousness that the peril was past, and then, with a mournful sigh, would she sink back again to try and regain sufficient self-control to betray nothing ; not even of him who had deserted her.

Week after week rolled by, and she made but slow progress towards recovery. There was not, it is true, what the doctors could pronounce to be malady—her heightened pulse alone was feverish—but a great shock had shaken her, and its effects remained in an utter apathy and indifference to everything around her.

She wished to be alone — to be left in complete solitude, and the room darkened. The merest stir or movement in the house jarred on her nerves and irritated her, and with this came back paroxysms of excitement that recalled the storm and the wreck. Sad, therefore, and sorrowful to see as were the long hours of her dreary apathy, they were less painful than these intervals of acute sensibility; and between the two her mind vibrated.

One evening about a month after the wreck, Emily came down to her aunt's room to say that she had been speaking about Joseph to Florry. "I was telling her how he was detained at Calcutta, and could not be here before the second mail from India; and her reply was, 'It is quite as well. He will be less shocked when he sees me.'"

"Has she never asked about Calvert?" asked the old lady.

"Never. Not once. I half suspect, however, that she overheard us that evening when we were talking of him, and wondering that he had never been seen again. For she said afterwards, 'Do not say before me what you desire me not to hear, for I hear frequently when I am unable to speak, or even make a sign in reply.'"

"But it is strange that nothing should ever be known of him."

"No, aunt. Carlo says several have been drowned in this lake whose bodies have never been found. He has some sort of explanation, about deep currents that set in amongst the rocks at the bottom, which I could not understand."

The days dragged on as before. Miss Grainger, after some struggles about how to accomplish the task, took courage, and wrote to Miss Sophia Calvert, to inform her of the disastrous event which had occurred and the loss of her cousin. The letter was, however, left without any acknowledgment whatever, and save in some chance whisperings between Emily and her aunt, the name of Calvert was never spoken of again.

Only a few days before Christmas a telegram told them that Loyd had reached Trieste, and would be with them in a few days. By this time Florence had recovered much of her strength and some of her looks. She was glad, very glad to hear that Joseph was coming; but her joy was not excessive. Her whole nature seemed to have been toned down by that terrible incident to a state of calm resignation to accept whatever came with little of joy or sorrow; to submit to rather than partake of, the changeful fortunes of life. It was thus Loyd found her when he came, and, to his thinking, she was more charming, more lovable than ever. The sudden caprices, which so often had worried him, were gone, and in their place there was a gentle tranquillity of character which suited every trait of his own nature, and rendered her more than ever companionable to him. Warned by her aunt and sister to avoid the topic of the storm, he never alluded to it in any shape to Florence; but one evening, as, after a long walk together, she lay down to rest before tea-time, he took Milly's arm and led her into the garden.

"She has told me all, Milly," said he, with some emotion; "at least, all that she can remember of that terrible day."

CHAPTER XXIV.

THE LAST AND THE SHORTEST.

LOYD was married to Florence; and they went to India, and in due time—even earlier than due time—he was promoted from rank to rank till he reached the dignity of chief judge of a district, a position which he filled with dignity and credit.

Few were more prosperous in all the relations of their lives. They were fortunate in almost everything, even to their residence near Simlah, on the slope of the Himalaya: they seemed to have all the goods of fortune at their feet. In India, where hospitality is less a virtue than a custom, Loyd's house was much frequented, his own agreeable manners, and the charming qualities of his wife, had given them a wide-spread notoriety, and few journeyed through their district without seeking their acquaintance.

"You don't know who is coming here to dinner, to-day, Florry," said Loyd, one morning at breakfast; "some one you will be glad to see, even for a memory of Europe—Stockwell."

"Stockwell? I don't remember Stockwell."

"Not remember him? And he so full of the charming reception you gave him at Orta, where he photographed the villa, and you and Emily in the porch, and Aunt Grainger washing her poodle in the flower-garden?"

"Oh, to be sure I do, but he would never let us have

a copy of it, he was so afraid Aunt Grainger would take it ill; and then he went away very suddenly; if I mistake not, he was called off by telegram on the very day he was to dine with us."

"Perhaps he'll have less compunctions now that your aunt is so unlikely to see herself so immortalised. I'm to go over to Behasana to fetch him, and I'll ask if he has a copy."

His day's duties over, Loyd went across to the camp where his friend Stockwell was staying. He brought him back, and the photographs were soon produced.

"My wife," said Loyd, "wishes to see some of her old Italian scenes. Have you any of those you took in Italy?"

"Yes, I have some half-dozen yonder. There they are, with their names on the back of them. This was the little inn you recommended me to stop at, with the vine terrace at the back of it. Here, you see the clump of cypress-trees next the boat-house."

"Ay, but she wants a little domestic scene at the villa, with her aunt making the morning toilet of her poodle. Have you got that?"

"To be sure I have; and—not exactly as a pendant to it, for it is terrific rather than droll—I have got a storm-scene that I took the morning I came away. The horses were just being harnessed, for I received a telegram informing me I must be at Ancona two days earlier than I looked for to catch the Indian mail, and I was taking the last view before I started. I was in a tremendous hurry, and the whole thing is smudged and scarce distinguishable. It was the grandest storm I ever witnessed. The whole sky grew black, and seemed to descend to meet the lake, as it was lashed to fury by the

16

wind.　I had to get a peasant to hold the instrument for me as I caught one effect—merely one.　The moment was happy, it was just when a great glare of lightning burst through the black mass of cloud, and lit up the centre of the lake, at the very moment that a dismasted boat was being drifted along to, I suppose, certain destruction.　Here it is, and here are, as well as I can make out, two figures. They are certainly figures, blurred as they are, and that is clearly a woman clinging to a man who is throwing her off: the action is plainly that. I have called it a Rent in a Cloud."

"Don't bring this to-day, Stockwell," said Loyd, as the cold sweat burst over his face and forehead ; "and when you talk of Orta to my wife, say nothing of the Rent in a Cloud."

ST. PATRICK'S EVE.

THE FIRST ERA.

IT was on the 16th of March, the eve of St. Patrick, not quite twenty years ago, that a little village on the bank of Lough Corrib was celebrating in its annual fair "the holy times," devoting one day to every species of enjoyment and pleasure, and on the next, by practising prayers and penance of various kinds, as it were to prepare their minds to resume their worldly duties in a frame of thought more seemly and becoming.

If a great and wealthy man might smile at the humble preparations for pleasure displayed on this occasion, he could scarcely scoff at the scene which surrounded them. The wide valley, encircled by lofty mountains, whose swelling outlines were tracked against the blue sky, or mingled gracefully with clouds, whose forms were little less fantastic and wild. The broad lake, stretching away into the distance, and either lost among the mountain-passes. or contracting as it approached the ancient city of Galway: a few, and but very few, islands marked its surface, and these rugged and rocky; on one alone a human trace was seen—the ruins of an ancient church; it was a mere gable now, but you could still track out the humble limits it had occupied—scarce space sufficient

for twenty persons; such were once, doubtless, the full
number of converts to the faith who frequented there.
There was a wild and savage grandeur in the whole: the
very aspect of the mountains proclaimed desolation, and
seemed to frown defiance at the efforts of man to subdue
them to his use; and even the herds of wild cattle seemed
to stray with caution among the cliffs and precipices of
this dreary region. Lower down, however, and as if in
compensation of the infertile tract above, the valley was
marked by patches of tillage and grassland, and studded
with cottages; which, if presenting at a nearer inspection
indubitable signs of poverty, yet to the distant eye bespoke
something of rural comfort, nestling as they often did be-
neath some large rock, and sheltered by the great turf-
stack, which even the poorest possessed. Many streams
wound their course through this valley; along whose
borders, amid a pasture brighter than the emerald, the
cattle grazed, and there, from time to time, some peasant
child sat fishing as he watched the herd.

Shut in by lake and mountain, this seemed a little
spot apart from all the world; and so, indeed, its inhabit-
ants found it. They were a poor but not unhappy race
of people, whose humble lives had taught them nothing
of the comforts and pleasures of richer communities. Po-
verty had, from habit, no terrors for them; short of actual
want, they never felt its pressure heavily.

Such were they who now were assembled to celebrate
the festival of their Patron Saint. It was drawing towards
evening; the sun was already low, and the red glare that
shone from behind the mountains showed that he was
near his setting. The business of the fair was almost con-
cluded; the little traffic so remote a region could supply,
the barter of a few sheep, the sale of a heifer, a moun-
tain pony, or a flock of goats, had all passed off, and

now the pleasures of the occasion were about to succeed. The votaries to amusement, as if annoyed at the protracted dealings of the more worldly minded, were somewhat rudely driving away the cattle that still continued to linger about; and pigs and poultry were beginning to discover that they were merely intruders. The canvas booths, erected as shelter against the night-air, were becoming crowded with visitors; and from more than one of the number the pleasant sounds of the bagpipe might now be heard, accompanied by the dull shuffling tramp of heavily-shod feet.

Various shows and exhibitions were also in preparation, and singular announcements were made by gentlemen in a mingled costume of Turk and Thimble-rigger, of "wonderful calves with two heads;" "six-legged pigs;" and an "infant of two years old that could drink a quart of spirits at a draught, if a respectable company were assembled to witness it;"—a feat which, for the honour of young Ireland, it should be added, was ever postponed from a deficiency in the annexed condition. Then there were "restaurants" on a scale of the most primitive simplicity, where boiled beef, or "spoleen," was sold from a huge pot, suspended over a fire in the open air, and which was invariably surrounded by a gourmand party of both sexes; gingerbread and cakes of every fashion and every degree of indigestion also abounded; while jugs and kegs flanked the entrance to each tent, reeking with a most unmistakable odour of that prime promoter of native drollery and fun—poteen. All was stir, movement, and bustle; old friends, separated since the last occasion of a similar festivity, were embracing cordially, the men kissing with an affectionate warmth no German ever equalled; pledges of love and friendship were taken in brimming glasses by many, who were perhaps to renew the opportunity for such testimonies hereafter, by a fight that very evening ; contracts ratified by whisky, until that moment not deemed binding ; and courtships, prosecuted with hopes, which the whole year previous had never suggested ; kind speeches and words of welcome went round ; while here and there some closely-gathered heads and scowling glances gave token, that other scores were to be acquitted on that night than merely those of commerce ; and in the firmly knitted brow, and more firmly grasped blackthorn, a practised observer could foresee, that some heads were to carry away deeper marks of that meeting, than simple memory can impress ;—and thus, in this wild sequestered spot, human passions were as rife as in the most busy communities of pampered civilisation. Love, hate, and hope, charity, fear, forgiveness, and malice ; long-smouldering revenge, long-subdued affection ; hearts pining beneath daily drudgery, suddenly awakened to a burst of pleasure and a renewal of happiness in the sight of old friends, for many a day lost sight of ; words of good cheer ; half mutterings of menace ; the whispered syllables of love ; the deeply-uttered tones of vengeance ; and amid all, the careless reckless glee of those, who appeared to feel the hour one snatched from the grasp of misery, and devoted to the very abandonment of pleasure. It seemed in vain that want and poverty had shed their chilling influence over hearts like these. The snow-drift and the storm might penetrate their frail dwellings ; the winter might blast, the hurricane might scatter their humble hoardings ; but still the bold high-beating spirit that lived within, beamed on throughout every trial ; and now, in the hour of long-sought enjoyment, blazed forth in a flame of joy, that was all but frantic.

The step that but yesterday fell wearily upon the

ground, now smote the earth with a proud beat, that told
of manhood's daring ; the voices were high, the eyes were
flashing ; long pent-up emotions of every shade and com-
plexion were there ; and it seemed a season where none
should wear disguise, but stand forth in all the fearless-
ness of avowed resolve ; and in the heart-home looks of
love, as well as in the fiery glances of hatred, none prac-
tised concealment. Here, went one with his arm round
his sweetheart's waist,—an evidence of accepted affection
none dared even to stare at ; there, went another, the skirt
of his long loose coat thrown over his arm, in whose
hand a stick was brandished—his gesture, even without
his wild hurroo ! an open declaration of battle, a challenge
to all who liked it. Mothers were met in close conclave,
interchanging family secrets and cares ; and daughters,
half conscious of the parts they themselves were playing
in the converse, passed looks of sly intelligence to each
other. And beggars were there too—beggars of a class
which even the eastern Dervish can scarcely vie with :
cripples brought many a mile away from their mountain-
homes to extort charity by exhibitions of dreadful de-
formity ; the halt, the blind, the muttering idiot, the
moping melancholy mad, mixed up with strange and mot-
ley figures in patched uniforms and rags—some, amusing
the crowd by their drolleries, some, singing a popular
ballad of the time—while through all, at every turn and
every corner, one huge fellow, without legs, rode upon an
ass, his wide chest ornamented by a picture of himself,
and a paragraph setting forth his infirmities. He, with
a voice deeper than a bassoon, bellowed forth his prayer
for alms, and seemed to monopolise far more than his
proportion of charity, doubtless owing to the more art-
istic development to which he had brought his profes-
sion. " De prayers of de holy Joseph be an yez, and re-

lieve de maimed; de prayers and blessins of all de saints on dem that assists de sufferin!" And there were pilgrims, some with heads venerable enough for the canvas of an old master, with flowing beards, and relics hung round their necks, objects of worship which failed not to create sentiments of devotion in the passers-by. But among these many sights and sounds, each calculated to appeal to different classes and ages of the motley mass, one object appeared to engross a more than ordinary share of attention; and although certainly not of a nature to draw marked notice elsewhere, was here sufficiently strange and uncommon to become actually a spectacle. This was neither more nor less than an English groom, who, mounted upon a thoroughbred horse, led another by the bridle, and slowly paraded backwards and forwards, in attendance on his master.

"Them's the iligant bastes, Darby," said one of the bystanders, as the horses moved past. "A finer pair than that I never seen."

"They're beauties, and no denying it," said the other; "and they've skins like a looking-glass."

"Arrah, botheration t' yez! what are ye saying about their skins?" cried a third, whose dress and manner betokened one of the rank of a small farmer. "'Tis the breeding that's in 'em; that's the raal beauty. Only look at their pasterns; and see how fine they run off over the quarter."

"Which is the best now, Phil?" said another, addressing the last speaker with a tone of some deference.

"The gray horse is worth two of the dark chestnut," replied Phil oracularly.

"Is he, then?" cried two or three in a breath. "Why is that, Phil?"

"Can't you perceive the signs of blood about the ears? They're long, and coming to a point——"

"You're wrong this time, my friend," said a sharp voice, with an accent which in Ireland would be called English. "You may be an excellent judge of an ass, but the horse you speak of, as the best, is not worth a fourth part of the value of the other." And so saying, a young and handsome man, attired in a riding costume, brushed somewhat rudely through the crowd, and seizing the rein of the led horse, vaulted lightly into the saddle and rode off, leaving Phil to the mockery and laughter of the crowd, whose reverence for the opinion of a gentleman was only beneath that they accorded to the priest himself.

"Faix, ye got it there, Phil!" "'Tis down on ye he was that time!" "Musha, but ye may well get red in the face!"

Such and such-like were the comments on one who but a moment before was rather a popular candidate for public honours.

"Who is he, then, at all?" said one among the rest, and who had come up too late to witness the scene.

"'Tis the young Mr. Leslie, the landlord's son, that's come over to fish the lakes," replied an old man reverentially.

"Begorra, he's no landlord of mine, anyhow," said Phil, now speaking for the first time. "I hould under Mister Martin, and his family was here before the Leslies was heard of." These words were said with a certain air of defiance, and a turn of the head around him, as though to imply, that if any one would gainsay the opinion, he was ready to stand by and maintain it. Happily for the peace of the particular moment, the crowd were nearly all Martins, and so, a simple buzz of approbation followed this announcement. Nor did their attention dwell much longer on the matter, as most were already occupied in watching the progress of the young man, who, at a fast swinging gallop, had taken to the fields beside the lake, and was now seen flying in succession over each dyke and wall before him, followed by his groom. The Irish passion for feats of horsemanship made this the most fascinating attraction of the fair; and already, opinions ran high among the crowd, that it was a race between the two horses, and more than one maintained, that "the little chap with the belt" was the better horse-man of the two. At last, having made a wide circuit of the village and the green, the riders were seen slowly moving down, as if returning to the fair.

There is no country where manly sports and daring exercises are held in higher repute than Ireland. The chivalry that has died out in richer lands still reigns there; and the full meed of approbation will ever be his, who can combine address and courage before an Irish crowd. It is needless to say, then, that many a word of praise and commendation was bestowed on young Leslie. His handsome features, his slight but well-formed figure, every particular of his dress and gesture, had found an advocate and an admirer; and while some were lavish in their epithets on the perfection of his horsemanship, others, who had seen him on foot, asserted, "that it was then he looked well entirely." There is a kind of epidemic character pertaining to praise. The snow-ball gathers not faster by rolling, than do the words of eulogy and approbation; and so now, many recited little anec-dotes of the youth's father, to show that he was a very pattern of landlords and country gentlemen, and had only one fault in life,—that he never lived among his tenantry.

"'Tis the first time I ever set eyes on him," cried one,

"and I hould my little place under him twenty-three years come Michaelmas."

"See now then, Barney," cried another, "I'd rather have a hard man that would stay here among us, than the finest landlord ever was seen that would be away from us. And what's the use of compassion and pity when the say would be between us? 'Tis the agent we have to look to."

"Agent! 'Tis wishing them, I am, the same agents! Them's the boys has no marcy for a poor man : I'm tould now "—and here the speaker assumed a tone of oracular seriousness that drew several listeners towards him—"I'm tould now, the agents get a guinea for every man, woman, and child they turn out of a houldin." A low murmur of indignant anger ran through the group, not one of whom ventured to disbelieve a testimony thus accredited.

"And sure when the landlords does come, divil a bit they know about us — no more nor if we were in Swayden ; didn't I hear the ould gentleman down there last summer, pitying the people for the distress. 'Ah,' says he, 'it's a hard sayson ye have, and obliged to tear the flax out of the ground, and it not long enough to cut !'"

A ready burst of laughter followed this anecdote, and many similar stories were recounted in corroboration of the opinion.

"That's the girl takes the shine out of the fair," said one of the younger men of the party, touching another by the arm, and pointing to a tall young girl, who, with features as straight and regular as a classic model, moved slowly past. She did not wear the scarlet cloak of the peasantry, but a large one of dark blue, lined with silk of the same colour ; a profusion of brown hair, dark and glossy, was braided on each side of her face, and turned up at the back of the head with the grace of an antique cameo. She seemed not more than nineteen years of age, and in the gaze of astonishment and pleasure she threw around her, it might be seen how new such scenes and sights were to her.

"That's Phil Joyce's sister, and a crooked disciple of a brother she has," said the other; "sorra bit if he'd ever let her come to the 'pattern' afore to-day; and she's the raal ornament of the place now she's in it."

"Just mind Phil, will ye! watch him now; see the frown he's giving the boys as they go by, for looking at his sister.   I wouldn't coort a girl that I couldn't look in the face and see what was in it, av she owned Ballina-hinch Castle," said the former.

"There now; what is he at now?" whispered the other; "he's left her in the tent there: and look at him, the way he's talking to ould Bill; he's telling him some-thing about a fight; never mind me agin, but there'll be 'wigs on the green' this night."

"I don't know where the Lynches and the Connors is to-day," said the other, casting a suspicious look around him, as if anxious to calculate the forces available in the event of a row.   "They gave the Joyces their own in Ballinrobe last fair.   I hope they're not afeard to come down here."

"Sorra bit, ma bouchal," said a voice from behind his shoulder; and at the same moment the speaker clapped his hands over the other's eyes: "who am I, now?"

"Arrah! Owen Connor; I know ye well," said the other; "and 'tis yourself ought not to be here to-day. The ould father of ye has nobody but yourself to look after him."

"I'd like to see ye call him ould to his face," said

Owen, laughing : " there he is now, in Poll Dawley's tent, dancing."

" Dancing ! " cried the other two in a breath.

" Aye, faix, dancing ' The little bould fox ; ' and may I never die in sin, if he hasn't a step that looks for all the world as if he made a hook and eye of his legs."

The young man who spoke these words was in mould and gesture the very ideal of an Irish peasant of the west ; somewhat above the middle size, rather slightly made, but with the light and neatly turned proportion that betokens activity, more than great strength, endurance, rather than the power of any single effort.   His face well became the character of his figure ; it was a handsome and an open one, where the expressions changed and crossed each other with lightning speed, now, beaming with good nature, now, flashing in anger, now, sparkling with some witty conception, or frowning a bold defiance as it met the glance of some member of a rival faction. He looked, as he was, one ready and willing to accept either part from fortune, and to exchange friendship and hard knocks with equal satisfaction.   Although in dress and appearance he was both cleanly and well clad, it was evident that he belonged to a very humble class among the peasantry.   Neither his hat nor his greatcoat, those un-erring signs of competence, had been new for many a day before ; and his shoes, in their patched and mended condition, betrayed the pains it had cost him to make even so respectable an appearance as he then presented.

" She didn't even give you a look to-day, Owen," said one of the former speakers ; " she turned her head the other way as she went by."

" Faix, I'm afeard ye've a bad chance," said the other, slily.

" Joke away, boys, and welcome," said Owen, reddening to the eyes as he spoke, and showing that his indifference to their banterings was very far from being real; "'tis little I mind what ye say,—as little as she herself would mind *me*," added he to himself.

"She's the purtiest girl in the town-land, and no second word to it,—and even if she hadn't a fortune——"

"Bad luck to the fortune!—that's what I say," cried Owen, suddenly; "'tis that same that breaks my rest night and day; sure if it wasn't for the money, there's many a dacent boy wouldn't be ashamed nor afeard to go up and coort her."

"She'll have two hundred, divil a less, I'm tould," interposed the other; "the ould man made a deal of money in the war-time."

"I wish he had it with him now," said Owen, bitterly.

"By all accounts he wouldn't mislike it himself. When Father John was giving him the rites, he says, 'Phil,' says he, 'how ould are ye now?' and the other didn't hear him, but went on muttering to himself; and the priest says agin, ''Tis how ould you are, I'm axing.' 'A hundred and forty-three,' says Phil, looking up at him. 'The saints be good to us,' says Father John, 'sure you're not that ould,—a hundred and forty-three?' 'A hundred and forty-seven.' 'Phew! he's more of it—a hundred and forty-seven!' 'A hundred and fifty,' cries Phil, and he gave the foot of the bed a little kick, this way—sorra more—and he died; and what was it but the guineas he was countin' in a stocking under the clothes all the while? ·Oh, musha! how the sowl was in the money, and he going to leave it all! I heerd Father John say, 'it was well they found it out, for there'd be a curse on them guineas, and every hand that would touch one of them *in secla seclorum;*' and they wer' all tuck away in a bag that night, and buried by the priest in a saycret place, where they'll never be found till the Day of Judgment."

Just as the story came to its end, the attention of the group was drawn off by seeing numbers of people running in a particular direction, while the sound of voices and the general excitement showed something new was going forward. The noise increased, and now, loud shouts were heard, mingled with the rattling of sticks and the utterance of those party cries so popular in an Irish fair. The young men stood still as if the affair was a mere momentary ebullition not deserving of attention, nor sufficiently important to merit the taking any farther interest in it; nor did they swerve from the resolve thus tacitly formed, as from time to time some three or four would emerge from the crowd, leading forth one, whose bleeding temples, or smashed head, made retreat no longer dishonourable.

"They're at it early," was the cool commentary of Owen Connor, as with a smile of superciliousness he looked towards the scene of strife.

"The Joyces is always the first to begin," remarked one of his companions.

"And the first to lave off too," said Owen; "two to one is what they call fair play."

"That's Phil's voice!—there now, do you hear him shouting?"

"'Tis that he's best at," said Owen, whose love for the pretty Mary Joyce was scarcely equalled by his dislike of her ill-tempered brother.

At this moment the shouts became louder and wilder, the screams of the women mingling with the uproar, which no longer seemed a mere passing skirmish, but a downright severe engagement.

"What is it all about, Christy?" said Owen, to a

young fellow led past between two friends, while the track of blood marked every step he went.

"'Tis well it becomes yez to ax," muttered the other, with his swollen and pallid lips, "when the Martins is beating your landlord's eldest son to smithereens."

"Mr. Leslie—young Mr. Leslie?" cried the three together; but a wild war-whoop from the crowd gave the answer back. "Hurroo! Martin for ever! Down with the Leslies! Ballinashough! Hurroo! Don't leave one of them livin! Beat their sowles out!"

"Leslie for ever!" yelled out Owen, with a voice heard over every part of the field; and with a spring into the air, and a wild flourish of his stick, he dashed into the crowd.

"Here's Owen Connor, make way for Owen;" cried the non-combatants, as they jostled and parted each other, to leave a free passage for one whose prowess was well known.

"He'll lave his mark on some of yez yet!" "That's the boy will give you music to dance to!" "Take that, Barney!" "Ha! Tarry, that made your nob ring like a forty-shilling pot!" Such and suck-like were the comments on him who now, reckless of his own safety, rushed madly into the very midst of the combatants, and fought his way onwards to where some seven or eight were desperately engaged over the fallen figure of a man. With a shrill yell no Indian could surpass, and a bound like a tiger, Owen came down in the midst of them, every stroke of his powerful blackthorn telling on his man as unerringly as though it were wielded by the hand of a giant.

"Save the young Master, Owen! Shelter him! Stand over him, Owen Connor!" were now the cries from all sides; and the stout-hearted peasant, striding over the body of young Leslie, cleared a space around him, and, as

he glanced defiance on all sides, called out, "Is that your
courage, to beat a young gentleman that never handled a
stick in his life? Oh, you cowardly set! Come and face
the men of your own barony if you dare! Come out on
the green and do it!—Pull him away—pull him away
quick," whispered he to his own party eagerly. "Tear-
an-ages! get him out of this before they're down on me."

As he spoke, the Joyces rushed forward with a cheer,
their party now trebly as strong as the enemy. They
bore down with a force that nothing could resist. Poor
Owen—the mark for every weapon—fell almost the first,
his head and face one indistinguishable mass of blood
and bruises, but not before some three or four of his
friends had rescued young Leslie from his danger, and
carried him to the outskirts of the fair. The fray now
became general, neutrality was impossible, and self-defence
almost suggested some participation in the battle. The
victory was, however, with the Joyces. They were on
their own territory; they mustered every moment stronger;
and in less than half-an-hour they had swept the enemy
from the field, save where a lingering wounded man re-
mained, whose maimed and crippled condition had
already removed him from all the animosities of combat.

"Where's the young master?" were the first words
Owen Connor spoke, as his friends carried him on the
door of a cabin, hastily unhinged for the purpose, towards
his home.

"Erra! he's safe enough, Owen," said one of his
bearers, who was by no means pleased that Mr. Leslie
had made the best of his way out of the fair, instead of
remaining to see the fight out.

"God be praised for that same, anyhow!" said Owen
piously. "His life was not worth a 'trawneen' when I
seen him first."

17

"It may be supposed from this speech, and the previous conduct of him who uttered it, that Owen Connor was an old and devoted adherent to the Leslie family, from whom he had received many benefits, and to whom he was linked by long acquaintance. Far from it. He neither knew Mr. Leslie nor his father. The former he saw for the first time as he stood over him in the fair; the latter he had never so much as set eyes upon, at any time; neither had he or his been favoured by them. The sole tie that subsisted between them—the one link that bound the poor man to the rich one—was that of the tenant to his landlord. Owen's father and grandfather before him had been cottiers on the estate; but being very poor and humble men, and the little farm they rented, a half-tilled half-reclaimed mountain tract, exempt from all prospect of improvement, and situated in a remote and unfrequented place, they were merely known by their names on the rent-roll. Except for this, their existence had been as totally forgotten, as though they had made part of the wild heath upon the mountain.

While Mr. Leslie lived in ignorance that such people existed on his property, they looked up to him with a degree of reverence almost devotional. The owner of the soil was a character actually sacred in their eyes; for what respect and what submission were enough for one, who held in his hands the destinies of so many; who could raise them to affluence, or depress them to want, and by his mere word control the agent himself, the most dreaded of all those who exerted an influence on their fortunes?

There was a feudalism, too, in this sentiment that gave the reverence a feeling of strong allegiance. The landlord was the head of a clan, as it were: he was the culminating point of that pyramid of which they formed the base; and they were proud of every display of his wealth and his power, which they deemed as ever reflecting credit upon themselves. And then, his position in the county—his rank—his titles—the amount of his property—his house—his retinue—his very equipage, were all subjects on which they descanted with eager delight, and proudly exalted in contrast with less favoured proprietors. At the time we speak of absentecism had only begun to impair the warmth of this affection ; the traditions of a resident landlord were yet fresh in the memory of the young ; and a hundred traits of kindness and good-nature were mingled in their minds with stories of grandeur and extravagance, which, to the Irish peasant's ear, are themes as grateful as ever the gorgeous pictures of Eastern splendour were to the heightened imagination and burning fancies of Oriental listeners.

Owen Connor was a firm disciple of this creed. Perhaps his lone sequestered life among the mountains, with no companionship save that of his old father, had made him longer retain these convictions in all their force, than if, by admixture with his equals, and greater intercourse with the world, he had conformed his opinions to the gradually changed tone of the country. It was of little moment to him what might be the temper or the habits of his landlord. The monarchy—and not the monarch of the soil—was the object of his loyalty ; and he would have deemed himself disgraced and dishonoured had he shown the slightest backwardness in his fealty. He would as soon have expected that the tall fern that grew wild in the valley should have changed into a blooming crop of wheat, as that the performance of such a service could have met with any requital. It was, to his thinking, a simple act of duty, and required not any prompting of high principle, still less any suggestion of self-interest. Poor Owen, therefore, had not even a sentiment of heroism to cheer him, as they bore him slowly along, every inequality of the ground sending a pang through his aching head that was actually torture.

"That's a mark you'll carry to your dying day, Owen, my boy," said one of the bearers, as they stopped for a moment to take breath. "I can see the bone there shining this minute."

"It must be good stuff anyways the same head," said Owen, with a sickly attempt to smile. "They never put a star in it yet; and faix I seen the sticks cracking like dry wood in the frost."

"It's well it didn't come lower down," said another, examining the deep cut, which gashed his forehead from the hair down to the eyebrow. "You know what the Widow Glynn said at Peter Henessy's wake, when she saw the stroke of the scythe that laid his head open—it just come, like yer own, down to that—'Ayeh!' says she, 'but he's the fine corpse; and wasn't it the Lord spared his eye!'"

"Stop, and good luck to you, Freney, and don't be making me laugh; the pain goes through my brain like the stick of a knife," said Owen, as he lifted his trembling hands and pressed them on either side of his head.

They wetted his lips with water, and resumed their way, not speaking aloud as before, but in a low undertone, only audible to Owen at intervals; for he had sunk into a half-stupid state, they believed to be sleep. The path each moment grew steeper; for, leaving the wild "boreen" road, which led to a large bog on the mountain-side, it wound now upwards, zigzagging between masses of granite rock and deep tufts of heather, where sometimes the foot sunk to the instep. The wet and spongy soil increased the difficulty greatly; and although all strong and powerful men, they were often obliged to halt and rest themselves.

"It's an iligant view, sure enough," said one, wiping his dripping forehead with the tail of his coat. "See there! look down where the fair is, now! it isn't the size of a good griddle, the whole of it. How purty the lights look shining in the water!"

"And the boats, too! Musha! they're coming up more of them. There'll be good divarshin there, this night." These last words, uttered with a half sigh, showed with what a heavy heart the speaker saw himself debarred from participating in the festivity.

"'Twas a dhroll place to build a house then, up there," said another, pointing to the dark speck, far, far away on the mountain, where Owen Connor's cabin stood.

"Owen says yez can see Galway of a fine day, and the boats going out from the Claddagh; and of an evening, when the sun is going down, you'll see across the bay, over to Clare, the big cliffs of Mogher."

"Now, then! are ye in earnest? I don't wonder he's so fond of the place after all. It's an iligant thing to see the whole world, and fine company besides. Look at Lough Mask! Now, boys, isn't that beautiful with the sun on it?"

"Come, it's getting late, Freney, and the poor boy ought to be at home before night;" and once more they lifted their burden and moved forward.

For a considerable time they continued to ascend without speaking, when one of the party in a low cautious voice remarked, "Poor Owen will think worse of it, when he hears the reason of the fight, than for the cut on the head—bad as it is."

"Musha; then he needn't," replied another; "for if

ye mane about Mary Joyce, he never had a chance of her."

"I'm not saying that he had," said the first speaker; "but he's just as fond of her; do you mind the way he never gave back one of Phil s blows, but let him hammer away as fast as he plazed?"

"What was it at all, that Mr. Leslie did?" asked another; "I didn't hear how it begun yet."

"Nor I either, rightly; but I believe Mary was standing looking at the dance, for she never foots a step herself—maybe she's too ginteel—and the young gentleman comes up and axes her for a partner; and something she said; but what does he do, but put his arm round her waist and gives her a kiss; and, ye see, the other girls laughed hearty, because they say Mary's so proud and high, and thinking herself above them all. Phil wasn't there at the time; but he heerd it afterwards, and come up to the tent, as young Mr. Leslie was laving it, and stood before him and wouldn't let him pass. 'I've a word to say to ye,' says Phil, and he scarce able to spake with passion; 'that was my sister ye had the impudence to take a liberty with.' 'Out of the way, ye bogtrotter,' says Leslie; them's the very words he said; 'out of the way, ye bog-trotter, or I'll lay my whip across your shoulders.' 'Take that first,' says Phil; and he put his fist between his two eyes, neat and clean;—down went the squire as if he was shot. You know the rest yourselves. The boys didn't lose any time, and if 'twas only two hours later, maybe the Joyces would have got as good as they gave."

A heavy groan from poor Owen now stopped the conversation, and they halted to ascertain if he were worse—but no; he seemed still sunk in the same heavy sleep as before, and apparently unconscious of all about him. Such, however, was not really the case; by some strange phenomenon of sickness, the ear had taken in each low and whispered word, at the time it would have been deaf to louder sounds; and every syllable they had spoken had already sunk deeply into his heart; happily for him, this was but a momentary pang; the grief stunned him at once, and he became insensible.

It was dark night as they reached the lonely cabin where Owen lived, miles away from any other dwelling, and standing at an elevation of more than a thousand feet above the plain. The short, sharp barking of a sheep-dog was the only sound that welcomed them; for the old man had not heard of his son's misfortune until long after they quitted the fair. The door was hasped and fastened with a stick; precaution enough in such a place, and for all that it contained, too. Opening this, they carried the young man in, and laid him upon the bed; and, while some busied themselves in kindling a fire upon the hearth, the others endeavoured, with such skill as they possessed, to dress his wounds, an operation which, if not strictly surgical in all its details, had at least the recommendation of tolerable experience in such matters.

" It's a nate little place when you're at it, then," said one of them, as with a piece of lighted bog-pine he took a very leisurely and accurate view of the interior.

The opinion, however, must be taken by the reader, as rather reflecting on the judgment of him who pronounced it, than in absolute praise of the object itself. The cabin consisted of a single room, and which, though remarkably clean in comparison with similar ones, had no evidence of anything above very narrow circumstances. A little dresser occupied the wall in front of the door, with its usual complement of crockery, cracked and whole; an old chest of drawers, the pride of the house, flanked this on one side; a low settle-bed on the other; various prints in very florid colouring decorated the walls, all religious subjects, where the apostles figured in garments like bathing-dresses; these were intermixed with ballads, dying speeches, and such-like ghostly literature, as form the most interesting reading of an Irish peasant; a few seats of unpainted deal, and a large straw chair for the old man, were the principal articles of furniture. There was a gun, minus the lock, suspended over the fireplace; and two fishing-rods, with a gaff and landing-net, were stretched upon wooden pegs; while over the bed was an earthenware crucifix, with its little cup beneath, for holy water; the whole surmounted by a picture of St. Francis Xavier in the act of blessing somebody: though, if the gesture were to be understood without the explanatory letter-press, he rather looked like a swimmer preparing for a dive. The oars, mast, and spritsail of a boat were lashed to the rafters overhead; for, strange as it may seem, there was a lake at that elevation of the mountain, and one which abounded in trout and perch, affording many a day's sport to both Owen and his father.

Such were the details which, sheltered beneath a warm roof of mountain-fern, called forth the praise we have mentioned; and, poor as they may seem to the reader, they were many degrees in comfort beyond the majority of Irish cabins.

The boys—for so the unmarried men of whatever age are called—having left one of the party to watch over Owen, now quitted the house, and began their return homeward. It was past midnight when the old man returned; and although endeavouring to master any appearance of emotion before the "strange boy," he could with difficulty control his feelings on beholding his son. The shirt matted with blood, contrasting with the livid colourless cheek—the heavy irregular breathing—the frequent startings as he slept—were all sore trials to the old man's nerve; but he managed to seem calm and collected, and to treat the occurrence as an ordinary one.

"Harry Joyce and his brother Luke—big Luke as they call him—has sore bones to-night; they tell me that Owen didn't lave breath in their bodies," said he with a grim smile, as he took his place by the fire.

"I heerd the ribs of them smashing like an ould turf creel," replied the other.

"'Tis himself can do it," said the old fellow, with eyes glistening with delight; "fair play and good ground, and I'd back him agin the Glen."

"And so you might, and farther too; he has the speret in him—that's better nor strength, any day."

And thus consoled by the recollection of Owen's prowess, and gratified by the hearty concurrence of his guest, the old father smoked and chatted away till day-break. It was not that he felt any want of affection for his son, or that his heart was untouched by the sad spectacle he presented—far from this; the poor old man had no other tie to life—no other object of hope or love than Owen; but years of a solitary life had taught him rather to conceal his emotions within his own bosom, than seek for consolation beyond it; besides that, even in his grief the old sentiment of faction-hatred was strong, and vengeance had its share in his thoughts also.

It would form no part of our object in this story, to dwell longer either on this theme, or the subject of Owen's illness; it will be enough to say, that he soon got better, far sooner perhaps than if all the appliances of luxury had ministered to his recovery; most certainly sooner than if his brain had been ordinarily occupied by thoughts and cares of a higher order than his were. The con-flict, however, had left a deeper scar behind than the ghastly wound that marked his brow. The poor fellow dwelt upon the portions of the conversation he overheard as they carried him up the mountain; and whatever might have been his fears before, now he was convinced that all prospect of gaining Mary's love was lost to him for ever.

This depression, natural to one after so severe an injury, excited little remark from the old man; and although he wished Owen might make some effort to exert himself, or even move about in the air, he left him to himself and his own time, well knowing that he never was disposed to yield an hour to sickness, beyond what he felt unavoidable.

It was about eight or nine days after the fair, that the father was sitting mending a fishing-net at the door of his cabin, to catch the last light of the fading day. Owen was seated near him, sometimes watching the progress of the work, sometimes patting the old sheep-dog that nestled close by, when the sound of voices attracted them: they listened, and could distinctly hear persons talking at the opposite side of the cliff, along which the pathway led; and before they could even hazard a guess as to who they were, the strangers appeared at the angle of the rock. The party consisted of two persons; one, a gentleman somewhat advanced in life, mounted on a stout but rough-looking pony—the other, was a countryman, who held the beast by the bridle, and seemed to take the greatest precaution for the rider's safety.

The very few visitors Owen and his father met with were for the most part people coming to fish the mountain-lake, who usually hired ponies in the valley for the ascent; so that when they perceived the animal coming slowly along, they scarce bestowed a second glance upon them, the old man merely remarking, "They're three weeks too early for this water, any how;" a sentiment concurred in by his son. In less than five minutes after the rider and his guide stood before the door.

"Is this where Owen Connor lives?" asked the gentleman.

"That same, yer honour," said old Owen, uncovering his head, as he rose respectfully from his low stool.

"And where is Owen Connor himself?"

"'Tis me, Sir," replied he; "that's my name."

"Yes, but it can scarcely be you that I am looking for; have you a son of that name?"

"Yes, Sir, I'm young Owen," said the young man, rising, but not without difficulty; while he steadied himself by holding the door-post.

"So then I am all right: Tracy, lead the pony about, till I call you;" and so saying, he dismounted and entered the cabin.

"Sit down, Owen; yes, yes—I insist upon it, and do you also. I have come up here to-day to have a few moments' talk with you about an occurrence that took place last week at the fair. There was a young gentleman, Mr. Leslie, got roughly treated by some of the people: let me hear your account of it."

Owen and his father exchanged glances; the same idea flashed across the minds of both, that the visitor was a magistrate come to take information against the Joyces for an assault; and however gladly they would have embraced any course that promised retaliation for their injuries, the notion of recurring to the law was a degree of baseness they would have scorned to adopt.

"I'll take the 'vestment' I never seen it at all," said the old man eagerly, and evidently delighted that no manner of cross-questioning or badgering could convert him into an informer.

"And the little I saw," said Owen, "they knocked out of my memory with this;" and he pointed to the half-healed gash on his forehead.

"But you know something of how the row begun?"

"No, yer honour, I was at the other side of the fair."

"Was young Mr. Leslie in fault—did you hear that?"

"I never heerd that he did any thing—unagreeable," said Owen, after hesitating for a few seconds in his choice of a word.

"So then, I'm not likely to obtain any information from either of you."

They made no reply, but their looks gave as palpable a concurrence to this speech, as though they swore to its truth.

"Well, I have another question to ask. It was you saved this young gentleman, I understand; what was your motive for doing so? when, as by your own confession, you were at a distance when the fight begun."

"He was my landlord's son," said Owen, half roughly; "I hope there is no law agin that."

"I sincerely trust not," ejaculated the gentleman; "have you been long on the estate?"

"Three generations of us now, yer honour," said the old man.

"And what rent do you pay?"

"Oh, musha, we pay enough! we pay fifteen shillings an acre for the bit of callows below, near the lake, and we give ten pounds a year for the mountain—and bad luck to it for a mountain—it's breaking my heart trying to make something out of it."

"Then I suppose you'd be well pleased to exchange your farm, and take one in a better and more profitable part of the country?"

Another suspicion here shot across the old man's

mind; and turning to Owen he said in Irish: "He wants to get the mountain for sporting over; but I'll not lave it."

The gentleman repeated his question.

"Troth, no then, yer honour; we've lived here so long we'll just stay our time in it."

"But the rent is heavy, you say."

"Well, we'll pay it, plaze God."

"And I'm sure it's a strange wild place in winter."

"It's wholesome, any how," was the short reply.

"I believe I must go back again as wise as I came," muttered the gentleman. "Come, my good old man,— and you, Owen; I want to know how I can best serve you, for what you've done for me: it was my son you rescued in the fair——"

"Are you the landlord—is yer honour Mr. Leslie?" exclaimed both as they rose from their seats as horrified as if they had taken such a liberty before royalty.

"Yes, Owen; and I grieve to say, that I should cause so much surprise to any tenant, at seeing me. I ought to be better known on my property; and I hope to become so: but it grows late, and I must reach the valley before night. Tell me, are you really attached to this farm, or have I any other, out of lease at this time, you like better?"

"1 would not leave the ould spot, with yer honour's permission, to get a demesne and a brick house; nor Owen neither."

"Well, then, be it so; I can only say, if you ever change your mind, you'll find me both ready and willing to serve you; meanwhile you must pay no more rent here."

"No more rent!"

"Not a farthing; I'm sorry the favour is so slight a

one, for indeed the mountain seems a bleak and profit-less tract."

"There is not its equal for mutton——"

"I'm glad of it, Owen; and it only remains for me to make the shepherd something more comfortable;— well, take this; and when I next come up here, which I intend to do, to fish the lake, I hope to find you in a better house;" and he pressed a pocket-book into the old man's hand as he said this, and left the cabin: while both Owen and his father were barely able to mutter a blessing upon him, so overwhelming and unexpected was the whole occurrence.

THE SECOND ERA.

ROM no man's life, perhaps, is hope more rigidly excluded than from that of the Irish peasant of a poor district. The shipwrecked mariner upon his raft, the convict in his cell, the lingering sufferer on a sick bed, may hope; but he must not.

Daily labour, barely sufficient to produce the commonest necessaries of life, points to no period of rest or repose; year succeeds year in the same dull routine of toil and privation; nor can he look around him and see one who has risen from that life of misery, to a position of even comparative comfort.

The whole study of his existence, the whole philosophy of his life, is, how to endure; to struggle on under poverty and sickness; in seasons of famine, in times of national calamity, to hoard up the little pittance for his landlord and the payment for his priest, and he has nothing more to seek for. Were it our object here, it would not be difficult to pursue this theme further, and examine, if much of the imputed slothfulness and indolence of the people was not in reality due to that very hopelessness. How little energy would be left to life, if you take away its ambitions; how few would enter upon the race, if there were no goal before them! Our present aim, however, is rather with the fortunes of those we

have so lately left. To these poor men, now, a new
existence opened. Not the sun of spring could more
suddenly illumine the landscape where winter so late
had thrown its shadows, than did prosperity fall brightly
on their hearts, endowing life with pleasures and en-
joyments, of which they had not dared to dream before.

In preferring this mountain-tract to some rich lowland
farm, they were rather guided by that spirit of attach-
ment to the home of their fathers—so characteristic a
trait in the Irish peasant—than by the promptings of
self-interest. The mountain was indeed a wild and
bleak expanse, scarce affording herbage for a few sheep
and goats; the callows at its foot, deeply flooded in
winter, and even by the rains of autumn, made tillage
precarious and uncertain; yet the fact that these were
rent-free, that of its labour and its fruits all was now
their own, inspired hope and sweetened toil. They no
longer felt the dreary monotony of daily exertion, by
which hour was linked to hour, and year to year, in one
unbroken succession;—no; they now could look for-
ward, they could lift up their hearts and strain their eyes
to a future, where honest industry had laid up its store
for the decline of life; they could already fancy the en-
joyments of the summer season, when they should look
down upon their own crops and herds, or think of the
winter nights, and the howling of the storm without, re-
minding them of the blessings of a home.

How little to the mind teeming with its bright and
ambitious aspirings would seem the history of their
humble hopes! how insignificant and how narrow might
appear the little plans and plots they laid for that new
road in life, in which they were now to travel! The
great man might scoff at these, the moralist might frown
at their worldliness; but there is nothing sordid or mean

in the spirit of manly independence ; and they who know the Irish people, will never accuse them of receiving worldly benefits with any forgetfulness of their true and only source. And now to our story.

The little cabin upon the mountain was speedily added to, and fashioned into a comfortable-looking farm-house of the humbler class. Both father and son would willingly have left it as it was ; but the landlord's wish had laid a command upon them, and they felt it would have been a misapplication of his bounty, had they not done as he had desired. So closely, indeed, did they adhere to his injunctions, that a little room was added specially for his use and accommodation, whenever he came on that promised excursion he hinted at. Every detail of this little chamber interested them deeply ; and many a night, as they sat over their fire, did they eagerly discuss the habits and tastes of the " quality," anxious to be wanting in nothing which should make it suitable for one like him. Sufficient money remained above all this ex-penditure to purchase some sheep, and even a cow ; and already their changed fortunes had excited the interest and curiosity of the little world in which they lived.

There is one blessing, and it is a great one, attendant on humble life. The amelioration of condition requires not that a man should leave the friends and companions he has so long sojourned with, and seek, in a new order, others to supply their place ; the spirit of class does not descend to him, or rather, he is far above it ; his altered state suggests comparatively few enjoyments or comforts in which his old associates cannot participate ; and thus the Connors' cabin was each Sunday thronged by the country people, who came to see with their own eyes, and hear with their own ears, the wonderful good for-tune that befell them.

18

Had the landlord been an angel of light, the blessings invoked upon him could not have been more frequent or fervent; each measured the munificence of the act by his own short standard of worldly possessions; and individual murmurings for real or fancied wrongs were hushed in the presence of one such deed of benevolence.

This is no exaggerated picture. Such was peasant-gratitude once; and such, O landlords of Ireland! it might still have been, if you had not deserted the people. The meanest of your favours, the poorest show of your good-feeling, were acts of grace for which nothing was deemed requital. Your presence in the poor man's cabin—your kind word to him upon the highway—your aid in sickness—your counsel in trouble, were ties which bound him more closely to your interest, and made him more surely yours, than all the parchments of your attorney, or all the papers of your agent. He knew you then as something more than the recipient of his earnings. That was a time, when neither the hireling patriot nor the calumnious press could sow discord between you. If it be otherwise now, ask yourselves, are you all blameless? Did you ever hope that affection could be transmitted through your agent, like the proceeds of your property? Did you expect that the attachments of a people were to reach you by the post? Or was it not natural, that, in their desertion by you, they should seek succour elsewhere? that in their difficulties and their trials they should turn to any who might feel or feign compassion for them? Nor is it wonderful that, amid the benefits thus bestowed, they should imbibe principles and opinions fatally in contrast with interests like yours.

There were few on whom good fortune could have fallen, without exciting more envious and jealous feelings on the part of others, than on the Connors. The rugged independent character of the father — the gay light-hearted nature of the son, had given them few enemies and many friends. The whole neighbourhood flocked about them to offer their good wishes and congratulations on their bettered condition, and with an honesty of purpose and a sincerity that might have shamed a more elevated sphere. The Joyces alone showed no participation in this sentiment, or rather, that small fraction of them more immediately linked with Phil Joyce. At first, they affected to sneer at the stories of the Connors' good fortune; and when denial became absurd, they half-hinted that it was a new custom in Ireland for men "to fight for money." These mocking speeches were not slow to reach the ears of the old man and his son; and many thought that the next fair-day would bring with it a heavy retribution for the calamities of the last. In this, however, they were mistaken. Neither Owen nor his father appeared that day; the mustering of their faction was strong and powerful, but they, whose wrongs were the cause of the gathering, never came forward to head them.

This was an indignity not to be passed over in silence; and the murmurs, at first low and subdued, grew louder and louder, until denunciations heavy and deep fell upon the two who "wouldn't come out and right themselves like men." The faction, discomfited and angered, soon broke up; and returning homeward in their several directions, they left the field to the enemy without even a blow. On the succeeding day, when the observances of religion had taken place of the riotous and disorderly proceedings of the fair, it was not customary for the younger men to remain. The frequenters of the place were mostly women; the few of the other sex were either old and feeble men, or such objects of compassion

18—2

as traded on the pious feelings of the votaries so opportunely evoked. It was with great difficulty the worthy priest of the parish had succeeded in dividing the secular from the holy customs of the time, and thus allowing the pilgrims, as all were called on that day, an uninterrupted period for their devotions. He was firm and resolute, however, in his purpose, and spared no pains to effect it: menacing this one—persuading that; suiting the measure of his arguments to the comprehension of each, he either cajoled or coerced, as the circumstance might warrant. His first care was to remove all the temptations to dissipation and excess ; and for this purpose, he banished every show and exhibition, and every tent where gambling and drinking went forward ;— his next, a more difficult task, was the exclusion of all those doubtful characters, who, in every walk of life, are suggestive of even more vice than they embody in themselves. These, however, abandoned the place, of their own accord, so .soon as they discovered how few were the inducements to remain ; until at length, by a tacit understanding, it seemed arranged, that the day of penance and mortification should suffer neither molestation nor interruption from those indisposed to partake of its benefits. So rigid was the priest in exacting compliance in this matter, that he compelled the tents to be struck by daybreak, except by those few, trusted and privileged individuals, whose ministerings to human wants were permitted during the day of sanctity.

And thus the whole picture was suddenly changed. The wild and riotous uproar of the fair, the tumult of voices and music, dancing, drinking, and fighting, were gone ; and the low monotonous sound of the pilgrims' prayers was heard, as they moved along upon their knees to some holy well or shrine, to offer up a prayer, or return a thanksgiving for blessings bestowed. The scene was a strange and picturesque one; the long lines of kneeling figures, where the rich scarlet cloak of the women predominated, crossed and recrossed each other as they wended their way to the destined altar; their muttered words blending with the louder and more boisterous appeals of the mendicants,—who, stationed at every convenient angle or turning, besieged each devotee with unremitting entreaty,—deep and heartfelt devotion in every face, every lineament and feature impressed with religious zeal and piety; but still, as group met group going and returning, they interchanged their greetings between their prayers, and mingled the worldly salutations with aspirations heavenward, and their " Paters," and Aves," and " Credos," were blended with enquiries for the " childer," or questions about the " crops."

" Isn't that Owen Connor, avich, that's going there, towards the Yallow-well?" said an old crone as she ceased to count her beads.

"You're right enough, Biddy; 'tis himself, and no other; it's a turn he took to devotion since he grew rich."

"Ayeh! ayeh! the Lord be good to us! how fond we all be of life, when we've the bit of bacon to the fore!" And with that she resumed her pious avocations with redoubled energy, to make up for lost time.

The old ladies were as sharp-sighted as such functionaries usually are in any sphere of society. It was Owen Connor himself, performing his first pilgrimage. The commands of his landlord had expressly forbidden him to engage in any disturbance at the fair; the only mode of complying with which, he rightly judged, was by absenting himself altogether. How this conduct was construed by others, we have briefly hinted at. As for himself, poor fellow, if a day of mortification could have availed him any thing, he needn't have appeared among the pilgrims;—a period of such sorrow and suffering he had never undergone before. But in justice it must be confessed it was devotion of a very questionable character that brought him there that morning. Since the fair-day, Mary Joyce had never deigned to notice him; and though he had been several times at mass, she either affected not to be aware of his presence, or designedly looked in another direction. The few words of greeting she once gave him on every Sunday morning—the smile she bestowed—dwelt the whole week in his heart, and made him long for the return of the time, when, even for a second or two, she would be near, and speak to him. He was not slow in supposing how the circumstances under which he rescued the landlord's son might be used against him by his enemies; and he well knew that she was not surrounded by any others than such. It was, then, with a heavy heart poor Owen witnessed how fatally his improved fortune had dashed hopes far dearer than all worldly advantage. Not only did the new comforts about him become distasteful, but he even accused them to himself as the source of all his present calamity; and half suspected that it was a judgment on him for receiving a reward in such a cause. To see her—to speak to her if possible—was now his wish, morn and night; to tell her that he cared more for one look, one glance, than for all the favours fortune did or could bestow; this, and to undeceive her as to any knowledge of young Leslie's rudeness to herself, was the sole aim of his thoughts. Stationing himself therefore in an angle of the ruined church, which formed one of the resting-places for prayer, he waited for hours for Mary's coming;

and at last, with a heart half sickened with deferred hope, he saw her pale but beautiful features, shaded by the large blue hood of her cloak, as with downcast eyes she followed in the train.

"Give me your place, acushla; God will reward you for it; I'm late at the station," said he, to an old ill-favoured hag that followed next to Mary; and at the same time, to aid his request, slipped half-a-crown into her hand.

The wrinkled face brightened into a kind of wicked intelligence as she muttered in Irish: "'Tis a gould guinea the same place is worth; but I'll give it to you for the sake of yer people;" and at the same time pocketing the coin in a canvas pouch, among relics and holy clay, she moved off, to admit him in the line.

Owen's heart beat almost to bursting, as he found himself so close to Mary; and all his former impatience to justify himself, and to speak to her, fled in the happiness he now enjoyed. No devotee ever regarded the relic of a saint with more trembling ecstasy than did he the folds of that heavy mantle that fell at his knees; he touched it as men would do a sacred thing. The live-long day he followed her, visiting in turn each shrine and holy spot; and ever, as he was ready to speak to her, some fear that, by a word, he might dispel the dream of bliss he revelled in, stopped him, and he was silent.

It was as the evening drew near, and the pilgrims were turning towards the lake, beside which, at a small thorn-tree, the last "station" of all was performed, that an old beggar, whose importunity suffered none to escape, blocked up the path, and prevented Mary from proceeding until she had given him something. All her money had been long since bestowed ; and she said so, hurriedly, and endeavoured to move forward.

"Let Owen Connor, behind you, give it, acushla ! He's rich now, and can well afford it," said the cripple.

She turned round at the words ; the action was involuntary, and their eyes met. There are glances which reveal the whole secret of a lifetime ; there are looks which dwell in the heart longer and deeper than words. Their eyes met for merely a few seconds ; and while in *her* face offended pride was depicted, poor Owen's sorrow-struck and broken aspect spoke of long suffering and grief so powerfully, that, ere she turned away, her heart had half forgiven him.

"You wrong me hardly, Mary," said he, in a low, broken voice, as the train moved on. "The Lord, he knows my heart this b!essed day ! *Pater noster, qui es in cœlis !*" added he, louder, as he perceived that his immediate follower had ceased his prayers to listen to him. " He knows that I'd rather live and died the poorest— *Beneficat tuum nomen !*" cried he, louder. And then, turning abruptly, said,—

" Av it's plazing to you, Sir, don't be trampin' on my heels. I can't mind my devotions, an' one so near me."

" It's not so unconvaynient, maybe, when they're afore you," muttered the old fellow, with a grin of sly malice. And though Owen overheard the taunt, he felt no inclination to notice it.

" Four long years I've loved ye, Mary Joyce ; and the sorra more encouragement I ever got nor the smile ye used to give me. And if ye take *that* from me, now— Are ye listening to me, Mary ? do ye hear me, asthore ? —Bad scran to ye, ye ould varmint ! why don't ye keep behind ? How is a man to save his sowl, an' you making him blasphame every minit ?"

"I was only listenin' to that iligant prayer ye were saying," said the old fellow, drily.

"'Tis betther you'd mind your own, then," said Owen, fiercely; "or, by the blessed day, I'll teach ye a new penance ye never heerd of afore!"

The man dropped back, frightened at the sudden determination these words were uttered in; and Owen resumed his place.

"I may never see ye again, Mary. 'Tis the last time you'll hear me spake to you. I'll lave the ould man. God look to him! I'll lave him now, and go be a sodger. Here we are now, coming to this holy well; and I'll swear an oath before the Queen of Heaven, that before this time to-morrow——"

"How is one to mind their prayers at all, Owen Connor, if ye be talking to yourself, so loud?" said Mary, in a whisper, but one which lost not a syllable, as it fell on Owen's ear.

"My own sweet darling, the light of my eyes, ye are!" cried he, as with clasped hands he muttered blessings upon her head; and with such vehemence of gesture, and such unfeigned signs of rapture, as to evoke remarks from some beggars near, highly laudatory of his zeal.

"Look at the fine young man there, prayin' wid all his might. Ayeh, the saints give ye the benefit of your pilgrimage!"

"Musha! but ye'r a credit to the station; ye put yer sowl in it, anyhow!" said an old Jezebel, whose hard features seemed to defy emotion.

Owen looked up; and directly in front of him, with his back against a tree, and his arms crossed on his breast, stood Phil Joyce; his brow was dark with passion, and his eyes glared like those of a maniac. A cold thrill ran through Owen's heart, lest the anger thus displayed should fall on Mary; for he well knew with what tyranny the poor girl was treated. He therefore took the moment of the pilgrims' approach to the holy tree, to move from his place, and, by a slightly circuitous path, came up to where Joyce was standing.

"I've a word for you, Phil Joyce," said he, in a low voice, where every trace of emotion was carefully subdued. "Can I spake it to you here?"

Owen's wan and sickly aspect, if it did not shock, it at least astonished Joyce, for he looked at him for some seconds without speaking; then said, half rudely,—

" Ay, here will do as well as anywhere, since ye didn't like to say it yesterday."

There was no mistaking this taunt; the sneer on Owen's want of courage was too plain to be misconstrued; and although for a moment he looked as if disposed to resent it, he merely shook his head mournfully, and replied: "It is not about that I came to speak; it's about your sister, Mary Joyce."

Phil turned upon him a stare of amazement, as quickly followed by a laugh, whose insulting mockery made Owen's cheek crimson with shame.

"True enough, Phil Joyce; I know your meanin' well," said he, with an immense effort to subdue his passion. "I'm a poor cottier, wid a bit of mountain-land— sorra more—and has no right to look up to one like her. But listen to me, Phil," and here he grasped his arm, and spoke with a thick guttural accent: "Listen to me! Av the girl wasn't what she is, but only your sister, I'd scorn her as I do yourself;" and, with that, he pushed him from him with a force that made him stagger. Before he had well recovered, Owen was again at his side, and continued :—" And now, one word more, and all's ended between us. For you, and your likings or mislikings, I never cared a rush; but 'tis Mary herself refused me, so there's no more about it; only don't be wreaking your temper on her, for she has no fault in it."

"Av a sister of mine ever bestowed a thought on the likes o' ye, I'd give her the outside of the door this night," said Joyce, whose courage now rose from seeing several of his faction attracted to the spot, by observing that he and Connor were conversing. "'Tis a disgrace —divil a less than a disgrace to spake of it!"

"Well, we won't do so any more, plaze God!" said Owen, with a smile of very fearful meaning. "It will be another little matter we'll have to settle when we meet next. There's a score there not paid off yet:" and at the word he lifted his hat, and disclosed the deep mark of the scarce-closed gash on his forehead: "and so, goodbye to ye."

A rude nod from Phil Joyce was all the reply, and Owen turned homewards.

If prosperity could suggest the frame of mind to enjoy it, the rich would always be happy; but such is not the dispensation of Providence. Acquisition is but a stage on the road of ambition; it lightens the way, but brings the goal no nearer. Owen never returned to his mountain-home with a sadder heart. He passed without regarding them, the little fields, now green with the coming spring; he bestowed no look nor thought upon the herds that already speckled the mountain-side; disappointment had embittered his spirit; and even love itself now gave way to faction-hate, the old and cherished animosity of party.

If the war of rival factions did not originally spring from the personal quarrels of men of rank and station, who stimulated their followers and adherents to acts of aggression and reprisal, it assuredly was perpetuated, if not with their concurrence, at least permission; and many

were not ashamed to avow, that in these savage encoun-
ters the "bad blood" of the country was "let out" at less
cost and trouble than by any other means. When legal
proceedings were recurred to, the landlord, in his capa-
city of magistrate, maintained the cause of his tenants;
and, however disposed to lean heavily on them himself,
in the true spirit of tyranny he opposed pressure from
any other hand than his own. The people were grateful
for this advocacy—far more, indeed, than they often
proved for less questionable kindness. They regarded
the law with so much dread—they awaited its decisions
with such uncertainty—that he who would conduct them
through its mazes was indeed a friend. But, was the
administration of justice, some forty or fifty years back
in Ireland, such as to excite or justify other sentiments?
Was it not this tampering with right and wrong, this
recurrence to patronage, that made legal redress seem an
act of meanness and cowardice among the people? No
cause was decided upon its own merits. The influence
of the great man—the interest he was disposed to take
in the case—the momentary condition of county politics
—with the general character of the individuals at issue,
usually determined the matter; and it could scarcely be
expected that a triumph thus obtained should have exer-
cised any peaceful sway among the people.

"He wouldn't be so bould to-day, av his landlord
wasn't to the fore," was Owen Connor's oft-repeated re-
flection, as he ascended the narrow pathway towards his
cabin; "'tis the good backing makes us brave, God help
us!" From that hour forward the gay light-hearted pea-
sant became dark, moody, and depressed; the very cir-
cumstances which might be supposed calculated to have
suggested a happier frame of mind, only increased and
embittered his gloom. His prosperity made daily labour

no longer a necessity. Industry, it is true, would have brought more comforts about him, and surrounded him with more appliances of enjoyment; but long habits of endurance had made him easily satisfied on this score, and there were no examples for his imitation which should make him strive for better. So far, then, from the landlord's benevolence working for good, its operation was directly the reverse; his leniency had indeed taken away the hardship of a difficult and onerous payment, but the relief suggested no desire for an equivalent amelioration of condition. The first pleasurable emotions of gratitude over, they soon recurred to the old customs in everything, and gradually fell back into all the observances of their former state, the only difference being, that less exertion on their parts was now called for than before.

Had the landlord been a resident on his property—acquainting himself daily and hourly with the condition of his tenants—holding up examples for their imitation—rewarding the deserving—discountenancing the unworthy—extending the benefits of education among the young, and fostering habits of order and good conduct among all, Owen would have striven among the first for a place of credit and honour, and speedily have distinguished himself above his equals. But, alas! no; Mr. Leslie, when not abroad, lived in England. Of his Irish estates he knew nothing, save through the half-yearly accounts of his agent. He was conscious of excellent intentions; he was a kind, even a benevolent man; and in the society of his set, remarkable for more than ordinary sympathies with the poor. To have ventured on any reflection on a landlord before him, would have been deemed a downright absurdity.

He was a living refutation of all such calumnies; yet how was it that, in the district he owned, the misery of

the people was a thing to shudder at? that there were
hovels excavated in the bogs, within which human beings
lingered on between life and death, their existence like
some terrible passage in a dream? that beneath these
frail roofs famine and fever dwelt, until suffering, and star-
vation itself, had ceased to prey upon minds on which
no ray of hope ever shone? Simply he did not know
of these things; he saw them not; he never heard of
them.   He was aware that seasons of unusual distress oc-
curred, and that a more than ordinary degree of want was
experienced by a failure of the potato crop; but on these
occasions he read his name, with a subscription of a hun-
dred pounds annexed, and was not that a receipt in full
for all the claims of conscience?   He ran his eyes over
a list in which royal and princely titles figured, and he
expressed himself grateful for so much sympathy with
Ireland! But did he ask himself the question, whether
if he had resided among his people, such necessities for
alms-giving had ever arisen? Did he enquire how far his
own desertion of his tenantry—his ignorance of their
state—his indifference to their condition—had fostered
these growing evils? Could he acquit himself of the
guilt of deriving all the appliances of his ease and en-
joyment, from those whose struggles to supply them were
made under the pressure of disease and hunger? Was
unconsciousness of all this an excuse sufficient to stifle
remorse? Oh, it is not the moneyed wealth dispensed by
the resident great man; it is not the stream of affluence,
flowing in its thousand tiny rills, and fertilising as it
goes, we want. It is far more the kindly influence
of those virtues which find their congenial soil in easy
circumstances; benevolence, sympathy, succour in sick-
ness, friendly counsel in distress, timely aid in trouble,
encouragement to the faint-hearted, caution to the over·

eager: these are gifts, which, giving, makes the bestower richer; and these are the benefits which, better than gold, foster the charities of life among a people, and bind up the human family in a holy and indissoluble league. No benevolence from afar, no well wishings from distant lands, compensate for the want of them. To neglect such duties is to fail in the great social compact by which the rich and poor are united, and, what some may deem of more moment still, to resign the rightful influence of property into the hands of dangerous and designing men.

It is in vain to suppose that traditionary deservings will elicit gratitude when the present generation are neglectful. On the contrary, the comparison of the once resident, now absent landlord, excites very different feelings ; the murmurings of discontent swell into the louder language of menace ; and evils, over which no protective power of human origin could avail, are ascribed to that class, who, forgetful of one great duty, are now accused of causing every calamity. If not present to exercise the duties their position demands, their absence exaggerates every accusation against them ; and from the very men, too, who have, by the fact of their desertion, succeeded in obtaining the influence that should be theirs.

Owen felt this desertion sorely. Had Mr. Leslie been at home, he would at once have had recourse to him. Mr. French, the agent, lived on the property—but Mr. French was "a hard man," and never liked the Connors; indeed, he never forgave them for not relinquishing the mountain-farm they held, in exchange for another he offered them, as he was anxious to preserve the mountain for his own shooting. At the time we speak of, intemperance was an Irish vice, and one which prevailed largely. Whisky entered into every circumstance and relation of life. It cemented friendships and ratified contracts; it celebrated the birth of the newly-born, it consoled the weeping relatives over the grave of the departed; it was a welcome and a bond of kindness, and as the stirrup-cup, was the last pledge at parting. Men commemorated their prosperity by drink, and none dared to face gloomy fortune without it. Owen Connor had recourse to it, as to a friend that never betrayed. The easy circumstances, in comparison with many others, he enjoyed, left him both means and leisure for such a course; and few days passed without his paying a visit to the "shebeen-house" of the village. If the old man noticed this new habit, his old prejudices were too strong to make him prompt in condemning it. Indeed, he rather regarded it as a natural consequence of their bettered fortune, that Owen should frequent these places; and as he never returned actually drunk, and always brought back with him the current rumours of the day, as gathered from news-papers and passing gossip, his father relied on such scraps of information for his evening's amusement over the fire.

It was somewhat later than usual that Owen was returning home one night, and the old man, anxious and uneasy at his absence, had wandered part of the way to meet him, when he saw him coming slowly forward, with that heavy weariness of step deep grief and pre-occupation inspire. When the young man had come within speaking distance of his father, he halted suddenly, and looking up at him, exclaimed, "There's sorrowful news for ye to-night, father!"

"I knew it! I knew it well!" said the old man, as he clasped his hands before him, and seemed preparing himself to bear the shock with courage. "I had a dhrame of it last night; and 'tis death, wherever it is."

" You're right there.   The master's dead ! "

Not another word was spoken by either, as side by side they slowly ascended the mountain-path.   It was only when seated at the fireside that Owen regained sufficient collectedness to detail the particulars he had learned in the village.   Mr. Leslie had died of the cholera at Paris.   The malady had just broken out in that city, and he was among its earliest victims.   The terrors which that dreadful pestilence inspired, reached every remote part of Europe, and at last, with all the aggravated horrors of its devastating career, swept across Ireland.   The same letter which brought the tidings of Mr. Leslie's death, was the first intelligence of the plague.   A scourge so awful needed not the fears of the ignorant to exaggerate its terrors ; yet men seemed to vie with each other in their dreadful conjectures regarding it.

All the sad interest the landlord's sudden death would have occasioned under other circumstances was merged in the fearful malady of which he died.   Men heard with almost apathy of the events that were announced as likely to succeed, in the management of the property ; and only listened with eagerness if the pestilence were mentioned. Already its arrival in England was declared ; and the last lingering hope of the devotee was, that the holy island of St. Patrick might escape its ravages.   Few cared to hear what a few weeks back had been welcome news— that the old agent was to be dismissed, and a new one appointed.   The speculations which once would have been rife enough, were now silent.   There was but one terrible topic in every heart and on every tongue—the cholera.

The inhabitants of great cities, with wide sources of information available, and free conversation with each other, can scarcely estimate the additional degree of terror the prospect of a dreadful epidemic inspires among the dwellers in unfrequented rural districts. The cloud, not bigger than a man's hand at first, gradually expands itself, until the whole surface of earth is darkened by its shadow. The business of life stands still; the care for the morrow is lost; the proneness to indulge in the gloomiest anticipations common calamity invariably suggests, heightens the real evil, and disease finds its victims more than doomed at its first approach. In this state of agonising suspense, when rumours arose to be contradicted, reasserted, and again disproved, came the tidings that the cholera was in Dublin. The same week it had broken out in many other places; at last the report went, that a poor man, who had gone into the market of Galway to sell his turf, was found dead on the steps of the chapel. Then, followed the whole array of precautionary measures, and advices, and boards of health. Then, it was announced that the plague was raging fearfully—the hospitals crowded—death in every street.

Terrible and appalling as these tidings were, the fearful fact never realised itself in the little district we speak of, until a death occurred in the town close by. He was a shopkeeper in Oughterarde, and known to the whole neighbourhood. This solitary instance brought with it more of dreadful meaning than all the shock of distant calamity. The heart-rending wail of those who listened to the news smote many more with the cold tremor of coming death. Another case soon followed, a third, and a fourth succeeded, all fatal; and the disease was among them.

It is only when a malady, generally fatal, is associated with the terrors of contagion, that the measure of horror and dread flows over. When the sympathy which suffering sickness calls for is yielded in a spirit of almost despair, and the ministerings to the dying are but the prelude to the same state, then indeed death is armed with all his terrors. No people are more remarkable for the charities of the sick-bed than the poor Irish. It is with them less a sentiment than a religious instinct ; and though they watched the course of the pestilence, and saw few, if any, escape death who took it, their devotion never failed them. They practised with such skill as they possessed, every remedy in turn. They, who trembled but an hour before at the word when spoken, faced the danger itself with a bold heart ; and while the insidious signs of the disease were already upon them—while their wearied limbs and clammy hands bespoke that their own hour was come, they did not desist from their good offices, until past the power to render them.

It was spring-time, the season more than usually mild, the prospects of the year were already favourable, and all the signs of abundance rife in the land. What a contrast the scene without to that presented by the interior of each dwelling ! There, death and dismay were met with at every step. The old man and the infant prostrated by the same stroke ; the strong and vigorous youth who went forth to labour in the morning—at noon, a feeble, broken-spirited creature—at sunset, a corpse.

As the minds and temperaments of men were fashioned, so did fear operate upon them. Some, it made reckless and desperate, careless of what should happen, and in- different to every measure of precaution ; some, became paralysed with fear, and seemed unable to make an effort for safety, were it even attainable ; others, exaggerating every care and caution, lived a life of unceasing terror and anxiety ; while a few—they were unfortunately a very few—summoned courage to meet the danger in a spirit of calm and resolute determination ; while in their re- formed habits t might be seen how thoroughly they felt

9—2

that their own hour might be a brief one. Among these was Owen Connor. From the day the malady appeared in the neighbourhood, he never entered the public-house of the village, but devoting himself to the work of kindness the emergency called for, went from cabin to cabin rendering every service in his power. The poorest depended on him for the supply of such little comforts as they possessed, for at every market-day he sold a sheep or a lamb to provide them; the better-off looked to him for advice and counsel, following his directions as implicitly as though he were a physician of great skill. All recognised his devotedness in their cause, and his very name was a talisman for courage in every humble cabin around. His little ass-cart, the only wheeled vehicle that ever ascended the mountain where he lived, was seen each morning moving from door to door, while Owen brought either some small purchase he was commissioned to make at Oughterarde, or left with the more humble some offering of his own benevolence.

"There's the salt ye bid me buy, Mary Cooney; and here's fourpence out of it,—do ye all be well, still?"

"We are, and thank ye, Owen."

"The Lord keep ye so! How's Ned Daly?"

"He's off, Owen dear; his brother James is making the coffin; poor boy, he looks very weak himself this morning."

The cart moved on, and at length stopped at a small hovel built against the side of a clay ditch. It was a mere assemblage of wet sods with the grass still growing, and covered by some branches of trees and loose straw over them. Owen halted the ass at the opening of the miserable den, through which the smoke now issued, and at the same moment a man, stooping double to permit him to pass out into the open air, came forward: he was apparently about fifty years of age—his real age was not thirty; originally a well-formed and stout-built fellow, starvation and want had made him a mere skeleton. His clothes were, a ragged coat, which he wore next his skin, for shirt he had none, and a pair of worn corduroy trousers; he had neither hat, shoes, nor stockings; but still, all these signs of destitution were nothing in comparison with the misery displayed in his countenance. Except that his lip trembled with a convulsive shiver, not a feature moved—the cheeks were livid and flattened— the dull gray eyes had lost all the light of intelligence, and stared vacantly before him.

"Well, Martin, how is she?"

"I don't know, Owen, dear," said he, in a faltering voice; "maybe 'tis sleeping she is."

Owen followed him within the hut, and stooping down to the fire, lighted a piece of bogwood to enable him to see. On the ground, covered only by a ragged frieze coat, lay a young woman quite dead : her arm, emaciated and livid, was wrapped round a little child of about three years old, still sleeping on the cold bosom of its mother.

"You must take little Patsy away," said Owen in a whisper, as he lifted the boy in his arms ; "*she's* happy now."

The young man fell upon his knees and kissed the corpse, but spoke not a word; grief had stupified his senses, and he was like one but half awake. "Come with me, Martin; come with me, and I'll settle everything for you." He obeyed mechanically, and before quitting the cabin, placed some turf upon the fire, as he was wont to do. The action was a simple one, but it brought the tears into Owen's eyes. "I'll take care of Patsy for you till you want him. He's fond of me of ould, and won't be lonesome with me ; " and Owen wrapped the child in his greatcoat, and moved forwards.

When they had advanced a few paces, Martin stopped suddenly and muttered, "She has nothing to drink !" and then, as if remembering vaguely what had happened, added, " It's a long sleep, Ellen dear !"

Owen gave the directions for the funeral, and leaving poor Martin in the house of one of the cottiers near, where he sat down beside the hearth, and never uttered a word ; he went on his way, with little Patsy still asleep within his arms.

" Where are you going, Peggy ?" asked Owen, as an old lame woman moved past as rapidly as her infirmity would permit : " you're in a hurry this morning."

" So I am, Owen Connor—these is the busy times wid me — I streaked five to-day, early as it is, and I'm going now over to Phil Joyce's. What's the matter wid yourself, Owen ? sit down, avich, and taste this."

" What's wrong at Phil's ?" asked Owen, with a choking fulness in his throat.

" It's the little brother he has ; Billy's got it, they say."

" Is Mary Joyce well—did ye hear ? "

" Errah ! she's well enough now, but she may be low before night," muttered the crone ; while she added, with a fiendish laugh, " her purty faytures won't save her now, no more nor the rest of us."

" There's a bottle of port wine, Peggy ; take it with ye, dear. 'Tis the finest thing at all, I'm tould, for keeping it off—get Mary to take a glass of it ; but mind now, for the love o' ye, never say it was me gav it. There's bad blood between the Joyces and me, ye understand."

" Ay, ay, I know well enough," said the hag, clutching the bottle eagerly, while opening a gate on the road-side, she hobbled on her way towards Phil Joyce's cabin.

It was near evening as Owen was enabled to turn homewards; for besides having a great many places to visit, he was obliged to stop twice to get poor Patsy something to eat, the little fellow being almost in a state of starvation. At length he faced towards the mountain, and with a sad heart and weary step plodded along.

"Is poor Ellen buried?" said he, as he passed the carpenter's door, where the coffin had been ordered.

"She's just laid in the mould—awhile ago."

"I hope Martin bears up better;—did you see him lately?"

"This is for him," said the carpenter, striking a board with his hammer; "he's at peace now."

"Martin! sure he's not dead? — Martin Neale, I mean."

"So do I too; he had it on him since morning, they say; but he just slipped away without a word or a moan."

"O God, be good to us, but the times is dreadful!" ejaculated Owen.

"Some says it's the ind of the world's comin'," said an old man, that sat moving his stick listlessly among the shavings; "and 'twould be well for most of us it was too."

"Thrue for you, Billy; there's no help for the poor."

No sentiment could meet more general acceptance than this—none less likely to provoke denial. Thrown upon each other for acts of kindness and benevolence, they felt from how narrow a store each contributed to another's wants, and knew well all the privations that charity like this necessitated, at the same time that they felt themselves deserted by those whose generosity might have been exercised without sacrificing a single enjoyment, or interfering with the pursuit of any accustomed pleasure.

There is no more common theme than the ingratitude of the poor—their selfishness and hard-heartedness ; and unquestionably a life of poverty is but an indifferent teacher of fine feelings or gentle emotions. The dreary monotony of their daily lives, the unvarying sameness of the life-long struggle between labour and want, are little suggestive of any other spirit than a dark and brooding melancholy : and it were well, besides, to ask, if they who call themselves benefactors have been really generous, and not merely just ? We speak more particularly of the relations which exist between the owner of the land and those who till it ; and where benevolence is a duty, and not a virtue depending on the will : not that they in whose behalf it is ever exercised, regard it in this light—very far from it ! Their thankfulness for benefits is generally most disproportioned to their extent ; but we are dissatisfied because our charity has not changed the whole current of their fortunes, and that the favours which cost us so little to bestow, should not become the ruling principle of their lives.

Owen reflected deeply on these things as he ascended the mountain-road. The orphan child he carried in his arms pressed such thoughts upon him, and he wondered why rich men denied themselves the pleasures of benevolence. He did not know that many great men enjoyed the happiness, but that it was made conformable to their high estate by institutions and establishments ; by boards, and committees, and guardians ; by all the pomp and circumstance of stuccoed buildings and liveried attendants. That to save themselves the burden of memory, their good deeds were chronicled in lists of "founders" and "life-subscribers," and their names set forth in newspapers; while, to protect their finer natures from the rude assaults of actual misery, they deputed others to be the stewards of their bounty.

Owen did not know all this, or he had doubtless been less unjust regarding such persons. He never so much as heard of the pains that are taken to ward off the very sight of poverty, and all the appliances employed to exclude suffering from the gaze of the wealthy. All his little experience told him was, how much of good might be done within the sphere around him by one possessed of affluence. There was not a cabin around, where he could not point to some object claiming aid or assistance. Even in seasons of comparative comfort and abundance, what a deal of misery still existed; and what a blessing it would bring on him who sought it out, to compassionate and relieve it! So Owen thought, and so he felt too; not the less strongly that another heart then beat against his own, the little pulses sending a gush of wild delight through his bosom as he revelled in the ecstasy of benevolence. The child awoke, and looked wildly about him; but when he recognised in whose arms he was, he smiled happily, and cried, "Nony, Nony," the name by which Owen was known among all the children of the village and its neighbourhood.

"Yes, Patsy," said Owen, kissing him, "your own Nony! you're coming home with him to see what a nice house he has upon the mountain for you, and the purty lake near it, and the fish swimming in it."

The little fellow clapped his hands with glee, and seemed delighted at all he heard.

"Poor darlin'," muttered Owen, sorrowfully; "he doesn't know 'tis the sad day for him;" and as he spoke, the wind from the valley bore on it the mournful cadence of a death-cry, as a funeral moved along the road.

" His father's berrin' ! " added he.   " God help us ! how fast misfortune does be overtaking us at the time our heart's happiest ! It will be many a day before he knows all this morning cost him."

The little child meanwhile caught the sounds, and starting up in Owen's arms, he strained his eyes to watch the funeral procession as it slowly passed on. Owen held him up for a few seconds to see it, and wiped the large tears that started to his own eyes. " Maybe Martin and poor Ellen's looking down on us now ! " and with that he laid the little boy back in his arms and plodded forward.

It was but seldom that Owen Connor ascended that steep way without halting to look down on the wide valley, and the lake, and the distant mountains beyond it.   The scene was one of which he never wearied ; indeed, its familiarity had charms for him greater and higher than mere picturesque beauty can bestow. Each humble cabin with its little family was known to him ; he was well read in the story of their lives ; he had mingled in all their hopes and fears from childhood to old age ; and, as the lights trembled through the dark night and spangled the broad expanse, he could bring before his mind's eye the humble hearths round which they sat, and think he almost heard their voices. Now, he heeded not these things, but steadily bent his steps towards home.

At last, the twinkle of a star-like light showed that he was near his journey's end. It shone from the deep shadow of a little glen, in which his cabin stood. The seclusion of the spot was in Owen's eyes its greatest charm. Like all men who have lived much alone, he set no common store by the pleasures of solitude, and fancied that most if not all of his happiness was derived from this source. At this moment his gratitude was more than usual, as he muttered to himself, " Thank God for it ! we've a snug little place away from the sickness, and no house near us at all ; " and with this comforting reflection he drew near the cabin. The door, contrary to custom at nightfall, lay open ; and Owen, painfully alive to any suspicious sign, from the state of anxiety his mind had suffered, entered hastily.

" Father ! where are you ? " said he quickly, not seeing the old man in his accustomed place beside the fire ; but there was no answer. Laying the child down, Owen passed into the little chamber which served as the old man's bed-room, and where now he lay stretched upon the bed in his clothes. " Are ye sick, father ? What ails ye, father dear ? " asked the young man, as he took his hand in his own.

" I'm glad ye've come at last, Owen," replied his father feebly. " I've got the sickness, and am going fast."

" No — no, father ! don't be down-hearted ! " cried Owen, with a desperate effort to suggest the courage he did not feel ; for the touch of the cold wet hand had already told him the sad secret. 'Tis a turn ye have."

" Well, maybe so," said he, with a sigh ; " but there's a cowld feeling about my heart I never knew afore. Get me a warm drink, anyway."

While Owen prepared some cordial from the little store he usually dispensed among the people, his father told him, that a boy from a sick house had called at the cabin that morning to seek for Owen, and from him, in all likelihood, he must have caught the malady. " I remember," said the old man, " that he was quite dark in the skin, and was weak in his limbs as he walked."

"Ayeh!" muttered Owen, "av it was the 'disease' he had, sorra bit of this mountain he'd ever get up. The strongest men can't lift a cup of wather to their lips, when it's on them; but there's a great scarcity in the glen, and maybe the boy eat nothing before he set out."

Although Owen's explanation was the correct one, it did not satisfy the old man's mind, who, besides feeling convinced of his having the malady, could not credit his taking it by other means than contagion. Owen never quitted his side, and multiplied cares and attentions of every kind; but it was plain the disease was gaining ground, for ere midnight the old man's strength was greatly gone, and his voice sunk to a mere whisper. Yet the malady was characterised by none of the symptoms of the prevailing epidemic, save slight cramps, of which from time to time he complained. His case seemed one of utter exhaustion. His mind was clear and calm; and although unable to speak, except in short and broken sentences, no trait of wandering intellect appeared. His malady was a common one among those whose fears, greatly excited by the disease, usually induced symptoms of prostration and debility, as great, if not as rapid, as those of actual cholera. Meanwhile his thoughts were alternately turning from his own condition to that of the people in the glen, for whom he felt the deepest compassion. "God help them!" was his constant expression. "Sickness is the sore thing; but starvation makes it dreadful. And so Luke Clancy's dead! Poor ould Luke! he was seventy-one in Michaelmas. And Martin, too! he was a fine man."

The old man slept, or seemed to sleep, for some hours, and on waking it was clear daylight. "Owen, dear! I wish," said he, "I could see the priest; but you mustn't lave me; I couldn't bear that now."

Poor Owen's thoughts were that moment occupied on the same subject, and he was torturing himself to think ot any means of obtaining Father John's assistance, without being obliged to go for him himself.

"I'll go, and be back here in an hour—ay, or less," said he, eagerly; for terrible as death was to him, the thought of seeing his father die unanointed, was still more so.

"In an hour—where'll I be in an hour, Owen dear? the blessed Virgin knows well, it wasn't my fault—I'd have the priest av I could—and sure, Owen, you'll not be-grudge me masses, when I'm gone. What's that? It's like a child crying out there."

"'Tis poor Martin's little boy I took home with me —he's lost father and mother this day;" and so saying, Owen hastened to see what ailed the child. " Yer sarvent, Sir," said Owen, as he perceived a stout-built, coarse-looking man, with a bull-terrier at his heels, standing in the middle of the floor. "Yer sarvent, Sir. Who do ye want here ? "

"Are you Owen Connor?" said the man, gruffly.

"That same," replied Owen, as sturdily.

"Then this is notice for you to come up to Mr. Lucas's office in Galway before the twenty-fifth, with your rent, or the receipt for it, which ever you like best."

"And who is Mr. Lucas when he's at home?" said Owen, half-sneeringly.

"You'll know him when you see him," rejoined the other, turning to leave the cabin, as he threw a printed paper on the dresser; and then, as if thinking he had not been formal enough in his mission, added, " Mr. Lucas is agent to your landlord, Mr. Leslie; and I'll give you a bit of advice, keep a civil tongue in your head with him, and it will do you no harm."

This counsel, delivered much more in a tone of menace than of friendly advice, concluded the interview, for having spoken, the fellow left the cabin, and began to descend the mountain.

Owen's heart swelled fiercely—a flood of conflicting emotions were warring within it; and as he turned to throw the paper into the fire, his eye caught the date, 16th March. "St. Patrick's Eve, the very day I saved his life," said he bitterly. "Sure I knew well enough how it would be when the landlord died! Well, well, if my poor ould father doesn't know it, it's no matter.—Well, Patsy, acushla, what are ye crying for? There, my boy, don't be afeard, 'tis Nony's with ye."

The accents so kindly uttered quieted the little fellow in a moment, and in a few minutes after he was again asleep in the old straw chair beside the fire. Brief as Owen's absence had been, the old man seemed much worse as he entered the room. "God forgive me, Owen darling," said he, "but it wasn't my poor sowl I was thinking of that minit. I was thinking that you must get a letter wrote to the young landlord about this little place —I'm sure he'll never say a word about rent, no more nor his father; and as the times wasn't good lately——"

"There, there, father," interrupted Owen, who felt shocked at the old man's not turning his thoughts in another direction; "never mind those things," said he; "who knows which of us will be left? the sickness doesn't spare the young, no more than the ould."

"Nor the rich, no more nor the poor," chimed in the old man, with a kind of bitter satisfaction, as he thought on the landlord's death; for of such incongruous motives is man made up, that calamities come lighter when they involve the fall of those in station above our own. "'Tis a fine day, seemingly," said he, suddenly changing the current of his thoughts; "and iligant weather for the country; we'll have to turn in the sheep over that wheat; it will be too rank: ayeh," cried he, with a deep sigh, "I'll not be here to see it:" and for once, the emotions no dread of futurity could awaken, were realised by worldly considerations, and the old man wept like a child.

"What time of the month is it?" asked he, after a long interval in which neither spoke; for Owen was not really sorry that even thus painfully the old man's thoughts should be turned towards eternity.

"'Tis the seventeenth, father, a holy-day all over Ireland!"

"Is there many at the 'station?'—look out at the door and see."

Owen ascended a little rising ground in front of the cabin, from which the whole valley was visible; but except a group that followed a funeral upon the road, he could see no human thing around. The green where the "stations" were celebrated was totally deserted. There were neither tents nor people; the panic of the plague had driven all ideas of revelry from the minds of the most reckless; and, even to observe the duties of religion, men feared to assemble in numbers. So long as the misfortune was at a distance, they could mingle their prayers in common, and entreat for mercy; but when death knocked at every door, the terror became almost despair.

"Is the 'stations' going on?" asked the old man eagerly, as Owen re-entered the room. "Is the people at the holy well?"

"I don't see many stirring at all, to-day," was the cautious answer; for Owen scrupled to inflict any avoidable pain upon his mind.

"Lift me up, then!" cried he suddenly, and, with a

voice stronger, from a violent effort of his will. "Lift me up to the window, till I see the blessed cross; and maybe I'd get a prayer among them. Come, be quick, Owen!"

Owen hastened to comply with his request; but already the old man's eyes were glazed and filmy. The effort had but hastened the moment of his doom; and with a low faint sigh, he lay back, and died.

To the Irish peasantry, who, more than any other people of Europe, are accustomed to bestow care and attention on the funerals of their friends and relatives, the cholera, in its necessity for speedy interment, was increased in terrors tenfold. The honours which they were wont to lavish on the dead—the ceremonial of the wake—the mingled merriment and sorrow—the profusion with which they spent the hoarded gains of hard-working labour — and lastly, the long train to the churchyard, evidencing the respect entertained for the departed, should all be foregone; for had not prudence forbid their assembling in numbers, and thus incurring the chances of contagion, which, whether real or not, they firmly believed in, the work of death was too widely disseminated to make such gatherings possible. Each had some one to lament within the limits of his own family, and private sorrow left little room for public sympathy. No longer then was the road filled by people on horseback and foot, as the funeral procession moved forth. The death-wail sounded no more. To chant the *requiem* of the departed, a few—a very few—immediate friends followed the body to the grave, in silence unbroken. Sad hearts, indeed, they brought, and broken spirits; for in this season of pestilence few dared to hope.

By noon, Owen was seen descending the mountain to the village, to make the last preparations for the old man's funeral. He carried little Patsy in his arms; for he could not leave the poor child alone, and in the house of death. The claims of infancy would seem never stronger than in the heart sorrowing over death. The grief that carries the sufferer in his mind's eye over the limits of this world, is arrested by the tender ties which bind him to life in the young. There is besides a hopefulness in early life — it is, perhaps, its chief characteristic — that combats sorrow, better than all the caresses of friendship, and all the consolations of age. Owen felt this now— he never knew it before. But yesterday, and his father's death had left him without one in the world on whom to fix a hope; and already, from his misery, there arose that one gleam, that now twinkled like a star in the sky of midnight. The little child he had taken for his own was a world to him; and as he went, he prayed fervently that poor Patsy might be spared to him through this terrible pestilence.

When Owen reached the carpenter's, there were several people there; some, standing moodily brooding over recent bereavements; others, spoke in low whispers, as if fearful of disturbing the silence; but all were sorrow-struck and sad.

" How is the ould man, Owen ? " said one of the group, as he came forward.

" He's better off than us, I trust in God ! " said Owen, with a quivering lip. " He went to rest this morning."

A muttered prayer from all around showed how general was the feeling of kindness entertained towards the Connors.

" When did he take it, Owen ? "

" I don't know that he tuk it at all; but when I came home last night he was lying on the bed, weak and powerless, and he slept away, with scarce a pain, till day-break ; then——"

20

"He's in glory now, I pray God!" muttered an old man with a white beard. "We were born in the same year, and I knew him since I was a child, like that in your arms; and a good man he was."

"Whose is the child, Owen?" said another in the crowd.

"Martin Neal's," whispered Owen; for he feared that the little fellow might catch the words. "What's the matter with Miles? he looks very low this morning."

This question referred to a large powerful-looking man, who, with a smith's apron twisted round his waist, sat without speaking in a corner of the shop.

"I'm afeard he's in a bad way," whispered the man to whom he spoke. "There was a process-server, or a bailiff, or something of the kind, serving notices through the townland yesterday, and he lost a shoe off his baste, and would have Miles out, to put it on, tho' we all tould him that he buried his daughter—a fine grown girl— that mornin'. And what does the fellow do, but goes and knocks at the forge till Miles comes out. You know Miles Regan, so I needn't say there wasn't many words passed between them. In less nor two minutes—whatever the bailiff said—Miles tuck him by the throat, and pulled him down from the horse, and dragged him along to the lake, and flung him in. 'Twas the Lord's marcy he knew how to swim; but we don't know what'll be done to Miles yet, for he was the new agent's man."

"Was he a big fellow, with a bull-dog following him?" asked Owen.

"No; that's another; sure there's three or four of them goin' about. We hear, that bad as ould French was, the new one is worse."

"Well—well, it's the will of God!" said Owen, in that tone of voice which bespoke a willingness for all endurance, so long as the consolation remained, that the ill was not unrecorded above; while he felt that all the evils of poverty were little in comparison with the loss of those nearest and dearest. "Come, Patsy, my boy!" said he at last, as he placed the coffin in the ass-cart, and turned towards the mountain; and, leading the little fellow by the hand, he set out on his way—"Come home."

It was not until he arrived at that part of the road from which the cabin was visible, that Owen knew the whole extent of his bereavement; then, when he looked up and saw the door hasped on the outside, and the chimney from which no smoke ascended, the full measure of his lone condition came at once before him, and he bent over the coffin and wept bitterly. All the old man's affection for him, his kind indulgence and forbearance, his happy nature, his simple-heartedness, gushed forth from his memory, and he wondered why he had not loved his father, in life, a thousand times more, so deeply was he now penetrated by his loss. If this theme did not assuage his sorrows, it at least so moulded his heart as to bear them in a better spirit; and when, having placed the body in the coffin, he knelt down beside it to pray, it was in a calmer and more submissive frame of mind than he had yet known.

It was late in the afternoon ere Owen was once more on the road down the mountain; for it was necessary— or at least believed so—that interment should take place on the day of death.

" I never thought it would be this way you'd go to your last home, father dear," said Owen aloud, and in a voice almost stifled with sobs; for the absence of all his friends and relatives at such a moment, now smote on the poor fellow's heart, as he walked beside the little cart on which the coffin was laid. It was indeed a sight to move a sterner nature than his; the coffin, not reverently carried by bearers, and followed by its long train of mourners, but laid slant-wise in the cart, the spade and shovel to dig the grave beside it, and Patsy seated on the back of the ass, watching with infant glee the motion of the animal, as with careful foot he descended the rugged mountain. Poor child! how your guileless laughter shook that strong man's heart with agony!

It was a long and weary way to the old churchyard. The narrow road, too, was deeply rutted and worn by wheel-tracks; for, alas, it had been trodden by many, of late. The gray daylight was fast fading as Owen pushed wide the old gate and entered. What a change to his eyes did the aspect of the place present! The green mounds of earth which marked the resting-place of village patriarchs, were gone; and heaps of fresh-turned clay were seen on every side, no longer decorated, as of old, with little emblems of affectionate sorrow; no tree, nor stone, not even a wild flower, spoke of the regrets of those who remained. The graves were rudely fashioned, as if in haste—for so it was—few dared to linger there!

Seeking out a lone spot near the ruins, Owen began to dig the grave, while the little child, in mute astonish·ment at all he saw, looked on.

"Why wouldn't you stay out in the road, Patsy, and play there, till I come to you? This is a cowld damp place for you, my boy."

"Nony! Nony!" cried the child, looking at him with an affectionate smile, as though to say he'd rather be near him.

"Well, well, who knows but you're right? if it's the will of God to take me, maybe you might as well go too. It's a sore thing to be alone in the world, like me now!"

And as he muttered the last few words he ceased digging, and rested his head on the cross of the spade.

"Was that you, Patsy? I heard a voice somewhere."

The child shook his head in token of dissent.

"Aych! it was only the wind through the ould walls; but sure it might be nat'ral enough for sighs and sobs to be here: there's many a one has floated over this damp clay."

He resumed his work once more. The night was falling fast as Owen stepped from the deep grave, and knelt down to say a prayer ere he committed the body to the earth.

"Kneel down, darlin', here by my side," said he placing his arm round the little fellow's waist; "'tis the likes of you God loves best;" and joining the tiny hands with his own, he uttered a deep and fervent prayer for the soul of the departed. "There, father!" said he, as he arose at last, and in a voice as if addressing a living person at his side; "there, father: the Lord, he knows my heart inside me; and if walking the world barefoot would give ye peace or ease, I'd do it, for you were a kind man and a good father to me." He kissed the coffin as he spoke, and stood silently gazing on it.

Arousing himself with a kind of struggle, he untied the cords, and lifted the coffin from the cart. For some seconds he busied himself in arranging the ropes beneath it, and then ceased suddenly, on remembering that he could not lower it into the grave unassisted.

"I'll have to go down the road for some one," muttered he to himself; but as he said this, he perceived at some distance off in the churchyard the figure of a man, as if kneeling over a grave. "The Lord help him, he has his grief too!" ejaculated Owen, as he moved towards him. On coming nearer he perceived that the grave was newly made, and from its size evidently that of a child.

"I ax your pardon," said Owen, in a timid voice, after waiting for several minutes in the vain expectation that the man would look up; "I ax your pardon for disturbing you, but maybe you'll be kind enough to help me to lay this coffin in the ground. I have nobody with me but a child."

The man started and looked round. Their eyes met; it was Phil Joyce and Owen who now confronted each other. But how unlike were both to what they were at their last parting! Then, vindictive passion, outraged pride, and vengeance, swelled every feature and tingled in every fibre of their frames. Now, each stood pale, care-worn, and dispirited, wearied out by sorrow, and almost broken-hearted. Owen was the first to speak.

"I axed your pardon before I saw you, Phil Joyce, and I ax it again now, for disturbing you; but I didn't know you, and I wanted to put my poor father's body in the grave."

"I didn't know he was dead," said Phil, in a hollow voice, like one speaking to himself. "This is poor little Billy here," and he pointed to the mound at his feet.

"The heavens be his bed this night!" said Owen, piously; "Good-night!" and he turned to go away; then stopping suddenly, he added, "Maybe, after all, you'll not refuse me, and the Lord might be more merciful to us both, than if we were to part like enemies."

"Owen Connor, I ask your forgiveness," said Phil, stretching forth his hand, while his voice trembled like a sick child's. "I didn't think the day would come I'd ever do it; but my heart is humble enough now, and maybe 'twill be lower soon. Will you take my hand?"

"Will I, Phil? will I, is it? ay, and however ye may

change to me after this night, I'll never forget this." And he grasped the cold fingers in both hands, and pressed them ardently, and the two men fell into each other's arms and wept.

Is it a proud or a humiliating confession for humanity—assuredly it is a true one—that the finest and best traits of our nature are elicited in our troubles, and not in our joys? that we come out purer through trials than prosperity? Does the chastisement of Heaven teach us better than the blessings lavished upon us? or are these gifts the compensation sent us for our afflictions, that when poorest before man we should be richest before God? Few hearts there are which sorrow makes not wiser—none which are not better for it. So it was here. These men, in the continuance of good fortune, had been enemies for life; mutual hatred had grown up between them, so that each yearned for vengeance on the other; and now they walked like brothers, only seeking forgiveness of each other, and asking pardon for the past.

The old man was laid in his grave, and they turned to leave the churchyard.

"Won't ye come home with me, Owen?" said Phil, as they came to where their roads separated; "won't ye come and eat your supper with us?"

Owen's throat filled up: he could only mutter, "Not to-night, Phil—another time, plaze God." He had not ventured even to ask for Mary, nor did he know whether Phil Joyce in his reconciliation might wish a renewal of any intimacy with his sister. Such was the reason of Owen's refusal; for, however strange it may seem to some, there is a delicacy of the heart as well as of good breeding, and one advantage it possesses—it is of all lands, and the fashion never changes.

Poor Owen would have shed his best blood to be able

to ask after Mary—to learn how she was, and how she bore up under the disasters of the time; but he never mentioned her name: and as for Phil Joyce, his gloomy thoughts had left no room for others, and he parted from Owen without a single allusion to her. "Good-night, Owen," said he, "and don't forget your promise to come and see us soon."

"Good-night, Phil," was the answer; "and I pray a blessing on you and yours." A slight quivering of the voice at the last word was all he suffered to escape him; and they parted.

THE THIRD ERA.

ROM that day, the pestilence began to abate in violence. The cases of disease became fewer and less fatal, and at last, like a spent bolt, the malady ceased to work its mischief. Men were slow enough to recognise this bettered aspect of their fortune. Calamity had weighed too heavily on them to make them rally at once. They still walked like those who felt the shadow of death upon them, and were fearful lest any imprudent act or word might bring back the plague among them.

With time, however, these features passed off: people gradually resumed their wonted habits; and, except where the work of death had been more than ordinarily destructive, the malady was now treated as " a thing that had been."

If Owen Connor had not escaped the common misfortune of the land, he could at least date one happy event from that sad period—his reconciliation with Phil Joyce. This was no passing friendship. The dreadful scenes he had witnessed about him had made Phil an altered character. The devotion of Owen—his manly indifference to personal risk whenever his services were wanted by another—his unsparing benevolence,—all these traits, the mention of which at first only irritated and vexed his soul, were now remembered in the day of reconciliation ; and none felt prouder to acknowledge his friendship than his former enemy.

Notwithstanding all this, Owen did not dare to found a hope upon his change of fortune ; for Mary was even more distant and cold to him than ever, as though to show that, whatever expectations he might conceive from her brother's friendship, he should not reckon too confidently on her feelings. Owen knew not how far he had himself to blame for this ; he was not aware that his own constrained manner, his over-acted reserve, had offended Mary to the quick ; and thus, both mutually retreated in misconception and distrust. The game of love is the same, whether the players be clad in velvet or in hodden gray. Beneath the gilded ceilings of a palace, or the lowly rafters of a cabin, there are the same hopes and fears, the same jealousies, and distrusts, and despondings ; the wiles and stratagems are all alike ; for, after all, the stake is human happiness, whether he who risks it be a peer or a peasant !

While Owen vacillated between hope and fear, now, resolving to hazard an avowal of his love and take his stand on the result, now, deeming it better to trust to time and longer intimacy, other events were happening around, which could not fail to interest him deeply. The new agent had commenced his campaign with an activity before unknown. Arrears of rent were demanded to be peremptorily paid up ; leases, whose exact conditions had not been fulfilled, were declared void ; tenants occupying sub-let land were noticed to quit ; and all the threatening signs of that rigid management displayed, by which an estate is assumed to be " admirably regulated," and the agent's duty most creditably discharged.

Many of the arrears were concessions made by the landlord in seasons of hardship and distress, but were unrecorded as such in the rent-roll or the tenant's receipt. There had been no intention of ever re-demanding them; and both parties had lost sight of the transaction until the sharp glance of a "new agent" discovered their existence. So of the leases: covenants to build, or plant, or drain, were inserted rather as contingencies, which prosperity might empower, than as actual conditions essential to be fulfilled; and as for sub-letting, it was simply the act by which a son or a daughter was portioned in the world, and enabled to commence the work of self-maintenance.

This slovenly system inflicted many evils. The demand of an extravagant rent rendered an abatement not a boon, but an act of imperative necessity; and while the overhanging debt supplied the landlord with a means of tyranny, it deprived the tenant of all desire to improve his condition. "Why should I labour," said he, "when the benefit never can be mine?" The landlord then declaimed against ingratitude, at the time that the peasant spoke against oppression. Could they both be right? The impossibility of ever becoming independent soon suggested that dogged indifference, too often confounded with indolent habits. Sustenance was enough for him, who, if he earned more, should surrender it; hence the poor man became chained to his poverty. It was a weight which grew with his strength; privations might as well be incurred with little labour as with great; and he sunk down to the condition of a mere drudge, careless and despondent. "He can only take all I have!" was the cottier's philosophy; and the maxim suggested a corollary, that the "all" should be as little as might be.

But there were other grievances flowing from this source. The extent of these abatements usually depended on the representation of the tenants themselves, and such evidences as they could produce of their poverty and destitution. Hence a whole world of falsehood and dissimulation was fostered. Cabins were suffered to stand half-roofed; children left to shiver in rags and nakedness; age and infirmity exhibited in attitudes of afflicting privations; habits of mendicity encouraged;—all, that they might impose upon the proprietor, and make him believe that any sum wrung from such as these must be an act of cruelty. If these schemes were sometimes successful, so in their failure they fell as heavy penalties upon the really destitute, for whose privations no pity was felt. Their misery, confounded in the general mass of dissimulation, was neglected; and for one who prospered in his falsehood, many were visited in their affliction.

That men in such circumstances as these should listen with greedy ears to any representation which reflected heavily on their wealthier neighbours, is little to be wondered at. The triumph of knavery and falsehood is a bad lesson for any people; but the fruitlessness of honest industry is, if possible, a worse one. Both were well taught by this system. And these things took place, not, be it observed, when the landlord or his agent were cruel and exacting—very far from it. They were the instances so popularly expatiated on by newspapers and journals; they were the cases headed—" Example for Landlords!" "Timely Benevolence!" and paragraphed thus:— "We learn, with the greatest pleasure, that Mr. Muldrennin, of Kilbally-drennin, has, in consideration of the failure of the potato-crop, and the severe pressure of the season, kindly abated five per cent of all his rents. Let this admirable example be generally followed, and we shall once more see," &c. &c. There was no explanatory note to state the actual condition of that tenantry, or the amount of that rent from which the deduction was made. Mr. Muldrennin was then free to run his career of active puffery throughout the kingdom, and his tenantry to starve on as before.

Of all worldly judgments there is one that never fails. No man was ever instrumental, either actively or through neglect, to another's demoralisation, that he was not made to feel the recoil of his conduct on himself. Such had been palpably the result here. The confidence of the people lost, they had taken to themselves the only advisers in their power, and taught themselves to suppose that relief can only be effected by legislative enactments, or their own efforts. This lesson once learned, and they were politicians for life. The consequence has been, isolation from him to whom once all respect and attachment were rendered ; distrust and dislike follow— would that the catalogue went no further !

And again to our story. Owen was at last reminded, by the conversation of those about, that he too had received a summons from the new agent to attend at his office in Galway—a visit which, somehow or other, he had at first totally neglected ; and, as the summons was not repeated, he finally supposed had been withdrawn by the agent, on learning the condition of his holding. As September drew to a close, however, he accompanied Phil Joyce on his way to Galway, prepared, if need be, to pay the half-year's rent, but ardently hoping the while it might never be demanded. It was a happy morning for poor Owen—the happiest of his whole life. He had gone over early to breakfast at Joyce's, and on reaching

the house found Mary alone, getting ready the meal.
Their usual distance in manner continued for some time;
each talked of what their thoughts were least occupied
on ; and at last, after many a look from the window to
see   Phil was coming, and wondering why he did not
arrive, Owen drew a heavy sigh and said, "It's no use,
Mary ; divil a longer can I be suffering this way ; take
me or refuse me you must this morning ! I know well
enough you don't care for me ; but if ye don't like
any one else better, who knows but in time, and with
God's blessin', but ye'll be as fond of me, as I am of
you ?"

"And who told ye I didn't like some one else?" said
Mary, with a sly glance ; and her handsome features
brightened up with a more than common brilliancy.

"The heavens make him good enough to desarve ye,
I pray this day !" said Owen, with a trembling lip. "I'll
go now ! that's enough !"

"Won't ye wait for yer breakfast, Owen Connor ?
Won't ye stay a bit for my brother ?"

"No, thank ye, Ma'am. I'll not go into Galway
to-day."

"Well, but don't go without your breakfast. Take a
cup of tay anyhow, Owen dear !"

"Owen dear ! O Mary, jewel ! don't say them words,
and I laving you for ever."

The young girl blushed deeply and turned away her
head, but her crimsoned neck showed that her shame
was not departed. At the moment, Phil burst into the
room, and standing for a second with his eyes fixed on
each in turn, he said, " Bad scran to ye, for women ; but
there's nothing but decate and wickedness in ye ; divil a
peace or ease I ever got when I quarrelled with Owen,
and now that we're friends, ye're as cross and discon-

tented as ever. Try what you can do with her yourself, Owen, my boy; for I give her up."

"'Tis not for me to thry it," said Owen, despondingly; "'tis another has the betther luck."

"That's not true, anyhow," cried Phil; "for she told me so herself."

"What! Mary, did ye say that?" said Owen, with a spring across the room; "did ye tell him that, darling?"

"Sure if I did, ye wouldn't believe me," said Mary, with a side-look; "women is nothing but deceit and wickedness."

"Sorra else," cried Owen, throwing his arm round her neck and kissing her; "and I'll never believe ye again, when ye say ye don't love me."

"'Tis a nice way to boil the eggs hard," said Phil, testily; "arrah, come over here and eat your breakfast, man; you'll have time enough for courting when we come back."

There needed not many words to a bargain which was already ratified; and before they left the house, the day of the wedding was actually fixed.

It was not without reason, then, that I said it was a happy day for Owen. Never did the long miles of the road seem so short as now; while, with many a plan for the future, and many a day-dream of happiness to come, he went at Phil's side scarce crediting his good fortune to be real.

When they arrived at the agent's office in the square at Galway, they found a great many of their neighbours and friends already there; some, moody and depressed, yet lingered about the door, though they had apparently finished the business which brought them; others, anxious-looking and troubled, were waiting for their turn to enter. They were all gathered into little groups and parties, conversing eagerly together in Irish; and as each came out of the office, he was speedily surrounded by several others, questioning him as to how he had fared, and what success he met with.

Few came forth satisfied — not one happy-looking. Some, who were deficient a few shillings, were sent back again, and appeared with the money still in their hands, which they counted over and over, as if hoping to make it more. Others, trusting to promptitude in their payments, were seeking renewal of their tenures at the same rent, and found their requests coldly received, and no pledge returned. Others, again, met with severe reproaches as to the condition of their dwellings and the neglected appearance of their farms, with significant hints that slovenly tenants would meet with little favour, and, although pleading sickness and distress, found the apology but slightly regarded.

"We thought the ould agent bad enough; but, faix, this one bates him out, entirely." Such was the comment of each and all, at the treatment met with, and such the general testimony of the crowd.

"Owen Connor! Owen Connor!" called out a voice, which Owen in a moment recognised as that of the fellow who had visited his cabin; and passing through the densely crowded hall, Owen forced his way into the small front parlour, where two clerks were seated at a table, writing.

"Over here; this way, if you please," said one of them, pointing with his pen to the place he should stand in. "What's your name?"

"Owen Connor, Sir."

"What's the name of your holding?"

"Ballydorery, Knockshaughlin, and Cushaglin, is

the townlands, and the mountain is Slieve-na-vick, Sir."

" Owen Connor, Owen Connor?" said the clerk, repeating the name three or four times over. " Oh, I remember; there has been no rent paid on your farm for some years."

" You're right there, Sir," said Owen; " the landlord, God be good to him! tould my poor father——"

" Well, well, I have nothing to do with that—step inside—Mr. Lucas will speak to you himself;—show this man inside, Luffey;" and the grim bailiff led the way into the back parlour, where two gentlemen were standing with their backs to the fire, chatting; they were both young and good-looking, and to Owen's eyes, as unlike agents as could be.

" Well, what does this honest fellow want?—no abatement, I hope ; a fellow with as good a coat as you have, can't be very ill off."

" True for you, yer honour, and I am not," said Owen in reply to the speaker, who seemed a few years younger than the other. " I was bid spake to yer honour about the little place I have up the mountains, and that Mr. Leslie gave my father rent-free——"

" Oh, you are the man from Maam, aint you ?"

" The same, Sir ; Owen Connor."

" That's the mountain I told you of, major," said Lucas in a whisper; then turning to Owen, resumed : " Well, I wished to see you very much, and speak to you. I've heard the story about your getting the land rent-free, and all that; but I find no mention of the matter in the books of the estate ; there is not the slightest note nor memorandum that I can see, on the subject ; and except your own word—which of course, as far as it goes, is all very well—I have nothing in your favour."

21

While these words were being spoken, Owen went through a thousand tortures ; and many a deep conflicting passion warred within him. "Well, Sir," said he at last, with a heavily drawn sigh, "well, Sir, with God's blessin', I'll do my best ; and whatever your honour says is fair, I'll thry and pay it : I suppose I'm undher rent since March last ?"

"March ! why, my good fellow, there's six years due last twenty-fifth ; what are you thinking of ?"

"Sure you don't mean I'm to pay, for what was given to me and my father ? " said Owen, with a wild look that almost startled the agent.

"I mean precisely what I say," said Lucas, reddening with anger at the tone Owen assumed. "I mean that you owe six years and a half of rent ; for which, if you neither produce receipt nor money, you'll never owe another half year for the same holding."

"And that's flat !" said the major, laughing.

"And that's flat !" echoed Lucas, joining in the mirth.

Owen looked from one to the other of the speakers, and although never indisposed to enjoy a jest, he could not, for the life of him, conceive what possible occasion for merriment existed at the present moment.

"Plenty of grouse on that mountain, aint there ?" said the major, tapping his boot with his cane.

But, although the question was addressed to Owen, he was too deeply sunk in his own sad musings to pay it any attention.

"Don't you hear, my good fellow ? Major Lynedock asks, if there are not plenty of grouse on the mountain."

"Did the present landlord say that I was to pay this back rent ?" said Owen deliberately, after a moment of deep thought.

"Mr. Leslie never gave me any particular instructions on your account," said Lucas smiling; "nor do I suppose that his intentions regarding you are different from those respecting other tenants."

"I saved his life, then!" said Owen; and his eyes flashed with indignation as he spoke.

"And you saved a devilish good fellow, I can tell you," said the major, smiling complacently, as though to hint that the act was a very sufficient reward for its own performance.

"The sorra much chance he had of coming to the property that day, anyhow, till I came up," said Owen, in a half soliloquy.

"What! were the savages about to scalp him? Eh!" asked the major.

Owen turned a scowl towards him that stopped the already-begun laugh; while Lucas, amazed at the peasant's effrontery, said, "You needn't wait any longer, my good fellow; I have nothing more to say."

"I was going to ask yer honour, Sir," said Owen, civilly, "if I paid the last half-year—I have it with me —if ye'll let me stay in the place till ye'll ask Mr. Leslie——"

"But you forget, my friend, that a receipt for the last half-year is a receipt in full," said Lucas, interrupting.

"Sure, I don't want the receipt!" said Owen hurriedly; "keep it yourself. It isn't mistrusting the word of a gentleman I'd be."

"Eh, Lucas! blarney! I say, blarney, and no mistake!" cried the major, half-suffocated with his own drollery.

"By my sowl! it's little blarney I'd give you, av I had ye at the side of Slieve-na-vick," said Owen; and the look he threw towards him left little doubt of his sincerity.

"Leave the room, Sir! leave the room!" said Lucas, with a gesture towards the door.

"Dare I ax you where Mr. Leslie is now, Sir?" said Owen, calmly.

"He's in London: No. 18, Belgrave Square."

"Would yer honour be so kind as to write it on a bit of paper for me?" said Owen, almost obsequiously.

Lucas sat down and wrote the address upon a card, handing it to Owen without a word.

"I humbly ax yer pardon, gentlemen, if I was rude to either of ye," said Owen, with a bow, as he moved towards the door; "but distress of mind doesn't improve a man's manners, if even he had more nor I have; but if I get the little place yet, and that ye care for a day's sport——"

"Eh, damme, you're not so bad, after all," said the major: "I say, Lucas—is he, now?"

"Your servant, gentlemen," said Owen, who felt too indignant at the cool insolence with which his generous proposal was accepted, to trust himself with more; and with that, he left the room.

"Well, Owen, my boy," said Phil, who long since having paid his own rent, was becoming impatient at his friend's absence; "well, Owen, ye might have settled about the whole estate by this time. Why did they keep you so long?"

In a voice tremulous with agitation, Owen repeated the result of his interview, adding, as he concluded, "And now, there's nothing for it, Phil, but to see the landlord himself, and spake to him. I've got the name of the place he's in, here—it's somewhere in London; and I'll never turn my steps to home, before I get a sight of him. I've the half-year's rent here in my pocket, so that I'll have money enough, and to spare; and I only ax ye, Phil, to tell Mary how the whole case is, and to take care of little Patsy for me till I come back—he's at your house now."

"Never fear, we'll take care of him, Owen; and I believe you're doing the best thing, after all."

The two friends passed the evening together, at least until the time arrived, when Owen took his departure by the mail. It was a sad termination to a day which opened so joyfully, and not all Phil's endeavours to rally and encourage his friend could dispossess Owen's mind of a gloomy foreboding that it was but the beginning of misfortune. "I have it over me," was his constant expression as they talked; "I have it over me, that something bad will come out of this;" and although his fears were vague and indescribable, they darkened his thoughts as effectually as real evils.

The last moment came, and Phil, with a hearty "God speed you," shook his friend's hand, and he was gone.

It would but protract my story, without fulfilling any of its objects, to speak of Owen's journey to England and on to London. It was a season of great distress in the manufacturing districts; several large failures had occurred —great stagnation of trade existed, and a general depression was observable over the population of the great trading cities. There were daily meetings to consider the condition of the working classes, and the newspapers were crammed with speeches and resolutions in their favour. Placards were carried about the streets, with terrible announcements of distress and privation, and processions of wretched-looking men were met with on every side.

Owen, who, from motives of economy, prosecuted his journey on foot, had frequent opportunities of entering the dwellings of the poor, and observing their habits and modes of life. The everlasting complaints of suffering and want rung in his ears from morning till night; and yet to his unaccustomed eyes the evidences betrayed few, if any, of the evils of great poverty. The majority were not without bread—the very poorest had a sufficiency of potatoes. Their dwellings were neat-looking and comfortable, and, in comparison with what he was used to, actually luxurious. Neither were their clothes like the ragged and tattered coverings Owen had seen at home. The fustian jackets of the men were generally whole and well cared for; but the children more than all struck him. In Ireland the young are usually the first to feel the pressure of hardship—their scanty clothing rather the requirement of decency, than a protection against weather; here, the children were cleanly and comfortably dressed —none were in rags, few without shoes and stockings.

What could such people mean by talking of distress, Owen could by no means comprehend. " I wish we had a little of this kind of poverty in ould Ireland !" was the constant theme of his thoughts. " 'Tis little they know what distress is. Faix, I wondher what they'd say if they saw Connemarra?" And yet, the privations they endured were such as had not been known for many years previous. Their sufferings were really great, and the interval between their ordinary habits as wide as ever presented itself in the fortunes of the poor Irishman's life. But poverty, after all, is merely relative; and they felt that as " starvation" which Paddy would hail as a season of blessing and abundance.

" With a fine slated house over them, and plenty of furniture inside, and warm clothes, and enough to eat,— that's what they call distress ! Musha ! I'd like to see them when they think they're comfortable," thought Owen, who at last lost all patience with such undeserved complainings, and could with difficulty restrain himself from an open attack on their injustice.

He arrived in London at last, and the same evening hastened to Belgrave Square; for his thoughts were now, as his journey drew to a close, painfully excited at the near prospect of seeing his landlord. He found the house without difficulty: it was a splendid town-mansion, well befitting a man of large fortune; and Owen experienced an Irishman's gratification in the spacious and handsome building he saw before him. He knocked, at first timidly, and then, as no answer was returned, more boldly; but it was not before a third summons that the door was opened; and an old mean-looking woman asked him what he wanted.

"I want to see the masther, Ma'am, av it's plazing to ye!" said Owen, leaning against the door-jamb as he spoke.

"The master? What do you mean?"

"Mr. Leslie himself, the landlord."

"Mr. Leslie is abroad—in Italy."

"Abroad! abroad!" echoed Owen, while a sickly faintness spread itself through his frame. "He's not out of England, is he?"

"I've told you he's in Italy, my good man."

"Erra! where's that at all?" cried Owen, despairingly.

"I'm sure I don't know; but I can give you the address, if you want it."

"No, thank ye, Ma'am—it's too late for that, now," said he. The old woman closed the door, and the poor fellow sat down upon the steps, overcome by this sad and unlooked-for result.

It was evening. The streets were crowded with people —some on foot, some on horseback and in carriages. The glare of splendid equipages, the glittering of wealth—the great human tide rolled past, unnoticed by Owen, for his own sorrows filled his whole heart.

Men in all their worldliness,—some on errands of pleasure, some care-worn and thoughtful, some brimful of expectation, and others downcast and dejected—moved past: scarcely one remarked that poor peasant, whose travelled and tired look, equally with his humble dress, bespoke one who came from afar.

"Well, God help me, what's best for me to do now?" said Owen Connor, as he sat ruminating on his fortune; and, unable to find any answer to his own question, he arose and walked slowly along, not knowing nor caring whither.

There is no such desolation as that of a large and crowded city to him who, friendless and alone, finds himself a wanderer within its walls. The man of education and taste looks around him for objects of interest or amusement, yet saddened by the thought that he is cut off from all intercourse with his fellow-men; but, to the poor unlettered stranger how doubly depressing are all these things! Far from speculating on the wealth and prosperity around him, he feels crushed and humiliated in its presence. His own humble condition appears even more lowly in contrast with such evidences of splendour; and instinctively he retreats from the regions where fashion, and rank, and riches abound, to the gloomy abodes of less-favoured fortunes.

When Owen awoke the following morning, and looked about him in the humble lodging he had selected, he could scarcely believe that already the end of his long journey had been met by failure. Again and again he endeavoured to remember if he had seen his landlord, and what reply he had received; but except a vague sense of disappointment, he could fix on nothing. It was only as he drew near the great mansion once more that he could thoroughly recollect all that had happened ; and then the truth flashed on his mind, and he felt all the bitterness of his misfortune. I need not dwell on this theme. The poor man turned again homeward ; why, he could not well have answered, had any been cruel enough to ask him. The hope that buoyed him up before, now spent and exhausted, his step was slow and his heart heavy, while his mind, racked with anxieties and dreads, increased his bodily debility, and made each mile of the way seem ten.

On the fourth day of his journey—wet through from morning till late in the evening—he was seized with a shivering-fit, followed soon after by symptoms of fever. The people in whose house he had taken shelter for the night, had him at once conveyed to the infirmary, where for eight weeks he lay dangerously ill ; a relapse of his malady, on the day before he was to be pronounced convalescent, occurred, and the third month was nigh its close ere Owen left the hospital.

It was more than a week ere he could proceed on his journey, which he did at last, moving only a few miles each day, and halting before nightfall. Thus wearily plodding on, he reached Liverpool at last, and about the middle of January arrived in his native country once more.

His strength regained, his bodily vigour restored, he had made a long day's journey to reach home, and it was about ten o'clock of a bright and starry night that he crossed the mountains that lie between Ballinrobe and Maam. To Owen, the separation from his home seemed like a thing of years long ; and his heart was full to bursting as each well-remembered spot appeared, bringing back a thousand associations of his former life. As he

strode along he stopped frequently to look down towards
the village, where, in each light that twinkled, he could
mark the different cabins of his old friends. At length,
the long low farm-house of the Joyces came into view—
he could trace it by the line of light that glittered from
every window—and from this Owen could not easily tear
himself away. Muttering a heartfelt prayer for those be-
neath that roof, he at last moved on, and near midnight
gained the little glen where his cabin stood. Scarcely,
however, had he reached the spot, when the fierce chal-
lenge of a dog attracted him. It was not his own poor
colley—he knew his voice well—and Owen's blood ran
chilly at the sound of that strange bark. He walked on,
however, resolutely grasping his stick in his hand, and
suddenly, as he turned the angle of the cliff, there stood
his cabin, with a light gleaming from the little window.

"'Tis Phil Joyce maybe has put somebody in, to take
care of the place," said he; but his fears gave no cre-
dence to the surmise.

Again the dog challenged, and at the same moment
the door was opened, and a man's voice called out, "Who
comes there?" The glare of the fire at his back showed
that he held a musket in his hand.

"'Tis me, Owen Connor," answered Owen half sulkily,
for he felt that indescribable annoyance a man will ex-
perience at any question, as to his approaching his own
dwelling, even though in incognito.

"Stay back, then," cried the other; "if you advance
another step, I'll send a bullet through you."

"Send a bullet through me!" cried Owen, scornfully,
yet even more astonished than indignant. "Why, isn't
a man to be let go to his own house, without being fired
at?

"I'll be as good as my word," said the fellow; and

as he spoke, Owen saw him lift the gun to his shoulder and steadily hold it there. "Move one step now, and you'll see if I'm not."

Owen's first impulse was to rush forward at any hazard, and if not wounded to grapple with his adversary; but he reflected for a second that some great change must have occurred in his absence, which, in all likelihood, no act of daring on his part could avert or alter. "I'll wait for morning, anyhow," thought he; and without another word, or deigning any answer to the other, he slowly turned and retraced his steps down the mountain.

There was a small mud hovel at the foot of the mountain, where Owen determined to pass the night. The old man who lived there had been a herd formerly, but age and rheumatism had left him a cripple, and he now lived on the charity of the neighbours.

"Poor Larry! I don't half like disturbing ye," said Owen as he arrived at the miserable contrivance of wattles that served for a door; but the chill night air, and his weary feet decided the difficulty, and he called out, "Larry—Larry Daly! open the door for me—Owen Connor. 'Tis me!"

The old man slept with the light slumber of age, and despite the consequences of his malady, managed to hobble to the door in a few seconds. "Oh! wirra, wirra! Owen, my son!" cried he, in Irish; "I hoped I'd never see ye here again—my own darlin'."

"That's a dhroll welcome, anyhow, Larry, for a man coming back among his own people."

"'Tis a thrue one, as sure as I live in sin. The Lord help us, this is bad fortune."

"What do you mean, Larry? What did I ever do to disgrace my name, that I wouldn't come back here?"

"'Tisn't what ye done, honey, but what's done upon

ye. Oh, wirra, wirra; 'tis a black day that led ye home here."

It was some time before Owen could induce the old man to moderate his sorrows, and relate the events which had occurred in his absence. I will not weary my reader by retailing the old man's prolixity, but tell them in the fewest words I am able, premising, that I must accompany the narrative by such explanations as I may feel necessary.

Soon after Owen's departure for England, certain disturbances occurred through the country. The houses of the gentry were broken open at night and searched for arms by men with blackened faces and in various disguises to escape recognition. Threatening notices were served on many of the resident families, menacing them with the worst if they did not speedily comply with certain conditions, either in the discharge of some obnoxious individuals from their employment, or the restoration of some plot of ground to its former holder. Awful denunciations were uttered against any who should dare to occupy land from which a former tenant was ejected; and so terrible was the vengeance exacted, and so sudden its execution, that few dared to transgress the orders of these savage denunciators. The law of the land seemed to stand still, justice appeared appalled and affrighted, by acts which bespoke deep and wide-spread conspiracy. The magistrates assembled to deliberate on what was to be done; and the only one who ventured to propose a bold and vigorous course of acting was murdered on his way homeward. Meanwhile, Mr. Lucas, whose stern exactions had given great discontent, seemed determined to carry through his measures at any risk. By influence with the government he succeeded in obtaining a considerable police-force, and, under cover of these, he issued his distress-warrants and executions, distrained and sold, probably with a severity increased by the very opposition he met with.

The measures undertaken by government to suppress outrage failed most signally. The difficulty of arresting a suspected individual was great in a country where a large force was always necessary. The difficulty of procuring evidence against him was still greater; for even such as were not banded in the conspiracy, had a greater dread of the reproach of informer, than of any other imputation; and when these two conditions were overcome, the last and greatest of all difficulties remained behind,—no jury could be found to convict, when their own lives might pay the penalty of their honesty. While thus, on one side, went the agent, with his cumbrous accompaniments of law-officers and parchments, police constables and bailiffs, to effect a distress or an ejectment; the midnight party with arms patrolled the country, firing the haggards and the farmhouses, setting all law at defiance, and asserting in their own bloody vengeance the supremacy of massacre.

Not a day went over without its chronicle of crime; the very calendar was red with murder. Friends parted with a fervour of feeling, that showed none knew if they would meet on the morrow; and a dark, gloomy suspicion prevailed through the land, each dreading his neighbour, and deeming his isolation more secure than all the ties of friendship. All the bonds of former love, all the relations of kindred and affection, were severed by this terrible league. Brothers, fathers, and sons were arrayed against each other. A despotism was thus set up, which even they who detested dared not oppose. The very defiance it hurled at superior power, awed and terrified themselves. Nor was this feeling lessened when they saw that these dreadful acts— acts so horrible as to make men shudder at the name of

Ireland when heard in the farthest corner of Europe—
that these had their apologists in the press, that even a
designation was invented for them, and murder could
be spoken of patriotically as the "Wild Justice" of the
people.

There is a terrible contagion in crime. The man whose
pure heart had never harboured a bad thought cannot live
untainted where wickedness is rife. The really base and
depraved were probably not many; but there were hard-
ships and sufferings every where; misery abounded in the
land—misery too dreadful to contemplate. It was not
difficult to connect such sufferings with the oppressions,
real or supposed, of the wealthier classes. Some, believed
the theory with all the avidity of men who grasp at straws
when drowning; others, felt a savage pleasure at the bare
thought of reversing the game of sufferance; while many,
mixed up their own wrongs with what they regarded as
national grievances, and converted their private vengeance
into a patriotic daring. Few stood utterly aloof, and even
of these, none would betray the rest.

The temporary success of murder, too, became a hor-
rible incentive to its commission. The agent shot, the
law he had set in motion stood still, the process fell
powerless; the "Wild Justice" superseded the slower
footsteps of common law, and the murderer saw himself
installed in safety, when he ratified his bond in the blood
of his victim.

Habitual poverty involves so much of degradation, that
recklessness of life is its almost invariable accompaniment;
and thus, many of these men ceased to speculate on the
future, and followed the dictates of their leaders in blind
and dogged submission. There were many, too, who felt
a kind of savage enthusiasm in the career of danger, and
actually loved the very hazard of the game. Many more

had private wrongs—old debts of injury to wipe out—and grasped at the occasion to acquit them; but even when no direct motives existed, the terror of evil consequences induced great numbers to ally themselves with this terrible conspiracy, and when not active partisans, at least to be faithful and secret confidants.

Among the many dispossessed by the agent was Owen Connor. Scarcely had he left the neighbourhood, than an ejectment was served against him; and the bailiff, by whose representations Owen was made to appear a man of dangerous character, installed in his mountain-farm. This fellow was one of those bold, devil-may-care ruffians, who survive in every contest longer than men of more circumspect courage; and Lucas was not sorry to find that he could establish such an outpost in this wild and dreary region. Well armed, and provided with a sufficiency of ammunition, he promised to maintain his stronghold against any force—a boast not so unreasonable, as there was only one approach to the cabin, and that, a narrow path on the very verge of a precipice. Owen's unexpected appearance was in his eyes, therefore, a signal for battle; he supposed that he was come back to assert his ancient right, and in this spirit it was, he menaced him with instant death if he advanced another step. Indeed, he had been more than once threatened that Owen's return would be a "dark day" for him, and prepared himself for a meeting with him, as an occasion which might prove fatal to either. These threats, not sparingly bandied by those who felt little inclination to do battle on their own account, had become so frequent, that many looked for Owen's reappearance as for an event of some moment.

Old Larry often heard these reports, and well knowing Owen's ardent disposition and passionate temper, and how easily he became the tool of others, when any deed of more than ordinary hazard was presented to him, grieved deeply over the consequences such promptings might lead to; and thus it was, that he received him with that outburst of sorrow for which Owen was little prepared.

If Owen was shocked as he listened first to the tale of anarchy and bloodshed the old man revealed, a savage pleasure came over him afterwards, to think, what terror these midnight maraudings were making in the hearts of those who lived in great houses, and had wealth and influence. His own wrongs rankled too deeply in his breast to make him an impartial hearer; and already, many of his sympathies were with the insurgents.

It was almost daybreak ere he could close his eyes; for although tired and worn out, the exciting themes he was revolving banished every thought of sleep, and made him restless and fretful. His last words to Larry, as he lay down to rest, were a desire that he might remain for a day or two concealed in his cabin, and that none of the neighbours should learn anything of his arrival. The truth was, he had not courage to face his former friends, nor could he bear to meet the Joyces: what step he purposed to take in the mean while, and how to fashion his future course, it is hard to say: for the present, he only asked time.

The whole of the following day he remained within the little hut; and when night came, at last ventured forth to breathe the fresh air and move his cramped limbs. His first object, then, was to go over to Joyce's house, with no intention of visiting its inmates—far from it. The poor fellow had conceived a shrinking horror of the avowal he should be compelled to make of his own failure, and did not dare to expose himself to such a test.

The night was dark and starless: that heavy, clouded darkness which follows a day of rain in our western climate, and makes the atmosphere seem loaded and weighty. To one less accustomed than was Owen, the pathway would have been difficult to discover; but he knew it well in every turning and winding, every dip of the ground, and every rock and streamlet in the course. There was the stillness of death on every side; and although Owen stopped more than once to listen, not the slightest sound could be heard. The gloom and dreariness suited well the "habit of his soul." His own thoughts were not of the brightest, and his step was slow and his head downcast as he went.

At last the glimmering of light, hazy and indistinct from the foggy atmosphere, came into view, and a few minutes after, he entered the little enclosure of the small garden which flanked one side of the cabin. The quick bark of a dog gave token of his approach, and Owen found some difficulty in making himself recognised by the animal, although an old acquaintance. This done, he crept stealthily to the window from which the gleam of light issued. The shutters were closed, but between their joinings he obtained a view of all within.

At one side of the fire was Mary—his own Mary, when last he parted with her. She was seated at a spinning-wheel, but seemed less occupied with the work, than bent on listening to some noise without. Phil also stood in the attitude of one inclining his ear to catch a sound, and held a musket in his hand like one ready to resist attack. A farm-servant, a lad of some eighteen, stood at his side, armed with a horse-pistol, his features betraying no very equivocal expression of fear and anxiety. Little Patsy nestled at Mary's side, and with his tiny hands had grasped her arm closely.

22

'They stood there, as if spell-bound. It was evident they were afraid, by the slightest stir, to lose the chance of hearing any noise without; and when Mary at last lifted up her head, as if to speak, a quick motion of her brother's hand warned her to be silent. What a history did that group reveal to Owen, as, with a heart throbbing fiercely, he gazed upon it! But a few short months back, and the inmates of that happy home knew not if at night the door was even latched; the thought of attack or danger never crossed their minds. The lordly dwellers in a castle felt less security in their slumbers than did these peasants; now, each night brought a renewal of their terrors. It came no longer the season of mutual greeting around the wintry hearth, the hour of rest and repose; but a time of anxiety and dread, a gloomy period of doubt, harassed by every breeze that stirred, and every branch that moved.

"''Tis nothing *this time*," said Phil, at last. "Thank God for that same!" and he replaced his gun above the chimney, while Mary blessed herself devoutly, and seemed to repeat a prayer to herself. Owen gave one parting look, and retired as noiselessly as he came.

To creep forth with the dark hours, and stand at this window, became with Owen, now, the whole business of life. The weary hours of the day were passed in the expectancy of that brief season—the only respite he enjoyed from the corroding cares of his own hard fortune. The dog, recognising him, no longer barked as he approached: and he could stand unmolested and look at that hearth, beside which he was wont once to sit and feel at home.

'Thus was it, as the third week was drawing to a close, when old Larry, who had ventured down to the village to make some little purchase, brought back the news, that information had been sworn by the bailiff against Owen Connor, for threatening him with death, on pain of his not abandoning his farm. The people would none of them give any credit to the oath, as none knew of Owen's return; and the allegation was only regarded as another instance of the perjury resorted to by their opponents, to crush and oppress them.

"They'll have the police out to-morrow, I hear, to search after ye; and sure the way ye've kept hid will be a bad job, if they find ye after all."

"*If* they do, Larry!" said Owen, laughing; "but I think it will puzzle them to do so." And the very spirit of defiance prevented Owen at once surrendering himself to the charge against him. He knew every cave and hiding-place of the mountain, from childhood upwards, and felt proud to think how he could baffle all pursuit, no matter how persevering his enemies. It was essential, however, that he should leave his present hiding-place at once: and no sooner was it dark, than Owen took leave of old Larry and issued forth. The rain was falling in torrents, accompanied by a perfect hurricane, as he left the cabin; fierce gusty blasts swept down the bleak mountain-side, and with wild and melancholy cadence poured along the valley; the waters of the lake plashed and beat upon the rocky shore: the rushing torrents, as they forced their way down the mountain, swelled the uproar, in which the sound of crashing branches and even rocks were mingled.

" 'Tis a dreary time to take to the cowld mountain for a home," said Owen, as he drew his thick frieze coat around him, and turned his shoulder to the storm. "I hardly think the police, or the king's throops either, will try a chase after me this night."

There was more of gratified pride in this muttered re-

22—2

flection than at first sight might appear; for Owen felt a kind of heroism in his own daring at that moment, that supported and actually encouraged him in his course. The old spirit of bold defiance, which for ages has characterised the people; the resolute resistance to authority, or to tyranny, which centuries have not erased, was strong in his hardy nature; and he asked for nothing better, than to pit his own skill, ingenuity, and endurance against his opponents for the mere pleasure of the encounter.

As there was little question on Owen's mind that no pursuit of him would take place on such a night, he resolved to pass the time till daybreak within the walls of the old churchyard, the only spot he could think of which promised any shelter. There was a little cell or crypt there, where he could safely remain till morning. An hour's walking brought him to the little gate, the last time he had entered which, was at his poor father's funeral.

His reflection, now, was rather on his own altered condition since that day; but even on that thought he suffered himself not to dwell. In fact, a hardy determination to face the future, in utter forgetfulness of the past, was the part he proposed to himself; and he did his utmost to bend his mind to the effort.

As he drew near the little crypt I have mentioned, he was amazed to see the faint flickering of a fire within it. At first a superstitious fear held him back, and he rapidly repeated some prayers to himself; but the emotion was soon over, and he advanced boldly toward it. "Who's there? stand! or give the word!" said a gruff voice from within. Owen stood still, but spoke not. The challenge was like that of a sentry, and he half-feared he had unwittingly strayed within the precincts of a patrol.

"Give the word at once! or you'll never spake another," was the savage speech which, accompanied by a deep curse, now met his ears, while the click of a gun-cock was distinctly audible.

"I'm a poor man, without a home or a shelter," said Owen, calmly; "and what's worse, I'm without arms, or maybe you wouldn't talk so brave."

"What's yer name? Where are ye from?"

"I'm Owen Connor; that's enough for ye, whoever ye are,' replied he, resolutely: "it's a name I'm not ashamed or afraid to say, anywhere."

The man within the cell threw a handful of dry furze upon the smouldering flame, and while he remained con-cealed himself, took a deliberate survey of Owen as he stood close to the doorway. "You're welcome, Owen," said he, in an altered voice, and one which Owen imme-diately recognised as that of the old blacksmith, Miles Regan; "you're welcome, my boy! better late than never, anyhow!"

"What do you mean, Miles? 'Tisn't expecting me here ye were, I suppose?"

"'Tis just that same then, I was expecting this many a day," said Miles, as with a rugged grasp of both hands he drew Owen within the narrow cell. "And 't'aint me only was expecting it, but everyone else. Here, avich, taste this—ye're wet and cowld both; that will put life in ye—and it never ped the king sixpence."

And he handed Owen a quart bottle as he spoke, the odour of which was unmistakable enough, to bear testi-mony to his words.

"And what brings you here, Miles, in the name of God?" said Owen, for his surprise at the meeting in-creased every moment.

"'Tis your own case, only worse," said the other,

with a drunken laugh, for the poteen had already affected his head.

"And what's that, if I might make bould?" said Owen, rather angrily.

"Just that I got the turn-out, my boy. That new chap, they have over the property, sould me out, root and branch; and as I didn't go quiet, ye see, they brought the polis down, and there was a bit of a fight, to take the two cows away; and somehow"—here he snatched the bottle rudely from Owen's hand, and swallowed a copious draught of it—"and, somehow, the corporal was killed, and I thought it better to be away for awhile—for, at the inquest, though the boys would take 'the vestment' they seen him shot by one of his comrades, there was a bit of a smash in his skull, ye see"—here he gave a low fearful laugh—"that fitted neatly to the top of my eleven-pound hammer; ye comprehend?"

Owen's blood ran cold as he said, "Ye don't mean it was you that killed him?"

"I do then," replied the other, with a savage grin, as he placed his face within a few inches of Owen's. "There's a hundred pounds blood-money for ye, now, if ye give the information! A hundred pounds," muttered he to himself: "musha, I never thought they'd give ten shillings for my own four bones before!"

Owen scorned to reply to the insinuation of his turning informer, and sat moodily thinking over the event.

"Well, I'll be going, anyhow," said he rising, for his abhorrence of his companion made him feel the storm and the hurricane a far preferable alternative.

"The divil a one foot ye'll leave this, my boy," said Miles, grasping him with the grip of his gigantic hand; "no, no, ma bouchal, 'tisn't so easy airned as ye think; a hundred pounds, naboclish!"

"Leave me free! let go my arm!" said Owen, whose anger now rose at the insolence of this taunt.

"I'll break it across my knee, first," said the infuriated ruffian, as he half imitated by a gesture his horrid threat.

There was no comparison in point of bodily strength between them; for although Owen was not half the other's age, and had the advantage of being perfectly sober, the smith was a man of enormous power, and held him, as though he were a child in his grasp.

"So that's what you'd be at, my boy, is it?" said Miles, scoffing; "it's the fine thrade you choose! but maybe it's not so pleasant, after all. Stay still there— be quiet, I say—by——" and here he uttered a most awful oath — "if you rouse me, I'll paste your brains against that wall:" and as he spoke, he dashed his closed fist against the rude and crumbling masonry, with a force that shook several large stones from their places, and left his knuckles one indistinguishable mass of blood and gore.

"That's brave, anyhow," said Owen, with a bitter mockery, for his own danger, at the moment, could not repress his contempt for the savage conduct of the other.

Fortunately, the besotted intellect of the smith made him accept the speech in a very different sense, and he said, "There never was the man yet, I wouldn't give him two blows at me, for one at him, and mine to be the last."

"I often heard of that before," said Owen, who saw that any attempt to escape by main force was completely out of the question, and that stratagem alone could present a chance.

"Did ye ever hear of Dan Lenahan?" said Miles, with a grin; "what I did to Dan: I was to fight him

wid one hand, and the other tied behind my back; and
when he came up to shake hands wid me before the fight,
I just put my thumb in my hand, that way, and I smashed
his four fingers over it."

"There was no fight that day, anyhow, Miles."

"Thrue for ye, boy; the sport was soon over—raich
me over the bottle," and with that, Miles finished the
poteen at a draught, and then lay back against the wall,
as if to sleep.   Still, he never relinquished his grasp, but,
as he fell off asleep, held him as in a vice.

As Owen sat thus a prisoner, turning over in his mind
every possible chance of escape, he heard the sound of
feet and men's voices rapidly approaching: and, in a few
moments, several men turned into the churchyard, and
came towards the crypt.   They were conversing in a low
but hurried voice, which was quickly hushed as they
came nearer.

"What's this!" cried one, as he entered the cell;
"Miles has a prisoner here!"

"Faix, he has so, Mickey;" answered Owen, for he
recognised in the speaker an old friend and schoolfellow.
The rest came hurriedly forward at the words, and soon
Owen found himself among a number of his former com-
panions.   Two or three of the party were namesakes and
relations.

The explanation of his capture was speedily given,
and they all laughed heartily at Owen's account of his
ingenious efforts at flattery.

"Av the poteen held out, Owen dear, ye wouldn't
have had much trouble; but he can drink two quarts
before he loses his strength."

In return for his narrative, they freely and frankly told
their own story.   They had been out arms-hunting—un-
successfully, however—their only exploit being the burn-

ing of a haggard belonging to a farmer who refused to join the " rising."

Owen felt greatly relieved to discover, that his old friends regarded the smith with a horror fully as great as his own. But they excused themselves for the companionship by saying, "What are we to do with the crayture? Ye wouldn't have us let him be taken?" And thus they were compelled to practise every measure for the security of one they had no love for, and whose own excesses increased the hazard tenfold.

The marauding exploits they told of, were, to Owen's ears, not devoid of a strange interest, the danger alone had its fascination for him ; and, artfully interwoven as their stories were with sentiments of affected patriotism and noble aspirations for the cause of their country, they affected him strongly.

For, strange as it may seem, a devotion to country— a mistaken sense of national honour—prompted many to these lawless courses. Vague notions of confiscated lands to be restored to their rightful possessors ; ancient privileges reconferred ; their church once more endowed with its long-lost wealth and power : such were the motives of the more high-spirited and independent. Others sought redress for personal grievances ; some real or imaginary hardship they laboured under ; or, perhaps, as was not unfrequent, they bore the memory of some old grudge or malice, which they hoped now to have an opportunity of requiting. Many were there, who, like the weak-minded in all popular commotions, float with the strong tide, whichever way it may run. They knew not the objects aimed at ; they were ignorant of the intentions of their leaders ; but would not lie under the stain of cowardice among their companions, nor shrink from any cause where there was danger, if only for that very reason. Thus was the mass made up, of men differing in various ways; but all held together by the common tie of a church and a country. It might be supposed that the leaders in such a movement would be those who, having suffered some grievous wrong, were reckless enough to adventure on any course that promised vengeance;—very far from this. The principal promoters of the insurrection were of the class of farmers—men well to do, and reputed, in many cases, wealthy. The instruments by which they worked were indeed of the very poorer class—the cottier, whose want and misery had eat into his nature, and who had as little room for fear as for hope in his chilled heart. Some injury sustained by one of these, some piece of justice denied him; his ejection from his tenement; a chance word, perhaps, spoken to him in anger by his landlord or the agent, were the springs which moved a man like this, and brought him into confederacy with those who promised him a speedy repayment of his wrongs, and flattered him into the belief that his individual case had all the weight and importance of a national question. Many insurrectionary movements have grown into the magnitude of systematic rebellion from the mere assumption on the part of others, that they were prearranged and predetermined. The self-importance suggested by a bold opposition to the law, is a strong agent in arming men against its terrors. The mock martyrdom of Ireland is in this way, perhaps, her greatest and least curable evil.

Owen was, of all others, the man they most wished for amongst them. Independent of his personal courage and daring, he was regarded as one fruitful in expedients, and never deterred by difficulties. This mingled character of cool determination and headlong impulse,

made him exactly suited to become a leader; and
many a plot was thought of, to draw him into their
snares, when the circumstances of his fortune thus antici-
pated their intentions.

It would not forward the object of my little tale to
dwell upon the life he now led. It was indeed an
existence full of misery and suffering. To exaggerate
the danger of his position, his companions asserted that
the greatest efforts were making for his capture, rewards
offered, and spies scattered far and wide through the
country; and while they agreed with him that nothing
could be laid to his charge, they still insisted, that were
he once taken, false-swearing and perjury would bring
him to the gallows, "as it did many a brave boy before
him."

Half-starved, and harassed by incessant change of
place; tortured by the fevered agony of a mind halting
between a deep purpose of vengeance and a conscious
sense of innocence, his own daily sufferings soon brought
down his mind to that sluggish state of gloomy despera-
tion, in which the very instincts of our better nature
seem dulled and blunted. "I cannot be worse!" was
his constant expression, as he wandered alone by some
unfrequented mountain-path, or along the verge of some
lonely ravine. "I cannot be worse!" It is an evil
moment that suggests a thought like this!

Each night he was accustomed to repair to the old
churchyard, where some of the "boys," as they called
themselves, assembled to deliberate on future measures,
or talk over the past. It was less in sympathy with
their plans that Owen came, than for the very want of
human companionship. His utter solitude gave him a
longing to hear their voices, and see their faces; while
in their recitals of outrage, he felt that strange pleasure

the sense of injury supplies, at any tale of sorrow and suffering.

At these meetings the whisky-bottle was never forgotten; and while some were under a pledge not to take more than a certain quantity—a vow they kept most religiously—others drank deeply. Among these was Owen. The few moments of reckless forgetfulness he then enjoyed were the coveted minutes of his long dreary day, and he wished for night to come as the last solace that was left him.

His companions knew him too well, to endeavour by any active influence to implicate him in their proceedings. They cunningly left the work to time and his own gloomy thoughts; watching, however, with eager anxiety, how, gradually, he became more and more interested in all their doings; how, by degrees he ceased even the half-remonstrance against some deed of unnecessary cruelty; and listened with animation where before he but heard with apathy, if not repugnance. The weeds of evil grow rankest in the rich soil of a heart whose nature, once noble, has been perverted and debased. Ere many weeks passed over, Owen, so far from disliking the theme of violence and outrage, became half-angry with his comrades, that they neither proposed any undertaking to him, nor even asked his assistance amongst them.

This spirit grew hourly stronger in him; offended pride worked within his heart during the tedious days he spent alone, and he could scarcely refrain from demanding what lack of courage and daring they saw in him, that he should be thus forgotten and neglected.

In this frame of mind, irresolute as to whether he should not propose himself for some hazardous scheme, or still remain a mere spectator of others, he arrived one evening in the old churchyard. Of late, "the boys," from preconcerted arrangements among themselves, had rather made a show of cold and careless indifference in their manner to Owen—conduct which deeply wounded him.

As he approached now the little crypt, he perceived that a greater number than usual were assembled through the churchyard, and many were gathered in little knots and groups, talking eagerly together; a half-nod, a scarcely muttered "Good-even," was all the salutation he met, as he moved towards the little cell, where, by the blaze of a piece of bog-pine, a party were regaling themselves—the custom and privilege of those who had been last out on any marauding expedition. A smoking pot of potatoes and some bottles of whisky formed the entertainment, at which Owen stood a longing and famished spectator.

"Will yez never be done there eatin' and crammin' yerselves?" said a gruff voice from the crowd to the party within; "and ye know well enough there's business to be done to-night."

"And aint we doing it?" answered one of the feasters. "Here's your health, Peter!" and so saying, he took a very lengthened draught from the "poteen" bottle.

"'Tis the thrade ye like best, anyhow," retorted the other. "Come, boys; be quick now!"

The party did not wait a second bidding, but arose from the place, and removing the big pot to make more room, they prepared the little cell for the reception of some other visitors.

"That's it now! We'll not be long about it. Larry, have yez the 'deck,' my boy?"

"There's the book, darlint," said a short, little, decrepid creature, speaking with an asthmatic effort, as he produced a pack of cards, which, if one were to judge from the dirt, made the skill of the game consist as much in deciphering as playing them.

"Where's Sam M'Guire?" called out the first speaker, in a voice loud enough to be heard over the whole space around; and the name was repeated from voice to voice, till it was replied to by one who cried—

"Here, Sir; am I wanted?"

"You are, Sam; and 'tis yourself's always to the fore when we need yez."

"I hope so indeed," said Sam, as he came forward, a flush of gratified pride on his hardy cheek. He was a young, athletic fellow, with a fine manly countenance, expressive of frankness and candour.

"Luke Heffernan! where's Luke?" said the other.

"I'm here beside ye," answered a dark-visaged, middle-aged man, with the collar of his frieze coat buttoned high on his face; "ye needn't be shouting my name that way—there may be more bad than good among uz."

"There's not an informer, any way—if that's what ye mean," said the other quickly. "Gavan Daly! Call Gavan Daly, will ye, out there?" And the words were passed from mouth to mouth in a minute, but no one replied to the summons.

"He's not here—Gavan's not here!" was the murmured answer of the crowd, given in a tone that boded very little in favour of its absent owner.

"Not here!" said the leader, as he crushed the piece of paper, from which he read, in his hand; "not here! Where is he, then? Does any of yez know where's Gavan Daly?"

But there was no answer.

"Can no body tell?—is he sick?—or is any belonging to him sick and dying, that he isn't here this night, as he swore to be?"

"I saw him wid a new coat on him this morning early in Oughterarde, and he said he was going to see a cousin of his down below Oranmore," said a young lad from the outside of the crowd, and the speaker was in a moment surrounded by several, anxious to find out some other particulars of the absent man. It was evident that the boy's story was far from being satisfactory, and the circumstance of Daly's wearing a new coat, was one freely commented on by those who well knew how thoroughly they were in the power of any who should betray them.

"He's in the black list this night," said the leader, as he motioned the rest to be silent; "that's where I put him now; and see, all of yez—mind my words—if any of uz comes to harm, it will go hard but some will be spared; and if there was only one remaining, he wouldn't be the cowardly villain not to see vengeance on Gavan Daly, for what he's done."

A murmur of indignation at the imputed treachery of the absent man buzzed through the crowd; while one fellow, with a face flushed by drink, and eyes bleared and bloodshot, cried out:

"And are ye to stop here all night, calling for the boy that's gone down to bethray yez? Is there none of yez will take his place?"

"I will! I will! I'm ready and willin'!" were uttered by full twenty, in a breath.

"Who will ye have with yez? take your own choice!" said the leader, turning towards M'Guire and Heffernan, who stood whispering eagerly together.

"There's the boy I'd take out of five hundred, av he

was the same I knew once," said M'Guire, laying his hand on Owen's shoulder.

"Begorra then, I wondher what ye seen in him lately to give you a consate out of him," cried Heffernan, with a rude laugh. "'Tisn't all he's done for the cause any-way."

Owen started, and fixed his eyes first on one, then on the other of the speakers; but his look was rather the vacant stare of one awakening from a heavy sleep, than the expression of any angry passion—for want and privation had gone far to sap his spirit, as well as his bodily strength.

"There, avich, taste that," said a man beside him, who was struck by his pale and wasted cheek, and miserable appearance.

Owen almost mechanically took the bottle, and drank freely, though the contents was strong poteen.

"Are ye any betther now?" said Heffernan, with a sneering accent.

"I am," said Owen, calmly, for he was unconscious of the insolence passed off on him; "I'm a deal better."

"Come along, ma bouchal!" cried M'Guire; "come into the little place with us, here."

"What do ye want with me, boys?" asked Owen, looking about him through the crowd.

"'Tis to take a hand at the cards, divil a more," said an old fellow near, and the speech sent a savage laugh among the rest.

"I'm ready and willin'," said Owen; "but sorra farthen I've left me to play; and if the stakes is high——"

"Faix, that's what they're not," said Heffernan; "they're the lowest ever ye played for."

"Tell me what it is, anyway," cried Owen.

"Just, the meanest thing at all—the life of the blaguard that turned yerself out of yer houldin'—Lucas the agent."

"To kill Lucas?"

"That same : and if ye don't like the game, turn away and make room for a boy that has more spirit in him."

"Who says I ever was afeard?" said Owen, on whom now the whisky was working. "Is it Luke Heffernan dares to face me down?—come out here, fair, and see will ye say it again."

"If you won't join the cause, you mustn't be bringing bad blood among us," cried the leader, in a determined tone; "there's many a brave boy here to-night would give his right hand to get the offer you did."

"I'm ready—here I am, ready now," shouted Owen wildly; "tell me what you want me to do, and see whether I will or no."

A cheer broke from the crowd at these words, and all within his reach stretched out their hands to grasp Owen's; and commendations were poured on him from every side.

Meanwhile Heffernan and his companion had cleared the little crypt of its former occupants, and having heaped fresh wood upon the fire, sat down before the blaze, and called out for Owen to join them. Owen took another draught from one of the many bottles offered by the by-standers, and hastened to obey the summons.

"Stand back now, and don't speak a word," cried the leader, keeping off the anxious crowd that pressed eagerly forward to witness the game; the hushed murmuring of the voices showing how deeply interested they felt.

The three players bent their heads forward as they sat, while Heffernan spoke some words in a low whisper, to which the others responded by a muttered assent. "Well, here's success to the undhertakin' anyhow," cried,

23

he aloud, and filling out a glass of whisky, drank it off; then passing the liquor to the two others, they followed his example.

"Will ye like to deal, Owen?" said M'Guire; "you're the new-comer, and we'll give ye the choice."

"No, thank ye, boys," said Owen; "do it yerselves, one of ye; I'm sure of fair play."

Heffernan then took the cards, and wetting his thumb for the convenience of better distributing them, slowly laid five cards before each player; he paused for a second before he turned the trump, and in a low voice said: "If any man's faint-hearted, let him say it now——"

"Turn the card round, and don't be bothering us," cried M'Guire; "one 'ud think we never played a game before."

"Come, be alive," said Owen, in whom the liquor had stimulated the passion for play.

"What's the thrump—is it a diamond? look over and tell us," murmured the crowd nearest the entrance.

"'Tis a spade!—I lay fourpence 'tis a spade!"

"Why wouldn't it be?" said another; "it's the same spade will dig Lucas's grave this night!"

"Look! see!" whispered another, "Owen Connor's won the first thrick! Watch him now! Mind the way he lays the card down, with a stroke of his fist!"

"I wish he wouldn't be drinking so fast!" said another.

"Who won that? who took that thrick?"

"Ould Heffernan, divil fear him! I never see him lose yet."

"There's another; that's Owen's!"

"No; by Jonas! 'tis Luke again has it."

"That's Sam M'Guire's! See how aizy he takes them up."

"Now for it, boys! whisht! here's the last round!" and at this moment, a breathless silence prevailed among the crowd; for while such as were nearest were eagerly bent on observing the progress of the game, the more distant bent their heads to catch every sound that might indicate its fortune.

"See how Luke grins! watch his face!" whispered a low voice. "He doesn't care how it goes, now, he's out of it!" and so it was. Heffernan had already won two of the five tricks, and was safe whatever the result of the last one. The trial lay between M'Guire and Owen.

"Come, Owen, my hearty!" said M'Guire, as he held a card ready to play, "you or I for it now; we'll soon see which the devil's fondest of. There's the two of clubs for ye!"

"There's the three, then!" said Owen, with a crash of his hand, as he placed the card over the other.

"And there's the four!" said Heffernan, "and the thrick is Sam M'Guire's."

"Owen Connor's lost!" "Owen's lost!" murmured the crowd; and, whether in half-compassion for his defeat, or grief that so hazardous a deed should be entrusted to a doubtful hand, the sensation created was evidently of gloom and dissatisfaction.

"You've a right to take either of us wid ye, Owen," said M'Guire, slapping him on the shoulder. "Luke or myself must go, if ye want us."

"No; I'll do it myself," said Owen, in a low hollow voice.

"There's the tool, then!" said Heffernan, producing from the breast of his frieze coat a long horse-pistol, the stock of which was mended by a clasp of iron belted round it; "and if it doesn't do its work, 'tis the first time it ever failed. Ould Miles Cregan, of Gurtane, was the last that heard it spake."

Owen took the weapon, and examined it leisurely, opening the pan and settling the priming, with a finger that never trembled. As he drew forth the ramrod to try the barrel, Heffernan said, with a half-grin, "There's two bullets in it, avich !—enough's as good as a feast."

Owen sat still and spoke not, while the leader and Heffernan explained to him the circumstances of the plot against the life of Mr. Lucas. Information had been obtained by some of the party, that the agent would leave Galway on the following evening, on his way to Westport, passing through Oughterarde and their own village, about midnight. He usually travelled in his gig, with relays of horses ready at different stations of the way, one of which was about two miles distant from the old ruin, on the edge of the lake—a wild and dreary spot, where stood a solitary cabin, inhabited by a poor man who earned his livelihood by fishing. No other house was within a mile of this ; and here, it was determined, while in the act of changing horses, the murder should be effected. The bleak common beside the lake was studded with furze and brambles, beneath which it was easy to obtain shelter, though pursuit was not to be apprehended—at least they judged that the servant would not venture to leave his master at such a moment ; and as for the fisherman, although not a sworn member of their party, they well knew he would not dare to inform against the meanest amongst them.

Owen listened attentively to all these details, and the accurate directions by which they instructed him on every step he should take. From the moment he should set foot within the cover to the very instant of firing, each little event had its warning.

"Mind!" repeated Heffernan, with a slow, distinct whisper, "he never goes into the house at all; but if the night's cowld—as it's sure to be this sayson—he'll be moving up and down, to keep his feet warm. Cover him as he turns round; but don't fire the first cover, but wait till he comes back to the same place again, and then blaze. Don't stir then, till ye see if he falls: if he does, be off down the common; but if he's only wounded—but sure ye'll do better than that!"

"I'll go bail he will!" said M'Guire. "Sorra fear that Owen Connor's heart would fail him! and sure if he likes me to be wid him——"

"No, no!" said Owen, in the same hollow voice as before, "I'll do it all by myself; I want nobody."

"'Tis the very words I said when I shot Lambert of Kilclunah!" said M'Guire. "I didn't know him by looks, and the boys wanted me to take some one to point him out. 'Sorra bit!' says I, 'leave that to me;' and so I waited in the gripe of the ditch all day, till, about four in the evening, I seen a stout man wid a white hat coming across the fields, to where the men was planting potatoes. So I ups to him wid a letter in my hand, this way, and my hat off—'Is yer honner Mr. Lambert?' says I. 'Yes,' says he; 'what do ye want with me?' ''Tis a bit of a note I've for yer honner,' says I; and I gav him the paper. He tuck it and opened it; but troth it was little matter there was no writin' in it, for he wouldn't have lived to read it through. I sent the ball through his heart, as near as I stand to ye; the wadding was burning his waistcoat when I left him. 'God save you!' says the men, as I went across the potato-field. 'Save you kindly!' says I. 'Was that a shot we heard?' says another. 'Yes,' says I; 'I was fright'ning the crows;' and sorra bit, but that's a saying they have against me ever since." These last few words were said in a simper of modesty, which, whether real or affected, was a strange sentiment at the conclusion of such a tale.

The party soon after separated, not to meet again for several nights; for the news of Lucas's death would of course be the signal for a general search through the country, and the most active measures to trace the murderer. It behoved them, then, to be more than usually careful not to be absent from their homes and their daily duties for some days at least: after which they could assemble in safety as before.

Grief has been known to change the hair to gray in a single night; the announcement of a sudden misfortune has palsied the hand that held the ill-omened letter; but I question if the hours that are passed before the commission of a great crime, planned and meditated beforehand, do not work more fearful devastation on the human heart, than all the sorrows that ever crushed humanity. Ere night came, Owen Connor seemed to have grown years older. In the tortured doubtings of his harassed mind he appeared to have spent almost a lifetime since the sun last rose. He had passed in review before him each phase of his former existence, from childhood—free, careless, and happy childhood—to days of boyish sport and revelry; then came the period of his first manhood, with its new ambitions and hopes. He thought of these, and how, amid the humble circumstances of his lowly fortune, he was happy. What would he have thought of him who should predict such a future as this for him? How could he have believed it? And yet the worst of all remained to come. He tried to rally his courage and steel his heart, by repeating over the phrases so frequent among his companions. "Sure, aint I driven to it? is it my fault if I take to this, or theirs that compelled me?" and such like. But these words came with no persuasive force in the still hour of conscience: they were only effectual amid the excitement and tumult of a multitude, when men's passions were high, and their resolutions daring. " It is too late to go back," muttered he, as he arose from the spot, where, awaiting nightfall, he had lain hid for several hours; "they mustn't call me a coward, any way."

As Owen reached the valley the darkness spread far and near; not a star could be seen; great masses of cloud covered the sky, and hung down heavily, midway upon the mountains. There was no rain; but on the wind came from time to time a drifted mist, which showed that the air was charged with moisture. The ground was still wet and plashy from recent heavy rain. It was indeed a cheerless night and a cheerless hour; but not more so than the heart of him who now, bent upon his deadly purpose, moved slowly on towards the common.

On descending towards the lake-side, he caught a passing view of the little village, where a few lights yet twinkled, and flickering stars that shone within some humble home. What would he not have given to be but the meanest peasant there, the poorest creature that toiled and sickened on his dreary way! He turned away hurriedly, and with his hand pressed heavily on his swelling heart walked rapidly on. " It will soon be over now," said Owen; he was about to add, with the accustomed piety of his class, "thank God for it," but the words stopped in his throat, and the dreadful thought flashed on him, ' Is it when I am about to shed His creature's blood, I should say this ? "

He sat down upon a large stone beside the lake, at a spot where the road came down to the water's edge, and where none could pass unobserved by him. He had often fished from that very rock when a boy, and eaten his little dinner of potatoes beneath its shelter. Here he sat once more, saying to himself as he did so, " 'Tis an ould friend, any way, and I'll just spend my last night with him ;" for so in his mind he already regarded his condition. The murder effected, he determined to make no effort to escape. Life was of no value to him. The snares of the conspiracy had entangled him, but his heart was not in it.

As the night wore on, the clouds lifted, and the wind, increasing to a storm, bore them hurriedly through the air ; the waters of the lake, lashed into waves, beat heavily on the low shore ; while the howling blast swept through the mountain-passes, and over the bleak wide plain, with a rushing sound. The thin crescent of a new moon could be seen from time to time as the clouds rolled past : too faint to shed any light upon the earth, it merely gave form to the dark masses that moved before it.

" I will do it here," said Owen, as he stood and looked upon the dark water that beat against the foot of the rock ; " here, on this spot."

He sat for some moments with his ear bent to listen, but the storm was loud enough to make all other sounds inaudible ; yet, in every noise he thought he heard the sound of wheels, and the rapid tramp of a horse's feet. The motionless attitude, the cold of the night, but more than either, the debility brought on by long fasting and hunger, benumbed his limbs, so that he felt almost unable to make the least exertion, should any such be called for.

He therefore descended from the rock and moved along the road ; at first, only thinking of restoring lost animation to his frame, but at length, in a half unconsciousness, he had wandered upwards of two miles beyond the little hovel where the change of horses was to take place. Just as he was on the point of returning, he perceived at a little distance, in front, the walls of a now ruined cabin, once the home of the old smith. Part of the roof had fallen in, the doors and windows were gone, the fragment of an old shutter alone remained, and this banged heavily back and forwards as the storm rushed through the wretched hut.

Almost without knowing it, Owen entered the cabin, and sat down beside the spot where once the forge-fire used to burn. He had been there, too, when a boy many a time—many a story had he listened to in that same corner; but why think of this now? The cold blast seemed to freeze his very blood—he felt his heart as if congealed within him. He sat cowering from the piercing blast for some time; and at last, unable to bear the sensation longer, determined to kindle a fire with the fragments of the old shutter. For this purpose he drew the charge of the pistol, in which there were three bullets, and not merely two, as Heffernan had told him. Laying these carefully down in his handkerchief, he kindled a light with some powder, and with the dexterity of one not unaccustomed to such operations, soon saw the dry sticks blazing on the hearth. On looking about he discovered a few sods of turf and some dry furze, with which he replenished his fire, till it gradually became a warm and cheering blaze. Owen now reloaded the pistol, just as he had found it. There was a sense of duty in his mind to follow out every instruction he received, and deviate in nothing. This done, he held his numbed fingers over the blaze, and bared his chest to the warm glow of the fire.

The sudden change from the cold night-air to the warmth of the cabin soon made him drowsy. Fatigue and watching aiding the inclination to sleep, he was obliged to move about the hut, and even expose himself to the chill blast, to resist its influence. The very purpose on which he was bent, so far from dispelling sleep, rather induced its approach; for, strange as it may seem, the concentration with which the mind brings its power to bear on any object will overcome all the interest and anxiety of our natures, and bring on sleep from very weariness.

He slept, at first, calmly and peacefully—exhaustion would have its debt acquitted—and he breathed as softly as an infant. At last, when the extreme of fatigue was passed, his brain began to busy itself with flitting thoughts and fancies,—some long-forgotten day of boyhood, some little scene of childish gaiety, flashed across him, and he dreamed of the old mountain-lake, where so often he watched the wide circles of the leaping trout, or tracked with his eye the foamy path of the wild water-hen, as she skimmed the surface. Then suddenly his chest heaved and fell with a strong motion, for with lightning's speed the current of his thoughts was changed; his heart was in the mad tumult of a faction-fight, loud shouts were ringing in his ears, the crash of sticks, the cries of pain, entreaties for mercy, execrations and threats, rung around him, when one figure moved slowly before his astonished gaze, with a sweet smile upon her lips, and love in her long-lashed eyes. She murmured his name; and now he slept with a low-drawn breath, his quivering lips repeating, " Mary !"

Another and a sadder change was coming. He was on the mountains, in the midst of a large assemblage of wild-looking and haggard men, whose violent speech and savage gestures well suited their reckless air. A loud shout welcomed him as he came amongst them, and a cry of "Here's Owen Connor—Owen at last!" and a hundred hands were stretched out to grasp his, but as suddenly withdrawn, on seeing that his hands were not bloodstained nor gory.

He shuddered as he looked upon their dripping fingers; but he shuddered still more as they called him "Coward!" What he said he knew not; but in a moment they were gathered round him, and clasping him in their arms; and now, his hands, his cheeks, his clothes, were streaked with blood; he tried to wipe the foul-stains out, but his fingers grew clotted, and his feet seemed to plash in the red stream, and his savage comrades laughed fiercely at his efforts, and mocked him.

"What am I, that you should clasp me thus?" he cried; and a voice from his inmost heart replied, "A murderer!" The cold sweat rolled in great drops down his brow, while the foam of agony dewed his pallid lips, and his frame trembled in a terrible convulsion. Confused and fearful images of bloodshed and its penalty, the crime and the scaffold, commingled, worked in his maddened brain. He heard the rush of feet, as if thousands were hurrying on, to see him die, and voices that swelled like the sea at midnight. Nor was the vision all unreal: for already two men had entered the hut.

The dreadful torture of his thoughts had now reached its climax, and with a bound Owen sprang from his sleep, and cried in a shriek of heart-wrung anguish, "No, never—I am not a murderer. Owen Connor can meet his death like a man, but not with blood upon him."

"Owen Connor! Owen Connor, did you say?" repeated one of the two who stood before him; "are you, then, Owen Connor?"

"I am," replied Owen, whose dreams were still the last impression on his mind. "I give myself up;—do what ye will with me;—hang, imprison, or transport me; I'll never gainsay you."

"Owen, do you not know me?" said the other, removing his travelling cap, and brushing back the hair from his forehead.

"No, I know nothing of you," said he, fiercely.

"Not remember your old friend—your landlord's son, Owen?"

Owen stared at him without speaking; his parted lips and fixed gaze evidencing the amazement which came over him.

"You saved my life, Owen," said the young man, horror-struck by the withered and wasted form of the peasant.

"And you have made me this," muttered Owen, as he let fall the pistol from his bosom. "Yes," cried he, with an energy very different from before, "I came out this night, sworn to murder that man beside you—your agent, Lucas; my soul is perjured if my hands are not bloody."

Lucas instantly took a pistol from the breast of his coat, and cocked it; while the ghastly whiteness of his cheek showed he did not think the danger was yet over.

"Put up your weapon," said Owen, contemptuously. "What would I care for it, if I wanted to take your life? Do you think the likes of me has any hould on the world?" and he laughed a scornful and bitter laugh.

"How is this, then?" cried Leslie; "is murder so light a crime that a man like this does not shrink from it?"

"The country," whispered Lucas, "is indeed in a fearful state. The rights of property no longer exist among us. That fellow—because he lost his farm——"

"Stop, Sir!" cried Owen, fiercely; "I will deny nothing of my guilt—but lay not more to my charge than is true. Want and misery have brought me low—destitution and recklessness still lower—but if I swore to have your life this night, it was not for any vengeance of my own."

"Ha! then there is a conspiracy!" cried Lucas, hastily. "We must have it out of you—every word of it—or it will go harder with yourself."

Owen's only reply was a bitter laugh; and from that moment he never uttered another word. All Lucas's threats, all Leslie's entreaties, were powerless and vain. The very allusion to becoming an informer was too revolting to be forgiven, and he firmly resolved to brave any and everything, rather than endure the mere proposal.

They returned to Galway as soon as the post-boys had succeeded in repairing the accidental breakage of the harness, which led to the opportune appearance of the landlord and his agent in the hut; Owen accompanying them without a word or a gesture.

So long as Lucas was present, Owen never opened his lips; the dread of committing himself, or in any way implicating one amongst his companions, deterred him; but when Leslie sent for him, alone, and asked him the circumstances which led him to the eve of so great a crime, he confessed all—omitting nothing, save such passages as might involve others—and even to Leslie he was guarded on this topic.

The young landlord listened with astonishment and sorrow to the peasant's story. Never till now did he conceive the mischiefs neglect and abandonment can pro-pagate, nor of how many sins mere poverty can be the parent. He knew not before that the very endurance of want can teach another endurance, and make men hardened against the terrors of the law and its inflictions. He was not aware of the condition of his tenantry; he wished them all well off and happy; he had no self-accusings of a grudging nature, nor an oppressive disposition, and he absolved himself of any hardships that originated with "the agent."

The cases brought before his notice rather disposed him to regard the people as wily and treacherous, false in their pledges and unmindful of favours; and many, doubtless, were so; but he never enquired how far their experience had taught them, that dishonesty was the best policy, and that trick and subtlety are the only aids to the poor man. He forgot, above all, that they had neither examples to look up to nor imitate, and that when once a people have become sunk in misery, they are the ready tools of any wicked enough to use them for violence, and false enough to persuade them that outrage can be their welfare; and, lastly, he overlooked the great fact, that in a corrupt and debased social condition, the evils which, under other circumstances, would be borne with a patient trust in future relief, are resented in a spirit of recklessness; and that men soon cease to shudder at a crime, when frequency has accustomed them to discuss its details.

I must not—I dare not dwell longer on this theme. Leslie felt all the accusations of an awakened conscience. He saw himself the origin of many misfortunes—of evils of whose very existence he never heard before. Ere Owen concluded his sad story, his mind was opened to some of the miseries of Ireland; and when he had ended he cried, "I will live at home with ye, amongst ye all, Owen! I will try if Irishmen cannot learn to know who is their true friend; and while repairing some of my own faults, mayhap I may remedy some of theirs."

"Oh! why did you not do this before I came to my ruin?" cried Owen, in a passionate burst of grief; for the poor fellow all along had given himself up for lost, and imagined that his own plea of guilt must bring him to the gallows. Nor was it till after much persuasion and great trouble that Leslie could reconcile him to himself, and assure him that his own fortunate repentance had saved him from destruction.

"You shall go back to your mountain-cabin, Owen : you shall have your own farm again, and be as happy as ever," said the young man. "The law must deal with those who break it, and no one will go farther than myself to vindicate the law; but I will also try if kindness and fair-dealing will not save many from the promptings of their own hearts, and teach men that, even here, the breach of God's commandments can bring neither peace nor happiness."

My object in this little story being to trace the career of one humble man through the trials and temptations incident to his lot in life, I must not dwell upon the wider theme of national disturbance. I have endeavoured—how weakly, I am well aware—to show, that social disorganisation, rather than political grievances, are the source of Irish outrage; that neglect and abandonment of the people on the part of those who stood in the position of friends and advisers towards them, have disseminated evils deeper and greater than even a tyranny could have engendered. But for this desertion of their duties, there had been no loss of their rightful influence, nor would the foul crime of assassination now stain the name of our land. With an educated and resident proprietary, Ireland could never have become what she now is; personal comfort, if no higher motive could be appealed to, would have necessitated a watchful observance of the habits of the people—the tares would have been weeded from the wheat; the evil influence of bad men would not have been suffered to spread its contagion through the land.

Let me not be supposed for a moment as joining in the popular cry against the landlords of Ireland. As regards the management of their estates, and the liberality of their dealings with their tenantry, they are, of course, with the exceptions which every country exhibits, a class as blameless and irreproachable as can be found anywhere—their real dereliction being, in my mind, their desertion of the people. To this cause, I believe, can be traced every one of the long catalogue of disasters to which Ireland is a prey: the despairing poverty, reckless habits, indifference to the mandates of the law, have their source here. The impassioned pursuit of any political privilege, which they are given to suppose will alleviate the evils of their state, has thrown them into the hands of the demagogue, and banded them in a league, which they assume to be national. You left them to drift on the waters, and you may now be shipwrecked among the floating fragments !

My tale is ended. I have only one record more to add. The exercise of the law, assisted by the energy and determination of a fearless and resident landlord, at length suppressed outrage and banished those who had been its originators. Through the evidence of Gavan Daly, whose treachery had been already suspected, several of the leaders were found guilty, and met the dreadful penalty of their crimes. The fact of an informer having been found amongst them, did, however, far more to break up this unholy league that all the terrors of the law, unassisted by such aid ; but it was long before either peace or happiness shed their true blessings on that land : mutual distrust, the memory of some lost friend, and the sad conviction of their own iniquity, darkened many a day, and made even a gloomier depth than they had ever known in their poverty.

There came, however, a reverse for this. It was a fine day in spring—the mountain and the lake were bright in the sunshine—the valley, rich in the promise of the coming year, was already green with the young wheat—the pleasant sounds of happy labour rose from the fields fresh-turned by the plough—the blue smoke curled into thin air from many a cabin, no longer mean-looking and miserable as before, but with signs of comfort around, in the trim hedge of the little garden and the white walls that glistened in the sun.

Towards the great mountain above the lake, however, many an eye was turned from afar, and many a peasant lingered to gaze upon the scene which now marked its rugged face.

Along the winding path which traced its zigzag course from the lake-side to the little glen where Owen's cabin stood, a vast procession could be seen moving on foot and on horseback. Some in country cars, assisted up the steep ascent by men's strong shoulders; others mounted in twos and threes upon some slow-footed beast; but the greater number walking or rather clambering their way—for in their eagerness to get forward, they, each moment, deserted the path to breast the ferny mountain-side. The scarlet cloaks of the women, as they fluttered in the wind, and their white caps, gave a brilliancy to the picture, which, as the masses emerged from the depth of some little dell and disappeared again, had all the semblance of some gorgeous panorama. Nor was eye the only sense gladdened by the spectacle—for even in the valley could be heard the clear ringing laughter as they went along, and the wild cheer of merriment that ever and anon burst forth from happy hearts, while, high above all, the pleasant sounds of the bagpipe rose, as, seated upon an ass, and entrusted to the guidance of a boy, the musician

24

moved along : his inspiriting strains taken advantage of at every spot of level ground by some merry souls, who would not "lose so much good music."

As the head of the dense column wound its way upward, one little group could be seen by those below, and were saluted by many a cheer and the waving of handkerchiefs. These were a party, whose horses and gear seemed far better than the rest; and among them rode a gentleman mounted on a strong pony—his chief care was bestowed less on his own beast, than in guiding that of a young country girl, who rode beside him. She was enveloped in a long blue cloak of dark cloth, beneath which she wore a white dress; a white ribbon floated through her dark hair, too; but in her features and the happy smile upon her lip, the bride was written more palpably than in all these.

High above her head, upon a pinnacle of rock, a man stood gazing at the scene; at his side a little child of some four or five years old, whose frantic glee seemed perilous in such a place, while his wild accents drew many an upward glance from those below, as he cried—

"See, Nony, see! Mary is coming to us at last!"

This, too, was a "St. Patrick's Eve," and a happy one. May Ireland see many such !

THE END.

PRINTED BY W. H. SMITH AND SON, 186, STRAND, LONDON.
1—6—71.